BRUTAL FIGHTER

This is for every single person who has taken a beating from life, but keeps bouncing back up.

Sometimes, when life knocks you down, you need to take advantage of the position to nut punch life before you climb back to your feet.

When in doubt, remember the people who have your back. You are not alone.

SERIES SO FAR

82ND STREET
VANDALS

Savage Vandal
Vicious Rebel
Ruthless Traitor
Dirty Devil
Brutal Fighter
Dangerous Renegade

FOREWORD

Dear Reader,

Welcome to book five of the 82nd Street Vandals series. If you have not read the first four, stop. Do not pass Go. Grab book one: Savage Vandal, and start there.

Seriously.

This is a series that really must be read in order.

Okay, back to my welcome. Brutal Fighter finds us, and Emersyn, back with her beloved Vandals. While she may not label them her beloved *yet*, she is very much back with the guys who are ready to burn the world down for her.

There are so many characters active in this book and we're jumping right into the deep end. Picking up within a day of her return, the Vandals and Lainey are on guard and ready to act as Emersyn *and* Freddie adjust to the fallout from their time at Pinetree.

I honestly think one of the best parts about writing this series is the intensity of the different relationships. The Vandals are a tight brotherhood of incredibly diverse and strong personalities.

They argue. They disagree. Sometimes their personalities just clash and they come to blows. But never make the mistake of thinking you can go after one and not get them all. One thing they have proven over and over is that they have each others backs.

As I said in the previous book, they are very much on a journey through a lot of dark places. Emersyn's strength will be tested in new ways. Each book of this series has immersed me deeper and deeper into the lives of the Vandals.

Their lives are changing, sometimes in subtle ways and, at other times, they are seismic shifts. Please remember that this is a dark romance and there are definitely triggering moments with regard to abuse, assault, violence, and addiction. Take care of yourself.

And now, as always, the housekeeping notes:

For those of you who have never read a reverse harem before, first let me thank you for picking this up and giving it a shot. Second, a reverse harem means the heroine will not make a choice in this book or any other between the guys in her life. It may take her a while to reach that conclusion, but it's the journey that drives it. There are many ways to frame this kind of relationship, currently reverse harem fits it very well.

Also, this is the fifth book in a series. While there may be no specific happy endings at the end of each of these books, there will be one to the whole series, that I promise you. Some of these books will have cliffhangers, largely due to the size of the story, but the happy ending has to be earned as part of the journey.

xoxo

Heather

THE VANDALS

82nd Street Boys
    Jasper "Hawk" Horan
    Kellan "Kestrel" Traschel
    Rome "Hummingbird" Cleary
    Vaughn "Falcon" Westbrook
    Liam "Mockingbird" O'Connell
    Freddie "Unknown" Dunlap
    Milo "Raptor" Hardigan

Not a Vandal
    Mickey "Doc" James
    Emersyn "Dove, Sparrow, Starling, Swan, Little Bit, Boo-Boo" Sharpe

Other Characters
    Elaine "Lainey" Benedict
    Adam Reed
    Ezra Graham
    Ms. Stephanie

KELLAN

The sound of Sparrow's laughter carried up the hall. The huskiness of it held notes of strain. Or maybe it was left over from the tears the night before. The sobbing had ripped my fucking heart out. The happy tears had been fine, but when she and Lainey had locked themselves away in Emersyn's room—yeah, I'd parked myself between the door and everyone else, including Milo.

Maybe, yeah, no maybe about it. Especially Milo.

But that meant I had to listen to her tears. I could have put on headphones or turned up music, but I'd just sat there.

"Are we going to keep standing around staring at each other with our dicks in our hands, or are we talking?" Freddie asked into the melancholy silence gripping the kitchen.

Sitting on the counter, he had a giant coffee mug in his hand that said "Suck my Coffee's Dick" and a bleary look on his face. I wasn't the only one studying him either. Jasper was a few feet away, his coffee cup all but ignored as he watched Freddie.

Were his eyes a little bright? His voice a little fierce? His posture a little too loose? There were so many different signs to watch for, but all I could find were signs of exhaustion and maybe a desire for more sleep. Well, that and the rumpled hair that seemed to match the pillow imprint on his cheek.

Bruises marred his chest in a couple of places and he had a particularly noticeable one on his arm. But the needle marks he had were from the facility, not shooting up.

Not that shooting up had ever been his particular favorite.

"I'm waiting on Liam," I said, checking my watch.

After his disappearing act the night before, we hadn't heard from him. Rome might have, but he kept his own counsel. Currently, he sat in a chair closest to the doorway, head tipped back, and eyes closed. It would be a mistake to think he was sleeping.

"And Doc," I added. "He'll be here in ten minutes. So caffeine up."

Tension in the room ratcheted higher as Milo snapped his head up.

"Oh," Sparrow's voice washed over me. Freddie's expression brightened, Jasper's attention lasered to the door, and Vaughn rose. Pivoting, I controlled my every reaction as I glanced to where she and Lainey stood in the doorway.

Our girl and her best friend.

The best friend who glared at Milo like she was ready to take his damn arm off if he dared put it too close to her.

Good luck with that, I wished him mentally. Not for all

the money in the world would I get involved in that partic-ular cluster fuck. I was already too invested as it was.

"Hey," Sparrow said, giving us all an uncertain smile. That killed me.

More than her tears. More than the *fucking* scars on her arms, that uncertainty gutted me.

Sparrow was a fighter. Brutal. Determined. Gifted. This—fisting my temper in both hands, I buried it with ruthless determination. She didn't need our rage.

Not yet.

She would, but she sure as fuck didn't need it right now, and she didn't need it directed at her.

"Coffee, Boo-Boo?" Freddie asked as he hopped down, his eyes and demeanor far more alert than he had been just a moment ago. "Ball-Cracker?"

"Yes," the best friend said.

"I just want water," Sparrow said. "I was going to the studio—if that's okay?"

The stillness in Jasper and Vaughn promised me they'd heard it too. Milo shifted his weight and I moved. Vaughn and I blocked him at the same time. It wasn't subtle, but I met his furious gaze and shook my head once.

Not. Yet.

"Yes," Rome answered for all of us. His directness was exactly what she needed. "Should you eat first?"

"No," Emersyn answered him, the measure of relief in her voice a damn sucker punch.

"Because you don't want to strain your system," I suggested, trusting Vaughn to keep Milo in place as I glanced at our girl. The painful thinness was back. The intervening days didn't seem to have been long enough to do that, but then, she'd only just started filling out her thinner frame before she left.

The shyness in those eyes as she glanced down and the hint of a smile went a long way toward making me feel just a bit better. "More that I don't want to overdo it." She took the water bottle Freddie handed her. "I kind of threw up this morning already."

"What?" Freddie asked. "Are you still feeling sick?"

She shook her head. "I just—ate three of the donuts you guys left for me and I think I ate them too fast." Her wince when she offered that admission had the anger I'd leashed surging against the ties.

"Fuck," Jasper swore. No one had to ask, he'd gone out to get them for her earlier.

Lainey wrapped an arm around her shoulders. "It was just too much sugar too fast. You'll be able to enjoy the others later."

"I can always eat them for you, Boo-Boo," Freddie offered. "Probably just bad donuts or something."

Her genuine chuckle was a gift. "Pretty sure it was me, but I want to go and stretch. I haven't really moved in a while and I need to see how much muscle I've lost."

Then she stiffened, and what little animation she'd gained bled from her face. Rome rose from his chair and moved to stand at her back. He didn't touch her, didn't say anything, just stood there, and a beat later, Doc filled the doorway.

She didn't even look at him. "I'm going to the studio."

"I'm going with you," Lainey said. When Milo twitched, she flat-out snorted. "We're not leaving the building." Then she faced down Doc like he didn't have several inches in height on her. "Excuse us."

Face impassive, Doc withdrew a few steps and Lainey put herself between Emersyn and him. No one said a word.

Save for Rome, who just said, "I'll be back." Then he followed them.

The silence stretched, almost painfully, until the sound of the door closed in the distance. The studio was sound-proof—kind of ideal for our discussion.

"What the fuck did you do?" Jasper demanded as he rounded on Doc.

"Not right now, Jas," I said, stopping him with a hand on his chest. I had my own thoughts on this particular issue. Thoughts we'd all have to address sooner or later.

"Kel—"

"I know," I told him, meeting his gaze. "I do know. We have a lot on our plate and she's right at the top of the list. But this can wait."

Wait until we had more details.

Wait until she was less wary.

Wait until we'd erased some of the fear in her.

"Kellan's right," Milo said. The ripple of shock rolling through the guys would have amused me on any other day. "We have shit we need to do and we need to keep it quiet when she's around."

Glancing at me when he said the last, Milo raised his brows. I nodded. "Sparrow needs to focus on herself. We need to give her the space to do that." Then we needed to figure out exactly what the fuck they'd done to her. Freddie knew some of it, but not all.

Doc's tests would tell us some too.

The only one who knew the whole story was Emersyn. Until she was ready to tell us, we'd have to fight this in the dark and without weapons.

That was fine. We'd handled worse odds.

Rome returned as Doc finally dragged a chair out from

the table. Vaughn just slapped a cup of coffee in front of him without a care for how it sloshed over the sides.

"Then let's get started," Jasper snarled, retreating, and that was something.

"We're still waiting on Liam," I said and pulled out my phone. It had buzzed when Sparrow had been in the room, but I didn't want the distraction.

A single message on the screen.

Ten minutes.

"Everyone get coffee, take a leak, shake off your shit and get ready to listen. When Liam gets here, we are going to settle some shit." That got everyone's attention. Freddie peered at me curiously. "What?"

"Who died and made you boss?"

"No one died," Milo said gruffly. "Kel's taking over."

Dead silence blanketed the room.

Rome shrugged. Vaughn only nodded. Jasper frowned, but didn't say a word. Unsurprisingly, Doc gave me a long hard stare. "Since when?"

"Since we discussed it," I told him. "This is done and not open for debate. We have too many irons in the fire and too many fronts we're defending on. That means we're done chasing our tails. Eat. Coffee. Piss. Whatever you need to do. You have nine minutes."

Then we were going to sort this shit out—starting with us and moving our way out to eliminate the threats we could eliminate right now. Her uncle had used our blindspots against us to get to her.

That wasn't happening again.

1

EMERSYN

Not even Lainey's arm linked with mine could slow the wild beat of my heart. I couldn't even bring myself to look at Doc. Not after that exam. Not after...

Rome reached past me, just barely brushing my arm with his, to open the door to the studio. A shiver skated over my skin, but this was one of apprehension. Stealing a look up at him, I smiled. "Thank you."

It came out far less wavering than I'd worried it would. A smile touched his own lips, brief, but the warmth never left his eyes. "I want to talk to you." Though, he didn't look at Lainey, he added, "Alone."

While not framed as a question, it also didn't register as a demand. Lainey chuckled. "I'll be inside, staring at myself in the mirrors."

She took the water bottle from my hand before she slid away and closed the door. Lainey seemed to like Rome.

Which was good, cause he'd been in our bed the night before. Turning, I looked up at him. "Hi."

"Hi." Raising his hand, he waited until I took a step closer before he traced a finger under my eye. They were so sore that even that light contact reminded me of how puffy they were. "What do you need?"

Closing my eyes, I leaned into him and then he wrapped his arms around me. Pressing my forehead to his chest, I just stayed right there. The hug offered security, safety, and even comfort. It was also a promise.

"I don't know," I admitted. It was so fucking hard to admit that too. A part of me couldn't even believe I admitted to throwing up, then again, they were all so worried. You could have sliced a knife at the tension present in that room.

Rome stroked a hand over my hair, the light petting sensation accompanied by his nails gently massaging my scalp had my eyelids fluttering. "Do you still feel sick?"

Not answering immediately, I considered how I was feeling. Between the jumbled emotional and physical reactions, my head was a mess. "I like being back."

It wasn't a lot, but—that part was true. Tipping my head back, I looked up at him. "Thank you for coming in last night."

Lainey being there had been wonderful, but when the dreams came...

"Kel doesn't know. He was sleeping."

I didn't laugh because Rome sounded pleased with himself.

"He was guarding the door."

My amusement fled at that sentiment. Guarding me.

He'd been guarding me.

With a light touch, Rome lifted my chin up so I'd look at him again. "He cares."

"I know." So did I. But I was... Steeling myself, I said, "Broken isn't bad."

"It's not, Starling."

Burying my face against his chest again, I threaded my arms around him. The scars ached today. I'd had cramps too. Then we'd found the donuts and I'd been so excited and hungry.

Rome said nothing as I clung to him. But I couldn't hide here forever, no matter if he'd let me. I really was glad to be back.

"I am glad to be back," I said, hoping he could hear me even if I was talking to his chest. "Just not sure I know how to be back yet."

"You will." Simple. Pure. Confidence. "Are you going to dance?"

"Yes." I'd meant it earlier. I needed to know how much I'd lost. How much muscle, how much flexibility—how much skill. If I'd lost too much... "Dancing is all I know."

"You know how to fly," he whispered against my hair, and I smiled at that. "We can mend wings, Starling."

That sounded amazing.

"Okay."

Another squeeze, then I made myself let him go. He loosened his grip, but when his gaze dipped to my lips once and then back to me, I rose on my tiptoes to meet his kiss. The first brush of his mouth to mine was gentle, the lightest of touches. He raised his hands to cup my cheeks.

Lips parting, I darted my tongue against his and then he deepened the kiss until all I could taste was Rome. He chased away every shadow that lingered from the night before, from the nightmares haunting me, from the endless days in Pinetree and...

My uncle's face flashed in my eyes, and I pulled back. Rome didn't hold me captive, but there was no mistaking the concern he wore. I licked my lips and tried to summon a smile. It failed miserably, but Rome cupped my cheek.

"I'm here," he promised. "I won't leave."

Not, I won't leave without telling you. No, just, I won't leave.

"Thank you." I touched his hand with mine and then he let me go as I turned to the studio door. Another glance at him, though, I couldn't help myself. His eyes. The color. It was what I'd searched for while I'd been in Pinetree before... "Maybe we can have lunch in a few hours?"

"Yes." No hesitation. "What do you want?"

I chuckled. Food sounded horrific at the moment, but— I needed to eat. "Think I can get a salad? A big one—like a Chef or a Cobb salad?"

Neither sounded appealing, but they'd be lighter and I could eat around anything my stomach didn't want.

"Yes. Dressing?"

I shook my head. Nope. Not tempting fate with that one.

Reaching around me, he opened the door again. "Be careful?"

"Yes."

That satisfied him. Lainey glanced over from where she leaned against the barre when the door opened.

"Do you want lunch?" Rome asked her.

"As long as it isn't greasy or made from processed foods." The lightness in her tone practically dared someone to challenge her. Making a face at her, I glanced back at Rome.

"She likes the same kind of salads I do. Please."

He flashed me a smile, and a nod, then closed the door and left us alone. I stared at it for a long moment, a sliver of longing alongside loneliness. Squaring my shoulders, I dragged my attention around to find Lainey giving me a sympathetic look.

"You don't have to do this, you know," she counseled, and I shook my head. "You just got back, and while you haven't told me what happened…"

"I did," I argued.

"You told me a little," she flung the ball back into my court. "I know when someone is guarding their words to protect me."

From anyone else, that might have sounded like an attack, but this was Lainey…

Moving to the floor, I slid down into a split. The pull on my thighs, my hamstrings, and my groin was intense. But I didn't force it, I just went down inch by inch as muscle memory helped muscle elasticity.

This was going to hurt.

"Em, when are you going to trust me?"

"I trust you." When she said nothing, I finished the stretch and held it until my muscles stopped trembling. Two-plus weeks was a lot of physical ground to make up. Finally, I glanced over at her. "Lainey, I do trust you."

"You were going through hell—all these years—you were in *Hell*. Why didn't you tell me?" It was the one question she hadn't asked. The one she'd given me room to breathe on since I'd found her in the clubhouse.

Coffee in one hand and my water in the other, she crossed to where I stretched and sank down on the floor in front of me. Pain flickered in her eyes and I had to blink back more tears. I'd cried more in the last few days than I think I had in my whole life.

At least more than I could remember.

"The clinic," she said slowly, but I could read the question amongst the pain in her eyes.

I shook my head. "I don't know if it was his or Eric's. I never wanted to know. I just—I couldn't."

"I hate that I didn't know. I knew he—"

I hated that she was in pain over this. "Lainey, I couldn't tell you. It was never about trust. Ever." I reached out to grip her hand and she fisted mine.

"But I knew something was wrong. I *knew* he was hurting you." The absolute conviction in her expression arrested me. "I wanted so badly to help you—but I didn't know how." Then the pain flickering there turned to fury. "And fucking Adam..."

She didn't finish the thought, taking a sip of her coffee instead. "Lainey..."

"Do not defend him to me," she said with such absolute rancor.

"He tried to help me. Well..." I sighed. "It's difficult to explain, but he did offer."

Her frown was swift. "What did he do?"

"He came to see me on the tour—about a week before it came to Braxton Harbor."

Surprise flickered across her face.

"He was really the last person I expected to see. Beyond —when I saw him with you and what you said about him, he and I aren't friends."

Weariness crashed through me and I leaned to the right, forcing myself to keep stretching. I needed to move. Keep moving or collapse into a fetal ball.

Fuck, I didn't want to cry anymore.

"What did he want?" Lainey asked when I didn't say anything.

"He asked me to marry him." That whole conversation had been so fucking weird.

"He did *what?*" Shock registered first, her chin rising, her eyes flashing, and even her voice climbing in pitch.

"I said no," I told her with a wry smile. "I couldn't. But he didn't want my answer then. And I know it's not funny, but Lainey, you look like you're going to turn into one of those cartoon steam kettles with the whistle screaming."

"Good, then I look like I feel. What do you mean he asked you to marry him?"

Shifting to stretch the other way, I let out a breath. "It's been a few months, so bear with me, and I'm still a little —fuzzy."

Fuzzy was a kind word for it. The anger drained out of her expression. "You don't—"

"I do, I've wanted to tell you since it happened. But..." I gestured to the studio. "This wasn't something I could tell you in a secret text message."

"I get it."

"Please, don't be mad at me."

"Oh, trust me," she said in a tone of velvet steel. "*You* are not the one I'm angry with." Then she blew out a breath. "Tell me. I can handle it. After the last few days..." An entirely different light came into her eyes. "I can handle anything."

Sorry, Adam, I apologized mentally. My thighs burned as I shifted my stretch and pointed my toes.

We had to talk about the last few days too. Why they had kept her here. We'd talked about so much and nothing at the same time. All the cracked shards seemed to tremble inside of me. Nothing held them together at the moment, not really.

One step at a time, I cautioned myself.

Broken isn't bad.

"Like I said, he came to see me while I was on the tour. Honestly, when he knocked on my hotel door—he was the last person I expected to see." Looking back, I could barely remember what I'd been thinking at the time. "It was weird —I was...I was bruised up. Eric had been particularly unkind a couple of days before and when he saw the bruises, he offered to take care of it for me."

Huh. I'd almost forgotten that part. I squeezed Lainey's fingers once before letting go and moved to pull my legs from the splits. Instead, I went into cobbler's pose, pressing the bottoms of my feet together. My hips protested it, but my body and I had a long, long acquaintance with pain and discomfort.

"Did he?" Lainey asked.

I shook my head. "No."

Her expression turned dark.

"And the problem isn't a problem anymore." I wouldn't say another word about it. The guys had taken care of it. The Vandals. Jasper. Kellan. Vaughn.

They'd ended that particular problem, and I still had not one fuck left to give for how Eric died.

Good riddance.

"I hope from the expression on your face that mad crew of violent misfits made sure that problem suffered on his way out."

I cut my gaze to the mirror and the hint of a smile I wore surprised me.

"The thought of me torturing him turns you on, doesn't it..."

The whisper of Jasper's question from a few months

earlier teased me. It was like a puzzle piece sliding into place. Maybe I should ask them how they did it.

Or would that be weird?

When I flicked a look back to Lainey, I caught her raised eyebrows, and I lifted my shoulders a little. "I'm just glad he's not my problem anymore."

So. Fucking. Glad.

"Me too."

We shared a small grin and then I pressed forward, leaning over my feet and elongating my back.

"Anyway… When he showed up, at first, I thought it was about you and that something had happened. He assured me you were safe though, and I sent you a text later and you answered. Oh…" I straightened. I had sent her a text. Good.

It was kind of hazy that night. Like I watched it happen through some gauzy veil.

"He was being—weird. I guess that is the only word I can use for it. When I told him to get to the point, he said he'd come to ask me to marry him, and honestly, I thought it was a joke at first. He pointed out I was eighteen and there was a lot he could do for me…"

Her lips compressed.

Straightening, I looked her in the eye. "When I asked him what, he said a lot. That he could 'protect' me and make sure I would never be hurt again."

Not that I'd believed him.

"When I asked him why, he said he'd tell me after I married him."

"What an asshole," she said with a grim look.

I shrugged. "I told him I couldn't—no matter what he could do for me—not without talking to you first."

Her smile was fleeting. "Bet that pissed him off."

I shook my head. "I don't know. He said to not answer him then and to think about it. He'd call me in a couple of weeks..."

And then, well, then I wasn't there to be called. I'd been here, safe and hidden with my Vandals even if I hadn't understood how safe I'd been.

That seemed so long ago.

So very, very long ago.

"I think he meant it," I finally said. "For what it's worth."

"That he wanted to marry you?"

"Well, I don't think it had anything to do with me." I shook my head. "But what I think he meant was the protecting me part."

She snorted.

"Lainey...I'm sorry."

"Nothing for you to be sorry about, Em. Not a damn thing." Her gaze went distant for a moment, then rocketed back to me. "Adam and I were a fable, a fairy tale, a stupid, stupid childish dream. I hope he did mean he'd protect you. That would at least make him less of an asshole. Not much less, but definitely less."

"Maybe. Then again," I said, bracing my hands on the floor and prepping myself for the pain as I pushed all my weight up onto them. Fire raced along the nerves in my forearms and everything trembled. Damaged tissue. Scar tissue. Abused muscles. "The only reason he could want to protect me would be *for* you."

2

Sweat dripped off every part of me before I collapsed on the floor to stare up at the ceiling. The room was hot, humid, and stank of my sweat. I was pretty sure I was going to puke again.

Lainey appeared in my periphery. A moment later, she pressed a bottle against my cheek and it was so deliciously cool. Closing my eyes, I tried to get my panting under control.

"I'm so fucking out of shape," I complained, though it came out broken. Sweat stung my eyes as I forced them open and then took the bottle. Sitting up took me a hot minute. I didn't even protest when Lainey helped.

My muscles wobbled like Jell-O. Even focusing on Lainey took real effort. Concern flickered across her face. "I think you overdid it."

The layering of understatement in that light, almost airy tone sent a ripple of amusement through me. Laughing, I nearly fumbled opening the water bottle. I could barely close my fingers on the cap.

Lainey steadied my grip and helped me open it. I took a couple of swallows. The water wasn't really cold, which was good. In this instance, cold water would be the worst thing for me.

Some distant part of my mind recognized this. The part of me who'd been dancing almost all of my life, who lived for the stage, thrived on it—because when I was there—I wasn't me. That part, that part damn well knew I wasn't ready for what I was doing.

But I didn't care.

I needed this.

Another swallow of water as I fought for control of my breathing. The rapid pounding of my heart bashed against my ribs. Sliding down next to me, Lainey let me lean on her.

"I'm all sweaty," I protested.

"I don't care," she retorted. "I'm not going to die because you got sweat on me."

Another laugh escaped me. My arms hurt. My back ached. My legs burned. I hadn't even gone up in the silks. Broken wings might heal, but I couldn't afford to be a grounded bird.

"You're still healing." Despite the lightness of her tone, it definitely held an element of scolding. "You can afford to not kill yourself on day one."

I shook my head. "I'll be fine." My heart rate was coming down and I wasn't quite gasping anymore. "It always takes a bit of work to get back into it after a break—"

"This wasn't a *break*, Em." She cupped my wrist, and I tried not to notice how much I continued to tremble. With care, she turned my arm over. The pink scars were absolutely livid. "They *hurt* you."

I didn't even try to shrug. "I have to heal, Lainey. I have to. Dancing is—"

"Your escape," she finished for me. "It's your way out. I remember. Even when you wouldn't tell me why or what was happening. I knew it was the key to your freedom. Goddammit, Em, I wish you'd told me."

"He'd have hurt you," I told her. "From the beginning, he made it clear I was to stay away from you."

"I hate that son of a bitch," she swore. "When I get back—"

"You won't do a damn thing." It was my turn to take the hard line. I didn't back down from the rage in her eyes. What fueled that rage was terror. "You can't. You have to promise me that you won't try."

"No chance in hell am I making that promise. Grandfather has..."

"Lainey." I stressed her name as I turned my hand over to capture hers. "You *can't*. Believe me when I say I hate him with every fiber of my being, but he is dangerous. I know he's killed people or had them killed."

"Then why are you protecting him?"

I scoffed. "I'm not protecting him. He could die tomorrow, and I'd go ask Freddie to pee on his grave for me." Tears clawed at the back of my throat, but I swallowed against the urge. "Every person—every person I've ever told has died."

And I still hadn't told her everything. The stricken look on her face shredded me. "Em..."

"Every. Single. One." Until now. "When you want to know why I couldn't tell you—this is why. It's why I won't tell you all of it now. I don't want you to have that in your mind. I could—I could distance myself for a long time. But if he hurt you…" It was why I'd gone back. He'd threatened all of those men out there. Good men.

Maybe not good by anyone else's definition, but they were good by mine. Good because they looked after each other. Good because they protected each other. Good, because for some damn reason, they decided I was worth protecting.

Setting the water bottle down, I turned my hands over to look at the angry scars and then up at Lainey.

"These will heal. I will dance. I will fly. But I can't lose you. I don't even dare risk you. At the same time, I'm selfish because I'm glad you're here."

Closing her eyes, Lainey dragged me in for a hug. "I could throttle you," she said in a voice misty with unshed tears. "I love you."

"I love you, too," I whispered, clinging to her. "You have saved me so many times."

"Not enough," she complained and I chuckled.

"More than you know."

Her arms tightened around me.

"Please, promise me." I couldn't let this go. "You can't do anything, and you can't let him know you know—"

"Can I break his legs?"

Pulling back, I lifted my shoulders. "I hurt him."

"Yeah?" She swiped at her face. "Bad?"

"He had to have surgery."

Mouth falling open, she stared at me. "Seriously?"

"Liam gave me a few lessons. And I put them to good use." I hoped he could never walk right again. "I should have done more…"

"Good, I hope it *hurt* a lot."

Me too.

"Now," she said as she climbed to her feet and held her hand out to me. "You stink."

"I love you, too," I said, chuckling even though I still kind of wanted to cry. Could you want to laugh and cry at the same time? Still, I let her pull me up and I winced at the drag on my arms.

My legs were less than happy with me. I was really going to hurt later.

"Think you can try to eat again after you shower?" Worry decorated those syllables. "I mean, we can get something bland from somewhere. Though if they have delivery, no one has been polite enough to share it."

My first step was a hobbling one. Fucking ow. My feet were cramping. I forced one step and flattened my foot. Then the next. I wouldn't let the toes keep curling.

"I'll try," I said. "Food would be good. Though... my stomach still isn't fond of a lot of things." Probably from the lack of food, but I kept that comment to myself. "I would like some coffee, though. After another couple of bottles of water."

I needed to ask the guys for some liniment. I didn't know if they had that here or what. Maybe some bananas. The potassium would be good for my muscles.

Limping forward, I made it three steps before Lainey slid an arm around me. "Lean on me."

"I'll be okay," I assured her, no matter how grateful I was for her company. "Really—this isn't the worst..."

The darkening of her expression silenced me from going into any further details. "You do know pain is a *bad* thing, right?"

"You're not alive if it doesn't hurt," I countered. "Art is pain."

The absolute snort of disdain she released made me

grin, but I let her help me to the door. Opening it, we let in a rush of fresh cool air from the hallway. Oh, and that just emphasized how bad my stink really was.

It took real effort to flatten my feet out cause my toes kept cramping and curling. Pushing open the door, the sound rushed in. I'd almost forgotten the soundproofing they'd done to the studio.

The raised voices had us both pausing. "Are you fucking kidding me right now?" Jasper demanded, and there was no mistaking the absolute fury in his voice. I started forward, but Lainey gripped me a little tighter.

"Maybe we shouldn't." It wasn't fear on her face but guarded worry.

"No," I said steadily. "We shouldn't. But I need to." I had no idea what they were fighting about, but I hadn't heard Jasper that aggrieved in weeks and weeks. "Go on up, I'll be up in a minute."

She scowled. "You really think I'm letting you walk in there without backup?"

A laugh escaped me. "No, I didn't think that, but you don't have to protect me from them."

Skeptical didn't begin to cover her response or the roll of her eyes at my suggestion. Something crashed and I wasn't the only one who jumped.

"Jas," Kellan said in a crisp, whip-crack tone. "Let him finish."

When Lainey didn't back down, I nodded. "Stay behind me."

Then I started forward without leaning on her. The absolute huff of disgust damn near ruined my quiet approach because I wanted to laugh. Fuck, I'd missed her. It was like having my arm back to have her here. I had no idea how long she'd get to stay, so often our visits were brief.

Selfishly, I never wanted her to go back. But that wasn't my call. The silence ahead didn't bode well. Normally one of the guys stood where they could see the hall, even if they were in the kitchen or the living room.

I didn't see anyone.

It wasn't until I cleared the stairs and the wall, that I found out why.

The majority of the Vandals stood in a half-circle, except for Freddie, who leaned back against the far wall behind a newcomer, playing with his knife.

There was nothing playful in his gaze, though. If anything, he looked angrier than Jasper had sounded.

Rome and Vaughn were nearest to me, their backs turned. Liam was also closer to the center, almost toe to toe with Jasper, and the air around them crackled. Milo and Doc both glared at all of them, arms folded.

In fact, it was Milo who noticed our arrival. I couldn't see Kellan, but since I'd heard him, he had to be here. Milo's gaze sharpened on me. When he flicked a look at Lainey, then back to me before giving a nod away, I was pretty sure I got the message.

He didn't want Lainey here. Before I could parse that though, a too familiar voice said, "You're all wasting time. I came here to get her and I'm not leaving without her."

Oh.

Shit.

Lainey stiffened next to me. "Fuck off, Adam. No one asked you to come here."

Right, that took care of that.

Doc was suddenly right there, catching my elbow lightly. I'd been swaying and until he'd steadied me, I hadn't realized it.

"Lainey," Adam snapped.

"Don't you Lainey me," she snarled back, and I groaned.

"I'm okay," I told Doc, not yanking my arm away from him but only because the last thing I wanted was to fall. My calves were starting to cramp and only forcing my feet flat was keeping that from happening.

Dried sweat made me sticky, and I ignored what I was wearing or how I looked as I looped my free arm through Lainey's before she could charge forward.

Adam suddenly became visible as he cut across the room right at us and slammed into a brick wall known as Rome.

"Get the hell out of my way," Adam ordered. If I thought it had been a shit show before, it had nothing on now.

"No," Rome said in that steady voice of his and then Adam took a swing.

All Hell broke loose.

"Fuck no." Instead of letting me go, Doc wrapped a steel arm around my middle and then hauled me backward. Milo went from being on the other side of the room to right there, and though I lost my grip on Lainey, he didn't.

"Put me down," she ordered him, but Milo ignored her. Over his shoulder she went and he marched right up the hall, not even slowing as she slammed her fist against his kidneys.

I flinched. Doc didn't carry me up the stairs, just away from the battle. And fuck, it was a battle.

That fist Adam threw had connected; the impact of flesh on flesh was hard to miss. Rome didn't seem deterred cause he punched him. I'd seen Rome fight—Adam was going to die if he didn't stop. But then he lashed out with a foot and it caught Rome in the chest.

Vaughn was on him next with Jasper, but Liam hooked his arms under Adam's and locked his hands behind his neck as he dragged him back. A flash of silver had me struggling now. Not that Doc flinched.

"Freddie, don't!" Panic twisted through me. I'd never seen anyone as fast as Freddie.

Jasper caught him though, caught him at the last second even as the blade nicked Adam's face and left a bloody trickle in its wake.

"Calm the fuck down," Kellan roared. Maybe not roared, but it was louder than everyone else and while Adam had struggled, he finally stopped.

Liam didn't let him go. Vaughn hauled Rome up to his feet and Doc still wouldn't let me go to check on any of them.

"No, Little Bit," he said way too close to my ear. "Not while they're all worked up. One move in your direction, and they *will* kill him."

The information stopped my struggle instantly. He wasn't wrong. Violence permeated the air and turned it positively volcanic. Freddie's expression wasn't playful, nor was Jasper's. Even Vaughn looked grim. He had a hand on Rome's shoulder but checked me over with a glance.

All of them were still between me and Adam, except for Liam, who kept him trapped in a hold that he couldn't break out of.

"Do that again," Kellan said, stepping right up to a trapped Adam. "And I don't give a fuck what your last name is, no one will find enough body parts to identify you. Clear?"

A shiver rocked through my whole body at the absence of everything "Kellan" in his voice. Ice was warmer than his tone.

Adam locked eyes with him, then flicked a look at me before he nodded to Kellan. "Clear."

Still, Liam held him a moment longer before letting him go, only to push him all the way back to the wall. Whatever threat he issued was too quiet for me to hear. Jasper still had Freddie in hand.

"Let me go," I said in the softest voice I dared.

"You're safer here," Doc told me, and I didn't scoff. Weariness chased the adrenaline from my system.

"I'll be fine," I told him. "I'll stay here until they calm down, but let me go."

Now that the chaos had diminished, there was no escaping the warmth of him pressed against my back or the strength as he kept me locked to him. There was no way I was breaking free without his cooperation.

But I also didn't want to argue in case Jasper decided to kill him again. We'd been down that road once.

"Pl—" I started to say only Rome was in front of me, staring at Doc.

"She said to let her go." Nothing moved in his gaze and Doc let out a sigh as his arm loosened. He set me down with gentleness before he backed up a step.

Taking a deep breath, I flexed my feet to try and stay steady on them, but Rome dipped his gaze to me.

"Are you all right?" I asked before he could. The kick to the chest had to have hurt.

One nod. "You?"

"I kind of need a shower." It was inane, but it seemed to be the right thing to say. A smile flickered over his lips.

"Do you need help—"

"Emersyn," Adam said, and while I couldn't see him past Rome, he sounded like he was still on the other side of the room. "We need to talk."

Yeah.

We did.

Except—

"Please."

Adam Reed just said please to me and Lainey wasn't here to hear it. I sighed. Touching a hand to Rome's chest, I hoped he could read the question in my eyes. He must have because he shifted so I could take a couple of steps forward.

The Charley horse hit with a kind of violence that almost tore a whimper from me. Rome's hand shot out to steady me, and I dug what was left of my nails into his arm, but he didn't flinch.

It would pass.

It would pass.

It would pass.

Flattening my foot, I fought to keep from buckling. Strong fingers dug into the vicious knot. Tears burned in my eyes as the firm pressure worked the cramp until it released. Rome held me steady the whole time and then the pain released. Damn near sagging, I could have wept. Glancing down, I found Doc gazing up at me.

"Better, Little Bit?" There was no mistaking that concern.

"Yes," I admitted. "Thank you."

A flash of a smile warmed his face.

"Emersyn..." Adam tugged my attention back to him. "Can we talk... alone?"

So much for detente.

3

I t took effort to convince the guys to let me speak with Adam *at all*. Honestly, I didn't *really* want to talk to him. But despite all of Lainey's protestations and anger, I didn't want anything to happen to him either.

It would *hurt* her.

So, yes, I would talk to him, but not alone.

I wasn't afraid of Adam, not really. That said, I also didn't want to be alone with anyone I didn't trust fully. Of all of them, Jasper's reaction worried me the most, but he didn't flinch. His gaze tracked to Freddie, who stood next to him.

"We'll go grab lunch," he suggested, before glancing at me. "Hungry, yet?"

Honestly? No. But I needed to eat. "Something light?"

He nodded. When he cut a glance past me to where Milo vanished with Lainey, a headache beat behind my eye. I needed to go check on them. Yes, I nodded, Lainey needed to eat too. When I just tapped myself, he smiled. Whatever he got me would be fine for her.

With Freddie in tow, he paused next to me for a moment, but the moment I put a hand on his chest, he wrapped me into a hug and then kissed the top of my head. God, I was so disgusting. Not that it slowed him down. "Be back soon, Swan."

"Sorry, Boo-Boo," Freddie murmured, then he glanced at Adam before me. "You sure?"

"I'm sure. I'll be here."

He nodded, then looked at Adam again.

On impulse, I leaned up to whisper in Freddie's ear, "Tell me later how you'd do it?"

A grin flashed across his face. "Deal." He lifted his pinky and I hooked mine through it. Pinky swears counted.

Then he left with Jasper.

Two down.

"You sure you want to talk to him, Sparrow?" The fact Kellan just elongated the same question Freddie asked wasn't lost on me.

"Yes," I said, telling him the same thing I said to Freddie. "But will you stay?"

Adam shot me an impatient look, but Liam spoke before he could say anything, "I would like to as well."

"Okay." But that meant...

"It's fine, Dove," Vaughn told me, holding out a hand. I was so gross, but that didn't deter him from wrapping me up in a hug when I slid my palm over his. "We won't be far," he assured me in that silky, lyrical quality of his that hugged me almost as tight as he did.

I squeezed him, but when he let me go and I glanced at Rome, he had Doc blocked off again.

"We'll wait for you, Starling," Rome said without looking at me. Right...

"Thank you."

I didn't quite manage to hide my wince when I pivoted to face the guys, and Kellan's eyes narrowed. Then he nodded toward the kitchen. I limped ahead of all of them. I didn't want to be trapped in the corner at the table so I headed over toward the coffee.

"Sparrow?" The question from right behind me warned me of how close Kellan had approached.

"Do you mind if I sit on the counter?" I asked, glancing back at him. The expression on his face spoke volumes about how silly he thought the question was, but all he did was hold out his hands. Did I want help? "Please."

Normally, I could hop right up there but fuck, I hurt at the moment.

With care, he settled his hands on my hips and lifted me right up to sit. Though he didn't let his touch linger, he studied me for a long moment. Long enough for me to realize that Adam and Liam hadn't followed us yet.

"Ten minutes," he said, finally. "Then he goes."

That seemed totally reasonable to me, except... "I don't know if that will be enough time for him."

"Too fucking bad. He can make an appointment." The crack of command in his voice made my heart thump almost eagerly.

"I missed you," I admitted and some of the tension eased in his expression.

"Same, Sparrow," he promised, then brushed the back of one knuckle down my cheek. "We're agreed on the timing?"

"Can I have a half a cup of coffee?" My stomach wasn't jolting all over the place. "And some water?"

"You can have whatever you want."

"Then we're agreed."

He chuckled.

"I need a shower," I admitted and something close to amusement danced into his eyes.

"I didn't say a word."

"You're far too polite."

"Eh, you at your stinkiest still smells better than most other people at their finest."

The compliment was so off the cuff, that I couldn't help but smile. "Thank you."

"You're welcome, Sparrow." With one last brush of my cheek, he turned away to retrieve a fresh water bottle. It came from the cabinet and not the fridge. The little details they remembered. I still needed to cool down and icy water wasn't good for me—especially with my legs already cramping. "Take a minute and drink, we have time."

I unscrewed the cap as he moved to make fresh coffee. The rich scent had begun to fill the kitchen when a disgruntled Adam appeared in the doorway, Liam right behind him.

"You look like hell," he said without an ounce of preamble. "Are you alright?"

"I'm as well as I can be," I told him. The concern radiating off him was just—weird.

His lips compressed, but when he would have moved closer, Liam cut him off, and Kellan moved to lean against the counter next to me. "I'm not going to hurt her."

"Then it's not a problem if we're here," Liam said as though it were not the first time he'd made such a statement.

"Except, this conversation is between the two of us," Adam countered, and the cold look he favored Liam with held far more than ice. Venom poisoned his voice. "We *all* have our secrets, remember?"

This was going well. "Adam," I said in a voice as weary as I felt. "You can argue and protest, but I want them here."

Liam just smirked. "What Hellspawn wants..."

"...she gets," Kellan finished. "Shut up, Liam." Then he fixed Adam with a look. "You have ten minutes. Stop wasting her time, or you can go right back where you came from."

Impatience creased Adam's face, but he looked at me. "Pinetree?"

Kellan stiffened, and I pressed a hand to his shoulder. "Yes," I told him. "Apparently, everyone knows that place." No matter how light I kept my tone, I couldn't keep images from cycling through my vision like rapidly playing still frames.

Ice in my veins.

White noise.

Buzzing.

Blood on my face.

The stapler in my hand...

"It's popular in some circles," Adam said, the frost icing each word. "Too popular. Not your first visit."

I shrugged. "Some of that is still fuzzy." Focusing on Adam, I didn't dare look at Liam or Kellan right now.

"You should have called me." For the first time since I'd discovered he was here, his tone softened.

"One," I told him in the same tone he used with me. "You and I are not friends. We're acquaintances—*because* of Lainey."

Fire flashed in his eyes.

"Two," I continued. "There was no time to call you after I went back."

"Then how did—"

I raised a hand, though I could imagine what the rest of that question was.

"Three, Lainey is *my* friend. It's none of your business what she and I talk about."

He started forward a step. "It is my business when being involved with you can endanger her."

"Yes, I've always been a threat to her."

"Not you," he snapped. "You're just as pig-headed stubborn as she is. *You* are not the problem."

I almost smiled because the complete dismissal of me as a threat was almost sweet.

"That said, I don't want Lainey immersed in this any further than she already is."

"To be honest," I said, pausing to glance at the coffee maker when it stopped. The smell of fresh brew practically flavored the air and my stomach seemed almost cooperative.

"Think you can eat toast with that?" Kellan asked as he finally shifted and poured a cup.

My stomach actually growled and then made the most awkward bubbling noise. Heat flushed my face, but embarrassment aside, I was kind of hungry.

"Maybe one slice and dry?"

"You got it." He set the coffee cup next to me and moved over to the counter, then I glanced at Adam, whose expression had shifted.

"I'm sorry," he said abruptly. "I should let this wait."

"But Lainey," I finished for him, and he sighed before raking a weary hand over his face.

"Yeah. I didn't even know she was fucking here." He slanted a dark look at Liam. Undisturbed, Liam just shrugged. Adam looked at me again. "What do you need?"

"Right now?"

"Yes," he said with just a hint of impatience.

"That's not a short answer. How about we just settle on, I'm where I want to be." I didn't miss the way Kellan's shoulders relaxed or how Liam's chin dropped a fraction at my admission. "I know you're worried about Lainey—"

"I'm worried about you too. I'm not a total fucking monster."

Well, that was true.

"This," he continued, taking another step toward me. "This is why I came to see you on the tour, though."

"This—as in Pinetree?" I frowned.

Again, he simply said, "Yes. The offer still stands. It benefits both of us—or it will when I'm alive again."

Wait a minute...

"What?"

"He's playing dead for his own safety," Liam explained. "Not something you need to worry about right now, Hellspawn."

"My uncle didn't..."

"No," Adam and Liam said in one breath, and I shuddered. Kellan flicked a look over me, but I only nodded to him. I was okay. I could do this.

Then he set the napkin with a single slice of toast into my hand. Taking a bite from the corner of it, I bought myself some time.

"It's an unrelated issue," Liam continued. "Though your uncle..."

At my glance, he sighed.

"We'll discuss that later." He would give me time, but it wasn't going away. I could only wish for such luck.

"The point," Adam said, bringing my attention back to him. "You need help. I can help you."

"What offer?" Liam asked, cutting a glance to me then back to Adam.

"How do you two know each other?" I mean, if we were going to be asking questions.

Liam's mouth twisted. "I'm not the subject of this discussion, Hellspawn."

"I'm not the subject either," I countered, lifting my chin before taking another bite of the toast. Bread should not taste this damn good.

"Au contraire, Hellspawn," Liam said. "We'll agree to disagree. Adam's time is running out, though, so let's just focus on what offer Reed made and then I'll get this ass out of your hair."

Au contraire, my ass. I still didn't argue with him. "It doesn't matter. It wouldn't change anything now."

"Not immediately," Adam agreed with me, the unspoken "but" hanging off the end of that sentence. "The rest of that discussion can wait until you are up for it. And will be done privately."

"You're being allowed to talk to her because she wanted to speak to you," Kellan interjected. "Watch the attitude."

I took another bite of the toast; the more I ate, the better it tasted. Still, I didn't dare shove it all down.

"Then we're done?" Liam asked, straightening.

"Not until I've seen Lainey," Adam said.

"That's probably not a good idea," I warned him. To be perfectly fair, Lainey probably *didn't* want to talk to him. "I told her about the offer this morning."

He let out such an aggrieved sigh that I *almost* felt sorry for him. "Did you have to?"

"Of course, I did. I told you then, I wouldn't do anything she didn't know about. *She* is my friend. She deserves a lot better than you jerking her around and treating her like shit all the time."

Liam raised his brows but said nothing.

"Fine," Adam said as though he were doing everything he could to keep his temper in his grip. "One week."

"One week?"

"Yes, in one week. Have O'Connell bring you to where I am staying. We'll finish our discussion."

"Time's up. Out," Kellan ordered, and Liam gripped Adam.

"Let's go."

Instead of struggling, he just went and I stared after them. Kellan followed to the door. No sounds of argument or fighting drifted back. That didn't mean there wouldn't be fighting later. The blood on Adam's cheek had dried, but he hadn't even tried to clean it off.

"He's playing dead?" I asked Kellan when he returned to me.

"Sparrow, I don't fucking know. Liam just informed us of some of this while you were dancing... speaking of which." He canted his head to the side. "Did you injure yourself?"

I didn't roll my eyes. It wasn't an unfair question. "Too long in confinement. You lose muscle and stamina..." Then I looked at my arms. "Injuries don't help."

"Not an answer," he chided softly.

"I'll be fine. I've recovered from worse workouts."

"That," he said in a tone far too light. "Does not make me feel better."

"I'm sorry."

"You never have to be sorry, Sparrow." Closing the distance between us, he planted his hands on the counter on either side of me. "I need to know so I can keep you safe. I can't protect you—or *help* you if I don't know."

There was a lot more under that sentence than just my practicing. "I left."

"You did."

"I should have told you."

Blowing out a breath, Kellan flexed his fingers and looked down for a moment. "I wish you'd trusted me enough to tell me."

Hurt scraped through me. "Kellan..."

"It's okay, Sparrow. I was still earning your trust back." There was no mistaking the pain in his eyes for anything else. "My only true regret is that you were hurt at all."

"I had to—protect all of you."

"They told me." A wry smile twisted his lips. "I keep thinking that's all on us. We're the ones who protect you, not the other way around."

"But?"

"I like that you want to protect me, *but* I need you to never do it again if it endangers you."

"You would. You did in the garage that day..." It seemed a million years before. "When you sent me away with Rome after that man got in." Had he been one of my uncle's hunters? That left an unpleasant feeling in my stomach. "And at the hotel..."

"You are way too much like your brother," he told me and I wrinkled my nose.

"You don't have to be mean."

A genuine chuckle broke free from him. "It was a compliment."

"Are you sure?" Cause, I *liked* Milo, but...

"I'm positive." Telegraphing every single move, he

cupped my chin, then brushed his lips against mine. "You said you wanted to shower?"

A shiver skated over my skin. "I do."

"Then let's get that done for you and we'll go rescue your friend."

Shit. Lainey. "Milo won't hurt her."

"Pretty sure hurting her is very much the last thing on his mind."

I opened my mouth then snapped it shut. "Can we check on her first?"

"We can do anything you want, Sparrow."

He lifted me off the counter, and before he could put me down, I wrapped my arms around him and hugged him as tight as I could. "I really did miss all of you."

The weight of his sigh vibrated through me. "Fuck me, Sparrow, I've missed you too."

4

Holding her, I kept my reactions on firm lockdown. The desire to steal her, as far the fuck away from all of this as possible until that shattered look in her eyes had been completely erased, choked me. As much as I wanted it—wanted her—my ass had to stay in the passenger seat. She might let me guide the wheel, but she had to drive.

For now, I savored holding her. There was no mistaking the fine sense of trembling in her muscles. Even as I focused on her, the sound of masculine conversation in the distance faded. Liam was walking that asshole Reed right the fuck back out of here.

What the hell he'd been thinking bringing *him* right into the heart of the clubhouse—well, I knew what he'd been thinking. He'd been thinking about this little powerhouse I was holding.

Adam was another fucking ally in her corner. Not one I trusted. Nor did I want to see him take that high-handed fucking attitude anywhere near Lainey. We didn't know her well, but the attachment both of our Hardigans had for her —one firmly in place and the other fast-forming—meant we would be protecting her.

As her arms loosened, I set her on her feet. While I was careful, I kept my hands in place in case she stumbled at all. Together, we headed out of the kitchen. I stayed close but a half-step ahead. The guys were absent from the living room and the hall—even Doc.

The last surprised me more than the others. His attention on Emersyn unnerved her. Just one more thing for us to deal with this week. We were clearing the fucking decks.

Emersyn wavered a little on her feet, that little hitch to her step kept me on guard. At the stairs, she moved up carefully, wincing with every step.

"I'll be okay," she assured me, and I caught her glancing up at me.

"I worry about you, Sparrow."

The corner of her mouth kicked up into a hint of a smile. She put a hand on the wall at the top of the stairs. "You didn't like it when I limped when you were *just* the driver."

She wasn't wrong. Except... "Are you still angry with me about that?"

When the little sparrow paused and turned those wide brown eyes on me, I wanted to kick myself for asking the question in the first place. Literally, I'd wanted to strangle anyone looking to push her, and then what did I do but—

"Kel," she said on an exhale. "I got over being angry a long time ago. I know I was..." She fumbled for a moment. Checking the urge to reach out to her, I hesitated when I took a step nearer, but she didn't retreat. "I blamed you for being you. In my head, I'd—I'd gotten a crush because you were so nice to me without being…fake about it. You never looked at my body or my name. You looked at me."

"I looked at your body, Sparrow." Call a spade a fucking spade.

A flush touched her face, but then she laughed. "Well, that's fair. I looked at yours."

"Did you like what you saw?"

"Then?" She raised her brows and a hint of a real smile curved her lips. "Yes." With that, she began limping her way down the hall. "Now?"

When she took too long a pause on that, it was my turn to laugh. "Now you're being mean."

"Maybe just a little." At the door to my room, she paused then looked down the hallway. Milo's door was closed. "I don't hear any yelling."

"Nope." That was all I would offer on that unless she asked me a direct question.

"Can you give me one sec?"

"I'll give you all the time you need," I promised her. Then I waited as she took painful steps all the way to Milo's door, shoving my hands deep in my pockets to keep from just picking her up and carrying her.

At Milo's door, she knocked. "Guys—Adam is gone. I'm going to shower. Then I'd like my friend back, Milo. Lainey, if you need rescue, just shout."

Then she stole a glance back at me with the most mischievous look on her face. The expression was pure gold, and I couldn't have stopped my own grin if I tried.

She made a show of listening, then put a hand over her mouth as though smothering a laugh. Finally, she said, "All right, showering now. Be good."

With that, she limped her way back to me. I pushed open the door to my room to let her in and she gave me another fleeting grin. I closed up behind us, then checked my phone as she headed for her room. Instead of closing herself in though, she left the door open.

"Kel?"

I abandoned the phone. "Yes, Sparrow?"

"Did you want to know about the now?"

Teasing me. She was teasing me.

I liked it. "Only if you want to tell me."

She was in her bathroom, but like her bedroom door, she'd also left that open. Leaning against the bedroom door frame, I folded my arms.

The water turned on and when she appeared again, she was only in panties and that workout top. Bruises were still very visible against her skin. Marks that had been made by hands, like the one on the inside of her biceps.

I trained my gaze on her eyes. "Yes." Then she winced as she turned. "Dammit—ow."

Across the room in a flash, I put a hand on her side to steady her and she wore a pained look as she flattened her foot.

"Sparrow," I growled it out. I hadn't meant to, but fuck it. "You're killing me."

"Sorry," she said with a wince. "Not trying to. I wanted to make you smile."

"You do that by breathing," I promised. "Can I help?" I'd already begun to take my hands off her once she had a hand braced on the counter.

Steam had begun to billow out of the shower. She caught my gaze in the mirror that was rapidly fogging. "Did you mean it?"

"That I want to help?" Somehow, I didn't think that was the question.

"About wanting me before—whether I was hot and fucked right from Vaughn's bed or Jasper's or—"

Oh. That. Yeah, I didn't wait for her to finish listing all of them. I was well aware of my brothers. Looping my arm around her waist, I pulled her back against me and the erection I'd been steadily ignoring. Then I bent my head. Twisting, she met me halfway.

This kiss turned the one in the warehouse the day before into dust. Her mouth opened to the first brush of my tongue. Coffee, Emersyn, and a vague hint of peppermint flooded my senses. Wanting her too damn much *had* been the problem.

When we took her, I hadn't wanted her here because I never wanted her in this life. We did dark shit in dark places, it had always fundamentally been a part of us. What I hadn't understood then—that same fucking darkness had filled all the shadowy corners of her life as well.

A soft groan escaped her as I slid a hand up to close around her throat, and she didn't pull back. Even as I kept my grip light, she tilted her head and then her tongue dueled with mine. The wild beat of her pulse hammered against my thumb as I stroked it over the pulse point.

When she fisted my shirt and turned, I allowed it. Then I hooked an arm around her waist and lifted her to the counter. It put her head closer on the level to mine and took the pressure off her poor feet and legs.

Then she bit my lower lip and it was my turn to growl. I chased her mouth and she made the sweetest sound as our tongues collided. Her body seemed to go liquid; the frantic cadence of her heart never slowed. Pausing, as much to fist my own control as to give her a chance to catch her breath, I studied her flushed cheeks and the light in her eyes when she opened them to stare up at me.

I still had my hand on her throat. I should fucking remove it, but I liked how she felt there; how she looked.

How she *tasted*.

"Does that answer your question?" The words came out husky, almost too growly, and raw. "I want you, Sparrow. Freshly fucked from their beds or needing it in mine."

But...

"I'm also not a man driven by my needs. I can and will wait for you to be ready."

She let out a shuddering breath. "I'm selfish."

"I don't care." With care, I caressed her pulse point as it slowed. "The cage doors will never be closed, Sparrow. But you also aren't going to be alone again unless you want it." Then... well, fuck, one of us would still be there.

"I wish I knew what you guys all saw in me," she admitted. The vulnerability added another layer to the torture I was going to visit on that mother fucker who called himself her uncle.

"I can't imagine what you see in us, so we're even." Then I winked deliberately and slid my hand from her throat. A trembling smile turned up her lips. "Now, you need to shower and I need to know if you need Doc for your legs."

Her whole expression wrinkled into one of disgust. "I do *need* to talk to him...not sure I want to do it, though."

I sighed. "I don't know what happened between you." I raised a hand to forestall her saying anything. "I don't need to know unless he needs a bone or three broken. What I *do* know, is Doc cares. Mickey J could always be a bit of a dick when he needed to be. Doc—Doc is different."

She frowned.

"You never have to deal with anyone you don't want to,

understood? You just say the word to me or Jas or Vaughn—or fuck it—Liam and Rome. We'll take care of it."

"Not Freddie?" She tilted her head to the side. "Although, he was going to stab Adam earlier, so maybe not a good plan."

"Freddie's very protective of you. So, yeah, maybe only tell him if you don't care what happens to the other person."

That pulled another smile from her, one with a hint of laughter. "He did that at Pinetree...when we were leaving. The orderly tried to stop us." She gave a little shiver. "Freddie never stopped moving."

The barest dilation of her pupils worried me. "C'mon, Sparrow. Let's get you in the shower. I'll—"

"Don't go."

Right, war wouldn't get me out of here now. "Not going anywhere. But you're not ready for me yet."

"Will it bother you if I'm naked..."

"Bother is not the word I'd use."

She gave me another tremulous smile. "I don't want to be a tease."

"Right," I said with a click of my tongue. "Enough of that. Need me to strip you out of those clothes?"

Keeping it light, I let her make the call. She eased off the counter and slid down the front of me. There was no missing my erection.

"Dicks do that," she murmured, and I grinned.

"Yes, they do."

"I like that your dick does."

Chuckling, I gave her ass the lightest of pinches. She jerked a bit, but her grin only widened. "Get your beautiful ass in the shower, Sparrow, and stop giving my dick a hard time. He's already pissed at me."

Then she did something that stopped my whole fucking heart. She knelt at my feet and murmured to my groin, "Be a good boy, it's not Kellan's fault I can't play with you yet."

Fuck.

Me.

All the air backed up as she gazed up at me, all open and perfectly provocative.

"Shower," I ordered.

More of the tension leached out of her, and when she started to reach up, I held out my hand. She took it and I helped her to her feet.

With a will bound in iron, I stood there while she stripped off the rest of her clothes. The bare length of her was every bit as perfect, even if underweight. The jut of her ribs worried me. The scattering of old and new bruises on her skin. The evidence of burns on her back. I cataloged every single mark.

When she climbed into the shower, I moved to lean against the counter and found Rome sitting on the edge of her bed. I had no idea how long he'd been there, but he sat silently.

We locked gazes and I read the same promise of violence in him that currently roiled within me.

"Kel?"

"I'm still here," I said. "Do you need something?"

"Thank you."

"You never have to thank me, Sparrow."

"Maybe I *want* to," she said in that prim tone I hadn't heard in far too long. I stole a glance at the shower and found her looking at me. Water droplets were scattered over her face and more spray from the shower ran in rivulets over her shoulders.

"Then you're welcome," I murmured, and she smiled.

There wasn't much I wouldn't do for her to look at me like that. "Rome is here, by the way."

Her smile widened. "He's always here."

"Yes," he answered from where he sat. "I am."

She let out a little breath then disappeared behind the shower curtain again. My smile fell away and I cut a look back to Rome. He had his phone in his hand. I didn't have to wait long. My phone vibrated in my pocket.

The message on the screen said, *Doc is waiting in the hall.*

Blowing out a breath, I scrubbed a hand over my face. Doc wanted to see her.

We'd give her the choice when she finished the shower and then deal with whatever came next. We still had plans to make. Plans Liam derailed the discussion on when he showed up with Reed.

Then there was the offer he and Emersyn discussed. "Sparrow?"

"Hmm?" She sounded so relaxed, I almost didn't want to bring it up.

"The offer Reed mentioned. Do I need to know what it was?"

Rome cocked his head, listening probably as closely as I was.

"I don't think so," she answered.

Now I really wanted to know what it was. "If that changes…"

"I'll tell you," she said. "I promise."

"Thank you." Even if what I really wanted to say was just tell me anyway.

"You don't have to thank me," she fired back and I chuckled.

"You're a brat."

"Thank you!"

I didn't roll my eyes. I'd missed that mouth. The way she pushed back, challenged, teased, and even eviscerated with that tongue. I missed the wild spirit that beat in her breast.

Fuck was I glad she was home.

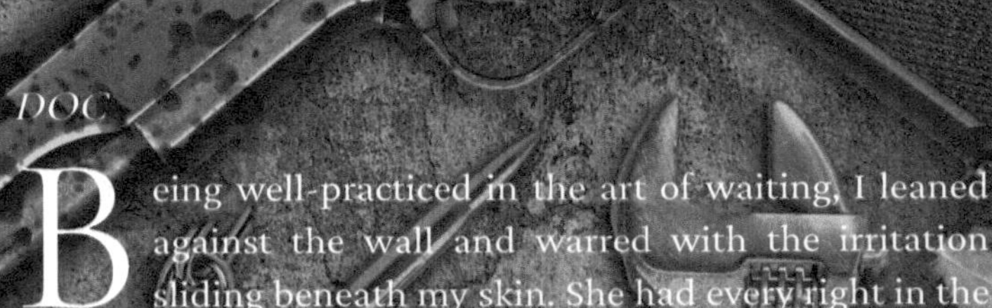

5

Being well-practiced in the art of waiting, I leaned against the wall and warred with the irritation sliding beneath my skin. She had every right in the world not to want to see me. Intellectually, I understood it.

Fuck, emotionally, I got it. I'd pushed her away. Deliberately. I wanted her to let go of the attachment she'd been forming because it seemed...

I don't fucking know what it seemed like at the time. Milo didn't buy my bullshit any more than Jasper had. To be fair, at least the hate often simmering in Jasper's eyes had dialed back. That had less to do with me than it had to do with that sweet girl in there who filled a gaping hole in this family they'd built for themselves.

Why shouldn't she? They'd constructed it around her. The last thing Milo needed was me perving on his sister. It had been bad enough when she'd just been this eighteen-year-old victim these idiots had kidnapped.

Now...

The door to Kellan's room opened and the man himself stood there. He gave me a long, assessing look. His expression betrayed nothing.

"Would she rather do this downstairs?" The room between Kellan's and Rome's was something akin to a cell. Even if it had its own bathroom and space.

"No," Emersyn answered from somewhere behind Kellan. "I don't."

At that, Kellan took a step to the side and motioned for me to enter. The door between Kellan's room and Emersyn's stood open. When she didn't appear to be in Kellan's, I followed the scent of steamy shower and the faint perfume of the shampoo she used. It had a touch of citrus and vanilla.

I found her standing near her open bathroom door, running a comb through wet hair. It was no surprise that Rome was also in the room. He sat on the foot of her bed, though he spared me a glance when I came in—a glance and a nod before he focused on her again.

While she didn't look at me and her attention was steadfast on the floor, I studied her posture. The cramps she'd had downstairs were indicative of the starvation she'd faced the last few weeks. It wasn't just the meds that needed to be out of her system, but she also needed to put better things back in.

I didn't have all the blood test results back yet, but I had some of the more important ones. I'd have the rest back by end of business the following day. Finished, she straightened and turned to put the comb back. She still favored one leg.

Clamping down on the pure rage of her mistreatment in a *medical* facility, I focused on what we needed to focus on. The here and the now. Patient first.

"Emersyn," I began, even if her name tasted odd on my tongue. This little bit had dug herself deeper inside of me than even I'd realized. "Do you want to do this in private or are the boys staying?"

Her reluctance to be alone with me at the clinic had stung, but it also made sense. She'd been through a trauma and the last time we'd seen each other, I'd been an asshole.

On purpose.

I was lucky she hadn't punched me.

Though, come to think of it, I would far prefer that to this. *It's not about you, Mickey. Suck it the fuck up and do your goddamn job.*

Chewing her lower lip, she peered at me. Did she want to know if it was good news or bad news? I had my bag with me. I'd already given her one round of antibiotics. "It's totally up to you," I told her, tacking the *little bit* on silently. "There are some things we need to talk about."

The crumpling of her expression gutted me, but she closed her eyes as she turned away.

"Medical or personal?" She kept her back to us, but her shoulders were already squaring and her chin coming up. There was so much fire in Little Bit. So much fire.

"Both," I confirmed. "One can wait, if you'd like. The other can't."

She sighed, then faced me again. Well, faced us.

"Kel? Do you and Rome mind if we talk...?"

"Of course, I don't. But do you think you can eat?" Yeah, I wasn't the only one not liking how wasted away she appeared.

"Jasper and Freddie were going to bring me something back. I don't know when..."

"I'll find out," Rome said as he stood. "If it's more than an hour then eat?"

A tremulous, if genuine smile touched her lips at the directness in that response. "Yes. I did have toast earlier."

Right. I didn't say a word.

"I'll get you coffee," Rome said, then motioned to the refillable water bottle on the dresser. "Fresh water. Cold, but not too cold."

Another smile. Then she gave him a light kiss. He brushed his knuckles down her cheek before he turned. The gentleness in his expression fled as he pinned me with a look.

Take care of her. I understood the unspoken order clearly. Like Rome, Kellan gave her a kiss, too, then he also favored me with a less than friendly stare.

Unlike Rome, however, he said, "Don't be a dick. I'll be right on the other side of that door."

That was as much for her as it was for me. At least Kellan kept his threats neutral. Then again, he always followed through. I just nodded.

After the door closed behind Kel, leaving me alone with Emersyn, I glanced back to find her watching me. She had her arms folded, her posture defensive.

"Little Bit," I said, then raised a hand when she lifted that chin and her eyes flashed. Yeah, I wanted to see that fire stoked, but this was about more than that. "Please, just hear me out?"

She glanced away, her focus on the door for a moment. I could rush her and push, but that was about just as much pushing as I intended to do. Kellan was right, she didn't deserve anyone being a dick to her.

When she faced me again, there was something unfathomable in those dark brown eyes. Despite having the same eye color as her brother, her eyes were so different. Or they had been, though I'd argue that the darkness that haunted them both was so different.

Maybe I just saw what I wanted to see.

"Okay," she agreed, and I let out a breath.

I motioned to the bed or the chair that sat on the far side near the wall of Rome's room. "Have a seat?"

Thankfully, she didn't offer an argument, just huffed a little impatiently, then circled the bed to take a seat. Yeah, that put her farther away, but I'd rather she took the time to let her muscles rest. Once she'd taken a seat, I circled the bed to follow her but I perched on the end of the bed.

With my bag set aside, I kept my hands visible and my palms open to her. The guarded look, the jumpiness when I'd first been treating her. The physiological and emotional signs of abuse had all been there, both in her actions and her responses.

We attributed all of it to her dance partner. He was definitely responsible for *some*, but not all. I saw the signs, I should have done more. Getting her to trust me had been the first step, then helping her had been the second.

"I'm sorry," I said, and surprise flickered over her face. "I was an asshole to you and I was an asshole on purpose."

Fresh shock registered.

Ripping the fucking Band-Aid off, I continued, "I also did it in the worst possible fucking way. Making you come was a fucking treat for me, then I stomped on your feelings so you would push me away. I was a dick."

She said nothing, staring at me with those bruised eyes.

"If you want to know why I did it, I will tell you, but I'm not going to force you to listen to me justify shit. There is no justification for it. But you did not deserve what I did...you never deserved that. I'm sorry."

The words tasted like so many shards of broken glass. I

refused to be deterred. If she never wanted to know why I did it, that was something I'd have to accept.

"Thank you," she said after a silence so long it had become almost profound. "I don't know if I want to know why you did it. It... hurt."

That slammed the blade in and twisted it deep. "I know, Little Bit. I wish I could go back and smack the shit out of myself for even thinking it was necessary."

A little nod. "Me too." Then lifted her shoulders. "There are a lot of things I wish I could go back for."

"Yeah," I agreed. "Same."

Then I lifted a hand to rub the back of my neck. The scar tissue was rough beneath my fingers, but I needed to alleviate the headache.

And the guilt.

The guilt was like a vicious little amoeba intent on devouring me from the inside out. But I fucking deserved it.

"That's the personal part," I said, exhaling a breath. "Now for the medical."

Her knuckles went white where she clasped her hands together. Reaching out, I put a hand on hers. It was not remotely professional, but I hated being a part of her suffering.

"You're not pregnant," I told her firmly. Tears filled her eyes, and she turned over one of her trembling hands and latched onto mine. "You do have a mild infection, but the shot I gave you should clear it up. I brought you a round of antibiotics to go ahead and take because we're going to make sure of it."

Her nails dug into the side of my palm, but I didn't flinch.

"The mild bruising and tearing in your vaginal region are going to take some time. It's probably uncomfortable when you pee, but I can give you something that will help with urination until this is all healed up. Your IUD is still in place, we verified that at the clinic."

She nodded.

"Now, let's talk about how undernourished you are... and what I want you to do to get you healthy again. Particularly when it comes to dehydrating yourself and pushing your muscles past the point of fatigue when you are not at a good fighting weight."

A tight line formed between her brows as she scowled at me. "I'm not giving up my dancing." Darkness continued to haunt those wounded eyes.

"I didn't say give it up, Little Bit. I said to get you back to fighting weight. There are also these..." I nodded to the scars on her arms. I had to *not* stare at them. They infuriated me. "Can you tell me how deep the cuts were? Did they compromise the muscles and tendons in your arms? There are things we can do to help with the scar tissue and then to work on the flexibility."

That pulled her back to me and refocused her attention. "They—" she broke off, hesitating. When she tugged her hand from mine, I opened my fingers to let her go and I sat back some to give her space again. "They—did it at my uncle's house." She licked her lips, then looked down at the scars running down her forearms. "He broke a glass then... cut me. I think they wanted it to look like I tried to kill myself."

Her voice wobbled at the end.

"Rome and Liam wanted his name..." She lifted her head, a tight smile on her face. "But I don't know how deep it was. I was—restrained a lot, and there were bandages and...then I'd go to the place with the white static."

That went with the burns I'd closed on her back and

along her neck. They were definitely healing but present. The fuckers had been using electro-shock. That also fits with what Milo's little spitfire told us.

Folding her arms, she hid the scars and then met my gaze. "I can't really tell you anything else. There was a fire, so if they had records, those are probably gone."

"Well, the full tox screen will come back soon, but it's also been a few days since they got you out, right?"

One nod.

"We'll start with what it tells us. Then we'll go from there. We can fix this, Little Bit."

"I have to dance, Doc," she said on a rushed exhale. "It's —my freedom. It's everything. I can't—if I can't…"

"You will," I told her and held out my hand again. "Look at me, Little Bit."

For a long moment, I thought she wouldn't as her breathing grew shallower. Anxiety could mask itself as a lot of things, but this wasn't anxiety.

This was fear.

It spiked the adrenaline and raked over me like the burning wreckage that spilled over me that day in the field. The burns that scalded my skin and fried my nerves. The excruciating pain that left you mute in agony because there were no words as it shredded even the thoughts you tried to form.

"Little Bit," I repeated. "Look at me."

She snapped at that, her gaze on me. "Don't tell me what to do."

"Then breathe with me," I informed her. "Breathe, slowly. Count for the inhale, hold, then release."

Her pupils were fat and blown, another sign of shock. That came with the fear.

"You're going to dance again, Little Bit. You danced this morning..."

"Not like I—"

"You danced." It wasn't a question. "It's a sport, it takes time and practice. Didn't you tell me the longer you were restricted, the more muscle tone you lost?"

The shallow dips in her breathing grew fewer as she took longer inhales.

"The longer it took you to get back to it, the longer it took to actually gain back the muscle and the flexibility." That wasn't a question. "So cut yourself some slack, there, Little Bit. You just got back. You had one workout and you pushed yourself harder than anyone should have. You could have injured yourself."

"I didn't."

A lone tear tracked down her cheek, and she swiped at it like it had offended her.

"But you could have, so we're going to talk diet, exercise, sleep regimen. Then we're going to talk about therapy for those arms and working on reducing that scar tissue."

"Is that even possible?" The question held more curiosity than it did anger or rebellion.

"Yes," I said, and when she finally set her hand in mine again, I traced a finger up the line of one angry scar. "Scar tissue is denser and it's less flexible. There are ointments we can apply every day that will help reduce the scar both in density and appearance. It will take time..."

"But it will go away?"

"Maybe not entirely, but enough that it won't be so visible or painful for you."

She bit her lower lip.

"But you need to take care of you. We need to rebalance

your electrolytes, and I brought a couple of vitamin shots so we can get a jump start on your system."

She searched my face and I waited her out even as I continued to trace the scar. "The infection?"

"Will be gone in a few days. Refrain from sex for a bit, not long, but enough to let you heal up. I can test you again in a week if you'd like. Okay—maybe not like but…"

"I get it," she assured me and then nodded slowly. "I don't want to hurt them."

"I know you don't, and so do they." The care they were all taking with her screamed that to anyone too stupid to notice it. That idiot this morning could have ended up dead and damn near had. "Will you let me help you?"

A half-nod. "Are you going to keep calling me Little Bit?"

My mouth twisted. "You asked me to stop. So I will." I didn't like it. "I might slip though, but I'll do my best…"

"It's okay."

Surprise sparked through me. "What's okay?"

"If you call me that. It's okay."

I frowned.

"You apologized for being a dick." A hint of a smile. "I haven't decided whether I forgive you or not yet but… you did apologize."

It was my turn to nod.

"So, it's okay. You can call me Little Bit."

"Will you call me Mickey?"

"I don't know if I'm there yet."

Honest answer.

"Okay." The vicious weight tearing me apart since I'd found out she was missing eased. It was far from gone. I'd burned bridges. Rebuilding them might take time. "Let's do those shots, then... we'll go see the boys so they know you're doing all right."

That wasn't what I'd intended to say, but she didn't need any more hits today except...

"Little Bit, listen to me?" At her nod, I locked my gaze on her. "I know this has been a trial, I can't imagine how it was for you and I won't pretend that I can. You can tell me anything, everything, or nothing. I'm not going anywhere. But I need you to remember that the fire inside of you is so much stronger than the fire they lit around you. You're here. You survived. Hold on to that and let that fire inside of you help heal you."

Some of the darkness in her eyes pulled back.

"That was almost poetic, Doc," she told me with a hint of a real smile. The first one to truly touch her eyes since I'd walked in. "What other secrets are you hiding?"

It was my turn to grin. "Get to know me," I invited. "You can find them all for yourself."

Maybe, just maybe, I could earn that forgiveness. First, we would get her body healed, then her spirit and her mind. If I was lucky, her heart would follow.

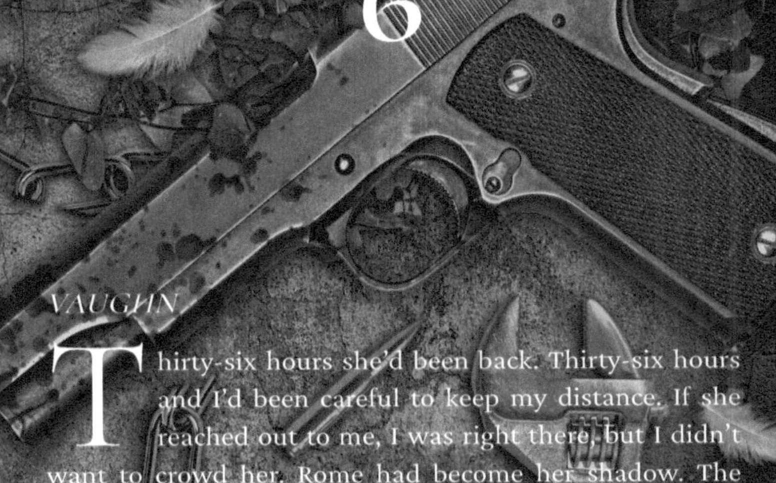

6

VAUGHN

Thirty-six hours she'd been back. Thirty-six hours and I'd been careful to keep my distance. If she reached out to me, I was right there, but I didn't want to crowd her. Rome had become her shadow. The relief whenever she sought him out with her gaze and found him close slaughtered any possible sense of jealousy.

Not that it didn't amuse me to find him letting himself out of Kellan's room—and more likely hers—when I was leaving mine to head down for coffee. He met my gaze with a nod.

"She okay?" I asked because, yeah, I did want to know. What I really wanted was to slip in there and steal her into my bed. Better to just have her choose to sleep there.

But her friend had given Milo the finger at dinner the night before, and the girls had gone upstairs—*alone*. So, I figured right now Lainey was who she needed.

Or maybe the girl needed her. Milo's irritation at the way Lainey blew him off had been entertaining. As had

Jasper's rumbled, "Don't you think you're a little old for her?"

If a head could have exploded, it would have been Milo's. As it was, he'd just stabbed his fork into his food and glared at him. "You looking for another round?"

Not missing a beat, Jasper smirked. "I'm not the one about to pop a blood vessel. But whatever you need..."

Yeah, I'd left them out in the warehouse pounding on each other. Cause that shit got boring after a while. They weren't going to kill each other and the rats scattered as soon as the fight started. What they didn't understand—the rats that was—and didn't need to, was that Jasper and Milo would never prolong a fight with a person they really wanted to kill.

They were both way too brutal for that.

What had begun as a real disagreement when Milo came home, had begun to resemble the old days when they took out their aggravations on each other to keep the edge off. In this case? To keep those tempers away from Dove.

I was fine with it.

"Yes," Rome answered my earlier question about how she was. He'd showered before leaving her room, and his hair was still damp. "Coffee?"

"I was just going down to make it, unless you plan on hiking four blocks over to get her the good stuff again."

Rome shrugged. "She likes the good stuff."

Grinning, I jerked my head to the hall. "Come on, I'll drive."

But Rome paused. He cut a glance back up the hallway.

"Jas is out, he went with Kel. They are going over every single truck. Kellan wanted a look at them himself." While he didn't work on the big rigs that often, he did know their engines. Someone had been fucking with the black boxes on them. Every single truck had been outfitted with a transponder.

When Kellan was done, they'd be outfitted with two.

Rome canted his head.

"I can go get the coffee, man. Stay here if she needs you here." Not leaving her alone was the plan. One of us would always be available to her. Kel made that damn clear *before* Liam derailed the meeting by bringing Reed into the mix.

Not that we'd needed the instruction. No one would smother her, but if one of us had been close at hand when her uncle pulled his approach, we could have prevented a lot of damage.

We learned from our mistakes.

"No," Rome said, then pivoted on his heel and strode down the hallway. He hit his fist against Milo's door in rapid succession. I was pretty sure no one would be asleep after that knock, except maybe the girls. But they had the insulation of Kellan and Rome's rooms to buffer the sounds.

Arms folded, I waited cause Rome was about to either make Milo's day or piss him off.

Maybe both.

The door yanked open and Milo glared, his disheveled hair a clear indicator he'd just gotten out of bed. The rumpled sweatpants were also a dead giveaway. Not that he'd just gotten out of bed, but that he'd been expecting someone different.

Scrubbing a hand over his face, Milo tried to wipe away the irritation, but it didn't help. Much.

"We're going to get Starling and her friend coffee. They aren't awake yet. Don't bother them. But be available if she needs you."

"Yes, sir," Milo drawled. "I'll be available. You plan on getting me coffee?"

Rome seemed to consider him. Then shook his head. "No."

I had to cover my mouth, or I'd have flat out fucking guffawed at the ripple of shock rioting over Milo's face. "What?"

"You wanted to send her away." He shrugged. "You have to earn coffee."

Then he pivoted and strode toward me. I met Milo's stunned gaze and just shrugged. I could get him coffee since I was going, but Rome had a point.

Besides, it was funny.

"Are you sure they're asleep?" Milo asked when Rome was a couple of steps away. "Do I have time to shower?"

"Maybe," Rome answered without looking back. "Starling was still sleeping dreamlessly when I got out of bed. Her friend snores. Pretty sure she's still asleep too." But his tone more than conveyed that whether she was or not, was not his problem.

I caught the shift in Milo's expression. "What do you mean when you got out of *bed*?"

"He's slept with the girls the last two nights," I answered before Rome could say a word. "If I were guessing, he's slept with Dove every night since they got her back."

Milo's mouth opened, but no sound came out.

"See you when we get back, Raptor."

Rome hadn't waited for his response. Not because he was afraid of it or even particularly worried about it. Rome didn't give a damn what people thought about him. Not even us.

Now, if accusations started flying—well, that was just one fight no one needed to have, cause Liam would get involved and Liam was the only one I'd ever seen take Milo and Jasper on *and* still be the one who walked away from the fight.

Thanks, but no thanks.

I'd never tested my size and strength against Liam, and I had no intentions of doing it now. Fighting each other wasn't a win. The ride to the coffee spot Rome favored didn't take long. Instead of the normal heat and morning sun, the day greeted us with heavy, lead-gray clouds and a damp breeze.

Autumn promised to be a wet one. We needed to make sure Dove had the right kinds of clothes and boots, especially if Rome planned to take her out for more painting.

"She needs a new design," he said as I pulled parallel to the curb nearest the shop and stopped on the street. Despite the earlier hour—and the only reason I was awake this early was for a chance to see her—traffic was heavy. There was no parking on this block.

"You want me to park or—"

"I got it." He was already out of the car. I rolled down the window as he was walking away.

"Don't forget to get one for me."

He waved a hand.

I kept an eye on the street and the traffic. Rome had a hoodie up over his head so I could make him out, but his hair wasn't visible. Didn't mean I'd relax my vigilance.

None of us were running alone either, if we could help it. Not that we couldn't look after ourselves, but the Sharpe family had a lot of money—and a lot of muscle—if they decided to bring the fight to our streets? Fine, let them bring it. We'd deal with them. But I didn't want any more surprises.

None of us dead.

That said, I wouldn't mind if her uncle would just show

up here. I'd like to take out the garbage and get back to enjoying her return. Movement on the street prickled my awareness. I scanned the area, uncertain of what triggered the warning.

Turning the phone in my hand, I fired a text to Rome.

Watch your back.

It could be absolutely nothing. Or it could be something. We were well within our territory, still… I gave every single person passing the car a solid look. No faces jumped out at me.

Shifting my gaze to the side mirrors, I scanned behind us, then the rearview, then the street.

Something—there.

The movement was moving up the opposite side of the street. His clothes were a wealthier cut. The shoes probably cost more than my car. His hair was unkempt and he had circles under his eyes like he'd been on a bender, but everything about him decried being in this part of Braxton Harbor at this time of day.

He was either doing the walk of shame…

Twice, he cast a look at the coffee shop and then glanced at my car. I kept an eye on him via the side mirror. Six foot plus, lean, expensive tastes—wrong day for this.

I warned him mentally, but the asshole didn't listen. Instead, he headed right for the cafe. All we'd wanted was coffee so we could take it back to Dove, and now this jackass. I snapped a picture of his profile and fired it off to Rome.

The *read* popped under the image, but he didn't say anything as the guy ducked inside.

Giving you 30.

Thirty seconds, I was already counting. If I didn't see or hear from Rome in that time, I was going in.

I was at twenty-six when the door to the shop opened, and Rome emerged with a tray of coffees in white cups with little green stoppers. He strode for the car, his expression grim.

Releasing the gun from where it was holstered next to the seat, I scanned behind him. Yep, here came the sore thumb. He wasn't even trying to look like he wasn't following Rome.

The passenger window was still open, letting in the sounds of morning traffic and the hum of a population waking up.

"Dodge," I told Rome as he got closer, but he shook his head.

"I got it." After setting the coffee inside securely, he straightened to greet the newcomer. "Liam told you to go home."

"Well, fuck Liam," the man responded. "He doesn't give me orders."

"This is the wrong place for you—"

This time, the flash of movement took me no time to track. "Down," I ordered and had the driver's side window open.

A fucking drive-by in the middle of rush-hour? They were going to kill someone.

"Get the fuck off me," the newcomer complained, but I didn't have time to worry about him. The gun pointing out of the driver's side window grew closer and closer. Passing traffic zoomed by.

I cut my gaze to the side mirror then back. So many fucking places for bullets to stray. I put two into the other vehicle—one right through that open window. The gun pointing out of it fell to the street as the driver went sideways and then his car slammed into a fire hydrant.

Pushing the driver's side door open, I ignored the squealing tires as cars ground to a halt. Water began to geyser, and I grabbed the gun from the street but doubled back to the car immediately at the sound of sirens in the distance.

"Time to go," I said, already putting the car in drive once I was behind the wheel again. The backdoor opened and a body landed on the seat. I barely had time to register that it was the idiot who followed Rome from the shop, before Rome was in the passenger seat with the coffee.

Right, we'd deal with him later. He wasn't moving. Hopefully, it wasn't body disposal. I really wanted to have some time with Dove, even if it was just to sit there with her.

I took the long way back to the clubhouse, one eye on the road behind us. The sirens didn't follow. There was every chance in the world someone got a look at me firing. But the locals would clean their cameras.

Still...

Fuck a goddamn duck. I called Kellan.

He answered at the end of the first ring. "What's up?"

"Shooter near the Dark and Roasted. Took care of it. But there was a body and a car, no time to clean it up."

I could picture his expression, almost hear the sigh. "Witnesses?"

"Probably. But it was fast."

"Any bystanders hurt?"

"No." It was why I'd targeted the driver. He had the weapon. Thankfully, he'd not hit anyone when he slammed into the hydrant. That was more dumb luck than skill.

"Get out of sight, I'll clean it up."

"Thanks—we may have a secondary problem."

"We don't," Rome said before Kellan could respond. "It's Liam's problem. We'll deal with it."

"Right. Let me know if I need to be involved."

Rome said nothing, so I just shook my head. "We'll take care of it. Soon as we get the coffee back to the girls."

"If you're too hot..." Kellan warned.

"I know." He didn't have to tell me. "I'll keep it on the down-low."

But I was not going dark anywhere *but* the clubhouse. The call ended without anything else needing to be said. Hell, just telling Kellan alleviated some of my concerns.

One more circle.

"We're clean," Rome said after a few more minutes, and I agreed. "The coffee is going to get cold."

"It won't." If it did, well, we'd figure that out too. "Maybe we should consider redecorating."

He gave me a look.

"What?" I shrugged. "We could add a real coffee maker like that fancy fucker at Liam's."

No comment came from him for a long moment, then he nodded. "I'll grab it the next time I'm there."

I didn't laugh. Cause Rome meant that.

Literally.

That would tweak Liam's balls. "It's for Dove."

"Yes," Rome agreed. "Liam won't mind."

A groan came from the backseat and I glanced back at him. "Is he going to be a problem?"

"Yes." Rome already had his phone in his hand. "For Liam."

7

The door closing softly behind Rome woke me. Or maybe it was his absence behind me. I'd been struggling to go to sleep, even with Lainey right there, when he slipped in and curled his arm around me. The moment his chest touched my back, I'd dropped into an almost dreamless sleep.

There had been a couple of moments, but Rome had always been there. Once, it had been Lainey who gripped my hands as Rome hugged me. I couldn't even remember the dream, just the shadows holding me down and the burn of white static.

"He really cares about you," Lainey said softly, and I stole a look over to where she'd opened her eyes and watched me. We were both lying on our sides. "They all do. Even Milo."

The last she said with a little wrinkle of her nose. Shifting, I hugged the pillow and studied her. "Do you want to talk to me about him?"

"Not really," Lainey said with a sigh. "Besides, you didn't want to know."

"You can—I mean, you were my friend first."

The corners of her mouth twitched. "Technically, he's been your brother since you were born."

"Technically, I didn't know he even existed before three months ago." Had it been three months? "Four months." Time seemed a little muddy, so I just shook my head. "You've been my best friend, hell—the closest thing to a real family I've ever had. So...if you need to talk to me, I'm here."

She sighed and rolled onto her back. "Em, I need to figure out what the hell I'm doing before I can talk about it."

Propping myself up on my elbows, I frowned. "He's not hurt—"

"No," she replied sharply, her expression fierce. "Not at all. I swear, he hasn't done a damn thing to me that I haven't enjoyed—or wanted."

Good. I hadn't remotely thought he would and I'd caught him looking at her.

"Just—I had plans and..."

It took everything I had not to grimace.

"Yeah." That I got. Slumping back to the bed, I sighed. "You didn't ask me about Adam."

"I have no intention of asking about him." The cool tone hid a lot of hurt. Next time, I was gonna kick Adam in the balls—just not when the guys were there. Cause, yeah, I didn't want to get him killed. "I swear he lives to order me around."

"He cares."

She scowled at me and I lifted my shoulders.

"Lainey, he cares. I know you don't see it."

"No, I see it," she corrected. "I also see the loathing that comes along with it. The burden of *caring* about me. Thanks, I'll pass. It was bad enough when my mother was just his father's mistress. Now that they're married? Fuck no."

"They got married already?" All the time here had begun to bleed together.

She gave me a wry smile. "A few months ago. We still didn't know where you were, just that you were missing."

Catching her hand, I squeezed it. "Sorry I wasn't there."

"You wouldn't have wanted to go to their wedding."

"No," I admitted. "Not really." I didn't like her mother. I didn't like how she made Lainey feel like she always had to prove herself. Not that mine was much better.

Chuckling, Lainey shook her head. "I didn't want to be there. Honestly, no one with a soul wanted to be there." The traces of laughter faded and a frown tightened her brow.

"You have to go back soon." It wasn't a question.

She nodded.

I didn't want her to go, but there was no point in saying that.

"You could always come with me," she offered. "Grandfather and I can..."

"No," I said, pushing myself upward. "I love you for saying so, and I know you would do everything you could, but no—I don't want to leave—I don't want to leave here again. I might have to someday, but..."

"You like these guys as much as they like you."

Heat rushed to my face and I lifted my shoulders. I was sore and more than a little stiff. My muscles protested as I climbed out of bed. "Can you really like so many different guys at once?"

Because I did, I needed to find Jasper today and talk to

him. To Vaughn too. They'd both been hanging back. Liam had practically vanished. Then again, he was busy with Adam. Still, if I wanted to find him, I bet Rome would help me.

"I don't see why not," Lainey said as she sat up and watched me open the drawers. "Granted, there's liking a few guys and then there's liking a *few* guys."

She wasn't wrong. Then, there was the conversation with Doc the day before. By the time we'd finished, she'd emerged, more than a little rumpled with beard burn on her cheeks and neck. I hadn't said anything and she hadn't told me.

But when it was time to go to bed last night, the vein in Milo's forehead had throbbed when Lainey said she was coming up with me. Milo was someone else I needed to spend time with.

All that longing while I was in Pinetree, and now I was nervous about it. What would he do if he found out the truth? The real truth? Could I tell him? I wanted to know *him,* though, and I wanted him to know *me,* not the image he built up or the one the world had.

But the real me.

"Em..." Lainey said softly, and I snapped back to the present. My heart drummed a harsh cadence. "It's going to be okay."

I hoped so. "I know," I said. "Until then..."

"Fake it until you can make it."

Pretty much.

She took a shower while I just brushed my teeth and braided my hair. The burns on my neck looked better. When I worried about loosening my hair to cover them, she'd stopped me.

"You wanted your hair in a braid. Fuck the rest."

Except the rest might infuriate them. The minute that thought alighted, I banished it. Almost all of them had seen the visible wounds, and a few had seen the others. They were going to be mad about those regardless.

They wouldn't be mad at me.

Freddie promised they got angry, but they also got over it. To be honest, my own experience told me the same. Only when Lainey was dressed did we leave the room.

I needed coffee. The weakness in my limbs hadn't totally vanished. The soreness of overdoing it had me walking slower, but I definitely needed a stretch even if I didn't go for a full routine.

Milo surprised me when we stepped out. "Good morning," he called, and I turned to find him striding down the hallway toward us. His gaze was definitely on my best friend and not on me.

"Good morning," I returned the greeting. His hair was slicked back from his face and he'd shaved. He dragged his gaze off Lainey with some effort and focused on me.

"You okay?" He paused.

"I'm going down to find the coffee," Lainey said. "You two should probably talk."

"We should," I agreed. "But we can talk later. No one wants to talk to me before coffee."

"Same."

Milo surprised me with a grin. "Rome and Vaughn went on a coffee hunt for you, but I started a regular pot. It might not be fancy, but it will do in a pinch."

"Kind of you," Lainey said after a moment.

"I can be," he returned and I clicked my tongue against my teeth. Right.

"I'm going for the coffee." I didn't make it two steps before Lainey clasped my hand, but we weren't alone. Milo walked down with us. By the second step, there was no mistaking the fresh scent of coffee, and it wrapped around me like a siren.

Even my stomach growled, and for the first time in days, I really was hungry. Not just aware of how empty my stomach was or warring with the swaying sensation of being nauseated. Even the toast and salad I'd eaten the day before had been an effort.

Maybe there would be donuts again.

Course, the last thing I wanted to do was throw up another round of them. That was a waste of delicious donuts. No one was in the living room or the kitchen as I followed the scent of coffee with Lainey in tow.

"It's not much," Milo said, and I glanced at him.

"It's fine," I filled my mug. "Don't get me wrong, the fancier coffee is great, but this is life's blood right here. When I was on tour, the only coffee we had backstage half the time could put hair on your chest."

"I hope not," Lainey said with a wrinkled nose. "Can you imagine waxing your nipples? A Brazilian is bad enough. Thankfully, laser is way more comfortable."

I snickered because Milo flat-out blanched. "I don't think Milo wants to listen to that discussion. That said, I prefer laser too—I suppose I need to think about things like appointments."

Granted, it had been a while since anything resembling a treatment, but I'd been on top of the grooming before.

"We can look around and see what they have here," Lainey told me, but her eyes weren't on me. "Waxing or lasering, you want someone who knows what they're doing."

"Stop picking on Milo," I told her as I carried my coffee over to the table. "We can look it up later."

"Maybe go to the same place you got your tattoo," she suggested.

"You have a tattoo?" Milo yanked his attention off Lainey to look at me and I smiled at him.

"Yeah, Vaughn did it for me." After setting the coffee aside, I stood up and pulled my shirt higher so he could see my abdomen. One of the few things they hadn't stripped away from me when I'd gone back. Maybe given some time, they would have.

"Head up," Milo read. "Wings out."

"I love it." Because Vaughn had done it for me. "It helps me to remember..."

"Remember what, Dove?" the man in question asked as he entered the kitchen with a tray of coffees. His gaze dipped to my abdomen, still on display, and a smile stole over my lips as his eyes warmed. The silky caress of his voice was another thing I'd missed.

"Just remember," I answered, letting go of my shirt and circling Milo to meet Vaughn. He all but thrust the coffees at my brother as I wrapped my arms around him.

My brother.

That thought sank in, adding another layer. With warm arms that caged around me like a security blanket, Vaughn hugged me. "I've been meaning to ask how it was," he murmured.

Tucking my head over his heart, I closed my eyes and soaked in his nearness. "It's fine. I think. It got yucky for a little while, but then the scab fell off. They were going to remove it with a laser—but they never got around to it."

Oh, they really had said they were going to get rid of it. My uncle hated the tattoo. Just the thought of him sent another prickle of unease through me and my skin went hot then cold, and finally clammy.

At my shiver, Vaughn half-picked me up. "Bring the coffee," he said as he carried me out to the living room.

"I'm okay," I told him and he settled onto the sofa with me in his lap.

"I know you are," he agreed. "But I'm not."

I frowned. "What's wrong?"

"I haven't gotten to really hold you in a few weeks. It's good to know you're here and you're all right." He spoke in a serious, low tone that had me wrapping him into a tighter hug.

"I'm sorry," I whispered.

"You don't have to be sorry." Even as he assured me, he ran his hand up and down my back. Tension I hadn't even realized had begun to knot my muscles loosened. "You never, ever have to be sorry, Dove. You made it, and you're back."

Milo cleared his throat, and I lifted my head to find him holding the tray with the coffees. Lainey hovered behind him, one of the white cups in her hand and a look of repleteness as she took a drink.

"Coffee?"

"You can have mine," Vaughn offered him.

"Rome's an ass," Milo grumped, but there was almost a smile on his lips as I took the coffee. When I would have moved over to sit next to him, Vaughn squeezed me gently.

"You're fine right here," he said. "Unless you need to sit elsewhere."

An out. He gave me an out and I glanced up to meet those gorgeous pale brown eyes of his. They were almost the shade of topaz, depending on the light. I loved looking at them.

"I'm good."

"Good." Then he brushed his lips to my forehead as Milo made a choked sound.

"Knock it off," Lainey commanded and I caught her slapping his biceps. "Look at how relaxed she is. Stop making it weird."

I bit my lip at the very heated look he sent her but he just set Vaughn's coffee on the table.

"I'll wait until Rome deems me worthy of coffee again."

"What did you do that you aren't worthy of it now?" Curiosity wriggled through me.

"Sent you away," Milo said dryly.

Oh.

I chewed my lip as he held up his hands, palm forward. "Not doing it again. But I do want to sit and talk to you if you can tear yourself away."

A sound rumbled through Vaughn, but I wasn't remotely deterred by the fierce look on Milo's face. "I've been here for two days," I informed him. "But you've been more interested in my best friend than me."

"Hey," Lainey said as Milo's ears actually seemed to flush. "Don't drag me into this. He does that enough as it is."

I giggled. Even irritated, Lainey seemed to sparkle. She and Milo might be at odds right now, but there was definitely chemistry there. He *really* better be good to her, or I was going...

"I need my stapler," I said, ignoring the surprise on their faces as I tried to stand. Vaughn had to put me on my feet as I looked around. "We didn't bring it with us, but I thought—I need to go to Liam's."

I needed my stapler.

"I'll get it," Rome said as he came down the hall. "Don't worry, Starling, I'll go get it."

My heart raced. "Can I go with you?" Two days. I'd left it there and then hadn't gone back for it.

I really needed it.

"Maybe stay here," Milo began, but I didn't want to stay.

"I'll be back," I promised him and Lainey. "I just need to go get it."

Vaughn and Rome shared a look and I swung my head, glancing between them.

"Please."

Rome held out his hand. "Come, we'll get it." Then he looked at Vaughn.

"Where did you…" Vaughn began, but Rome didn't slow as he guided me to the door. My pulse was so loud, it was like it thudded in my ears.

"In the office. Check for me?"

"Yeah," Vaughn said, an element of disappointment in his voice.

I paused, glancing back. At my cessation of movement, Rome stopped. "You can come with us," I offered, guilt tackling the wildness under my skin. Even just standing there was agitating. I couldn't believe I hadn't brought it with me.

"Not this time, Dove," he assured me. "Go get your— stapler. Rome has you." The last he said with an indecipherable look at Rome.

"Yes. We'll be back." Then Rome glanced down at me. "You ready, Starling?"

"Please."

"We're going."

I barely noticed anything else as he picked me up at the door and carried me over to a car. Rome even buckled my seatbelt for me and then set my coffee cup in the holder before closing the passenger door.

When had he taken the coffee? I'd had it in my hand, but I didn't recall setting it down. Ice frosted my skin and I hugged myself a little tighter. The sun slanted through the windows as Rome pulled out of the garage.

There were guys moving around outside and a truck parked alongside one of the huge bay doors. I recognized some of the rats, but I didn't want to think about them. No, just go. I hated the traffic, even as Rome took a different route, pulling around the thicker clog of cars. There must have been an accident.

The random ramble of thoughts wandered through my head as I tried to slow my shallow breathing. The closer we got though, the deeper my breaths became. But it wasn't until we were almost to Liam's before I realized I didn't have any shoes.

8

Fuck Adam Reed. A headache pulsed behind my eye. He was in a full-on fucking snit after I took him back to the house. Not that he'd have enjoyed the description. Still, that was exactly what it was.

"You have five days," he'd declared. "Five days then I'm getting Lainey, and we're getting the fuck out of here."

We'd talked strategy for hours, and that was only after I convinced him that we needed the time. Too many damn irons were in the fire. Ezra spiraled out of control. He'd blown my phone up with so many fucking messages, the voicemail was full.

Not good.

Especially when I had two missed calls from an unknown number. I'd already dumped the messages and sent a message to the King. If he'd been trying to reach me while I settled Adam's furious ass back down, we had more problems.

After a shower, I'd thrown on shorts and walked back to

the kitchen. Coffee, food, then sleep. Maybe just food and then sleep. Exhaustion wore at me. I'd been on the go since we got Hellspawn back.

There were fights this weekend.

"What offer did you make her?"

The question had been right there since the two had their cryptic exchange in the kitchen. Maybe not all that cryptic. Still, their conversation had excluded the actual item in the center of it. The fact she'd confided in her *friend* and not us chafed.

"We aren't discussing Emersyn Sharpe." The grim reply had done little to settle my irritation or curiosity. Adam's reaction to Emersyn's name the first time around had been telling.

His reaction to *seeing* her, even more so.

But it wasn't a romantic interest. No, his attention had been far too fucking respectful. The heat in his eyes had been saved for Lainey. Elaine Benedict. Goddammit, I should have recognized the name. Reed's father married her mother.

How the fuck were we all tangled up, and I'd somehow missed their connection to Milo's Ivy?

The coffee spluttered as the machine spat out two shots of espresso. I didn't bother to soften either one. The first, I shotgunned before I opened the fridge.

I'd missed the connection because Adam and Ezra did not bring up Lainey by name. Not once had I seen a mention of her with regard to Emersyn either. So, what Milo had known and when he'd known it, the cagey shit had kept to himself.

Pulling out one of the pre-prepared meals I kept on hand, I shoved it in the microwave and scrubbed a hand over my face. I should have called Rome to check on her, but I wanted to give her—

The alarm beeped a warning that it had disengaged a split second before the locks tumbled. Pulling the gun from the top of the fridge, I flicked off the light in the kitchen. The shades in the living room were down, blocking the mid-morning light...

"We're here," Rome said and some of the tension bled out of me. A moment later, Emersyn stepped through the open door. Pale, expression tight, and her teeth sunk into her lower lip like she planned to leave them there.

I stored the gun just in time because the microwave beeped it was finished and she flinched so hard I winced.

"Ease up, Hellspawn," I said by way of greeting. "It's just food."

Over her head, Rome glanced at me and he shook his head once. He didn't linger on the eye contact, his whole focus zeroing in on her.

"Sorry," she muttered, then fled. Fucking *fled* down deeper into the apartment. Instead of following her, Rome glanced at me again.

"What happened?" The last time I'd seen her, she'd been fine. Tired, more than a little worn out, but *fine*.

He shook his head. "She wanted the stapler."

As explanations went, that one was thin except—I got it. She'd been firm in holding onto it since we got her back.

"And Ezra is at the clubhouse."

"What?" That snapped my attention from the back bedroom to my other half.

Rome shrugged. "He followed me. Someone took a shot at us. Maybe at him. Vaughn took care of it, but your friend wasn't cooperating. He's secure in the office. Starling didn't see."

Fuck.

My.

Life.

I scrubbed a hand over my face again. All I wanted was a few hours of sleep. "Back up…"

"No. She needs…"

The discomfort leaking between his words had me packing away my own frustrations for the moment. He was worried about her.

"Her stapler. Give her a beat, Rome." I yanked open the nuke and pulled the food out. "Have you eaten?"

"Not hungry."

Right. Not really an answer. Putting the food on a plate, I slid it onto the counter. "Eat. I'll check on her in a minute. Tell me what happened."

His fingers twitched like he was drawing something, but then he curled them into a fist. "I don't know."

"You said someone took a shot at you," I reminded him. Currently, I had my own feelings on *that* subject tightly locked down. If someone took a shot at Rome, it could be related to me or the Vandals. It could have just been some punk on the street. But he said *Ezra* had been there…

Rome shrugged, but he didn't touch the food while I put more in the microwave. Instead, he studied my coffee machine. Yeah, I could put on a regular pot since they were here.

"The shooter is dead," was all he offered by explanation.

"And Ezra?"

"He's unconscious." That got a flicker of a smile, but I had no chance to pursue it because Hellspawn appeared in the doorway. Some of the color had returned to her face, she had her stapler firmly cradled in her arms, and there were traces of dampness on her cheeks and around her eyes.

"Who is?"

"No one," I said before Rome answered her. Directness could be a blessing and a curse. "Hungry, Hellspawn?"

She shrugged. Right. I was pulling the next meal out of the microwave, but Rome motioned her over to the plate I'd made for him. Wrinkling her nose, she blinked slowly. "Salmon for breakfast?"

"It's my dinner," I told her bluntly. "It's good for you."

Despite the encouragement, she still gave the food a look.

"It's good," Rome said. "I think." Then he took a bite. I wasn't the only one watching him, though I kept an eye on her as well.

The faint twitch to her lips when Rome couldn't help but grimace almost made me laugh for real. Resisting the urge, I plated the second meal. The lemon pepper chicken was one of my favorites. The brown rice and the carrots were also good.

"It's all right," Rome said finally.

"You don't like fish?" The genuine curiosity in her voice suggested that whatever fear had driven her to reclaim that stapler had eased. Or maybe she just wanted to make it easier for Rome.

He shrugged. "It's oily."

I snorted, but I wasn't the only one. Rome flashed her a smile.

"Do you want it?"

"Or you can have the chicken," I said patiently, ignoring the fact they were both being precious about the food. Not that I couldn't eat both meals, but if I had to... "I can always make an actual breakfast, Hellspawn, if dinner in the morning hours offends your sensibilities."

To take either plate, she was going to have to change her grip on the stapler or...

Fuck it. I put the plate down then moved over to the counter. "Come on, come sit. Then you can have it right next to you. I'll make coffee and if you don't want the chicken or the salmon, I'll make you an omelet and some bacon..."

If I hadn't been watching for it, I might have missed the faint grimace.

"Or some toast and maybe some poached eggs?" Not my favorite, but when your stomach wasn't cooperating, it would do.

Light seeped out of the shadows in her eyes.

Right, I moved from that counter to let her make her own call and set the chicken next to the salmon. Rome picked it up and took a bite, then dug in. I didn't comment. I could reheat the salmon after I got her something to eat.

One step at a time, she moved over to the counter then put the stapler down before she paused. I caught her actions in the reflection on the stainless steel. While the image blurred, her hesitation didn't.

Flattening her hands on the counter, she started to push up. It wasn't anywhere near the smoothness I'd seen her execute that move with before. Nor was it effortless.

Rome didn't move any more than I did. If she started to fall, we'd catch her. But she needed to know she could do this herself. Finally, she sat and scowled down at her arms.

I checked my need to comfort her or ask questions. For. The. Moment.

"What did Doc say?" Rome didn't. Another reason to love my mirror.

"That they will heal," she said slowly, fingering the scars. "That there are things we can do to reduce the scar tissue and to exercise the muscles—rehabilitate them."

Nothing in her tone suggested it was good news nor that she believed him.

"Did he give you the rest of your results?" I kept it light as I set the water to heat on the stove. The bread was ready to drop when I was ready.

The weight of her stare settled on me and I twisted to meet that look head-on.

"I'm not pregnant." A hot desert wind blew through me that she'd worried that had been an option.

"Okay."

Despite the fact that he seemed focused on his food, Rome undoubtedly listened to every single word she said.

And those she didn't.

Just like me.

"I have a bit of an infection," she added with a grimace. "The antibiotics are already working. He wants me to take more, though."

Right. I fisted my temper and parked it. People were going to be broken when I hit the ring this weekend. I needed the outlet. The question about her uncle was right there on my tongue, but I refused to make her explain shit to me.

I could torture it out of him.

Oh, I liked that plan.

I cracked two eggs, one at a time, into the boiling water. Then dropped the toast. Rome had nearly finished his food.

"Anything else you want to share?" Lots of ways to phrase that, but if she wanted to talk to us, I wasn't going to stop her.

"I hurt him."

"Doc?" I twisted to look at her again and a smile ghosted over her lips.

"No, not him. My uncle."

Oh. "Good."

She was chewing her lower lip again. Paying attention to the eggs and the toast, I got her breakfast together without smashing anything.

"I tried to get away." She wasn't looking at either of us this time. Instead, she rested a hand on the stapler. Rome went still. Everything about Hellspawn said wild animal, trapped, and hurt. One false move could startle her.

Worse, it could chase her off.

"I punched him in the dick." It was the almost wistful note in her voice that had me altering some plans where said bastard was concerned. "Then did that wrap his knee and jerk it move we worked on."

She swallowed, the convulsive motion in no way detracting from the solitary note of pride.

"Something cracked when he went down. I hurt him." The repeat of the last sentence stoked a sense of pride inside of me. When I held out the plate to her, she seemed to come back to us in the kitchen. Returning from whatever distant place she'd fled. "Thank you for showing me how to do that."

"You're welcome, Hellspawn. Give it another couple of days, and we'll start training again."

She gripped the plate, but I didn't let it go when she blinked in surprise. "Really?"

"I know you're not a hundred percent right now, but it's better to know what you can do no matter what condition you're in."

The sheer amount of chewing she kept doing to her

lower lip threatened to split the skin. Understanding kindled in her eyes and she nodded once. "Thank you."

"My pleasure. Remind me that I want to show you how to kill a man..." When she dipped her gaze to the stapler and red flushed her cheeks, I added, "Without the stapler."

There. The corners of her lips curved upwards in a real smile. There she was.

"I did pretty good with it," she admitted.

"You did amazing with it," I assured her, and when she tugged the plate, I let it go before handing her a fork. "But there's more than one way to skin an asshole."

Her nose wrinkled again. "At least you didn't say cat."

"Hellspawn, no one is skinning your pussy. Ever."

Rome huffed a breath, but it was Hellspawn's reaction that I wanted. The real smile came and went as if she fought with laughter. "Not even if I ask?"

"Ask me sometime and find out." What the fuck was I doing? The comment slipped out before I could reel it back in. But the mirth dancing in her eyes and the color in her cheeks was a thousand percent improvement from the pale, shaky woman who arrived with my other half.

I stole a glance at him and he nodded once—to me— then at her. But he was right. She responded to the teasing, to the tone, or maybe just to us.

Whatever.

Flirting with her wasn't a damn hardship. Still, I wasn't stepping on Rome's toes. She dug into the poached eggs and toast with some enthusiasm.

Satisfied, I got my food reheating then went about making coffee.

"Will you tell me how you know Adam?" she asked, but only after she'd cleaned her plate and turned down my offer for more.

The last thing I wanted to talk about was Adam.

"Sure," I countered. "Tell me what he offered you." I took her empty plate and passed her the fresh coffee. I'd made one for Rome too.

"You won't like it," she warned me.

That went without saying. "Then don't tell me." It was the best I could do.

"But I want to know how you know him."

Pulling out the food, I leaned back against the counter and sank the fork into the flaky, somewhat overcooked salmon, and shrugged. "I told you my price."

Rome could have told her. He knew. But she hadn't asked him. That, and I had a feeling he wanted to know what Reed had offered her too.

She sighed, staring into her coffee cup for a minute. "He asked me to marry him."

The plate cracked in my hand.

9

KELLAN

The latest message from Vaughn had me pinching the bridge of my nose. Emersyn had a panic attack of some kind. Rome had taken her to Liam's. Also, we had a guest at the clubhouse—though not inside, and it was someone *else* that Liam knew.

"Problem?" Jasper asked as he circled the truck carrying a couple of sodas. I'd been going over every single engine, then marking them as well as adding a secondary black box.

If someone wandered off with one of our trucks or tried to swap it with another by shifting the boxes, we'd know. The secondary only activated when the primary wasn't in range.

Not perfect by any stretch, but we needed more details. On my list of shit to get under control, the trucking business was near the top.

Near.

Sparrow was the top.

"Sparrow had a panic attack." I cracked open the can, then took a long drink from it. Jasper's knuckles whitened before he dragged out his cigarettes and lit one. Where that might have relaxed him, the tension around his eyes and in his jaw only seemed to sharpen. "And we have another guest at the clubhouse. Someone Liam knows."

"What the fuck is their deal? Have they told you?" Jasper asked, blowing out a stream of smoke. "And is she alright?"

"Rome took her to Liam's for something she left there, and I have some of the details on Liam and Milo's arrangement."

"Arrangement." Jasper spit and then glared off as I fired a message back to Vaughn. We'd be done here soon. If I had to go to Liam's to get Sparrow, I would.

The days of exiling her were done. If she *wanted* to stay there, it was one thing. I wouldn't like it, but I would make damn sure she knew she was welcome with us whenever and however she wanted.

"Not a fan of it, but I told you when this shit went down something wasn't right." It wasn't an "I told you so," and it didn't need to be.

I wanted to send her a message, too, but did she have her phone back yet? That had *also* been at Liam's. With that in mind, I sent Rome a text to make sure she picked up her phone while it was there. If not, I'd just get her a new one.

Shoving the phone back into my pocket, I knocked back half of the can of soda. It wasn't that hot today, but the work was also not clean and we had a lot of trucks. More than I realized. Jasper had done really fucking good with this business.

Another reason to be pissed off about someone fucking with it.

Jasper had gone silent, his gaze distant. "I get why they didn't trust me. But why didn't they tell you?"

"They didn't tell anyone, Jas," I reminded him, then bumped his shoulder with my fist before I resumed syncing the new black box with this last truck. "I think that was the point. They didn't pick and choose; they made a move and then waited to see how it played out."

Shaking my head, I could almost imagine that conversation. That was the problem. Milo and I had talked in a similar fashion once—when I'd told him I was leaving. It wasn't a conversation I'd had with anyone else.

"Milo took lead," I reminded both of us. "He led because we followed. He was the one who pulled us together, kept us together, and made sure we were all looked after."

Then he'd gone to prison.

I glanced at Jasper, he still stared away with an unreadable expression. "So, I get why they decided that in the beginning. But why did they let it play out?" I shrugged. "Milo wouldn't say anything once he was in prison, cause every single conversation was monitored."

Something we always had to be aware of.

"As for Liam..."

"He's a dick," Jasper commented. "Rome knew."

"Maybe. But they're brothers. Rome wouldn't abandon him any more than Liam would abandon Rome." No matter our differences, that loyalty Liam had to Rome remained unquestionable. It had been salty feelings on our side...

"Fuck, I hate secrets," Jasper snarled, then flicked the cigarette over to join the small but growing stack since we'd gotten out here. He'd clean them up before we left the truck yard. Not that it made much difference. When he was fighting with his own emotions, he smoked. "I hate all of their secrets."

"Sparrow had her reasons," I commented as I half climbed into the engine and found the spot on the far side of the engine block itself where I could secure the box to the frame. We'd need to check them periodically because they would be subject to vibrations from the road.

"That doesn't make me feel better," Jasper grumbled. "We ready to finish the test?"

"Almost—and it wasn't meant to make you feel better. I don't like the fact she went back and then went through hell any more than you do." Straightening, I cut a look at him. "But we had to earn her trust. We thought we knew what the fuck was going on with her—"

I blew out a breath. Fisting my temper and putting it back in the box. It helped abso-fucking-lutely no one if I lost my shit. It wasn't hard to get there, all I had to do was picture that hollow, wary look she'd worn when she climbed out of the car.

The fear.

If that didn't do it, the sound of her crying would have. That fucking nightmare she'd had. I should have figured it out *then*. It wasn't like we hadn't heard other kids crying at the group home. Not everyone there came from great backgrounds.

Jasper hadn't.

Fuck knew Freddie hadn't. Not that he'd ever said anything directly, but some of the pieces we'd put together. Especially after...

I set the tools aside and picked up the can to drain the soda. Right, I needed to not focus on this shit.

"We killed that asshole," Jasper reminded me. "And he went slow and painful."

"Every single fucking person who put that look on her face is going out the same way," I said in a low voice. It would take time and it would take patience. "Every. Single. One."

"No argument from me."

Milo had enough pieces, but he wasn't trying to look at them. Not yet. When he did—speaking of which...

"How are you so calm right now?" I studied him. Jasper's temper had always been hair-trigger. But not only was he holding it together, but he also seemed to have it on firm lockdown.

"No clue," he admitted, his expression grim. "I have a beehive buzzing under my skin. All I want to do is get my hands on the motherfucker that hurt her. But I can't—yet."

That was—probably one of the most mature things he'd ever said when it came to his temper. "Who are you, and what the fuck have you done with Jas?"

He lit another cigarette and flipped me off at the same time. "I don't want to scare her."

All of my humor dried up at that statement. "You don't scare her. She's seen you pretty pissed and just gotten right in your face about it."

A fleeting smile crossed his mouth. "She's a fighter."

"Yes, she is."

He cut another look at me. "I hate the fear in her eyes."

There wasn't much I could say to that except nod. Getting back to work, I secured the last box. "Run the test."

While he shifted his attention to the laptop we had set up, I wiped my hands before repacking my tools. There was a half-full bottle of water just inside my box. I drained it while I waited for Jasper to sign off. We needed to get the trucks back on the road.

The only people who knew what we were doing were Vandals. Vetting and re-vetting the drivers had taken time. But our guys were loyal. Then again, I would have said that about the missing drivers too. No, keeping this information compartmentalized was the way to go. It was why I'd come out here myself to get the installs done.

Every single one was coded to not only verify location but they would also signal when and if the other box had been tampered with. It wasn't just distance from the primary black box, but if the primary failed to respond to the check-ins.

It wasn't the most infallible plan, none of us were hackers. But I trusted my source for the backup black boxes and trusted my own skills at getting them in place.

My phone buzzed.

Two rats checking in. Look at JD. He'd managed to do something useful.

Cops at scene. No witnesses. Canvasing for video footage. So far so good.

Acknowledging it, I told him to keep an eye on things but don't stand out. I'd have another relieve him soon. If we rotated the rats, it gave us eyes on the street without drawing too much attention to themselves.

That said, our territory stayed relatively crime-free. We kept it that way. Then the shooting a few months ago at the club in Diamonds territory—Liam's club, and now this.

Was it Liam who was the target? Was that why they'd gone after Rome? Or did it have something to do with our new guest?

JD fired back an acknowledgement. We definitely wanted Vaughn to stay out of the spotlight for a bit. We looked after our community and they looked after us. Still...

"Looks good," Jasper said and I moved to glance at the screen. We had signals from all of them. They were in a resting state. "You know if they have a way to scan for electronics, we're fucked, right?"

"Yes and no." My phone buzzed in my hand, but I didn't glance at the screen yet. "If they have the materials and the wherewithal to scan, identify, and remove the secondary black boxes, we'll know about it from the ping or lack of one. But it will also give us a starting point for when it went dead and tell us the team we're dealing with is a lot more sophisticated than we think."

"I hope not," he admitted. "We have enough issues."

Agreed, but another piece of the puzzle was another piece. "The drivers ready for the changes?"

"Yeah, they aren't happy," he said as he shut down the laptop and packed it up. "But they're less happy about the idea of disappearing. We've got three drivers we can't account for. No one has any information on them. Still, I think they will appreciate the changes. Even if I'm not sure we can afford to maintain that level for more than a few months."

The trucks would be rolling out with the same buddy system we were using. Ambushing one truck might require coordination, but two? That increased the difficulty. The addition of backup drivers to literally ride shotgun? Hopefully, that would stack the odds in our favor. If not—we now had the backup black boxes.

Agitation marked his movements as he drained the last of his soda, then crushed the can. Like he had earlier, I scanned the area. The truck yard was a good distance from the warehouse. It was also owned under a different name not linked back to us. Jasper and Milo had moved the trucks here themselves.

We'd also get to work on moving the trucks back to pickup locations. Our drivers didn't own our trucks. We paid them a handsome fee for driving and they made a percentage from their hauls safely delivered. It gave them a vested interest and still kept the bulk of the profit for us.

It also meant we had to handle the bulk of the expenses. When it had just been two trucks, that hadn't been an issue, we'd always been tight. But we had a fleet of them now.

Even three down, we could handle the excess burden at the moment. Six months down the road, that could be a different story.

"We going to get her?" he asked once he slung the backpack over his shoulder.

"Not yet," I told him. "If she decides to stay there, we're going to need to shift security."

Jasper nodded. "I'll take tonight. I have to be on the road by late tomorrow, and I want her to hear that from me."

"Done."

I jerked a thumb to my car. "You want to start moving the trucks now?"

"Tomorrow morning is soon enough. I'm actually the first driver going out."

"Who's riding shotgun with you?"

He just gave me a look.

"Yeah, no shotgun, you're not going." I pointed at him. "Before you argue, remember, you're about to tell her you're going and coming back. Don't lie to her."

I left him chewing on that thought as I strode over to my baby. His teeth ground when he said, "You're a dick."

Chuckling, I slid into the driver's seat and started the engine. She purred for me. "I don't hear you disagreeing with me."

He dropped his bag into the backseat before he slouched into the passenger side. "Asshole."

The buzz of my phone reminded me I hadn't checked the next round of messages. Damn thing. Sometimes, it was quiet for days and others it never shut up.

A news alert flashed over the screen and I scrolled down it, half expecting to see something about the shooting, but it was a news alert for Jonathon Warrick.

Swiping up, I waited for the news page to load.

WARRICK PREVIEWS NEW CHARITY AT MOTHER'S BENEFIT

"What the fuck?" Jasper asked as he caught what was on my screen, but I didn't answer. Warrick's mother died? I must have missed the news. Scrolling through the article, I skimmed the details.

Noel Warrick had died at some event a few weeks earlier. Shellfish allergy, apparently. In the meanwhile, the family had asked for privacy during their time of grieving.

Now? They were raising money for a new charity to get kids off the streets and help domestic violence survivors find a way out.

I could read between the lines with the next person. Warrick traded in people. His charities were fronts. They kept the family nose clean while allowing them to rub elbows with the elite. In the meanwhile, they profited off blood and misery.

Clicking the phone screen dark, I set it aside before yanking on my seatbelt and putting the car in drive.

"I'm here," Jasper offered. He didn't add anything more. Didn't have to. Whatever move I made, he'd back me.

It was what we did.

The last person in the world I ever wanted to speak to was the person I actually needed to talk to and this stupid fucking charity announcement just gave me a way in.

Fuck.

10

Liam's reaction to Adam's offer had been stony silence in the wake of his destroyed plate. It and the food just went into the trash before he left Rome and me in the kitchen. I winced.

"Don't worry, Starling, he's not mad at you." Rome carried his now empty plate over to the sink and began to clean up.

A sigh escaped and I ran my hand over the stapler. The coolness of the metal soothed the wild agitation that had buzzed under my skin. I could think and breathe again.

The water cut off and Rome put a damp hand against my leg. At the silent request, I glanced at him.

"Did you tell him yes?"

Did I tell— "No." I shook my head. "The offer surprised the hell out of me, to be honest. Adam and I only know each other through Lainey. It's—hard to explain." Then, even though he hadn't asked, I added, "And it wasn't that I told him 'no,' either. He didn't want an answer from me. He wanted me to think about it and then we'd talk again."

"But you didn't talk again." That wasn't a question. The searching look in his eyes held me in place and I wouldn't look away for anything in the world.

"No, because the next stop on my tour was Braxton Harbor."

Understanding lit his expression. "Good." He gave my leg a squeeze before claiming my plate and washing it up too. That was it, just good. No explanations. No questions.

Rome had finished the cleanup when a freshly dressed Liam appeared in the doorway. His unreadable expression seemed set in stone and a muscle twitched in his jaw.

"I'm going to the clubhouse," he informed us. "You two stay here." With that, he pivoted and stalked away.

"Hey," I called, sliding off the counter. It wasn't graceful, but I didn't land on my ass. "Wait."

He was already at the door when he jerked around. "What?" He snapped the syllable so hard it might as well have cracked like the plate he'd held earlier. Despite the *very* obvious anger in his eyes and in his voice, he had his face locked. The rigidness alone would have made me back off a few months ago.

But Liam wouldn't hurt me.

"I'm not a dog, I don't sit and stay."

"Hellspawn," he growled, then glanced over my head and I didn't have to check to know Rome was there. Those indecipherable looks they shared always registered no matter how swift they were in passing. He blew out a breath. "I need to go to the clubhouse. I would prefer it if you two stayed here."

"Better," I complimented him. "But you didn't answer my question, and I paid your price." Fighting the urge to fold my arms, I flexed my hands. The stapler was behind me. It was right there if I needed it.

I didn't *need* it here.

Scrubbing a hand over his face, Liam glanced away from us and I swore the weariness seemed to just roll off him in waves.

"Not to mention," I continued. "You're exhausted. You were either getting ready for bed or just getting up when we got here..."

"It doesn't matter." Despite how he fired those words out, they carried a lot less anger than his earlier statements. "Hellspawn," he said, finally glancing at me, and it made my whole body ache as a piece of his mask slipped. "This— is not a conversation we need to have."

Maybe not. "Telling you about Adam's offer wasn't one either."

"No," he disagreed, fresh violence filling his eyes. "That one I definitely needed to know and trust me, I'll deal with Reed soon enough."

That boded well. Kellan's words of warning echoed in the back of my head.

"You don't have to deal with him," I said, choosing my words carefully. "He offered to help me. It had absolutely nothing to do with any of you."

His shoulders squared and his chin lifted. "Is that so?"

"Yes, it is." I didn't care how tall he and Rome were. Narrowing the distance between us, I lifted my chin to meet him, glare for glare. At least this was more familiar. "When Adam made that offer, I didn't even know who you were."

A frown rippled over his brow and his eyes narrowed. "Hellspawn."

"Don't you Hellspawn me," I said, jabbing a finger into the center of his chest. "I didn't know you or Jasper or

Kellan. I didn't know Rome or Freddie or Vaughn. I didn't know Doc or Milo. I didn't know *any of you.*"

An ache I barely recognized unfolded in my chest. A hollowness that had marked so much of my life.

"All of you were out here—watching over me—but you had no idea how alone I was. I had one person. One. Because of her, I had two others. Maybe they weren't *mine*, but they looked after me too."

His expression faltered. "Hellspawn…"

"Don't." It was my turn to snap. "You wanted to know when I said you wouldn't like it. And I told you because I'm trying to not keep secrets." Some… some I couldn't bring myself to repeat. But this one? This one I could. "Maybe if I'd known you guys were out here or if I'd known from the beginning… But maybes don't fix anything. I can't live my life that way. I have only ever had what I had when I had it. I lived my life for tours, for the time when I could be far away from everything I knew."

Those words resonated in me. I'd heard them some-where, but at the same time, I'd never truly understood what it meant until now.

"Adam coming to me that night was bizarre. I still don't know what prompted the offer. He wouldn't tell me until I accepted. But one thing I *do* know for damn certain…"

I still had a hand on the center of Liam's chest. When I would have pulled it away, he covered it with his own.

"What do you know, Hellspawn?" The growl was gone. Not the anger, no, that was still there but it had lessened and licked at the words rather than burned them.

"He saw the bruises that Eric gave me."

Glaciers were warmer than Liam's eyes at the mention of my former dancer partner. My now very dead dance partner. The tiniest flame of glee flared in that darkened hollow in my soul. He was dead because my guys had dealt with him and made sure he could never hurt me again.

They'd done it for me.

And yeah, it helped me sleep at night.

Or it had anyway.

I swallowed, shaking off those thoughts to focus on Liam again. "Adam and Ezra were very protective of Lainey. *Ridiculously* protective. Or at least, I used to think so." But the world wasn't quite so black and white. I didn't exist in the shadows while she was safe in the light.

Maybe she'd only ever been safe because they had made sure of it.

"They're not my friends, but they are my allies, or they have been. Adam offered to deal with him for me. He didn't know who or why or anything. He just saw the bruises and asked me if I needed it taken care of."

A laugh escaped me but there was no humor in it at all. None.

"I'd almost forgotten that. He had no reason to protect me outside of Lainey. And Lainey wasn't anywhere near me. But he still sought me out right after my birthday to make that offer. Whatever his motives were—I believe he didn't mean *me* harm. That means you don't get to *deal* with him."

Liam rubbed the back of my hand; the motion helped. I'd begun shaking again. The urge to cry burned in the back of my throat. I wouldn't give in to those tears. Could you be angry and elated and terrified and secure all at the same time?

"Without them—without Lainey, I was alone. So that means the only person who gets to *deal* with him is Lainey. Now, if she decides to kick his ass—feel free."

"Noted," Liam replied, the remnants of temper seemed to have drained away. "Any other orders—ma'am?"

He didn't have to be such a dick about it. I made a face but barely made it a step before he hauled me back, and then his mouth closed over mine and the flame guttered as a fluttering filled my chest. The firmness of his lips over mine and the hot brush of his tongue, coupled with the way his hands gripped me, tangled me up in the silks until I was dizzy from it.

All the breath backed up in my lungs, and I went from pressing my hand against his chest to fisting his shirt as I strained upward into the kiss. The thud of his heart echoed my own as it sped up and I groaned as he stroked his tongue against mine.

The world spun, but he lifted me off my feet and I clasped his neck. In all the hugs I'd received, Liam had kept his distance. But I drowned in the contact now, clinging to him as he all but devoured my mouth. The nip of his teeth against my lower lip carried the barest hint of sting and I dragged my eyes open.

He pulled back a few spare millimeters giving me a chance to catch my breath as he locked his gaze on mine. Heat flushed my face, heat and a spiraling sensation spread through me that I couldn't identify. It was like falling... only I wasn't in control.

"Hellspawn..." The ragged, trailing note scraped past my own confusion to dig its talons in deep. If not for being so close, I might have missed the flash of guilt in his eyes. Then he glanced past me as a hand drifted along my spine. Liam's arms were banded around me, one arm under my ass, the other around my shoulders while he had a hand on my nape.

Rome.

I tilted my head back, following Liam's glance, to find Rome right there. His eyes held not an ounce of rancor or remonstration. "You're not alone."

Not anymore.

"You're here," I whispered, not quite trusting my voice to collapse under it.

Rome nodded once. "I'm here." Then he covered Liam's hand on my nape, the brush of their fingertips different in temperatures—Liam's hot where Rome's were cool. The sensory overload sent shivers all the way through me. "So is Liam." The last was a promise.

Then he kissed me. The teasing tangle of his tongue sweeping over mine was a reminder every bit as much as his words. Comfort and need vied for dominance in the way he moved his lips over mine. I slid my own hand into Liam's hair, gripping him tighter.

A low groan vibrated in my throat as Rome tilted my head. No, they both did and another shudder went through me as I hitched my thighs to Liam's hips. The erection waiting for me sent a wildfire raging through my system.

What—

"Not alone," Rome repeated, his lips bare millimeters away. Liquid heat unspooled to travel the same spiral that had unraveled in me earlier. Then he turned his head and mine together so our cheeks brushed and we were both looking at Liam.

Hunger reflected in his eyes now. A hunger I recognized. "You're not alone," I whispered, echoing Rome's words. Cause he was right. That loneliness in Liam had been there from the moment I met him. Isolated and away from his brothers in a life he thrived in but didn't want.

"Dammit..." Liam muttered.

"No," Rome said. "Not alone. Starling. You. Me."

The firmness in his tone was undeniable and it carried far more weight than someone throwing a punch or yelling.

None of us was alone.

I swallowed, but I didn't retreat from Liam's searching gaze or pull away from the contact with Rome. This kind of vulnerability was dangerous. It was a threat, but they weren't.

The panic that swelled retreated at the same time. Rome's arms around me, along with Liam's, offered safety.

"She's your girl," Liam finally said, and hope crushed in me.

"She's herself," Rome corrected. "Starling?"

Another hard swallow, but the lump wouldn't go away. "Rome?"

"Do you want Liam?"

The question might have floored me, but it flattened Liam. His pupils constricted. But he didn't turn away. He couldn't. If he did, he'd either pull me from Rome or have to drop me.

Suddenly my heart squeezed for him.

These guys—all of them—I wanted *them*. I wanted that fierce loyalty and dedication. I wanted to deserve it. But I also—I just wanted to belong.

Admitting that was opening a vein. They could hurt me. Oh, God, could they hurt me.

Doc had.

But at the same time...

"Yes." I couldn't reject him. I didn't want to reject any of them. "I can't—"

"It's all right," Liam interrupted, but Rome slapped his shoulder, and we both jumped.

"Listen," he ordered, but his eyes were gentle when he glanced at me. "You can't?"

"I can't—I still have the infection." Oh, now I wanted to crawl into a hole and just die. "It's getting better, but I can't do anything more yet…"

Fear and embarrassment were a disgusting cocktail that left a trail of acid in my gut.

"But you want me?" Liam asked, his gaze hard on me.

"Us," Rome corrected and a half-drunken laugh escaped me.

Except, I wasn't remotely drunk.

"You want *us*," Liam repeated with a glance at Rome that held an element of warning.

"I want all of you," I admitted. If I was going to fall, I might as well fall with style. "I want—to belong. To you—to Rome…to Kellan and Jasper—"

He closed his eyes and fear cracked through me.

"I'm selfish, I know—"

But I didn't manage another word because Liam kissed me this time with a hell of a lot more force and a hint of bruising demand before he nipped my lower lip. None of it truly hurt, but it shut me up.

"Hellspawn…you have always *belonged*." He let out another groan, bending his forehead so his head touched mine and Rome shifted so we were a circle. Then his forehead rested against ours. It was sweet. "This is a fucking mess," Liam admitted.

"Doesn't matter," Rome said. "Our mess."

"Our girl," Liam added, then looked at me. "That means you're *never* marrying Reed."

I blinked.

"I—"

"Just say you agree, Hellspawn," Liam continued. "I don't care what his reasons were. You want to belong to us —with us? Then you never marry him."

Another bubble of laughter escaped me. It was wholly inappropriate for the level of intensity, and Liam narrowed his eyes on me.

"I never wanted to marry him. Not then. Not now." Then I giggled and Liam's lips compressed, but Rome let out a soft laugh and pressed a kiss to the side of my head.

"Someday, Hellspawn, I'm going to put you over my knee and paddle that ass of yours. The only thing I haven't decided is if it's before or after I play with it." That really shouldn't be a remotely attractive offer, but my pulse jumped not at the "threat" of spanking. It was more of the idea of him "playing" with my ass that still worried me.

Only the choking fear didn't erupt. It couldn't get to me through them.

"But today is not that day?" I went for levity because the urge to grind myself on him was growing. There were lots of things we could do but...

"No," he muttered. "It's not. Not that you aren't a tempting morsel and I'm more than willing to suit up to play with you, but—you need more time to heal."

"Kissing is all right," Rome told him. "Starling likes kisses."

I did, but what delighted me was Liam's sudden laugh. It came all the way up from his belly. "I figured that part out, Rome. Thanks." Then he grimaced. "As much as I'd like to continue this discussion of kisses, there's someone at the clubhouse we need to deal with."

We. Not I.

Affection, not relief, swarmed through me at his words.

"Do I want to know?"

"Probably," he said and there was such a sigh of regret as he watched me carefully. "Ezra is there."

My stomach bottomed out. "Lainey's Ezra?"

"Yep."

That was bad.

"Does Lainey know?"

"No," Rome answered.

That was really bad.

"Is he in trouble?"

"To be determined," Liam said, the weight of their regard rested on me. "Your call, Hellspawn, what do you want to do?"

11

The drive back to the clubhouse was so different from the drive to Liam's. For one, I had shoes on. A lot of my things were still in Rome's bedroom and the twins were adamant they could stay there for as long as I wanted them there. Liam's expression had shifted when I claimed Rome's bear to bring back with me along with the stapler—but only after I looked at Rome to make sure it was okay.

Embarrassment crept through me at first, but Liam had only said, "We'll just make sure they come back with you when you stay here."

Not if, but when.

The other thing that was different was the giant boxed espresso machine we'd stopped to buy on the way back. I thought they'd want to go directly back, but they'd been in another of those silent communication stares when I came back with the bear and my shoes.

When I'd asked why we had to stop now, all Liam had done was grin and say, "Trust me, Hellspawn."

I did. But why did I have to just trust him about a new coffee maker? Still... It was a lovely machine and the one Liam had made fantastic coffee. "What about..."

"No one is gonna touch him before I get there," Liam added before he closed the door to stride into the store, leaving me and Rome in the car. It took him almost no time to re-emerge with the machine. Apparently, he had called ahead.

My pulse spiked when we got near the warehouse. The speed of our earlier exit had left Lainey, Milo, and poor Vaughn in our wake. I needed to apologize to him for just taking off like that.

Freddie was the first thing I saw when we pulled inside. The nerves fled and urgency replaced them. I only waited until Rome put the car in park before I was out of the vehicle, stapler in hand.

"Boo-Boo!" He grinned, pocketing the knife he'd had in his hand and running his fingers through his blond hair. "You didn't run away again, right?"

"Nope," I told him, crossing my heart as I headed toward him. "Promise."

He dropped his gaze to the stapler in my hand. "Oh, had to go fetch the buddy."

I slowed a couple of steps away, but then he just spread his arms. Balancing the stapler and *not* wanting to crowd him, I gave him a one-armed hug. "I haven't seen you that much," I murmured.

"You must suck at hide and seek," he said in a too light tone as he gave me a little squeeze. But when he pulled back, his eyes were a little too bright. "I messed up a little."

Worry fisted inside of me. "Freddie..."

"Nah, not like that, Boo-Boo. At least not this time." He gave me a grin that verged a little on brittle. "Just needed to get my head straight."

"Did you?" I hugged the stapler to my chest.

"Nah," he assured me with a grin. "I'm still cracked, but pretty. You know."

I did. I really fucking did. Still, even with him making light of it...

"I'm good, Boo-Boo," Freddie said, crossing *his* heart with crossed fingers.

"That's not how that works."

He snorted then glanced past me. "Oh, it's a party. And they brought us a present."

"It's for Starling," Rome informed him as he moved past us and I bit my lip. He carried the espresso machine inside without slowing. "Wait for me."

I glanced up at Liam. "I can pay you back for it."

"If you offered, I might be insulted," he warned me. "So you won't offer, I won't be insulted, and Rome won't steal my coffee maker. It's all good."

"Oh hell yeah, we get the good stuff," Freddie said, offering me his fist to bump, and I tapped it lightly with my knuckles. "Though, it was kind of funny listening to the ball-cracker inform Raptor that his coffee sucks. Pretty sure it wasn't his coffee she was talking about, you know." The playful leer and waggling eyebrows made me laugh even as I shook my head.

"Eww," I informed him. "I don't want to know anything about Milo's brewing skills."

"I'm wounded," the man in question announced as he held the door open for Rome. "I thought you wanted to get to know me." The droll tone removed any sting from the question.

"I do, I just don't need to know why Lainey says your coffee sucks."

His lips compressed and maybe it was the light in here, but a flush of red touched his face as he transferred his look from me to Freddie. "Seriously?"

Unperturbed, Freddie spread his hands. "What can I say? Rome and Liam are taking care of Boo-Boo's coffee needs, double-teaming as it were. You could always ask someone for help with the ball-cracker's if you're stuck."

The absolute tongue-in-cheek wasn't lost on me. Nor Milo, not really. Despite his stormy expression, he seemed to be fighting a smile. "You little…"

"Temper, temper! Look at Boo-Boo." Freddie darted behind me. "Boo-Boo makes everything better."

A laugh bubbled out of me as I twisted to look at him. "I think you're fine."

"Nah, you are. I'm just a smart-ass."

Liam cleared his throat, a gentle, if firm, reminder that we'd actually returned to the clubhouse for an entirely different reason. Right. "Sorry," I told him.

"Don't have to be sorry, Hellspawn, but if you want to talk to him, we should go do it now."

"Talk to who?" Milo asked as Vaughn emerged from behind them.

Instead of answering Milo, I asked, "Where is Lainey?"

"Oh, she's locked in his room," Vaughn told me as he joined us and Milo scowled.

"You locked her in your room?" The outrage was immediate. "What the hell…?"

Milo glared at Vaughn. "Thanks for that."

To my surprise, Vaughn just grinned.

"And no, Ivy, I didn't lock her in there. She locked me out." He grumbled those last four words. One glance at

Vaughn confirmed the words. "Now, would you like to go convince her to unlock the door?"

I would except...

"We have to talk to someone first." I chewed my lower lip. "Then we should get her after we sort some things out."

That was how it ended up being a whole entourage that headed to the office. There was a room beyond it that had once held Eric and, thankfully, Ezra wasn't in there hanging by chains. Instead, he was secured to a desk by an ankle shackle.

A bruise marred the underside of his jaw and a second one mottled the side of his face though it had faded to green and yellow, so a lot older than the one on his jaw.

"You cock-sucking shitweed," Ezra snarled at Liam. It was definitely at Liam since he was the first one through the door.

Freddie snorted a laugh while Vaughn frowned. Rome stayed one step in front of me but angled so I could see. It meant peering between them.

"You can fuck right off, O'Connell. You and your fuc—Emersyn?" The wild swerve from rage to shock shifted everything about him. Ezra lunged to his feet and gave me a solid once over before he transferred his attention back to Liam.

The irreverent, if sometimes playful, smirk he often sported—well, at least when I was around—was nowhere in evidence.

"You're a goddamn traitor. You kidnapped Emersyn. That's why she's been missing all these months..." His teeth clicked together as he jerked his attention back to me again. "He took you and you had to call Lainey—did you assholes fucking take her too? Where the hell is Adam?"

And right back to rage.

"You finished, you drama queen?" Liam asked and unlike Ezra, he was cool. Too cool, it was almost cold. That wasn't fair.

"Ezra—"

The snap of his attention riveted on me like a laser. He took one step forward and I swore the guys closed in like a solid wall around me.

"Nope." I patted Rome's shoulder. I still had my stapler. I was fine. "Stop it," I said and when he glanced down at me, I added a, "please."

With a single nod, he shifted so I could see Ezra again. A fierce frown darkened his expression.

"*You're* with *them*?" Disappointment flecked the anger simmering in his tone.

"Yes," I told him truthfully, then pointed a finger at him when he opened his mouth. "My turn to talk, please."

He snapped it shut with a second click of his teeth.

"One, Liam did not kidnap me."

"It's Liam, is it?" Oh, he disapproved. How did Lainey put it? Too fucking bad.

"You heard me, don't be a dick just because you can be." Hugging my stapler, I added, "Two, he didn't, nor did anyone else here, kidnap Lainey."

"But you've seen her." He narrowed his eyes. "You're too calm, and she was a goddamn wreck after you went missing. You're supposed to be her best fucking friend..."

"Watch your mouth and your tone," Milo snapped. "You're worried, fine. Don't be an asshole."

"Or what?" Ezra sneered. Then he frowned. "Wait a fucking minute..."

Wait for...

"Ezra, Lainey is fine. I promise."

Once again, his attention lashed at me like a turbulent wind. "Where is she?"

"When you calm down, I'll tell her you want to see her." It was all I would offer him. "But I'm making no promises. You're being kind of an asshole, but you also have a shackle on your ankle. I'm trying to be understanding, so maybe be less of a dick?"

Freddie snickered. "Boo-Boo is a badass."

The shock and surprise fell away to be replaced by a genuinely fierce expression. "You're going to tell me where she is right now or..."

"Or nothing," Liam interrupted as Freddie came to stand right next to me. A flicker of motion in the corner of my eye caught my attention and I spotted the knife in his hand. Shifting my grip on the stapler, I dropped my hand to tap his pinky with mine.

Rome and Vaughn moved, allowing Milo to take my other side while they formed a near triangle around Ezra.

"Stop threatening people and starting shit, you hard-headed, arrogant jackass." The chill in Liam's voice cracked to give way to absolute exasperation. "I told you to go home before. What the hell are you doing in Braxton Harbor?"

"Following you," he said with an angrier smirk. "Look what I found, an heiress hidden away with your dirty secret family..."

I groaned.

"Not that I blame you, Em. I'd choose anyone over that bastard uncle of yours too."

Freddie finally hooked his pinky with mine and the flash of the knife vanished as he put it away. I squeezed his pinky and he returned the affection.

"You really know this asshat?" Freddie asked. "I mean, I thought you hung out with all the classy types."

"Fuck you, punk," Ezra snapped in response.

"Yeah," Freddie said slowly, tilting his head to rest it against mine lightly. "You're not my type. But keep it up and we're gonna have a front-row seat to your beatdown."

"What the hell is going on in here?" Kellan demanded and I shifted to look back. Kellan and Jasper stood just outside the open door to the office. "And is this how you take care of problems, Liam? I thought you understood the value of discretion."

This was going nowhere fast, but it was good to see them. Even better to have them all here. Everyone except… "We should call Doc," I suggested.

"You okay, Sparrow?" Kellan gave me a once over, the concern transforming the impatience in his expression to something far warmer.

"I'm better," I promised. "But Ezra has bruises and he may have hit his head."

"He didn't," Rome offered. "I did. But I was trying to keep him from being shot."

"What?" Ezra asked and I frowned.

Everyone started talking, and the noise rose, not that they were arguing. I didn't think. But Kellan was annoyed. Liam frustrated. Rome seemed almost calmer now. Vaughn didn't, there was an unfamiliar agitation to him. Milo's hostility, though somewhat decreased, was still a living entity in the room with us. Freddie tugged my pinky with his and I drifted back a step at his request.

Two steps back and I bumped into Jasper, who just threaded his arms around my middle. "This okay?" he asked in a tone that loosened knots in my spine I hadn't even realized were there.

"Yes."

I was still trying to brace the stapler, but Jasper shifted

one of his hands to rest over mine and the weight eased. He didn't take it away but helped me hold it.

Like a warm cloak, Jasper settled around me while Freddie muttered, "Ten bucks on Liam popping the new guy before this is over."

I winced. "I hope not."

"I'm betting Milo hits him before Liam does." Jasper might have a point. Liam was all ice, but Milo just radiated pissed off. The longer the conversation went on, the angrier he grew.

"Ten?" Freddie asked.

"Guys," I protested.

"Ten," Jasper agreed, then brushed the shell of my ear with a kiss. "Unless you want to place your own."

I laughed, but a whistle cut through the raucous din. It shut everyone up. Even Ezra.

"Enough," Kellan said in a far calmer tone. "We do not have time for this or any more Royals drama."

Royals...

"Liam, take him and get rid of him. I don't care if you dump him on the back of a fruit truck and send him on his way or put him on a plane..."

"Kel—" Liam began, but Ezra ran right over the top of him. "I'm not going anywhere without Lainey or Emersyn. They're ours anyway. If you know where Adam is, it's in your best interests to tell me. You don't want me as an enemy." Gone was the raging torrent of words to be replaced by an ice-cold venom.

This was going nowhere good.

Liam had said there was a plan and to let him handle Ezra, but I wasn't sure where this was going...

"You're better off giving her to us regardless," Ezra

continued as he cut a look back at Liam. "You've all but put a target on her back now, and you know what—"

I never found out what because Liam's fist crashed into Ezra's face and he went down. I flinched at the meaty slam of flesh on flesh. A bone cracked somewhere because the crunch of it echoed through the little room.

"Yes!" Freddie chortled, holding a hand out. "Pay up, Jas."

12

A low chuckle escaped me at Liam's very solid and effective delivery of "have a little more shut the fuck up." Emersyn let out a little sigh, the exhale more disappointed than angry. I gave her a little squeeze, and she leaned back into me. She weighed less than a damn feather, despite all the power housed in her body.

The fact that she trusted me to support her in the face of everything else settled something extremely primitive inside of me. Instead of turning me into gold or something with her touch, she transformed my anger into patience and my frustration into amusement.

I really didn't give two shits about this guy, though she seemed to care. The simple fact he wasn't one of us placed him on dangerous ground. That he was one of *them* and he wanted to claim *Emersyn*? Yeah, he could get fucked.

Half the reason I'd moved to wrap around her when Kel and I walked back into this interrogation, was to keep myself from chucking this new asshole into the fridge and locking him up. First that Reed prick, and now this jackass?

"Liam," Kellan said on the end of an aggrieved sigh. "Should we be expecting any more Bay Ridge Royals to show up?"

The absolute irritation on Liam's face almost made me smile. "Fuck, I hope not. These two are the only ones I can halfway stand." He scrubbed a hand over his face then glanced back at us. No, not us. Her. "I told you this wasn't going to go well, Hellspawn."

"I know," she murmured, her voice so low even I had to strain to hear her. "But we can't hurt him—not any more than we already have. I need to talk to him. Maybe without all of you hovering, he'll be more cooperative. The thing I don't get is why doesn't he know where Adam is?"

Liam cast a look at the ceiling. Yeah, someone's plotting and schemes were coming home to roost. I'd enjoy it more if it wasn't sweeping our girl into the middle of all this crap.

Then again, she'd always been at the center of it. Liam shifted his attention to me, and he flicked a look to Emersyn then back to me. Right. He wanted me to get her out of here.

Not that I minded stealing some time with her, I was more content right now just holding her than I'd been in weeks. But if he wanted me to get her out of here, I needed more reason than just a look.

His expression shifted, but it was Milo who turned away from the unconscious guy on the ground. "Ivy," he said, almost gently. "We don't know this guy..."

"I do," she informed him, which was news to him and me. "He's a... friend of Lainey's." The hint of hesitation around the word "friend" wasn't lost on me or Milo. He frowned, his jaw tightening.

Yeah, he didn't want this guy around Lainey or Emersyn.

"I know he is," Milo admitted, and I wasn't the only one surprised. Okay, so apparently *not* news to him. The room had gone quiet. "I met both him and the other—Adam—a few years ago."

"Wait... you..."

"I followed you to Florida. It was almost time for your birthday and I just wanted to see you. See how you were doing." That admission cost him.

"You followed me..."

He rubbed the back of his neck then glanced around the room. "I've been meaning to tell you," he admitted and it was the first time in my life I could swear he looked almost embarrassed. "You girls were adorable, and you played all over the park."

Silence greeted his statement and I stole a look downward. I'd been balancing the stapler, but she hadn't let it go. If anything, her knuckles were whiter now on it than they had been earlier. Freddie still had his pinkie locked around hers—or had because she raised that hand to hug the stapler more firmly.

"Ivy—"

"You know that's a little weird, right?" The question carried just the smallest amount of humor. Enough to rob it of any real sting. "It's also really cute."

He grimaced.

"So, you saw when Ezra and Adam caught up to us?"

I wasn't the only one now laser-focused on Milo. Liam shot a look between Ezra and Emersyn. He'd missed something and it irritated the fuck out of him.

Same, brother, I almost said aloud. But I kept it to myself. We'd all missed more than I cared to admit. We'd missed some really big shit. All at once, I just wanted to haul her out of here and steal her away somewhere safe where she never had to worry again.

Maybe Kellan was right. We needed to make some changes around here.

"Yes," he admitted. "They caught the fact I'd been watching you two as well."

She gave a little start in my arms. "Adam would have been pissed...but he didn't say anything to us."

"Your friend caught them in the act and told them off." Milo shrugged. "I didn't give two shits about them. As long as you were safe."

"Starling," Rome said, calling all of our attention to where the man groaned.

"Kellan," she said. "Can we do what we did with Adam?"

That chafed. She wanted to talk to the asshole without the rest of us.

"Not sure he's as stable as Reed," Kellan said, not that it said much. "He and Liam are definitely a lot more volatile."

Liam only shrugged. "Ezra's not so bad. But he is loyal as fuck, and he's convinced I have something to do with their disappearances..."

"You do," Ezra said with a pained sound. "You back-stabbing fucking traitor..."

"Ezra," Emersyn said, pulling away from me, and it took everything I had not to drag her back and right the fuck out of here. My instincts were to get the bat and just end the damn problem. I had to share her attention with my brothers, I didn't need this asshole and he sure as shit hadn't earned a spot.

Fisting my hands, I forced my muscles to relax as I let

her go. She took two steps forward then paused as she looked at the stapler in her hands.

"I got it," Freddie offered almost gallantly, and probably a good idea to keep his hands busy. They'd already twitched toward his knife more than once.

"Thank you," she said, surrendering the office supply. Yeah, I wasn't judging. Then blowing out a breath, she turned to face Ezra again. Those shoulders squared and her chin lifted. The guy was dragging himself upward with help from Liam, who didn't look any happier to be helping than the guy receiving it.

"Emersyn," the jerk said. "Why are you with these assholes?"

"Well, one of them is my brother, and the others all saved my life. As for the rest—it's a very long explanation."

"They're a gang."

Well, he wasn't wrong, but all Emersyn did was shrug. "So?"

The guy gaped at her and I grinned. My girl was not the type to back down from anyone. Even when she thought we were holding her prisoner, she'd stood up to us. That spirit was as vital and gorgeous as the rest of her.

"Did you really just say 'so?'" He straightened, wincing as he touched a hand to his face and then he glared at Liam before returning his attention to Emersyn. Fortunately for his continued health, he stopped scowling when he looked at her.

"Contrary to what you and Adam both believe, neither Lainey nor I are idiots. I know who they are."

He sighed. "Is she here, Emersyn?"

"She's fine, Ezra. Stop worrying about her. I'll tell her you want to see her and if she wants to see you, no one will stop her. But you have to stop being an asshole."

He frowned, then reached out a hand like he was going to touch her. I took a step forward and I wasn't the only one. The barest hint of calculation touched his eyes as he swept a look over us. Bastard was playing a dangerous game if he wanted to test us.

"Are you really okay?" the guy asked finally. "She was worried about you."

"I know, and I'm—okay. Stop fighting them for me, please. I'm not leaving again."

Some fist in my gut just let go and I was able to take a deeper breath.

He grunted. "Fine, but if that changes..."

"It won't."

"But *if* it does," he said, chewing those words like they were glass. "You say the word."

"Thank you." The perfect politeness in those two words were softened by a smile. "Will you listen to Liam now? Stop fighting him so hard?"

"You swear they're okay?"

If she did, then she admitted to seeing the other dickhead. Liam just shrugged when she glanced at him. He wasn't wrong. Even Kellan wasn't making a move to prevent it. Milo wasn't happy, but then again this guy already acted like he had some claim on her.

But I bet he was less thrilled about the claim on Lainey than he was on Emersyn. I gripped his shoulder to let him know we had his back. We'd have hers too. For him and for Emersyn.

The tension in Milo's shoulders didn't ease, but he gave me a nod. We didn't need the words. Though I had a feeling we needed to get our knuckles bloody sooner rather than later this week. Maybe he should go with me to ride shotgun.

It would at least give him something else to focus on. And I'd have backup. Kel was right.

I was telling her that I was coming back and I wasn't going to lie to her.

"I promise," she said. "They're both fine."

Slumping back against the wall, the guy looked exhausted, but he nodded. "Thank you."

"You're welcome." Then she looked at Rome before she glanced at Liam. "Can we let him go now?"

"Soon, Hellspawn. Ezra's got impulse control issues and we should probably have another conversation before giving him too much freedom."

She made a face. "Okay."

"You give us some time now?" It was a carefully worded question. Liam was giving her a measure of control.

"Please behave." The last she directed at Ezra but he just gave a noncommittal shrug in response. Right. Whatever, dickhead.

"Come on, Swan," I said, holding out a hand. "We'll let them deal with this."

To my surprise, she pressed a kiss to Liam's cheek and then to Rome's before she turned back to me. Vaughn got a kiss and so did Kellan. Pausing at Freddie, she raised her brows and he grinned.

"Bring it in, Boo-Boo."

Her answering smile echoed the brighter expression on his face. She pressed a kiss to his cheek and then held her cheek toward him and he dropped a quick peck there before he surrendered the stapler back to her.

Everyone, including the irritating shit in the corner, tracked her movements. Milo just gave her a dry look when she grinned up at him, but with an aggrieved sigh, he gave her a cheek and she kissed it. "Don't be grumpy, you know you love me."

The lightness in that statement was one thing, but the ownership was something else.

"I do," Milo admitted, the thunderclouds in his expression clearing for real. "Doesn't change that you're a brat."

"I know." Then she turned to me and slid her hand in mine. Everything she'd just done had been to send a message that not only was she happy with where she was, but she claimed us too.

I was more than fucking fine with that.

Interlocking my fingers with hers, I nodded to Kellan then flicked a look at Freddie. The last few weeks had been hard on him and I wanted everyone to keep an eye on him. Just for now. He was adjusting to being home again and having Emersyn back helped.

Fuck, it helped all of us.

"Will he be all right, you think?" she asked as we left the office and headed toward the clubhouse. A couple of rats were hanging out near the big roll-up door. There would be trucks heading this way soon. We had the rats deployed all over the neighborhood after this morning.

Running my thumb in little circles around the back of her hand, I said, "As long as he cooperates, he's not going to give them a reason."

She sighed again.

"Swan," I said as we went inside and I tugged her around to look up at me. "He's not your responsibility. He's a grown man. You told him how it was. Liam—as big of a prick as he can be—is not prone to just fucking someone up for the fun of it." As much as I hated defending him. "No one else there wants to hurt him either. So—let them figure it out. Okay?"

A hint of a smile teased at her lips.

"What?" I asked.

"You said something nice about Liam."

I grunted. "Not planning to make a habit of it." Her laugh was a reward all its own. And as much as it killed me to make the offer, I said, "Do you need to talk to your friend?"

Some of her mirth faded. "Yes, hopefully, she's still speaking to me after whatever happened between her and Milo."

"Okay, well, let me walk you down there—then, tonight? Will you sleep in my room?" At the faintest hint of her expression growing tense though, I added, "Or if you're not up for that, can I stay with you? I just want to hold you for a while, if that's all right. I'm leaving tomorrow..."

"Wait, you're leaving?"

"I'll be back, Swan, I promise. I might drag Milo with me. But I have to do a run and it's going to take a couple of days. Maybe three."

A frown marred her brow. "I—do you have to go?" That sound was so forlorn it shredded me. "No, ignore that. Of course, you do. If you didn't have to do it, you wouldn't be leaving. I just—"

"You just got back," I finished for her and then cupped her cheek. "Trust me, I know. I've been keeping my distance, giving you time—I know this is all overwhelming. But it's killing me a little, Swan."

"Yes."

"What?"

"Yes, I'll spend the night in your room. I just need to tell Lainey—and probably Rome. Though, he's been sleeping where I am. So, he might sneak into your room."

I snorted. "I can live with it. "

"Jasper?"

"I really can live with it, Swan, it's fine."

"No, I just—I am so—I want to be everywhere. I want to spend time with all of you and I feel like I'm already failing. I can't be in two places at the same time and I'm so greedy, that I want to be."

The plaintive note was my undoing. "You're not failing at anything. You've only been back a couple of days." Barely any time at all. Even if the world was infinitely brighter with her in it. "I know I'm feeling a bit greedy myself." More than a bit. "So, you be as selfish as you need to be. I *want* you to be selfish and I *want* you to tell us what you need."

"I missed you."

"Well, we're going to have to work on your aim." With care, I opened my arms. When she more than met me halfway, I wrapped her up tight. "I missed you too."

I had no idea how long we stood there, but she relaxed into me and I could have held that position all night if I had to. A little sound of disgruntlement escaped her. No matter how adorable it was, I didn't laugh.

"I need to put the stapler in my room and then find Lainey. Once I make sure she's okay, we'll do something? You and me?"

"I'd like that." Stroking a hand over her hair, I pressed a kiss to her temple before I drew back and met her gaze. "We can also send someone to grab pizza and salads, then settle in down here and watch movies with everyone."

That way, she could spend time with all of us. I suppose someone would call it growth, but I couldn't believe what I was about to ask.

"Do you want me to invite Doc?"

13

The next few days were a blur of exhausting activity mixed with staggering moments of darkness and doubt. I wasn't sure which days were worse. The ones where I couldn't catch my breath or the ones where it was like I relived every dark moment.

I'd slept with Jasper that night after speaking to Ezra. The next day, Jasper had left and taken Milo with him. While I was never alone, I felt their absence keenly. Lainey had been circumspect since her brief conversation with Ezra. Whatever was said between them had left her in a dark mood of her own.

Not long after, Liam left with Ezra, and I hadn't seen or heard from him. Vaughn was often there and I went looking for him more and more. Like Rome, I could just go and curl up with him and he would keep the shadows away.

I wanted more. I could play pretend with the best of them. Head up. Wings out. *Broken isn't bad*. Those words resonated with me. But it took more and more effort. The bear and the stapler appeared wherever I slept. If it was in Vaughn's room, they followed me because Rome made sure, though once Freddie had snagged them for me and on another occasion, Lainey brought them herself before she gave me a hug goodnight.

Every single day I danced. I pushed myself harder and harder. More than once, Lainey or Rome had come in to find me lying on the wooden floor, soaked in sweat and exhausted. I kept eyeing the silks, but each time I considered gripping one, I shied away.

My arms still ached so damn bad. Doc had called the day before, and now he was coming out to see me today. Though he had asked if I wanted to go to the clinic. Other than going to Liam's, I hadn't left the confines of the clubhouse at all.

While we'd watched movies, I'd avoided the news or regular stations. Kellan had been in and out. Though he always found me when he returned, twice he'd offered to let me go to the shop with him, but I didn't want to leave Lainey here alone.

No, it was better for Doc to come here. Then I'd have... backup. Lying on the floor of the dance studio, I flicked a look to where the silks hung. Curling upward, I did a crunch to sit up.

The music ended a few minutes earlier, but sweat soaked through my leotard and dance shorts. My hair was a sticky, matted mess. Or it would be if I hadn't braided it. Standing, I began the slow walk and cool down, stretching my feet and not letting my muscles go too lax, too fast.

A week I'd been home.

A week.

It didn't feel like it. It almost felt like…

The door opened, and I cut a look to the wall of mirrors. Vaughn eased inside with a large bottle of water in one hand and a bag of…

My stomach grumbled as I pivoted. "Burgers?"

He grinned. "I had one of the rats run down to that place on 78th that you liked." I swore I was drooling, and I ran a hand over my mouth to make sure it hadn't escaped. "You've been in here for a while and you didn't eat much at breakfast."

"Worried about me getting too skinny?" I meant it as a tease, but his sober expression and solemn topaz eyes were hard to dispute when I pivoted to walk toward him on my circuit.

"Yes," he said easily and I sighed. "Dove," he continued. "This isn't a criticism."

"I know that," I said, tapping my head. "In here, I know that."

"But it feels like it?" Warmth, not judgment, radiated off him as I came closer.

"Maybe?" That didn't seem fair. I shook my head. "That doesn't seem fair. I don't actually know what I feel, really."

"You don't have to know," he told me gently, handing me the water bottle when I paused in front of him.

It was room temperature and I smiled slowly as I twisted off the already loosened cap. "You remembered?"

"I did," he admitted. "There's a second one waiting for you that's colder, but we'll save that for after you eat and cool down… then maybe after a shower."

I tried to do a not so delicate sniff test, but all I could smell in the studio was the sweat from a hard workout. Seemingly undeterred, Vaughn cupped my chin gently then deposited the softest of kisses on the tip of my nose before he brushed my lips.

"Let me turn on the fan for you."

The light touch was so fleeting, I missed it before he even took his hand away. I downed the water in slow sips that turned into longer ones as I kept walking. Overhead, a fan cranked on. I'd half-forgotten that was up there. The push of cooler air began to move in the studio.

"I should probably remember to turn that on when I'm in here." After all, they'd gone to such extreme lengths to build me a studio. My path took me closer to the silks, but I kept moving.

Vaughn shrugged as he went to one of the hidden panel closets and opened it. Inside were boxes of my favorite dance shoes. Everything from jazz boots to toe shoes. Rome knew exactly which ones I'd liked and they'd gone to some lengths to stock them.

It must have cost them a small fortune to do all of this. Another scrape of guilt rubbed against the inside of my skin. Even when they'd gifted it to me in the first place, I hadn't understood *why*, just that it presented me with an opportunity to escape.

Ironic that the one place I'd been so fiercely determined to leave had become the sanctuary I was desperate to return to. A ruffle of fabric tugged my attention, followed by a couple of thumps. Turning, I continued to walk—only backwards this time—as I watched Vaughn setting up a couple of huge cushions on the floor.

"Those are new," I murmured and he grinned.

"We'd ordered them, it just took a while to come in…"

And then I'd been gone. I chewed my lower lip.

"Come on," he said, curling his fingers in a beckoning

motion as he settled onto one of the pillows. Unwilling to be so far away, I followed the inexorable tug toward him.

He sat on one cushion and I folded down to sit on the one opposite his in the v he'd formed with his legs. Rather than curl my legs in, I stretched them over his. "This all right?"

With a chuckle, he peeled off one dance paw, then the other, and I wiggled my toes at the sudden freedom. Then he rested a warm hand on my calf before passing me the bag. "Eat up, Dove."

The voracious rumble from my stomach gurgled at the soft order. There was no denying it. I was starving. The burger smelled fantastic. So did the fries. I pulled out a handful and offered them to Vaughn first.

Quirking a brow, he eyed the bag and then me.

"Yes, I get it, you brought them for me and I adore you for it. Now, let me share them with you."

The stretch of his lips as he smiled sent a shiver through me. With a shake of his head, he leaned forward and wrapped his lips around the six or so fries I held out in offering, as well as my fingers. The stroke of his tongue as he swiped away the salt sent another shudder through my system.

Leaning back, he chewed and then nodded me toward the fries. The tingling sensation from the caress of his mouth lingered as I devoured a dozen or so fries myself. They were piping hot still, but not so hot they burned my mouth. The salt was like manna from heaven, and then I dug into the bag to pull out the oversized cheddar burger.

So many calories, too many, and the carbs, but then again—I'd been working out. Hopefully, I could eat all of this. I hadn't thrown up in four days, so that was a good sign, right?

Shoving that thought right out of my head, I unwrapped the burger but then stole a look in the bag again. "Didn't you get anything?"

"I have what I want right here," he informed me. Heat flooded my face and I glanced down at the burger before taking a bite of it. At least if I was eating it, I didn't have to come up with something pithy to say.

A mini-orgasm exploded in my mouth. He was right about these burgers being one of my favorites. Kellan had brought me one of these one evening before a performance. A meal I should have totally turned down and at the same time, it had been amazing.

"I can't believe you guys remember these details," I admitted around the bite of food, careful to put a hand over my mouth. Nothing said attractive like sending little bits flying while you chewed.

He chuckled. "I try to remember everything about you, Dove. You notice stuff about us. We just have more practice and a longer history..."

True. They'd had years to know where I was and what I liked or didn't. I glanced down at the food again. The first bite definitely tasted like more, but I made myself take a drink before I tried another.

The pressure of his thumb stroking along my calf grew stronger. When the muscle started to knot, he dug his fingers in a little harder and I groaned. I wasn't sure what felt better, the food in my mouth or the massage he worked along my leg.

"Keep eating, Dove," he murmured. As the silken nature of his voice soothed me, he paused the massage until I opened my eyes. I hadn't even realized I'd closed them.

"That feels good," I admitted.

"I'm glad. You still need to eat. Finish that burger and I'll massage anything you want."

The sensual undertone in the offer wasn't lost on me. It had been over a week. I'd finished all the antibiotics but...

"Nothing has to happen, Dove," he continued in that calm voice. "I'm not asking you to give me anything..."

"I like having sex with you," I admitted.

His grin was pure sin. "That makes me very happy, because I love having sex with you too. But this isn't a race," he continued. While his voice still held every ounce of my attention with its magnetic tones, his expression was firm. "This isn't a quid pro quo. I don't know everything that happened—and I'm not asking you to tell me. I will listen. I will ask you to tell me when you're ready and then we're going to have a very long discussion about what touches you like and where you want to be touched."

I swallowed the bite of the burger slowly as I stared into his topaz eyes. "You already figured out part of it." I hated admitting that more than anything, but—they knew. Rome knew. Freddie knew.

Vaughn could know. Right?

"I think so," he said but then nodded to the burger again. Right, I needed to eat. I took a bite and he smiled. "But I'm not going to assume anything. That's not how this is going to work for us. We're going to talk and we're going to figure it out together. I never ever want you to suffer a touch you don't want again. Understood?"

The barest hint of command in his voice became absolute at the end there and I had to blink back the burn of tears that threatened to spill out of my eyes, even as my throat burned. Stuffing the food into my mouth, I bought myself some time and nodded.

"Good girl." Then he cradled my calf as he began to

work his hands up and down the muscle. They were huge against my leg and the warmth invading my system wasn't just from the massage.

We sat there in the quiet with the fan whirring for background noise as he worked the leg muscle until it was putty, then he moved over to my left leg. I finished the last of the burger and most of the fries. I couldn't eat it all. As it was, I felt almost too full.

With sips of water, I washed it down and then wiped my hands on one of the napkins from the bag.

"Done?"

At my nod, he took the bag with the trash and set it aside. Sliding his hands up my legs, he paused at my hips and waited for my nod. Another flush of pleasure went through me at his patience and kindness.

He lifted me up and right over onto his lap, then wrapped his arms around me. It was loose enough that I could slip away if I wanted but tight enough that I couldn't mistake his wanting me close for anything else.

"Thank you," I told him. It was hard to encompass all of it.

"My pleasure, Dove," he assured me, then nuzzled a kiss to my forehead.

I sighed.

"What is it? Too much?"

I couldn't deny the concern in those words. "No," I answered, trying to find the shreds of my courage and yanking them up like they could hide all my damaged bits. "I just—sometimes I wish none of you knew still."

"Why?" No judgment, simply a straightforward question.

"You knew about Eric, and that was bad enough—but I was also so uncertain of why I was here, or what was going to happen, I almost didn't care *then*." Which, I really couldn't put my finger on when that shifted exactly. "It was always safer that no one knew."

"It was *not* safer for you."

Cupping his jaw, I stroked my thumb along his cheek. "I survived. I always survived. I had before, and I could again." Even if I hated every single moment.

His eyes darkened.

"But it wasn't always safe for others. It was why I didn't dare tell people. I tried before—everyone I ever told died." Until now... The little voice reminded me. I'd told Freddie. I'd told Rome. They were still here. Then apprehension stalked through me like a rabid animal on the hunt. "It was easier to pretend, too, if no one knew. Then I could just be me...I could have sex when I wanted and with who I wanted. I could say how and why or no if I didn't want to."

He studied me for so long, that I was certain he'd already seen right through me. "I get it," he admitted after a protracted silence. "Sometimes—you have to pretend because to do anything else would be even more painful." With care, he rubbed my back in a slow circle. "Sometimes, you need it because it's how you put one foot in front of the other."

How... "I almost hate to ask how you know that," I admitted.

"You can ask," he said softly, then pressed another kiss to my temple. "Not sure I'm ready to answer yet, but I understand, Dove. I really do. I hate that you've been so alone that it was the better option for you. Just means we need to work harder, so you know that it isn't your only option anymore."

I liked that.

I liked that so much.

"Now," he continued, clearing his throat. "What would you say to a long hot shower, then a massage? You can even take a nap, and I'll keep watch for you."

"I think I'd say—that sounds like heaven."

"Then wings out, Dove," he advised as he stood, lifting me. "I'll clean this up later. Heaven awaits..."

14

The clubhouse wasn't quiet when we emerged from the dance studio. But I didn't let the conversation and laughter floating from the kitchen distract us. I headed straight for the stairs and climbed them two at a time. The soft weight of her arms looped around my neck and the relaxed expression on her face offered me a kind of relief I'd never experienced before.

Thankfully, we didn't run into anyone. Not that I begrudged the others their affection for her or from her. Hell, I didn't even mind sharing intimacy with her, but right now—I wanted to extend this moment of profound trust. I wanted to be greedy with it. Once inside my room, I shifted my grip only long enough to lock the door.

The moment the tumbler slotted into place, she lifted her head and I paused. "This still okay, Dove?" If she wanted it unlocked, then I'd just take my chances. Hell, she'd probably like it if one of the others joined us.

Something depthless in those brown eyes of hers teased

me. Her level of maturity had always astounded me. Moreover, the way she seemed to relate to us had been something of a mystery. Yes, the fucker she'd danced with had hurt her, and initially, the darkness in her seemed to be tied to that.

Now I knew better.

Yes, he'd influenced some of that darkness, but he wasn't the source. The world she'd inhabited had honed her to diamond toughness while not robbing her of her heart.

"I trust you," she whispered and those three words branded themselves on my heart. "And you're locking us in together."

"Yes, I am. But you can unlock it anytime you want."

She grinned, some of the humor creeping up to brighten her eyes. "So can Freddie and Rome."

A bark of laughter escaped me. "Probably Kel and Jas too, if we're being honest. We're all pretty familiar with picking locks."

"So, when you lock it... it's really not to keep them out."

No, I guess it wasn't.

"I like that we can trust them."

We. Yes. Definitely, we. "Me too." I brushed another kiss to her forehead then carried her into the bathroom. When I set her down on the cool countertop, she let out a little gasp then laughed.

"I'm hotter than I thought," she said in a too light tone before she fanned herself. Another chuckle worked its way out of me.

"You're fucking gorgeous, Dove. Inside and out." I touched a finger to her chin and lifted her face so I could brush another kiss over her lips.

Pink touched her cheeks, and I had to resist the urge to

linger on those fucking bitable lips until they were plump and swollen from my kisses. My dick thickened in my pants, but it wasn't like I didn't sport a semi around her all the fucking time. Even if I never fucked her again, I'd want her right where she was. The most exquisite torment wrapped in the most delightful package.

"What are you thinking about?" The whispered words pulled me back to the present, grounding me from my fantasies. Well, maybe not grounding me—more like tethering me back from the brink.

"You," I admitted, reaching for her dance shorts and hooking my fingers into place. "This still okay?"

The pink flush to her face only deepened. "You don't have to ask me at every single step..." Nothing in her tone indicated she truly minded.

Running my thumb back and forth along her side, I leaned in until our noses brushed. The scent of the burger on her breath could have been a turn-off if it had been anyone else. For me, it just meant I'd fed her and she'd enjoyed the food. Nothing about any of that could ever be a turn-off. Hell, nothing about *her* could dampen my desire for her.

"Maybe I want to," I explained rather than scolded. She'd get enough of that from Jasper. Not that it concerned me. He cared far too much about her to ever make her feel bad, but he would tease, scold, and probably taunt—though maybe that was more of a Liam maneuver. "I'd rather verify at each step that we're still on the same page, Dove. If you need me to slow down or speed up, we can adjust as we go."

Too much had been taken from her.

"Then yes, this is still okay." Acceptance. Pure and undiluted. Another reason to adore her so much. Bracing her hands on the countertop, she pushed upward. The obvious strain, coupled with the way her knuckles whitened, had me peeling the dance shorts down swiftly. Then she settled back on the counter with a little huff.

Her cheeks went ruddy and I paused to lift one of her hands, then ran my fingers over one scar. The barest flinch had me slowing the contact. I watched her face, but she had her gaze on her arm. When her breathing evened again, I began to do a slow massage of her forearm. Careful of the puckered skin, I worked the muscle on either side of it.

When her lips parted and she released a half-groaning sigh, I nodded to myself. Then I moved over to work the muscles on her other forearm. How deep these cuts had to have been to leave the brutal marring to her flesh, I didn't want to imagine. At the same time, I needed to help her feel better. Using those muscles had to be hard on her.

By the time I finished with her second arm, she had her head tilted back and her eyes closed. She half-swayed from the attention and I moved a hand to her thigh. "Still with me, Dove?"

"Hmm-hmm...and I thought I wasn't getting a massage until after my shower?" Drowsy, almost pleasure-drenched words in that sweet husky tone of hers was like a wrapped caress around my dick.

I made her feel like that. The possessiveness added to my craving for her, but I kept my eyes on the prize. In this case, making her *feel* better and taking care of *her* needs. Not mine.

Not yet.

"I just said a shower and a massage," I reminded her. "But if that's a complaint..."

Her eyes fluttered open and a true smile spread her lips. "Not even. Do I need to take the leotard off now?"

"Yes. Do you want me to stay for the shower or go?"

"Stay." No hesitation. Not even the slightest. "The first time we kissed was in here."

Yes, it had been and my cock hardened to stone at the memory. I'd been washing that bastard's blood off me when she came in. I wasn't sure if she ever noticed that part, and I sure as fuck wasn't bringing it up now. Maybe later.

Maybe.

"I'd like that," I said, responding to her invitation once I had my desire leashed properly. With care, I lifted her off the counter and only when she was steady on her feet, did I begin to peel off the leotard.

She tracked my every motion with her gaze. When I tugged it down to her ankles, I stole a look upward and watched her as she lifted first one foot, then the other.

Unlike her first sojourn with us, her bruises weren't everywhere. They were, however, darker in some places than others. The fading marks of restraints had already been visible, something I had to focus on *not* thinking about even as I cataloged them. The scars on her forearms and wrists were the worst—seemingly. But there were burn marks on her neck and on her shoulders.

Not lingering over any one mark too long, I ran my hands over her skin soothingly. The bare skin at the apex of her thighs wasn't marred. But there was a yellowish-green bruise to the inside of one thigh. I had to fist my temper because I swore it was in the shape of a hand. Or had been before it had begun to fade.

When she bit her lower lip, I halted my inspection and rose. "Whatever you need," I told her. "We can make it happen."

"Don't think about him here," she whispered. "I won't. I don't want to ever think about him again."

My heart just fucking shattered and I straightened to my full height. Cupping her face, I dipped my head and just kissed her. Her lips parted for me and I thrust into that kiss all my worry, anger, affection, and need. When she dug her fingers into my shirt and fisted it, my heart settled from a rapid race to a hard thud. She dragged me closer and I delved my tongue against hers, chasing it to play with it.

I kissed her until we were both breathless from it, then moved to rest my head against hers. "I'm only thinking of you," I promised. I would *only* ever think about her.

"Take the shower with me?"

"Dove..."

"Please."

I chuckled softly. "I wasn't saying no, sweetheart, I promise. I just want you to know nothing *has* to happen."

"Does that mean it can?" She stole a look up at me and I groaned.

"I can't tell you no," I admitted. I should. I absolutely should. Doc was due here today at some point. But... "How do you feel?"

"Honestly?"

I just looked at her and that smile of hers flickered away then back.

"Sorry, I meant that as a joke."

"I'll laugh later, I promise."

"Thank you."

Awareness of her nudity and the weight of her pressed against me made it impossible to focus on anything else.

"I'm—better." That didn't sound terribly certain. "I think. He warned me about soreness, but that seems gone, or maybe I just can't feel that past the ache in my legs."

Another attempt at a playful smile. Yes, as much as I wanted to give in to that, I didn't dare. Not yet. This was too important. She caught my fingers and carried my hand down to her thighs, then spread her legs so she could run them against the seam of her cunt.

She was soaked.

"I know I want you," she whispered. "But maybe we need a condom."

"Or I can just get a shot when Doc gets here," I admitted in a gruff tone. I really didn't want anything between us. "Unless you prefer…"

"I just want you," she admitted, and it began to hammer away at my restraint. "I want to feel you and no one else. I want—I just want to want you and have you want me."

Snapping a hand out, I dragged the shower curtain back and then got the water started. Not once did I ease my fingers from between her thighs. Instead, I began stroking her cunt, drawing the slickness up from her entrance to circle her clit. The slow, deliberate strokes of me delving deeper into her cunt with one finger had her head tilting back as she gripped the counter. Then she spread her legs.

The water kicked on and I continued the lazy caresses. "I can make you come as many times as you want," I promised.

It took a solid minute for the steam to waft out, and by then, I had two fingers speared into her and her clit under my thumb. The little bundle of nerves seemed to swell with every stroke and she clamped down on my fingers as I dragged them out and pushed them in. A little mewl of pleasure escaped her throat, and I leaned in closer, nibbling a kiss along her neck to her jaw.

"Does that feel good?"

Another soft sound escaped and I chuckled, halting my hand until I was barely touching her even though my fingers were plunged deep. The trembling muscles around them had me aching to replace my fingers with something far thicker and more satisfying for both of us, but I needed to know this wasn't hurting her.

"Words, Dove," I whispered, nipping the softness just behind the shell of her ear. "I need your words."

"It feels—amazing," she elongated the last word on a breathless little moan as I skated my thumb back against her clit. She clenched around my fingers as she clamped her thighs on my hand. The squeeze of her muscles was fucking intoxicating.

"Good," I teased, biting down gently before adding, "Play with those beautiful tits for me. They look so fucking suckable right now, but I want my hand where it is."

She whimpered but let go of me to cup her breasts. As she began to twist and tease her nipples, I licked my lips. She wasn't gentle; she would grip them tight enough to make them plump deeper with blood even as she moaned.

Fucking her with my hand was an experience, because she didn't hide her reactions. None of them. As her muscles began to spasm, I sucked against her earlobe and then rocked my hand, curling my fingers with every plunge to find that soft, textured, and spongy spot that had her thrash abruptly when I added pressure to her clit at the same time.

The rush of dampness over my hand as she let out a little scream was a fucking joy. I kept up the strokes as she trembled and shook until she whimpered again and then I captured her lips, swallowing that sound as eager as I was to taste her passion on her lips.

"Vaughn," she groaned in between kisses.

"We're not done, my sweet dove." It was as much an admonishment to the riot of hot need inside my body as it was to comfort her. "Hold on for me."

She wasn't alone in groaning when I tugged my fingers free and then I lifted her up to sit on the cold countertop. Not that it seemed to diminish one ounce of the flush suffusing her whole body. At this level, I nudged aside her hand and sucked one of her nipples against my teeth even as she gasped. So fucking responsive for me.

So perfect.

I stripped out of my clothes swiftly, then banded an arm around her and carried her right under the steaming water. She was right, the first time we'd kissed had been in this bathroom. The first time we'd fucked had been in here too.

I devoured her lips as she clung to me and I had us under the spray until we were both soaked. Only then did I set her on her feet. I kept my hands on her hips until she was steady and then lifted my head.

My cock pressed right against her belly and the satiny soft skin was a provocation all its own.

"You still want this?" I checked, and she wrapped a hand around my dick, tracing her fingertip over my piercing with such agonizing gentleness I bucked into her hand.

"Yes," she whispered. "Please fuck me, Vaughn. Just fuck me until the only thing I can feel is you."

Yep. That shattered any remaining reservations.

"Turn around, Dove," I ordered. "Hands on that wall, and hold on." I needed all my control. "Because if you want to feel me—you're going to feel me."

The beckoning in her eyes and the final stroke of her fingers was both a torture and tease, but I wanted all of it. I wanted her wild open sexuality and her freedom. I wanted her bendy body and her throaty laughter. I wanted her fucking trust and I wanted to live up to every single expectation.

As soon as she presented that sweet ass to me, I eyed it for a long time. That was next on my list to reclaim *for her.* No more fear for her.

Ever.

Then I fisted my dick, squeezing it hard enough to make pain twinge up my spine. Not that it softened the rock-hard erection. Not with her right there, but it did buy me a measure of control.

Nudging her feet apart, I teased the head of my cock against her cunt. She let out a low sound and then pressed her hands to the wall, though one began to slide downwards.

"Play with your clit," I ordered. "Touch yourself and make yourself come for me." The tips of her fingers dipped lower, long enough to tease at my piercing, then I shifted the angle, stepping back and pulling her ass toward me. She dipped like the elegant dancer she was, until her back was perfectly curved and arched.

"Hang on," I managed in a raw tone and then I pushed in—shallow, slow thrusts. Just the tip, then a little bit more. She let out a long huffing groan, like she couldn't catch her breath to even make the sound.

"Slow," I ordered, but she pushed back toward me and then I was fucking all the way inside that velvet-gloved heat, and she wrapped my cock up like the perfect package she was. Bracing her hip with one hand, I wrapped that braid around my free fist. It was the perfect length for this.

"Tell me what you want," I ordered and she let out another cry and slapped her hand against the tile.

"You, I want you."

"This?" I taunted, but only a little as I rocked my hips. It was agony and ecstasy. I'd already blown my fucking load like a teenager once with her, and I had a feeling the desire to flood her over and over again was always gonna be there.

"Yes, deeper," she begged. Goddammit, she begged. "Fuck me harder."

"Better," I complimented as her tone went fiercer and the demand harsher. "That's it, Dove, tell me what you fucking want."

"Fuck me, Vaughn. Fuck me so hard you're all I feel."

That was what I wanted. I tugged her hair to tilt her head back and tightened my hand on her hip. My control seemed in constant danger of eroding, but I'd pull out and jerk off against the wall or die from an everlasting hard-on if she asked it of me.

"Hang on," I repeated my command from earlier and then I dropped all pretense of holding back. I pulled out and then slammed back inside her. The sweet grip of her cunt was the best goddamn thing I'd ever known, and I wanted to stay here forever.

The only care I took was to check for even a hint of true pain as I rocked into her. My balls dragged up tight. I wasn't going to last long. But my sweet girl still had her hand on her clit and she was already spasming around me.

Fuck yes.

That was two.

I wanted a third one. This time I pressed her right against the tile, trusting the sensory play of cold and warmth against her nipples to help and then began short bursts of pumping, keeping my pierced tip as far into her as I could.

Her breathing grew shallower and shallower. I dragged her head back so I could see her eyes and her pupils were huge. This time when she came, I drank in the devout look of ecstasy on her face before I let go and then just rocked my hips. We came together again and again. She fought to keep me inside, and I fought to pull out and then thrust back in.

When the white-hot heat expanded and my own orgasm crashed through me, I plunged my head down to claim her mouth, tangling our tongues as I pumped every drop into her sweet, delicious cunt.

Together, we hung there, hearts slamming and her body trembling. Or maybe it was mine. Eventually, we would have to move, but first...

"Still good?" I asked in a raw tone.

"Yes," she exhaled the word, like it was an actual effort to release it. "But that felt like, can I have some more?"

A real laugh shook free from my chest, riding the effervescence of relief and delight. "Whatever you want. First, we get clean."

"Okay," she agreed. "I need to rest up anyway. I don't think I can move."

"You don't have to—I'll take care of everything."

Every damn thing she needed.

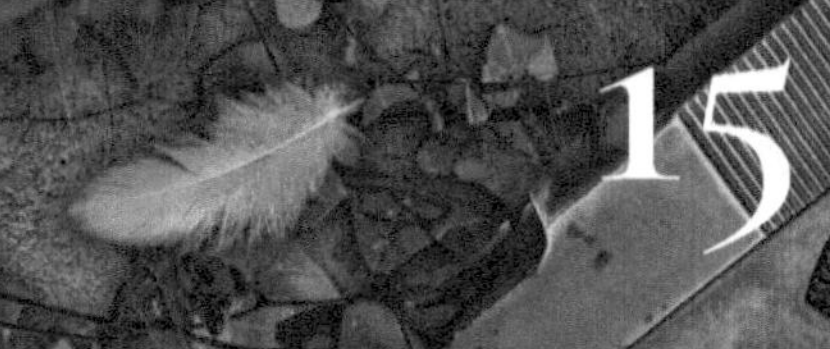

15

"You look happy," Lainey commented after she swung open the door to Milo's room and stepped back to let me in. The smile playing over my lips seemed to just grow. It was the most ridiculous thing.

It helped that I was practically boneless. Multiple orgasms were good for what ailed you. The amusement on Lainey's face was fleeting. "You don't."

She shrugged. I didn't miss how she glanced past me down the hall while I stepped inside. When she closed the door, she re-engaged the locks. "I'll be fine," she said as she waved toward the sofa. "Have a seat. You want coffee?"

"You actually have coffee here?" I tracked her as she picked up two empty pizza boxes and carried them to a large black trash sack. It was nearly full, but she just shoved the cardboard inside.

"It's nothing fancy," she answered, motioning to the little two-cup maker sitting on a low table near the bathroom. There was a fridge tucked up next to it.

I really hadn't looked at Milo's room. It weirded me out that it *was* Milo's room. But the pictures of me on the dresser were the biggest reason they'd probably never let me in here.

"No," I said, moving toward the dresser rather than the sofa. "I should probably hydrate."

Vaughn had definitely increased my exertion for the day. My cunt was sore in all the best ways. Even after cleaning up, I swore a little leaked with every step. It'd be gross, except it was Vaughn.

And I kind of liked it. Though, I really did need to make sure it was safe for him. A part of me really wished he hadn't risked himself, and at the same time—

Who was I kidding? There was a definite thrill that being with me was worth it to him. The oldest frame on the dresser was of a little boy and a woman who should be familiar.

She looked like me.

Our mother.

Our *biological* mother.

I should feel something for her, but I didn't. Instead, I focused on the little boy. The tilt to his chin, the brightness in his eyes, and the messy haircut just added to the adorable factor. It was hard to imagine Milo—big, jacked, and a little scary—as this sweetheart.

"Hydrate, huh?" Lainey asked as she joined me with a couple of water bottles in hand. "You're walking a little slow."

It wasn't a question, but I shot her a small smile as I took the water bottle then looked back at the photos again. The sweetheart of a little boy was a little older in another photo and holding a very tiny baby.

The grin on his face just shattered me, splintering those pieces I'd been trying to piece back together. It was like I was one of those puzzles Freddie, Bodhi, and I had been working on at Pinetree. There were a couple more with Milo and his—our—mother, but she looked ill in those pictures. None of them were with me. Then a scattering of photos with Milo and me, those also vanished.

In the older pictures, it was only me. More than one had been clipped from a magazine or a newspaper. They weren't even real photos, which just made me sad.

"Em..." Lainey said, wrapping an arm around me and leaning her head against mine as I sighed. Here it came.

"You have to go," I murmured.

"I wish—"

"But Andrea will be home soon?"

"Yes, but only for a few weeks, two months max, then she's back to school." Boarding schools. Just like Lainey.

Just like me.

Well, until I went to independent studies and home-schooling. I "graduated" when I was sixteen. "You have school, too, right?"

"I've been thinking about that," Lainey admitted. "Once I get Andrea settled, I can come back here. Back you up..."

I would love that, except... "You can't reposition your whole life because of me."

"Don't tell me what I can't do," she reminded me archly as she unscrewed the top of her water bottle. "You know how I feel about that."

A laugh escaped me as I gave her a squeeze. "You could take over the world if you decided you wanted to."

"Thank you," she said, pointing her bottle at me before taking a drink. "You're forgiven."

The photo of us at Disney World—it was the only photo that had Lainey and I both in it. The dichotomy of it being here... it was bright and colorful, our grins were wide and ridiculously happy. I already knew just how damn dark the world was even then, but it was better when Lainey was there.

When I could forget.

"I gave that to him," she admitted quietly.

"You saw him that day," I murmured. "You never said..."

"I didn't know he was your brother. But yes, I did see Adam and Ezra giving him a hard time. He also wasn't backing down. It was—kind of cool."

I quirked a brow at her. "Cool?"

She downed another long drink of water before drifting back to sit on the sofa. "Don't look at me like that. Everyone bowed to Adam and Ezra. No one crossed them, much less gave them shit. Then there's this guy with a pretty face and he's just—not taking their crap. I don't think it ever occurred to him that they were dangerous."

Turning with the photo in my hand, I studied her expression and the small smile curving her lips. This was a memory she'd enjoyed and it *clearly* left an impression. "Or maybe it never occurred to Adam or Ezra that Milo was dangerous."

So far, I didn't think they'd focused on him. Adam hadn't because Milo had hauled Lainey out of that confrontation. The rest of us had Ezra surrounded when Milo showed up—but he'd recognized Milo. Fuck, this was complicated.

They just all needed to behave around Lainey, or I would kick their asses. I had enough backup to do it. That thought triggered a laugh. I hugged the photo of us to my chest with one arm while I tried not to splutter water.

"You have a point," she commented after a long moment before focusing on me. "They still don't. Ezra's furious that I didn't just leave with him the other day."

I winced.

"He also wants you to reconsider staying here," she continued, but waved me off as I opened my mouth. "Don't worry. I told him to shut up about you. Now, if you *want* to leave, I'll have your back. I already told you, I'll sic my grandfather on your uncle. And we have friends..."

"I know, but I don't want to go back. Not just because of him." I sighed, crossing over to sink down on the sofa. Maybe all the sex had relaxed me enough that talking about this didn't gut me. At least not yet. Not that I wanted to linger on the subject. "I really do want to be here. I don't—I don't need to be Emersyn Sharpe anymore. I don't think I ever did. I've been running away from who she is my whole life. I just didn't understand that."

"I thought you'd say that," she admitted, then gave me a half-smile that I felt all the way to my soul. "I don't want to leave you behind either. If it wasn't..."

"You have to. She needs you. I know." Her sister was everything to her. Some girls might have resented her as the usurper, the golden child. The one her mother doted on and shared with her lover. The sister Adam and Lainey both shared through their respective parents. But not Lainey.

"She's such a brat," Lainey commented with a groan. "Impulsive, a little wild, but at the same time—too damn trusting. She doesn't understand the games or how they're played. Sometimes, I think she isn't even aware they're happening."

"How much of that is her?" I asked. "And how much of that is you, dealing with the problems before they become problems?" Because Lainey would. She would fix things, especially if she perceived a threat.

"I have no idea what you are referring to," she answered with a little shrug, then grinned. "Besides, you and I both know that information is power and power can be leveraged."

Yes, yes I did. "She's very lucky to have you."

This time her smile softened to something adoring. "I'm lucky to have her. She's so damn sweet sometimes, it makes my teeth ache. Then others, I love that we've been able to keep our world from touching her."

"Are you going to be alright when you go back?" This wasn't about Andrea now. "With leaving Milo?"

The open affection in her expression shuttered. "I'm leaving you," she said. "I don't like it, but I will survive so I can come back and help you too. I'll also be in a position to assist you there and before you tell me to stay out of it, tell me—if our roles were reversed, would you?"

Not a chance.

With a firm nod, she saluted me with her water. "Thank you for understanding."

"I love you," I whispered, not because the words were hard to say or especially new, but rather because they were admitting to the vulnerability we shared.

"I love you too." She reached over, and we clasped hands, her eyes nearly as misty as my own. "Now, help me plan my exodus. Your brother is being difficult and I'd rather not kick his balls up into his throat. The whole captivity thing was fun, but I do need to get back."

Fuck, I was really going to miss her. "I'd prefer not to discuss his balls at all."

"Killjoy."

"Bitch."

"Ha!" She grinned. "Your Freddie calls me Ball-Cracker."

That he did. Exhaling, I leaned on those endorphins some more. "When do you need to go?"

Lainey and I didn't get as long to talk as I would have liked when Freddie came looking for me. Doc was here. Dread curled in my stomach. Honestly, I wasn't even sure why. If it were bad news, he would have come sooner. Our last visit had cleared up a few things.

He waited for me out in the hall with Milo. Both straightened and Milo glanced at me. "Mickey said he needed to see you again. You're okay, right?"

"I am," I told him. After seeing the pictures in his room, my heart ached all over again. "Really, if it was something —I would tell you." Yes, it was a lie. But only a little one.

I was okay *now*. That was the important part. Milo scowled like he could hear my internal monologue then shook his head. "When you two are done, we're figuring out dinner and the plans for the rest of the weekend."

It was the weekend.

Wow.

"Okay." I'd lost track of the days of the week, but what did they matter? "We can do this in my room and then come down."

"You need any backup?" He kept the question quiet as he paused to press a kiss to my cheek. The affection was so damn sweet.

"I'm good," I told him. The very last place he needed to

be was in an appointment with me and Doc. "Really. Go make nice with Lainey, she needs to leave soon. As much as I would love to keep her here, she does have to go."

His scowl darkened. "We'll discuss it."

Right. That meant a fight. "Okay." I could handle that. I patted his arm and then glanced at Doc. His expression had barely shifted while we spoke. If anything, it remained firmly neutral.

Once we were shut into my room, I sat down on the edge of the bed. "Last results are in?"

"Yep. Everything looks good."

All the breath rushed out of me in a whoosh.

"You've still got an electrolyte imbalance and your sodium numbers are low. A little too low." He dragged the chair over to sit opposite me rather than sit on the bed. It was weird how he could fill up so much space with his size but also make himself smaller, easier to be around.

He'd done that from the beginning and I wasn't sure he even knew he was doing it. Hell, I'd barely noticed it at first except that I'd responded to it. I think. I had responded to it...

"Little Bit," he said, touching my knee gently, and I stopped bouncing my leg. I hadn't even realized I'd started. "You with me?"

"Yes, sorry—I was just thinking about how you always get down on my level. I'm right about that, right? If I'm sitting, you sit. If I'm standing, you don't always stand." I fumbled for the pieces. I couldn't see the side with the puzzle but these fit. "You even sit down on the floor if I'm on the floor—or in the bath."

"It's called reducing my threat level. It's especially important for those who've been through a trauma to find a certain amount of safety with their physicians."

"So, it's just cause you're a doctor."

That was—disappointing. Great, was I just going to keep embarrassing myself with him?

"No," he answered, then tucked a finger under my chin to lift my gaze back up to him. "I understand the philosophy and the principle because I'm a doctor. That's not the only reason I do it."

I grimaced. "I'm whining when I should be saying thank you."

Chuckling, he ran his thumb along my jaw. "You never have to thank me. You're also not whining. This has been a long and difficult week for you."

Another sigh escaped me. "Not as bad as the couple before it. Honestly, this week has been kind of great."

"I'm glad."

We locked gazes and I had to fight a smile.

"What?"

"Just—this is weird, and I have a weird question to ask you—the you that is the doctor but you're also...well, I don't know what we are exactly. Now I sound like a blithering idiot."

"You want to know if I need to treat one of the guys because someone got enthusiastic?"

Shock jolted through me. How the—

"You're walking a little slow," he answered my unspoken question. "Not like you do after you dance, but more like you've been thoroughly railed. Since you're in a fairly good mood, I'm guessing the interest was mutual and appreciated, but maybe a little too impulsive?"

Heat flooded my face and then another laugh erupted out of me. His grin softened, but it stayed in place. When I lifted my hands to cover my mouth, he drew back from touching me and just waited out my giggles.

"I'm sorry," I tried to say around gasps of laughter. Why was this so damn funny? "You said railed and—Mickey J, do you have a dirty mouth?"

"Anything is possible," he agreed, still smiling. "To answer the question, no, our enthusiastic knucklehead does not need to worry. You should be completely in the clear."

I exhaled. "He's not a knucklehead."

"That's a matter of opinion, Little Bit, and right now, the one that matters is yours. So... you ready to talk about some physical therapy and scar treatment?"

Just like that, reality doused me in icy water. I looked at my arms. "You think we can really fix the damage they did?"

"All of it?" He framed the question. "Unlikely. But can we make it easier for you and help you regain some flexibility and strength? Absolutely."

When he held out his hand, I stopped staring at the scars and settled my hand in his, then he drew my hand up to his arm. The left arm was covered in tattoos that hid the ridges of the scars but not from the touch. Tracing my fingers downward, he moved my hand from one swirling tattoo to another.

"The scars tell us we survived. Don't ever forget that." The gruffness in those words chased away my self-pity. "You can do this, Little Bit. I'll be with you every step of the way."

I pursed my lips then gripped his hand. "Okay."

"Okay?"

"Okay. Show me what I have to do."

He covered my hand with his free hand and then studied me for a long time.

"What?"

"You just never fail to amaze me, Little Bit." The hint of wonder lingered in his eyes, and I swore some little tiny piece of me glued itself back together. "Let's start with the basics," he said, squeezing my hands before he reached for his bag. "Scar care…"

"Thank you," Milo said as he opened the door to the car. My nerves spiked at getting into the vehicle, but he'd asked me to go meet this person and I'd said yes.

"You said she can't come here?" I tested the theory because I'd been fine until we walked out to one of the cars. The older Camaro had a classic look, but it was shiny and polished like it had rolled off the assembly line the week before. The color was a rustic kind of red with a black racing stripe.

"I said I'd prefer it if she didn't," Milo explained, leaning against the driver's side but not getting in the car. The weight of his gaze rested on me like a heavy pressure front rolling in. But was it bringing some rain or gearing up for a storm? "We have always kept her at a distance from our business. We do a lot of business here."

That made sense. "Kind of like you kept me at a distance?"

With a wince, he sighed and then scrubbed a hand over his face. "Ivy—I know it seems like I abandoned you. But I swear, it wasn't like that. I thought... I thought we had a damn good idea of what was going on with you, and most of the time, when I saw you—"

He cut off abruptly and I pressed up to the passenger door to meet his gaze over the roof of the car.

"I don't blame you."

Until those words passed my lips, I didn't realize how absolutely true they were. Milo opened his mouth and I shook my head.

"I don't," I repeated. "People who saw me daily had no idea about any of it." As much as I hated to admit it. "I was very good at keeping private matters private. Part of that was the isolation. When I was on the road with the tour, I only had a handful of people I could even 'think' of as friends. But none of them genuinely were."

I'd learned from my mistakes. I might have looked for allies, but never friends. Lainey had been enough. With everyone else, I'd undoubtedly respected the limitations of those relationships. The handful of mistakes I'd made had never lived long enough to regret offering me compassion.

Resting my chin against my hands, I sighed. "Lainey didn't know."

"She suspected," he countered. "She suspected *something* was wrong, and she knew about Pinetree."

"But she had no true evidence." Until the last ten days, I'd never talked to her about that part of my life. We'd always filed it away under the label of impossible family matters then just focused on ourselves.

He studied me for a long moment before nodding. "Then, yes, I suppose in some ways we keep her in the dark as we did you." The response circled us back to my earlier question. "It's safer for her, because what she doesn't know she can't testify to. While I don't doubt she wouldn't protect us with everything she has—"

"You don't want her to have to." I got that. "It's why I never told Lainey either."

Understanding creased the sadness in his eyes and he cut a look across the warehouse. "She hates that."

"I know." There wasn't much else to say to that. "She's the best."

He glanced over at me. "Warning me?"

I didn't flinch. "Yes."

A grin softened his whole expression. "You're fierce when you want to be."

"She's my best friend."

"I know something about that," he admitted, then shook his head. "But be that as it may, I do want to take you to see Miss Stephanie, and I don't want to ask her to come here."

Some of the nerves that had evaporated while we stood here slammed back into me. Sweat dampened my back, but I tried not to focus on that. "Just straight to her and back again?"

"If you prefer," he said slowly. "Ivy—I won't let anything happen to you."

I lifted my shoulders and fought for some measure of control. He already had enough to worry about. "Lainey needs to leave soon. I want to spend as much time with her as I can."

None of it was a lie, but his eyes shuttered and his lips compressed. "Let's go then. The sooner we go, the sooner we can get you back."

He slid into the driver's seat, leaving me little choice but to get into the passenger. It was that or run back inside and hide. While I didn't really want to do either, the former at least would be progress—right?

Curling my fingers into my palms, I sucked in a deep breath. I could do this. Pulling open the door, I climbed in before I could change my mind. Milo started the engine as soon as my butt hit the seat. It practically purred as it rumbled to life.

"Kel took good care of her for me while I was gone," Milo admitted as I strapped on my seat belt. As soon as it clicked into place, he hit a button to open the outer door then snapped his sunglasses into place. "There's an extra pair in the glove box if you need them."

An extra pair. I didn't even know where mine were. Maybe still at Liam's?

I found the pair and shoved them on. They were a little big on my face, but they helped to mute the blinding light outside. I held my breath as he tapped the accelerator, and we rolled out. The door was already closing when I dared a look back.

"You all do that thing with how you park. Back in or face the car toward the doors, so you don't have to back out."

"Makes for a faster exit when you need one," he said. "Every second you waste trying to turn a car around is..."

"...is a chance for someone to catch up?" I really didn't want him to police his words around me, but then—I could hardly blame him, could I?

"Something like that." He drove with a kind of aggressiveness I hadn't noticed in the others. Well, Rome maybe when we'd been on the bike riding away from Kellan's shop.

This was different. I didn't think we were in this much of a hurry. Yet, he accelerated down the alley a little faster than I expected and only tapped his brakes once before turning into the flow of traffic, sharp and smooth. It was like a spot just created itself for him and I gripped the door bar at the way he switched between lanes.

Traffic wasn't slow by any stretch, but he prowled between the vehicles and slid into spaces I didn't think we should fit and kept on going.

"Breathe, Ivy," Milo commented.

"Uh-huh."

"I'm not that bad of a driver," he complained and I laughed. I couldn't help it.

"Even if you were, I could hardly say anything. I'm not one to talk, I barely know the basics behind driving."

That earned me a look. "Didn't want to learn or didn't have time?"

I shrugged. "I was always on the road. New cities. Sometimes new continents. Just never seemed practical." Nor would my uncle have allowed it. "Drivers also provide security when I'm exhausted." I fought to not react to his next lane change.

Did he have a death wish? Or did he really think people would just get out of his way?

More the latter, I guessed, because they definitely tapped their brakes when he didn't touch his.

The sweat dotting the back of my neck seemed to intensify. "That was how I met Kellan—only he introduced himself as Kestrel. He was a *great* driver."

"Was he?" Milo almost sounded—grudging?

"Yes," I confirmed, then tried to just not watch where we were going. Only that just seemed infinitely worse, especially when he changed lanes so often. "He never let anyone jump in the car with me because they decided I needed company. Always got me to and from the venue. Even hung out when I was doing rehearsals off-site—huh." That all made so much more sense now. "That's almost embarrassing."

"What is?"

"I thought he was being so cautious and hanging out when I did rehearsals because he was into me." I made a face. "I even kind of made a pass at him."

No *kind of* about it, but Milo's choked sound said I was better off with the maybe than the definitive invite. The attentiveness and the kindness had kind of been my kryptonite.

"It stung when I thought he was just a kidnapper." I made a face. "Then it was worse when he told me I didn't belong in your world. He really wanted to get rid of me."

"And you're smiling about that?" Anger sparked in Milo's words and I looked at him, blinking.

"Yes. Because—he cared. He knew the secrets everyone was keeping and he didn't want to lead me on. It was sweet —in a really backhanded kind of way." I laughed. "I must have driven him crazy."

Milo just groaned. "So, this is payback? Driving me crazy?"

"Oh, shut up. You're hung up on my best friend and apparently fucking like rabbits, so you don't get to have an opinion."

I swore he just let out a long grunt of sound. It wasn't a no.

"Don't hurt her, Milo. I mean it." I loved her and I was beginning to adore him. It would kill me.

"You don't think much of me..."

"That's not true," I said before he could finish the

thought. "I don't *know* you. I want to...I do. But I love her. She dove right into everything with all of you, not even knowing who you were, because she wanted to help me. I wouldn't do any less for her."

"She's already planning on leaving, so I doubt you have much to worry about."

Rolling my head to the side, I stared at him. "Milo, she has to go home because she has a little sister who needs her and a family she doesn't trust to keep her safe because they are too preoccupied with themselves."

It wasn't a betrayal, but Lainey wouldn't tell him about Andrea. She wouldn't even bring her up.

"Her sister means the world to her. Has since the day she was born."

The whiteness in his knuckles vanished, and he stopped attacking every open space between the cars like it was a personal enemy.

"She's already planning on coming back *after* her sister goes back to school."

"A little sister?" The barest hint of hope crept into his voice.

"You know something about that, don't you? What you'd give up for a little sister."

He cut a look at me. "You know I do."

It was so weird to think of him with Lainey. It had been Adam for so long—for her. Maybe even for Ezra, though his reaction seemed to indicate something else altogether. That said, I kind of liked it too.

As long as our life didn't hurt her.

We'd left the city and it wasn't long before he pulled off a highway. As we passed a handful of traffic lights, the city gave way to suburbia.

Fast food restaurants scattered between gas stations,

box stores, and all kinds of places. There were like a dozen car washes. Who needed to wash their car that much? Then the little nail salons and I glanced at my fingers.

A manicure sounded lovely. But we turned away from the stores and shops onto quieter streets. There were bikes in some of the yards, just laying on their sides, not discarded. Waiting. Basketball hoops, manicured yards with gorgeous flowers, and others where the grass definitely needed a trim.

We passed older people out for a walk. A couple with a dog. Another lady was walking her dog and pushing a stroller with a couple of kids in it. "It's so weird," I murmured.

"Yeah," Milo agreed. "It's so—normal."

"Did we ever live in a house like one of these?"

"No," he admitted, taking a right at a stop sign. "We lived in an apartment about six blocks from where the clubhouse is now."

Oh.

"I'd show you, but they tore them down about ten years ago."

"That sucks."

"It was a shit hole," he said with a shrug, then pulled up neatly into a driveway. Though he put the car in park, he didn't turn off the engine. Instead, he studied the house in front of us. It was a lovely place. Though, the yard, like a few others, definitely needed mowing. "Miss Stephanie lives here. She—she saved my life more than I can describe. She introduced me to the guys, looked after us when—when our mother died."

"Was she a foster mom?" He hadn't really told me much about her. However, there had always been affection when he mentioned bringing me to meet this person.

"No, she was—is a social worker." Then he glanced at me. "She was our social worker. She helped place you with the Sharpes. Not directly, just—when the adoption offer came, she brought it to me and told me about it and was there when they came to meet you."

A chill crept through me.

"You want me to meet her?" Cause, honestly, I wasn't sure what I was supposed to think of anyone who gave me to the Sharpes. Mom and Dad weren't horrible people, but...

"Yes, I do. She's family, Ivy. Of all the people in my life, she has been among the steadiest and most steadfast. Even when I pled guilty, she didn't just throw me away. Trust takes time, you know?"

I did.

"But I think she can help you. She's helped all of us over the years. I know it could be tough for you, and I'm not asking you to tell her everything. You don't have to tell her anything. I just—I just want to give you a chance to meet someone I admire and respect."

With an endorsement like that...

"When you're ready to go, we can go." But he hesitated.

"What's wrong?"

"Her yard needs mowing, so, if you don't mind, I'd like to do that before we leave."

Oh.

That was so—sweet.

"I don't mind," I said. "I don't mind at all." Right now, we seemed a million miles away from Braxton Harbor, Pinetree, and the world I'd grown up in. We were also far enough away, it was almost like being on another planet.

I pushed the door open and climbed out. "Let's go," I said to him. "I saw the curtain move, so she knows we're out here."

And now, I was really curious about this woman Milo admired so much.

Very curious.

17

Milo waited for me to circle the car before walking up to the porch with me. I slid my hands into the back pockets of my jeans. This was—weird. I didn't have another word for it. Shifting, I glanced back at the street then to the little house again as he lifted a hand to knock, but a voice carried out before he touched the door.

"Come in, I unlocked it while you were in the car." The warm, feminine voice echoed with laughter. The effect on Milo was instantaneous. His mouth softened into a hint of a smile as the tips of his ears seemed to redden.

It was adorable.

Still, I couldn't shake the plummeting sensation from my stomach as he opened the door, then pushed it in and motioned for me to go in first. Despite the near instant change to his demeanor, he scanned the street and the tension in his shoulders hadn't vanished.

Pushing past my own hesitation, I stepped inside. The

foyer was small but neat. A coat rack stood to the right of the door, just blocking the four panes of glass that would otherwise allow someone to see in. There was also a row of coat hooks mounted on the wall. Shoes were lined up neatly in a row—four pairs of them—just below the hooks and then the foyer split off in two directions.

"I'm in the kitchen," our hostess called. "Come on through."

"Should we take our shoes off?" I asked, pitching my voice low. There was a formal living room to our right—okay, maybe not so formal. There were books overflowing on the shelves, a stack of magazines on the table, and a knitting basket next to one of the chairs.

"No," Milo said. "We would if we've just mowed, but our shoes are clean." He sounded almost excited. "Come on."

With a light touch to my lower back, he guided me ahead of him. I bypassed the living room and followed the sound of water turning on and the scent of coffee. The kitchen was a bright room filled with sunshine. There were plants on the windowsill that looked out into the yard and more greenery in boxes along the other windows near a table.

It was also a bright yellow color. It should be too much, but it just seemed to make the room shimmer with sunshine.

"Hey, Miss Stephanie," Milo said as he cut around me to greet the woman standing at the counter next to an electric kettle. She'd turned as soon as we came in. She was my height, maybe a little taller, dark brown hair with a scattering of gray, and light brown eyes.

"Well now, it's about time you came to see me," she said with a warm smile and a scolding, if not friendly, tone.

He dwarfed her in size, but when she opened her arms, he all but fell into them. I folded my own and glanced toward the windows. That seemed far too personal a moment. "I've missed you, boyo, but I knew you'd survive and come out stronger. But I'm glad to have that place well behind you."

"Me too," he admitted in a deeper tone before clearing his throat as he straightened. "I would have come sooner, but—"

"You don't have to explain," she said with a cluck of her tongue. "But you can tell me who—"

I glanced over just as she cut off and her mouth opened into a circle.

Yeah. Recognition flared in her eyes and I shifted my weight.

"Miss Stephanie, this is Ivy—all grown up. Ivy—this is Miss Stephanie. She's a big sister, ass-kicker, sometimes mom to all of us."

"I'm a friend," she told him with another look before she focused on me. "You've been missing for a while."

"I wouldn't believe everything you see on television," I told her carefully. "Despite what they say, I'm not missing. Or crazy. Or…"

"She's been with us," Milo interjected. "With the guys, then with me when I came back."

Right, so we were skipping the whole exile to Liam's and my trip home? I could definitely live without mentioning the latter.

"Well, I'm glad. I admit, I followed the story and I worried. I would have come up to talk to you," she said to Milo. "But you were in solitary."

He dropped his chin a bit. "Yes, ma'am."

"Don't you ma'am me in that tone. I know you boys. I'm sure there's a lot you're not telling me, and I know better than to ask." The timer on the oven went off, and she raised a hand. "I'm going to make some tea. Would either of you like some? I've also got a couple of trays of cookies to put in."

"Chocolate chip?" Milo brightened.

"With peanut butter, yes, I was going to add some peanut butter chips since I saw it was you."

He grinned. "I'll skip the tea, although I could go for a soda or water if you have it."

"Water," she said. "In the fridge. And you—do you prefer Ivy or Emersyn, sweetheart?"

The ease with which she transferred her attention from Milo to me and the shift in her tone from familiar and warm to just kind, was impressive.

"Emersyn is fine." It hadn't really occurred to me until just now that I liked my name. Even if I hated the Sharpe part of it. I'd been Emersyn for as long as I could remember. Ivy—Ivy belonged to Milo.

He could call me Ivy.

"Emersyn it is." Easy as that. "Now, would you like some tea?"

"Actually, water is fine." My mouth was suddenly dry. "I've never been much of a tea drinker. More coffee than anything else."

"Well, I have some of that around here. I keep it for the boys when they visit and for my brother. He can drink a gallon all by himself." She gave another cluck of her tongue. "Go on, you two. Sit down. I'll get coffee started after I get these cookies in."

It wasn't until she motioned toward the trays she had set aside that I even noticed the cookies at all. Milo snagged a couple of bottles of water from the fridge. He unscrewed one before handing it to me and then nodded to the little table.

For her part, Miss Stephanie was an economy of motion. She got the trays of cookies in, then poured her water over the tea in her cup before she got the coffee brewing. It all smelled good and as I sat back in the chair, some of the tension left me, even if I couldn't really relax.

"Jasper was here a few weeks ago and Vaughn dropped by a couple of weeks back. But someone needs to bring Rome to see me. I know he comes by, I see the gifts, but he never seems to stick around to talk." She gave the most exasperated smile. "That boy is so talented. I wish he'd let me make arrangements for him to go to art school."

"Liam would have sent him a long time ago if he wanted it," Milo assured her. "You know as well as I do, no one makes Rome do anything he doesn't want to do."

I hid a smile.

"This is true. And how are Kellan and Freddie?" She gave me a glance as she added some lemon and honey to her tea. "Sorry, I rarely get to see Milo, so I thought I'd catch up with him while you decide what you think of me."

I blinked. I hadn't said a word, and Milo chuckled. "Be nice, Miss Stephanie. Ivy's got a reason to be wary of the world." As much as humor filled his tone, he still knocked his foot against mine. It was a quiet reminder that he was there. "I brought her here to meet you because you've always been good to us."

"Hmm," she said as she finished with her tea then got down another mug. This one was a stone-looking tumbler in varying shades of blue. "I'll accept that for now, but I do want to know how Kellan and Freddie are. I haven't seen Freddie at all since last summer."

I frowned.

"He's good. Had some stress lately—but I think he's handling it. Before you say anything," Milo cautioned in an almost soothing voice. For a guy who had been all snarls and growls when I first met him, this was just like a completely different side to him. He measured his words and his tone with Miss Stephanie. "We're all keeping an eye on him, Jasper especially. Kel's also fine, just tackling a lot of new projects."

He definitely cared about her, but more, he respected her. That didn't seem to be something he did easily. If anything, it gave her a boost in my estimation.

"Do you want any cream or sugar in your coffee, Emersyn?"

"Black is fine."

She made a face. "That's definitely an acquired taste, but then I'm not a huge fan of coffee. Of course," she continued as she carried the mugs over to the table.

"I've been drinking backstage coffee for years," I told her lightly as I accepted the mug. "Not that I don't like the good stuff, but if it will kick me in the ass and wake me up, I'll drink it."

She gave me a bemused look, then glanced at Milo. "I like her."

"Me too." He grinned at me. "She's a brat, though."

I just flipped him off while I took a sip of coffee. His laugh was worth it, but hers caught me off guard.

"You have spent way too much time with those boys if you're already picking up their mannerisms," she said and then settled in with her tea.

"No, these were all mine, to begin with. Stage kid, life on the road, performers are a rowdy bunch. They've all been pretty damn gentlemanly around me. Jasper's manners are impeccable. So are Vaughn's and Kellan's." I considered that for a moment. "Liam's could use some work, but then I think he likes baiting me, and I like to tweak him, so it's all good."

Surprise flickered across her face, then a much warmer smile. "I'm so glad they found you again. I know they've kept an eye out, yet I wasn't sure you were ever going to reach out to her."

I caught Milo's faint shake of his head.

"I'm glad they did, too," I told her. That much was very true. "I had a whole family out here I didn't know about."

"It happens that way sometimes." Genuine regret lingered in those words. "Adoptions are not always open. Once the final papers are signed and custody awarded, we have to leave it in their hands. Well, at least until you're eighteen. Your parents were so eager to take you home. Eager to shower you with everything." Another wistful sigh as she gave Milo an apologetic glance.

"I told you then, if they only wanted Ivy, I could deal with it. That hasn't changed." He comforted her and now I had to rethink how to ask my next questions.

"No, but you shouldn't have had to deal with it." She glanced at me, hesitating.

"I'd like to know," I told her, grasping all of my courage. "About the adoption—about them—then." Were they alone? I wanted to ask, but I couldn't bring myself to discuss him. Not with Milo right there.

"Well, there's not much to tell. As much as I'd like to say I was the one who vetted everything, that was above my pay grade. I did speak with the social worker in New York, they handled the home visit there and then there was the paperwork. But ultimately, the final decision was put in the hands of the family court." She glanced at Milo. "The judge looked at everything, their standing, their wealth, and they made a compelling case. They were truly enamored of you —especially Mrs. Sharpe."

Milo seemed to be studying his water bottle. "It was a closed adoption, I didn't really get what that meant then, but I do now. Miss Stephanie wasn't supposed to tell me about them or their names…"

"No, I absolutely was not supposed to do that." She made a face. The scent of baking cookies wreathed the air, softening it somehow. It was homey and warm in this bright yellow kitchen with this very kind woman and her kind eyes. "However, Milo deserved to know that you were going to be fine. If you'd just disappeared…"

She clucked her tongue and rose.

"That would not have been reassuring." She squeezed his shoulder then moved over to the oven, reaching it mere seconds before the timer went off. "So, he knew their names and where they'd gone to live. I just never in a million years could have imagined the life you had, young lady. A star and on the road as a child."

Instead of awe, disapproval clung to those words.

"I'm sure it seemed amazing to you, but the choice they made to let you do it seems—just at odds. They didn't travel with you." One tray came out, then another. "Well, what do I know—you have had a very interesting career and you're still a baby. Probably just being a little old-fashioned."

Not that I'd have labeled her old. She looked to be in her late thirties, maybe early forties, even with the sprinkle of gray amongst the brown strands.

"It definitely gave this one plenty to brag about." Though she tried to cover the earlier disapproval with cheerfulness, it hadn't vanished completely.

When she returned to the table, she had three hot

cookies on a plate for each of us. Yeah, I didn't think I could bring myself to eat something quite that sweet yet, but Milo tore right in.

His cookie fell apart, steaming and the chocolate and peanut butter melting.

"Hot," he said around a mouthful and just devoured the three in quick succession. When he glanced at my plate, I shoved it over.

"Please," I said. "You're way too fun to watch eat those."

For the first time all day, his eyes lit up. A bit of chocolate smeared the corner of his mouth and a crumb landed on his shirt—not that it stayed there long before he rescued it to eat. He grinned before tugging the plate closer to himself. "You don't know what you're missing."

No, I hadn't. But I had a brother now, and I caught Miss Stephanie smiling at us both. He was right about one thing.

I did like Miss Stephanie.

18

We swapped out shifts of eight hours, with one driving and the other catching rack time. Deploying the fleet of trucks was a calculated risk. I had to admit, Kellan had a point. We would have to bait the hook to get more answers. That was why I took the Canadian run myself.

The drive would take us two days there, a few hours to load, then two days back. Driving sixteen hours and scattering the other eight hours for fuel breaks meant we could move faster, but it also meant we were asking for trouble if—when—they came for us.

"I can hear you thinking up here, Hawk," Milo rumbled. It was his time to drive and I was supposed to be sleeping, but instead, I had a picture of Emersyn up on my phone after scrolling through the handful of messages we'd exchanged since we'd left. "You could always let Rosie and her five sisters get your mind off shit."

"I like you, man," I said with a grin as I shook my head. "But I am not jacking off while you're driving."

"Wouldn't bother me if you did."

I opened my mouth to comment, then shut it abruptly. That was some weird shit, but then—how much privacy had he been allowed for all those years in jail.

"Knock it off," he said over his shoulder without taking his gaze off the road. There were curtains I could close to block out the light, but I was too comfortable to move them. "Shit happened, I've moved on."

Right. Not that I said that aloud.

"Thanks for the offer, but I'm fine. It's not horniness keeping me awake anyway." Even if it was, after Emersyn, the idea of returning to my hand just held zero appeal. I could be patient.

"What's up?"

"Just playing out the scenarios in my head. We're not sure exactly where they're hitting the trucks. Though we are pretty sure that all the ones they've hit were taken either close to the border or just on the other side of it. I lean toward the other side."

"Give me your reasoning." The familiarity in that single sentence pulled another smile from me. I closed the messages and then turned off the screen to set the phone against my chest. Milo had always been the most rational of us. Always planning a dozen steps ahead, or at least thinking that far ahead.

So much of that had been missing in him since he'd come home. Moments like this reminded me he was coming back to us. Slow but steady.

Hooking an arm behind my head, I drummed my fingers against the phone on my chest. "Because for about fifteen minutes, give or take, the trucks go dark on the far side of the border crossing. The next tower for transmitting is near their weigh station. There are three exits between the border crossing and that weigh station."

"There's a rest stop?"

"Yep. I've been there myself. At least on this route. The other two routes also have rest stops, at different points—but they are also a little more intermittent with the signals." But there was a kicker to all of this. "The problem is, we'd have to be looking for the failed signal to catch it, and it's a small enough window of time it could just be a drop connect that is then picked up again."

Standard operating procedure. Technology was great, but none of it was infallible. That was why our backup right now included both a technological and human component.

"Makes sense," Milo murmured more to himself than to me. "But how do they know what we're picking up?" Yes, we did move some illegal goods and handled transport for a lot of others; jobs where we were hired to pick up items from one location then deliver them to another.

We were well-paid to keep our noses out of it. Our only two main rules were no hard drugs and no people. I wasn't a fan of moving guns and weapons, but I'd take those over people and drugs any damn day of the week.

So, the fact that not only were our shipments getting hijacked, they were then using our papers and our trucks to ship people? Fuck that. I just wanted to get my hands on the assholes who decided to do this. Follow it right up the chain to the top, then cut the fucking head off and shove it up their ass.

"That's the ten-thousand-dollar question. There're a few ways I can think of," I admitted, circling back to Milo's earlier question. "The problem is—there's a ton of risk in each one. So, either they're well prepared..."

"Or they don't care about collateral."

That was definitely the problem we faced because if they didn't care about collateral, they were likely to have more guns than us. Not that we were novices at this. We'd taken on plenty of bigger, stronger outfits who were better equipped.

"Just means we need to be ready to fight dirty," I said around a yawn.

"Is there really any other way to fight?"

"Nope." The dry observation helped me to relax. We had a few hours before the border crossing and I'd initially intended to push it, get over, pick up our load, then get back.

Now?

We'd get a place and sleep. The rest stop might be ideal, but we could also drop into a hotel. I was still planning when I drifted off to sleep. The release of air from the brakes woke me as the truck came to a stop.

"Gas, coffee, and piss break," Milo said, and I raised a thumb but stayed where I was. Part of our plan was to also *look* like we were driving solo.

If I needed to take a leak, I had a couple of empty jugs back here. Not my favorite, but it would do. When Milo returned, he had two huge bags of takeout and the smell had my stomach growling. I waited until we were back on the road before sitting up and reaching for a bag.

Roast beef sandwiches and curly fries. Fuck yes.

I checked the GPS then frowned. "Why the fuck didn't you wake me up?"

"Cause the first three hours, you didn't sleep," he answered easily. "And I'm not tired. We can trade out once we get to the border."

We weren't that far now. Maybe two hours, max. How

fucking fast had Mr. Lead Foot been driving. "You do know we can't afford the speeding tickets," I pointed out.

"Shut the fuck up. I'm barely going ten over the limit."

Asshole.

"My truck, my rules."

He didn't comment, but he did slow down a fraction. I scrubbed a hand over my face before going back to my food.

"Besides," Milo continued as he unwrapped a sandwich and kept one hand on the wheel. "I needed some time to think."

That never boded well. "About?" I kept my tone light. We had enough on our plates.

"Just stuff."

"Stuff like a certain brunette best friend with a lot of attitude?"

He didn't respond, and as tempted as I was to needle him a little, I let it go.

"Stuff like, I took Ivy to see Miss Stephanie."

"How'd that go?" I'd known when they'd gone, but I was still trying to give her all the space she needed. The fact that she'd sought me out twice suggested it was the right call. She'd also slept in my room a couple of times too. The minute my thoughts drifted to her, I wished we were already heading back home.

"Not sure," he admitted after another silence.

I finished my sandwich and a few more fries before I prodded him. "Not sure how? What were you expecting?"

"I don't know," he admitted. "Sometimes I feel like she's right there, trying to reach out to me and we're communicating across this huge chasm, and I can only hear about half of what she's saying. Worse, she can either not hear me at all or only gets bits and pieces."

After cleaning my hands with a wipe, I stuffed all the

trash into a bag, then climbed down into the passenger seat. There was a second soda waiting for me. I'd need to take a leak soon, but I needed a drink more.

"First, be patient. Hardest part of having her at the clubhouse in the first place, was I knew all this shit about her and she didn't have the first fucking clue about us." That still chafed some. "We've maintained this one-sided relationship she was utterly unaware of. We know a lot about her—but we don't know everything. Our, no, not our. *My* mistake was I assumed that I did know. The thing with the dance partner... pissed me the fuck off. We should have seen it sooner, then...once we had her there, I didn't want her to go back until she was healed."

"Then you didn't want her to go back." Milo shrugged. "I get that."

"Yeah, but the difference now is she *wants* to be here. She wants to get to know you—to know all of us. She's also *trusting* us to look after her." That quieted a lot of my internal objections.

"She has so many secrets," he admitted. "Mayhem is just as bad."

"Mayhem?"

"Lainey," he said with a chuckle. "She's a riot, and she is definitely good at causing mayhem."

"Word of unasked for advice, maybe don't call the girl you're interested in such an—interesting nickname?"

He chuckled. "Better for us both if we keep a healthier distance. Ivy is her priority."

Yeah. Right.

"Considering she's in your bed more often than in Emersyn's, I think you've already lost that argument."

He didn't say anything more about it and I let it go. Not because I didn't care, but honestly, emotional shit like this gave me hives if I had to pry it out of someone. They wanted to talk, I could definitely listen.

The only two I'd never had any trouble pursuing those dialogues with were Freddie and Emersyn. An hour later, we took another break—this time, to let me hit the bathrooms and then to take over the driving.

It was getting late. We made the border after dark. If we pushed, we *might* be able to pick up the load tonight. I turned that over in my head as I waited for our turn with the border guard.

I had both of our IDs and passport cards. We'd all gotten them when the trucking had begun to pick up. Fortunately, they were good for a few years, so Milo hadn't had to reapply.

When it was our turn, I climbed out on request and went to open the back. This was routine. We were on our way across to do a pick-up and we weren't transporting anything across.

"All good," the guy said after filling out the information and handing me a tear sheet for my logbook. "Be aware there's some road work going on, yeah. Probably best to go straight to your pick-up zone. The earlier exits are closed for a few miles."

Right. Interesting.

"Thanks. Might pull off for the night and do the pick-up in the morning." Call it a hunch, but now I was really curious.

"Sure thing," the guy said. He'd signed his name to the paperwork. I'd have to look at it. "There are a few places up the way. If you go on up to Moncrief, there are a couple of inexpensive places, clean and good food for breakfast."

"Thanks," I said, holding out a hand. He shook it, super

briefly, and I locked up the back before I headed to the driver's seat.

"What was that?" Milo asked after I got us moving and waved real friendly-like.

"Trusting my gut," I told him. "The inspector told me all the nearby exits are closed for construction. When I told him we might put in to sleep for the night, he told me to head on up to Moncrief. Suggestion, sure. Might be paranoid."

Milo didn't comment. The roads on this side of the border were nice, but we also had to deal with a lower speed limit.

"You think he's selling out potential targets." It didn't take him any time at all to get there.

"Maybe. Don't know. Like I said, just something rubbed me wrong."

"Go straight to the pick-up," he said after a moment, then he climbed into the sleeper. We had made some modifications. Keeping my eye on the road, I tracked his movements, putting up the bed and pulling out the guns.

He slid one up between the seats to me, and I tucked it into the holster on the seat. We'd have to store them again when it was time to cross back over... but he was right. The sooner we got the load and doubled back, the sooner we might have a problem.

It wasn't nerves or unease sliding through my system but excitement.

"You know you're grinning like a fucking crazy guy right now, don't you?" Milo was back in the passenger seat and my bat was now in the well next to his feet.

My grin grew. "Been a while since we had some fun."

His snort just made me laugh.

"Lighten up, Raptor," I informed him with a light smack

of my fist to his biceps. "This is going to be almost as good as sex."

"Nope," he said. "Considering I know where you've been putting your dick, that doesn't go on the table as a comparison. Ever."

I laughed.

Really, fucking laughed. "Man, you should only worry if I ever said it was better, and trust me, nothing is better."

"I will shoot you."

I wasn't worried.

"She'd kick your ass."

His muttered response just added to the hilarity. Fuck yes, I'd send a message to our contact when we were sixty minutes out. The adrenaline gave me a hell of an energy boost.

If all went well, we'd be back in Braxton Harbor with more info on this problem and I could spend more time coaxing Emersyn back into my bed to stay.

After cranking up the music, I took a drink from my soda and kept my head on a swivel. But I really wanted these fuckers to come for us.

I *really* wanted it.

19

M ilo played scarce in the sleeper of the truck while I went over the paperwork. Sure, the border agents had seen him and his paperwork. I was pretty sure our new *friend* Brendon Wyatt had likely already alerted whomever he would alert about the truck. Did they care about the crew?

The absolute lack of any evidence of our other drivers suggested that no, no they did not. The violence humming in my system surged in excitement. It took actual effort to stand fucking still and sign off the numbers on the pallets they were loading onto the truck.

Pharmaceuticals, including contraceptives. There were three pages detailing the types. I barely skimmed the list, making sure no one had added any oxy or similar products to the pickup. Insulin made up the bulk of it. Medical-grade equipment, including three ultrasound devices, with a fourth that was earmarked for special delivery.

That had to be for Doc. It was a therapy ultrasound

machine. I glanced to where the guys were adding the pallets. Four of them were medical, one of the four for Doc. I'd prefer they weren't on this run because if he needed them, I really didn't want to risk them.

At the same time, I couldn't turn them away. Three wrapped pallets were a private delivery. The storage facility address was listed on the sheet. It was a dummy address. The name was all I needed. There would be an email after I confirmed pick up and then we would get what we needed to do the drop-off.

These shipments were none of my fucking business, except the insurance on this one was listed at an astronomical price. It was also worth noting because anything that tipped our hand and our routes needed to be investigated.

The last set of pallets were a straight-up grocery run of dry goods that would be going to the port. That was the bread-and-butter of a transportation business. Getting goods from point A to point B without dealing with clients. We were a middle-man in the chain.

It paid damn good.

"The weight is off," I told Maurice. "You've got a hundred pounds extra here." It was forty-five kilos, but give or take, that was the same as a hundred pounds. "It doesn't add up."

I flipped to the other pages and did the mental math.

Maurice frowned. "We checked every pallet with the scale. Hang on..." He pulled the radio from his belt and called to someone in French. The rapid staccato answer popped over the two-way as the man he consulted with answered.

It took me only a minute to track which pallets were heavier than their listed contents.

Two of the medical supplies' pallets. Not the pharmaceuticals. Smart. That would definitely invite an inspection. But equipment could always be heavier—so why check it?

"We can pull the pallets and re-weigh them," Maurice offered, though his expression said it was the last thing he wanted to do. It was late, and the air was cold enough that I could see my breath. While I had a jacket on, he was in rolled-up shirtsleeves. Not that it seemed to be bothering him.

Running a hand over his beard, he half-glared to where one of the loaders had another pallet already on its way to the trailer. The irritation wasn't manufactured, neither was the grim expression. We'd be here longer if we pulled everything off and re-weighed. Then if it proved something was off, we might have to open one of the sealed pallets.

That could be problematic on many levels and not for me, because it meant the loaders had been compromised. I didn't envy him that conversation.

"Probably my math," I told him like it was my own mistake. "Everything standard on the drop-off?"

"Yeah, everything is normal from the paperwork to the check-in." He cut a glance at me. "You don't usually fuck up the math."

"Nope," I told him, then scrawled my signature on the bottom of the page before I tucked my copies away and handed him his. He stared at them a minute then at me. I clapped him on the shoulder. "Just do us both a favor, double-check the next loads?"

He gave a slow nod. The question was, what was he letting go of now, but I saluted him with two fingers before heading over to finish supervising the load. Well, I lit a cigarette and tracked each pallet they loaded. My job was transport.

An hour and three cigarettes later, I locked up the back

of the trailer and climbed up into the cab. Making a show of filling out my logbook, I kept one eye on the side mirror.

"How'd it go?"

"It's under the dash on the passenger side," Milo commented. "You were right."

I didn't shift to check for the tracker they'd put in the cab. Pretty fucking bold, but then—to hijack in the first place required a certain level of boldness. "Don't sound so surprised. I have my moments."

"Not surprised," Milo answered from the shadowy recesses where he'd waited out the duration of the loading process out of sight. "Annoyed that we had to leave that guy there."

Yeah. That I understood. "Don't worry. We have friends here too. Once this is done, we'll make sure we do a clean sweep."

"Not worried." The barely suppressed rage in his voice echoed my own thoughts on the matter. "You ready for the kind of fight this could be?"

I resisted the urge for a flip response. The bat was within reach and the gun was holstered. I'd have to slide it back to Milo when we got to the border. The way back in was a lot easier than leaving.

We had friends on this side of the border, though.

One of whom directed me toward the empty lane waiting for entrance. It took ten minutes and a peruse of the logbook. "Good to see you," Eastwood told me. "Been a few weeks."

"Just go where they send me," I told him with a careless shrug. "Above my pay grade, you know?"

"Ain't that the truth—you just crossed in tonight. Heading back already?" He peered up at me.

Milo was armed, but there was a witness so I just went

with it. "Got me a pretty little thing waiting. You know how it is."

Eastwood let out a laugh as he signed the book. "Man, I wish I knew how it was. After three kids, it turns my wife on more when I come home and take over so she can get a break."

"Hey," I said as he handed it back up to me and accepted the slide of cash under the book, pocketing it like it hadn't even been there. "She gave you three kids, I think she deserves a little pampering. Consider getting a babysitter and taking her out on a real date. I hear girls like that shit."

"Your girl like it?"

An image of Emersyn flashed through my head and the look of delight when I told her why I'd taken her up to the point. Even more, the look on her face when I caught her as she dropped from the silks.

"Yeah." I chuckled, keeping up the ruse. Only this one ventured way too close, so I didn't elaborate. "Thanks for the reminder."

"You got it bad."

"Maybe. We good?"

"Yep," he said, then waved to the guys ahead and I saluted. "Have a good one."

"You too." I left the window down and lit a cigarette before pulling forward.

No comments came from behind me, and it wasn't until we had put a good couple of miles between us and the border that he slid out and climbed into the passenger seat.

I half-expected him to say something, but he didn't. Instead, he kept his gaze on the road. He wasn't wrong, we needed to focus—

"You really are gone on her." It wasn't a question.

I put out the cigarette, then closed the window before I answered. "She's not a fling." Not from the moment I'd laid eyes on her again. Everything about the wild survivor in her eyes called to me. "You can get pissed about it. You can keep trying to knock my skull in, but I'm not letting go until the day she tells me to fuck off."

Probably wouldn't let her go even then. At least not go far without going after her and trying to win her back.

"I'm not a perfect guy, Milo."

"None of us are, Jas," he said on a sigh. "One thing I keep turning over in my head—I wanted her to have a better life. I thought she had it. Shiny world, lots of opportunities..."

"Money heals all wounds?" I suggested and he let out the most bitter laugh.

"Yeah. But it's all fucking lies."

"We learned that a long time ago," I pointed out, not to be a dick. "Just because some shit turned out bad, doesn't mean it all is."

"When the hell did you start looking at the bright side?"

Fuck if I knew. Maybe since Emersyn showed me there was one. "Hey, you've always believed in the best for us. Believed we were capable. Fuck, you had hope when I had none. Don't stop now."

"No promises." His sigh carried a lot of weight. "Look—"

Headlights approaching at speed behind us pulled my attention. Granted, it wasn't that late *yet*, but traffic coming in from the border was scarce. Most of us were going to be doing transport, with the occasional car, at least until we got a bit further south.

The car rocketed up next to us, then passed. It was

almost two truck lengths in front of us when it switched into our lane. But there were no brake lights.

There wasn't much on this stretch of road and there was another fifty miles to the first rest area on this side of the border. Another set of headlights filled my side mirror.

"That car is pacing us." Milo nodded to the car ahead. He wasn't wrong. Considering how fast they'd approached, caught up, and then passed—they'd adjusted their speed to stay exactly two car lengths ahead.

The headlights behind us were higher up—definitely another truck.

"You know how we used to head down to the docks on the weekends to make some extra money?"

"If you mean by picking fights and placing bets, yes, I do." His attention seemed as split as mine. "This is a little different."

"Not really." The more the tension amped up, the calmer I became. I lived for this shit. They wanted to come for me and mine. Well, they were about to meet my bat and my temper.

No one touched what was ours, and they sure as shit didn't get to take it away. We'd fought too long and too fucking hard to let it slip through our fingers.

These guys may not have wanted a fight, but they were about to get it.

"Two against two at the moment," I pointed out. "Really unfair odds—for them."

Milo laughed. "You are a crazy asshole."

"Sometimes."

Lights came on from the side of the road ahead and I moved over to give the car on the shoulder some space.

"Probably a good thing I am."

"Fuck me, that's more like ten to two," Milo muttered and I grinned.

"Good for them, now it's a fair fight."

The truck behind us had a pair of cars with it. The vehicles coming on from the shoulder where they'd stopped numbered another two. The car ahead of us was soon joined by two larger vehicles entering the road.

"It's like they set up a parade for us."

"Crunch and bump." Exactly. They were going to get us to stop by pulling an "accident." Totally reasonable for me to stop and make sure folks were all right. Especially if they staged it in the middle of the road.

Even being ready for it, I winced at the SUV clipping the smaller car and sending it careening into a spin. When it flipped, I shook my head.

I was already braking. They weren't even a half-mile ahead. Cutting it close. The air brakes screamed and Milo had the shotgun in hand and reached into the back to pull out a second gun.

"If we're wrong..."

"We're not." Like me, the other cars were slowing and pulling over. That accident was across the highway. We could get around it, but it wasn't etiquette. I checked the radio for signals and there were none.

That clinched it.

"We need one alive," Milo reminded me. Movement from the back of the trailer as a couple of guys rushed toward the driver's side had me nodding.

"One. Got it."

I opened the door and swung down. The light glinted off the gun one of the guys held, and I didn't wait for him to get to me—I just shot him.

The bullets slammed into his chest, knocking him back

into the man behind him and his gun went flying. The roar of the shotgun told me Milo was already engaged.

Kevlar.

How nice.

I snagged my bat before I left the shield of the car door and cracked the skull on the second guy before pivoting to take a swing at his friend.

He tried to dodge, but the beauty of a bat was I didn't need to hit you head-on. Cracking it against your side or your arm hurt damn near as much.

Sometimes worse.

The sound of his arm snapping under the weight of the swing cracked loudly. He went down, clutching his arm and letting out a wail. I kicked him in the jaw to both shut him up and knock him out. A scuffle of a shoe sounded behind me and I turned. The guy trying to climb into the truck didn't enjoy the bullet to his side.

He clasped a hand to himself and staggered backwards. I helped him along with another swing of the bat. Oh, fuck, it felt good to just let go. The steady blasts of the shotgun continued. Milo was fine, so I headed to the back of the truck.

There were a pair of guys there, one with a huge set of bolt cutters.

Fuckers.

One of them lunged right at me and I barely got a shot off before we hit the ground. The fucking gun went flying but I held onto the bat. We flipped over and I got the bat between us. The guy's hand kept slipping on the blood, slicking the end of it, but I forced it down against his throat.

In the dark, with only the scattered headlights for illumination, I could make out the guy's eyes. When they widened a fraction, I let him go and rolled. Hot blood spattered my face as the bolt cutters came down on that guy's head.

His friend staggered back and I yanked the bat to me as I rushed to my feet. With both hands on the grip, I swung it. A series of strikes drove the larger man back. Yeah, he might have a couple of inches and fifty pounds, but a solid, wooden bat had a lot going for it.

When his arms went up to shield his head, I went low and took out his knee. A bullet pinged off the back of the truck, the hot metal bouncing so fast I never saw it, but I sure as shit felt it grazing my cheek in a blaze of burning fire.

Retreating, I scanned for my gun and kept moving. Then I rolled right under the truck, coming out the other side with my gun in hand.

"Down," Milo ordered, and I hit the deck. The roar of the shotgun let loose above me and another figure crumpled.

"Five down up there. How many do you have?"

"Two definitely dead. One unconscious, and one crippled and trying to run." He wasn't getting far. "Also, that guy you just shot was mine. Not that we were keeping score or anything."

"Check the vehicles," he said, though there was the barest hint of laughter in his voice. "I'll get your not-runner."

"Just remember, I already tagged him."

"Yeah, yeah." Milo set off after the big guy and I jogged toward the trucks. They were empty, both in the front and the back. I snagged the logbooks from both.

Some habits were hard to break, even for hijackers. Then I helped myself to wallets and IDs. Milo had our "runner" tied up and secured in the hold. I dragged the guy I'd knocked out around to the back and between us, we hauled him up in there.

He was bloody and groaning. At least we had the big drop cloths in place. The last thing I wanted to do was clean blood off the merchandise.

I checked my watch.

"Fifteen minutes," I muttered. "Getting slow."

"Jas?"

'Yeah?"

"You're a fucking lunatic."

I grinned and saluted him with my bat. "Yes, I am, but I'm a smart fucking lunatic." The plan worked and Milo couldn't argue with it.

Course, now we had a huge fucking mess to clean up.

That might take a minute.

20

The phone's buzzing woke me. The phone was typically on *do not disturb* when I hit the bed. Especially since Emersyn came back. I wanted nothing to bother her. Running a hand over my face, I grabbed it to see who it was.

Milo.

Answering, I braced for it. They'd only be calling this late two, going on three, days into a drive for two reasons.

"We got 'em," he said in a voice that was neither harried nor breathless. "They made a move on us not twenty-two miles over the border with a full load. Ten men, of varying ages. Grabbed IDs and logbooks. We got pictures of all, packed up two of them to bring back—one might not make it. But we've got a bloody mess out here."

Fuck.

"And we were careful with what we touched."

That was something. "Give me the coordinates and then get the fuck out of there."

"You want us to leave it?" Milo sounded surprised.

"Sends a clear message," Jasper said in the background.

"If you're sure you didn't leave fingerprints, collect what you need and get out of there. How long since this went down?"

"Twenty minutes."

Yeah, they were fucking lucky and it was a bloodbath.

"Go, put miles between you and the scene, and change your route." From the sound of it, they'd switched me to speaker. I could hear Jasper as he blew out a breath.

Probably smoking.

"Already planned on it. They put a tracker inside the cab when we were at the pick-up."

Fuck.

"That means someone knows our depots. Because not all the pickups were from the same locations."

A secondary organization with access to equipment, men to make a drop, and then switch out what they were hauling?

"And Kel," Jasper continued. "One of these guys, I recognized him. He works for Warrick."

"Go," I said. "Get moving. Check-in." I needed to call for a cleanup, but Jasper was right. The mess of bodies and fallout sent a much louder message.

Fucking Warrick. I couldn't put off confronting the son of a bitch much longer.

We were going to have to do a full cleanup of our network of contacts. Fortunately, we did actually know people who did that. People who trusted us to handle big-ticket transport. All we had needed was *evidence*.

The door to Emersyn's room opened and she slipped through it like a shadow before she closed it. Granted, it could have been her friend, but the shadow moved like

Emersyn. The low lighting in the room prevented it from being truly dark, and my vision had adjusted already.

When she hesitated near the foot of the bed, I held out a hand to her.

"We're going," Milo said. The sound of the doors closing echoed down the line. "You don't have to deal with that asshole on your own."

Yes, I did. "Don't worry about it," I told them as Emersyn glided her hand into mine.

With care, I pulled her forward until she slid a knee on the bed. When I gave another gentle tug, she climbed right into my lap. I wrapped an arm around her as she tucked her cheek against my shoulder.

"Hey, guys," I said before they could end the call because we really weren't in the habit of lingering over goodbyes. "A little bird wants to say goodnight."

Then I moved the phone to her ear, savoring how the light and shadows played over her face. She lifted her gaze to mine in surprise. The rumble of their voices carried and a smile softened her whole face. "Just woke up," she said. "No bad dreams."

Well, that was good. I ran a hand over her back, rubbing in gentle circles. The door to her room opened, letting out another shadow. This one was dressed in more than just a t-shirt and panties. Rome came to crouch next to the bed. His hair was damp.

Ahh, that was what woke Sparrow up.

I lifted my chin to him and he nodded, waiting for her too.

"Okay, I'll see you when you get back. Drive safely—" Then a laugh. "Yes, I will absolutely say yes to a date."

I could hear Jasper's triumph from here.

"Bye…" She bit her lower lip then glanced at me as she passed the now darkened phone to me. "They hung up."

"It's fine," I assured her. "They were just checking in."

"It's a little late, isn't it?"

"They are probably swapping out drivers, which means they can go farther in a day." Still rubbing her back, I flicked a look at Rome. "You heading out?"

He nodded. "Liam."

I figured. He was the only person who could get him out of Emersyn's bed with any kind of willingness. It wasn't quite eleven. That meant Liam had fights.

"Need backup?"

He shook his head, then brushed his knuckles down Emersyn's cheek. "Stay with Kel?"

Yeah, sure, Rome. Just invite her to stay in my bed, why don't you? Not that I said anything.

"I'll be fine," she assured him. "Go watch Liam's back."

He nodded. "You will be fine. Stay with Kel."

It was interesting to have her shift that sweet ass against my lap as she tipped her face up to his. He gave her a kiss and then nodded to me before slipping out of my room. The light cut across the room would have blinded me if I hadn't already half-closed my eyes when he opened the door. I didn't have to check, I heard the turn of the lock on my door before he closed it.

"I guess I'm staying with you," she said in the drollest of tones, not that it did anything to hide her worry or her concern.

"A fate worse than death," I said with a gasp. "Stuck with me."

That earned me a genuine laugh. Better. When she curled up closer to my chest again and tucked her head into my shoulder, I resumed rubbing her back.

"I'm glad you didn't have bad dreams." The last time she'd had a nightmare was not something I'd forget anytime soon.

"Me too," she said with a sigh, then yawned. They'd only gone to bed a few hours earlier. Rome had probably not wanted to wake her up when he left, but he wouldn't let her wake up to him gone without a warning.

I got it. Navigating around her triggers was going to take time. We had to identify them, then disarm them—if we could. We were definitely killing the people behind each and every one. But we needed her to tell us.

Give us a direction. Point us in it.

Then we'd eradicate everything in our path.

But she didn't need blood-soaked vengeance yet.

"You want to go back to bed? Lainey is in there," I offered, but she shook her head against my shoulder.

Right.

"Okay, hold on a sec for me, okay?"

"Okay."

I opened a text message from Milo and copied the coordinates he'd sent. Then I sent a second message to one of our contacts in the State Highway Patrol for the state *next* to where they were driving. Let them know one of our drivers reported something weird on the road, but the insurance wouldn't let them stop.

It was a reasonable request.

Harvey responded within two minutes. It was an acknowledgement and a dollar figure. An expensive one, but he also had to deal with state lines and probably subcontracting. Whatever worked. Frankly, I didn't want to risk Jasper or Milo's freedom for a message. We had other ways of delivering those.

I flipped over to the banking app and sent the money

through a direct transaction. The money went to his sister's account. But it also tied her firmly to us, so it was in his best interests to honor all agreements. I wasn't worried.

When I went back to the message screen, he sent a thumbs up. That meant he got the money and he'd take care of it. I deleted the messages. Then logged into the service provider and deleted them there too.

By the time I'd finished, Emersyn had gone loose and warm, tucked against me. The soft little puffs of her breath tickled my neck. I set the phone down on the nightstand, then slid an arm under her legs.

"Just moving us to lay down, Sparrow," I murmured against her hair.

"Sorry," she said around a yawn, but she didn't pull away when I tucked us under the blanket. If anything, she stretched then curled right up to my side. "I didn't mean to fall asleep." Her voice was so sleep-drenched and her words almost a mumble.

"I don't mind," I whispered. "Go back to sleep."

"Kel?" Stubborn little sparrow.

"Have I mentioned how much I love the sound of my name on your lips?"

She curled her fingers against my chest. A hesitation. I waited her out, though. The one thing our little sparrow was good at was setting boundaries when she truly didn't like something. I kind of enjoyed the hell out of that.

"No," she drew the single syllable out, then flexed her fingers before she mirrored how I'd been rubbing her back by tracing her hand lightly against my chest. "So, you like it?"

"Hmm, love it."

"Kellan."

I chuckled at the barest hint of sass in that sleepy voice. "Yes, Sparrow?"

"Is everything *really* okay? I tried not to look at your phone."

"Everything is okay," I promised her. "We have some things we're sorting out. I'll tell you if you really need to know."

"But you don't want to tell me?" No hurt echoed in those words, so I closed my hand over hers on my chest and then tucked it right over my heart.

"It's not that I don't want to tell you *per se*," I answered, choosing my words carefully. "You're wrestling with a lot of stuff right now. I want your focus on you."

"What if I want my focus on you?"

I chuckled, pressing another kiss to the top of her head. My dick was already at full salute, but I ignored it. I had never been a victim of my own desires. I refused to start now.

"I would probably enjoy that," I admitted. "Are you ready to focus on me, Sparrow?"

Tracing little circles against the back of her hand, I let her turn that question over in her mind. She surprised me with a nuzzled kiss to my jaw.

"I want to be," she whispered.

I smiled into the dark. "That's more than enough for now."

A little sound of disgust escaped her and I couldn't help but chuckle at that scoff. "I hate feeling this way." That confession smothered my humor in an instant.

"I hate that you feel this way, too," I promised. Then risking it, I tumbled her over so I could press my nose to hers in the dark. This close, I could imagine every single one of her features.

She sucked in a breath in a sharp, slight inhale. Her pulse hammered beneath my fingertips as I wrapped a hand against her throat.

"Sparrow, I want you to listen to me." The sweet scent of her filled my nostrils and it would be so easy to nestle myself against her softness and warmth. Instead, I kept my weight off her, settling for just the collaring of her neck. "If it takes you a day, a week, a month, or a year—it takes as long as it takes. I *loathe* that anyone made you question yourself. I despise that you're hurting. I will kill anyone who ever hurts you again. I'll happily slaughter every single person who has ever hurt you."

Her shallow breaths deepened even if her pulse continued its staccato beat against my fingertips.

"I told you I want you in my bed. Right now, if that's just to sleep, then we'll sleep. If you need me to hold you and keep the dreams away, then I'll fucking drive them away. If you need me to bury my face in that cunt of yours and make you come until you cry so you can relax—well, we can do that too."

When she shuddered, I let myself smile. Because fuck, that really did sound good.

"I can use my fingers, my lips, my tongue—or nothing at all. Right now, I want you to focus on you. If you need it, you *tell* me. All right?"

She swallowed and then fisted my hair. When she tugged, I went at her request and claimed her lips with mine. The kiss was light and effortless but quickly caught fire as she tested her tongue against mine.

That's it, Sparrow. Fight your way back to us. When she arched her body to rub against mine, I endured the sensual torture but took control of the kiss. As much as she wanted to push herself, I wouldn't let her use me to do it.

Not when I could wait.

Gasping for air, she pulled away and I lifted my head instantly. It didn't matter how dark the room was, I was intimately aware of every inch of her.

Our breaths mingled as we panted, but she calmed almost instantly when I tightened my hand a fraction. The rapid cadence of her heart quieted.

"Feel better?" I asked, and fuck if my voice wasn't rough as hell.

"Not really," she admitted, then bumped her hips against mine. "You?"

"In Hell," I admitted with a laugh. "But it's the sweetest fucking torture, so I'm good with being here."

That pulled another genuine chuckle from her. Rolling onto my back, I let her come to me again. She followed, flowing against me like one of her silks and I wrapped her up.

"Now," I told her. "Go to sleep."

When she pressed a finger to my lips, I went silent. "I know you want me to focus on me, but I want you to know that I will help you in any way I can."

"I do know," I answered, pressing a kiss to that finger before capturing her hand and settling it on my chest again. "Now, sleep."

This time, she didn't buck the order, though she let out another huff of impatient breath. I wrapped her up, cradling her and keeping her tight to me. Surprisingly enough, though, her breath evened out almost immediately. Or maybe not so surprisingly.

Was that why Rome insisted on sleeping with her every night? She needed to be held. She needed to know she was safe.

Sweet Sparrow, whatever you need. Though I savored

her nearness and the way her breath feathered over my skin, sleep eluded me. Milo and Jasper were on the road and still at risk.

Vaughn was still lying low and the cops had been all over the neighborhood asking questions. Liam's work with the Royals may have been compromised, not to mention the issues with Reed and now the new guy. I still needed to deal with Warrick. That was a boil left too long.

And somewhere out there, we had enemies making moves against us *and* her. We were making our own moves now. But like Sparrow, I was impatient to be done with them all. No matter how much I disliked it, I refused to rush.

Rushing could mean missing something and making a mistake.

I wouldn't risk her.

I wouldn't risk any of them.

So tonight, I held her, and I planned.

21

"This would be easier at the clinic," Doc advised as he "scraped" the flat metal bar down my right forearm. I tried to breathe through the stretch it forced on the muscles beneath it. "Breathe."

"I am breathing." The fact that I panted the words didn't help. Doc had arrived shortly after breakfast to begin another therapy session. The two prior sessions had been delayed because I'd been dancing. Today, he'd told me to wait to do the therapy first.

Currently, I wanted to take the tool and hit him with it. As it was, I flexed my left hand and forced my breathing to even out. The pain was negligible, but it was also driving home just how tight my arms were and how much damage they'd inflicted.

"I know, nothing about this is comfortable." He moved the bar back to the crook of my elbow and began the downward roll again. We'd started the whole process with me flexing and stretching my arms as much as possible. "And it probably feels worse than it is."

"Are you sure?" I cut my gaze up from where he pushed the tool down the length of my forearm. Granted, I called it scraping, but he wasn't being *harsh*. I just hated every damn thing about these scars.

"Yes," he told me, his gaze firmly on me. How long had he been watching me? "I'm sure."

After another couple of passes, he held the tool out to me. Probably not wise since I had already considered smacking him with it.

At my questioning look, he said, "Take it. I want you to feel what I'm doing."

"Trust me," I told him. "I feel it."

The corners of his lips tipped upward. "Little Bit, just take the damn thing. You know what I meant."

I had to bite the inside corner of my mouth to keep from smiling back up at him. We were in the kitchen. The last couple of nights, I'd slept with Kellan because Rome had been absent. He sent me a message every day, but he had to help Liam. I wouldn't argue with that, and Kellan hadn't objected to me sleeping in his room.

Lainey found the whole thing hilarious, but she'd also retreated to Milo's room the night before, so she hadn't commented this morning when we came down for coffee. The only reason she hadn't stuck around for the "therapy" session was because I told her it was okay.

My issues with Doc were my issues. The therapy to help my arms I also needed. I needed them back.

Tool in hand, I eyed him and the corners of his mouth twitched again. "How close are you to swinging that thing at my head?"

I tested the weight of it. Despite being metal, it was

warm to the touch—maybe because he'd just been using it? And it wasn't heavy. Not really.

Not like my stapler.

The flash of blood splatter and brain matter danced across my vision, and I shook my head. "I'm not," I told him. Not anymore. No. That would—just no.

"Easy, Little Bit. I'm putting my hand over yours." I had no idea why he said that until his hand engulfed mine. The bar cut into my palm despite its rounded nature. "Relax your hand," Doc continued in a soothing tone. "You with me here?"

I tried to stop squeezing the bar. It took me a moment and some concentration to ease my grip. Doc slid it right out of my hand then turned my palm over. The red mark rippling over my palm was a hard indention in the shape of the bar. The half-moon crescents from my nails decorated one side of it.

Saying nothing, Doc massaged my palm with his thumbs. Even watching as he worked, it barely registered for a moment and then feeling rushed back into my fingers with a stinging sensation.

"Fuck," I muttered.

"It happens," Doc said, his tone easy and accepting. "We don't always know where the IEDs are until we trip them."

I tried to swallow around the lump in my throat, but it refused to budge. The words registered, but the letters—they should mean something, right? "What's an IED?"

"An improvised explosive device," he explained. "They are often camouflaged as something as simple as a coffee can, or maybe they are hidden in a soccer ball. Can even just be hidden under a couple of rocks in a road."

With every word, he kept spiraling his thumbs out in

circles over my palm before working his way up to my wrist. The biting, stinging sensation of pins and needles receded.

"They look harmless until you touch one. The force of the detonation is one thing, but it's what they pack inside—the shrapnel-that tears through you. That's what does the worst of the damage."

The lump still wouldn't move.

"If you're lucky, it's a dummy load."

Dragging my attention up from the hypnotic motion of his thumbs, I blinked at him. A frown had tightened his forehead and his eyebrows were turned almost down at the outside edges.

"If you're not lucky?"

His mouth dipped down at the sides and he sighed. "Well, if you're not lucky, then you hope that you can survive it long enough to get medical attention."

As he reached the crook of my elbow, he began massaging a path back down to my wrist.

"Survival, Little Bit, comes in different forms. There's the part where your heart keeps beating and your blood flows."

He stroked the line of the scar, every single puckered inch of it. The whole area was red, almost inflamed.

"Then there's the part where the pain registers. Pain is the body's way of telling us something is wrong, but it also tells us we're alive. There are different kinds of pain—the physical kind is the most obvious. The trauma. That is the one that holds all your attention. At first."

With care, he let go of that hand, then lifted my other. While I didn't have a bar mark across this palm, he went to work massaging it as he had the other. The contact sent more shivers than tingles this time. I could feel every single stroke of his skin on mine.

"The rest—that comes later. Often, after the gaping wounds are closed up and bound. The emotional damage. The mental anguish. That pain isn't so obvious. It haunts you, ties you up, and holds you hostage. Then it lashes out when you least expect it. Those wounds may not bleed like the physical, but they are no less deep and penetrating. Sometimes, they are worse."

I bit my lip.

"Because when a physical wound is infected, we can lance it, load you up with antibiotics—even debride it if we have to. But emotional and mental scars? They take an entirely different kind of work, you don't always know they're infected. At least not easily."

"That's—awful."

"It can be." Something in those three words pulled my attention back up to him. "Little Bit, I told you the scars tell us we survived. They can also mask other injuries, hidden ones."

I lifted my shoulders. "If they're hidden, do they have to be masked?"

One corner of his mouth lifted. "Unfortunately, yes."

That didn't make any sense. "I don't—I don't get that."

"Do you want to tell me about what happened here?" He ran his thumb up and down one of the scars.

The question was like a record scratch, and I jerked my hand back. Or I would have, if he hadn't shackled my wrist with his hand.

"Hidden. The physical trauma is right here, Little Bit. I can see it. I can touch it. I can even treat it."

A shudder ripped up my spine.

"But the damage that it hides? I only get glimpses of it."

I tugged my wrist again, and this time, Doc let me go. Standing abruptly, I retreated to the other side of the kitchen. I should have gone out the door. As it was, it put Doc between me and the door.

Folding my arms, I hid my scars against my chest. "I just want my arms to get better so I can dance."

"I know," he said, leaning back in the chair. Head canted, he studied me as he put his fingers on the metal bar he'd been using. "And I will do everything I can to help you with that. But—"

"No buts," I cut him off. "Just the scar tissue. Once it's gone or at least minimized, the rest won't matter."

And if it did, Doc was the absolute last person I wanted to talk to about any of this.

He sighed. "Little Bit…"

"Don't," I said with a shake of my head. "Just—I don't want to talk about that. Not with you. Not with anyone. You said you'd help me with the scars."

"And I will," he insisted, then stood, but he didn't try to get close to me. Instead, he just packed the items away in the kit he'd brought with him. "I've got a new ultrasound machine coming. When it gets here, you'll have to come to the clinic. But we're going to add that to the exercises I want you to do and the rest. We need to break down that scar tissue and make sure there are no adhesions."

It hadn't even been a few weeks since it happened. The smash of glass, the taut arms holding me still as they dragged the jagged point down my arm, was like a dousing in icy water.

"Little Bit—"

"Please don't," I asked him. I'd beg if I had to. "I don't want to talk about this."

"If I could let it go, I would. But I've seen wounds like these that if they go too long…"

"She said don't." Like a gift, Rome interrupted before Doc could finish following the path he'd begun. "Leave her alone."

Doc glanced at him. "I'm not trying to hurt her. But she can't ignore this."

"She said don't." He repeated the phrase as he moved to the center of the kitchen, planting himself between me and Doc. "You want to help. Help. But don't push."

"What if she needs pushing?" The dry question irritated me and I straightened this time.

"She's right here and doesn't appreciate being discussed in the third person." Still, I didn't try to go around Rome. Instead, I just moved up behind him, where I could meet Doc's gaze.

"Yes, you are," Doc agreed. "But you're also in full retreat. I won't corner you, Little Bit."

I made a face. "Then why did you keep asking…"

"Because I hate seeing you in pain."

Sighing, I pressed my forehead to Rome's biceps. His whole body was rigid, tense, and ready. He would take on Doc if I needed it and I hated the idea of any of them fighting. At the same time, the fact he was right there eased some of the tension in my gut and I could take a deeper breath.

"Not really a fan of it myself," I admitted finally. "But I don't like talking about it."

"I know." Those two words held such a wealth of weight that I found myself searching Doc's eyes. "No one wants to talk about something that hurt them. It leaves you vulnerable and raw. But you're seeing it again in your head.

It's right there, and when it swallows you whole like that, you're going through it—again."

Sweat slid down the back of my neck.

"You don't have to talk about it with me," Doc continued, but it was the sympathy in his eyes that held me captive. "But you do need to talk about it."

Rather than trust my voice, I just nodded. I had talked about it. Well, not all of it, but some of it. With Rome. With Freddie. With Lainey.

Exhaustion swarmed over me, and I leaned more into Rome. He lifted an arm and slid it around me. I didn't know whether he noticed me wavering on my feet or if he'd just wanted to hold me. Either way, it helped.

A lot.

"Right," Doc said, done with his packing. "Ice your arms. Alternate with heat. You should warm them up fully *before* you dance, then cool them down. The method we just used is gonna increase blood flow to that area and it could increase discomfort. If it gets too bad, call me. I know you don't want to take medication, but we can at least make you comfortable. We can also look into topicals."

"Like liniment?"

"Yes. There are others. Take tomorrow off of all physical activity. Then we'll do more the day after."

I wrinkled my nose. "I want to dance."

"If dancing was just you having fun and not punishing yourself at a brutal pace, I'd worry about it less. But you are going to injure yourself at the rate you're going. You damn near did that already." He pointed a finger at Rome. "And before you jump to her defense, be aware that if she tears muscles or ligaments, it could make it a lot worse for her. Sometimes, you have to be brutally honest to be kind."

He wasn't wrong. I just hated that he wasn't.

"Fine," I agreed, and Rome glanced down at me. The question was there in his eyes. Did I really want to do this? No. Did I need to? Yes. "I'm stubborn. But I'm also tough. I've trained and performed through far worse injuries."

"Maybe," Doc said. "The difference is, you don't have to. Now, I'm going to go. Think about what I said, call me if you need me. I'll see you soon."

Letting go of Rome, I took two steps after Doc as he exited the kitchen.

"Do—Mickey?"

He paused and glanced back at me.

"Thank you."

With a small smile, he nodded. "Take care of yourself, okay?" Then he glanced over my head. "Look after her."

Not waiting for a response, he left. It took some of the pressure out of the room with his absence and I could breathe. Rome settled his hands on my shoulders gently.

"Come out with me?"

The question caught me off-guard, and I pivoted to look up at him. "What?"

"Come out with me," he repeated. "You need to get out of here and I want to show you something."

My stomach dropped at the idea of going out. It was like I was a string pulled too tight, and I vibrated under the tension. "Right now?"

He opened his mouth then gave me a once over. "Change first. Then we go."

When he held out his hand to me, I took it. Another tremor went through me, and I tightened my grip.

"It'll be fun," he promised, and despite my unease, I smiled because he did.

Fun or not, I couldn't say no to Rome. Even if he would totally understand. He wanted to show me something.

I wanted to see it.

More, I needed to do anything that wasn't thinking about my scars—visible or hidden.

22

Starling's reluctance to leave the clubhouse seemed to wane as she changed. "Do I need layers? Or just a jacket?"

The weather had turned chilly again, but the wind was more the problem than the actual temperature. "Layers." If we were out in the sun, it would be okay.

When she went looking for her shoes, I pulled them out from under the bed. The fact her cheeks went red, gave her a glow that she'd been missing.

"Just going to tell Lainey we're leaving," she said after pulling her hair up into a ponytail. A grimace touched her face, though she turned away to try and hide it.

"Do you need to take something?"

"You see too much," she scolded rather than answer me, but her smile robbed the words of any harshness. After finding her retreating from Doc, I'd made the decision then and there to get her out of the clubhouse. Doc meant well, but he upset her and he didn't know why.

Or maybe he did.

I didn't care which it was, I just didn't want him to do it again.

"That doesn't answer my question."

She huffed a breath then glanced down at her forearms. The scars were hidden by the long sleeves of the sweatshirt she'd pulled on over her tank top. She'd been in dance shorts earlier, but she'd traded them for leggings that hugged her hips but fell loose below her knees to her ankles.

I was pretty sure she could dance in those too.

She could probably dance in anything.

"They hurt," she admitted.

"Then take something."

When she made a face again, I waited. Taking medication was not something she liked doing. She hadn't when it had been the antibiotics. Not even the aspirin we'd offered her at the hotel...

"You don't want to be drugged." Understanding flared.

"They kept giving me stuff—"

I nodded. "We have different kinds. We don't keep narcotics here."

"There's Kellan's weed."

"Not a narcotic." I shrugged. "And Freddie doesn't like it as much. I don't want you to hurt. So take one. I will bring the others with me so you can take more."

"Okay."

"Go tell your friend, and I'll get the pain relievers." Kellan would have some in his room. If he didn't, I'd get the ones from mine. We could go to Liam's if we needed. He kept everything there.

"Thank you, Rome." She pressed a hand to my chest then rose up on her toes, so I dipped my head to meet her kiss. I liked kissing Starling. This wasn't one of the longer, deeper ones where it felt like we were breathing for each other. Instead, it was more like a butterfly brushed my lips.

I liked that.

We needed to add more butterflies around here.

I followed her from the room—then paused to double back and grab her stapler. If we stayed at Liam's, it should be there. I considered the bear, then snagged him too. They'd both fit in my bag.

Kellan had a bottle of ibuprofen and a second one of naproxen in his bathroom cabinet. I took both, then snagged a marker to leave a message on his mirror.

Done, I went to my room. The door to Milo's was open and I could make out the sound of Starling talking to her friend. The other woman was leaving soon. Maybe I should ask at some point if we were supposed to drive her back.

Not today.

I grabbed my duffel and shifted the paint cans around, then put the stapler and bear in a different bag to protect them before putting them inside the duffel. I had ropes and hooks if we went out to the bridge. I wasn't planning to go there, but just in case.

Snagging my jacket, I dragged it on before draping the bag over my shoulder. If she got cold, I wanted something for her. Her laughter floated up the hallway when I stepped back out.

"I don't know—I don't, Lainey. Rome goes where he wants and if he wants me to go with him...well, I *want* to go."

The barest hint of uncertainty in her voice tugged at me. Since we'd come back, she'd stayed almost exclusively in the clubhouse, except for the day I took her to get the stapler and when Milo took her to see Miss Stephanie.

I'd followed but kept my distance. I didn't want them out there alone, but she didn't have to be afraid if she realized I'd followed them. Milo knew, and he'd only nodded.

When she was finally ready, I straightened and held out my hand. I'd never craved contact with another the way I did with her. She *fit*. Sometimes, even the others were a strain. Liam was the only one I'd never had to work to be around. Starling belonged, and I liked having her close.

It was better when it was all three of us, but Liam's fights were done. I could be with her again. Missing her the past two days hadn't been as bad as when she'd been at Pinetree, but I still didn't like it.

I led her out to the warehouse. There were rats working. Vaughn had his phone to his ear and faced us as we exited. Starling squeezed my hand, and I glanced down at her. When she nodded to Vaughn, I shifted our direction to head toward him.

"I have a whole crew here," Vaughn was saying as we approached. That explained all the rats. I spared them a look. A couple paused to glance in our direction, but they quickly found other things to do. "Kel will be back in a couple of hours. He had to go to the shop."

It was probably Milo and Jasper on the phone. They'd been on their way back.

"How far out are you?" Vaughn smiled down at Starling, and I let her go as she gave him a hug. He wrapped an arm around her and pressed a silent kiss to the top of her head. "We'll be ready. Rome's taking Dove out for the day."

A smile tugged at my lips at that announcement.

"Don't worry, Milo, we have your girl covered." That pulled a smile from Starling and she grinned over at me. My smile for her was as automatic as taking the next breath. "Yep. We'll be here. See you in a few hours—what? No. No."

When he added a third no in a slightly more impatient tone, Starling tilted her head back. "Right," Vaughn said, then rolled his eyes almost playfully at her. That made her smile again.

I frowned. If there was a problem, Vaughn would tell us.

"Yeah," he said. "Hanging up now. Bye."

Finished, he dipped his head and kissed Starling soundly. She curled her arm around his neck, and even though I knew it hurt, she didn't let go. Vaughn, however, didn't linger in the kiss, although clearly, he could have.

"You two off to get into trouble?" The question was light and his expression gentle—for her. The quick look he shot me held a warning as well as an inquiry.

"Maybe," Starling answered for both of us in a teasing tone. "But Rome said it will be fun."

"He did, huh?" He gave her a hug then raised his eyebrows at me. I shrugged and shook my head. I wasn't taking her anywhere dangerous and I wouldn't leave her alone. Not for a second.

But she needed out of the clubhouse. She needed to forget for a while.

When Vaughn tapped his phone asking for us to check-in, I nodded once. That seemed to satisfy him and he loosened his grip on her. "Well, go have fun. I'll stay here and work."

"You could come with us," she offered and I didn't even mind. It was still getting her out of here.

"I wish, Dove." He sighed then lifted his chin to motion to the rats. "Gotta hang out here. We've got a couple of trucks coming in, and we're gonna need to offload and then set up deliveries."

Not his favorite thing.

"And you're looking after Lainey."

"Yep. Go on, go have fun with Rome." He brushed his fingers down her cheek. "Just be safe, all right?"

"I will if you will." Her promise was easily given and her earlier reluctance was nowhere in view.

"Deal." He winked and then she grinned. Talking to Vaughn had made her feel better. I liked that. When she reached for my hand again, I slid my fingers between hers.

We headed not for the exit but for the car. At her surprise, I shrugged. "It's too cold to walk all the way." We could, but I liked the idea of her being cold far less than I did having to take a car.

I spotted easily another half-dozen rats on our way out. They were on the corner, above on a fire escape and more toward the street. Kel was taking no chances with anything.

"Are they going to be all right if we're not there?" she asked as we got to the end of the alley and I glanced at her.

"They'll be fine, Starling. That's why they have a whole crew." They would be less distracted if she were there too. The rats didn't need to be around her. "If you don't want to go..."

"I do," she said, shifting in her seat to face me. "I guess I'm... I don't know what I am."

"You're healing."

"Am I?"

"Yes."

That seemed to settle it. We didn't have that far to drive. Most of the area had been undergoing "recovery efforts." People buying old properties and converting them. Some we didn't care about. The one or two we had—Liam had purchased.

He thought I didn't know. Or maybe he didn't care. There was one I wanted to show Starling. Less than ten blocks away, I pulled over into public parking. We had passes—all the cars did. So, I ignored the little box where we could pay.

She looked around, her expression alternating between apprehensive and curious.

"I'm here," I reminded her and she shot me a smile. "You don't have to pretend."

"I'm not—I mean, I don't mean to."

Caressing her cheek with two fingers, I studied her. "I know." I didn't need her to explain. If she wanted to, I would listen. "You ready?"

When she leaned into my touch and closed her eyes, I cupped her face and waited for her. The measured breaths she took slowed as though she exerted her own will over them. Serenity replaced unease and color warmed her face. It fascinated me, the way the light played over her delicate features and shifted the shadows.

She was like one of those shadows that danced in and out of view, one you could only ever truly see from the corner of your eye. Then she opened her eyes and the transformation dazzled me as her whole expression warmed.

"Ready."

Trust shimmered in her eyes and spilled over into mine. Guided more by impulse, I kissed her. The press of my lips on hers, not seeking to delve my tongue into her mouth or to drag her closer, just holding there as if I could share some of me with some of her.

The curving of her lips against the kiss before she mirrored my touch in cupping my cheek pulled a smile from me. Then she giggled, an almost spring-like sound in its effervescence.

"I feel like we're going to clack teeth," she whispered, not pulling away. The movement of her mouth as she formed the words added an intimacy to the contact.

"Maybe," I conceded, then kissed her lightly once more before brushing another to the tip of her nose. "I want to do more than that."

"We can."

A hot wind blew through me at those two words. "Yes?" I lifted my head to search her eyes.

"Yes." Then she bit her lower lip. "But maybe not right here."

"No." I agreed. "I want you where no one else can see or touch."

She shivered. Still cupping her face, I traced my thumb over her lips.

"Doc said it was safe?"

A slow nod.

"Good." I wanted no fear in her. Then, before I could change my mind and pull out of the lot, I kissed her once more. "Come."

It wasn't until I was almost out of the car before she said on a breathless little exhale, "I hope so—but you first."

The odd wording made me laugh. Circling the car, I opened her door. The bracing chill of the wind rushed against me. She made a face, but only briefly before she laughed. The wind slapped her ponytail and I frowned toward the sky.

Still sunny, with only a few clouds and most of them moving swiftly. The air had a wetness to it.

"It's going to rain," I said. "We need to be quick."

She frowned. "The sun is still out."

"I know. Come on." Locking the car, I tugged her to follow me and she fell into step. "The wind is coming from the water."

It often blew in fiercer before the storm, like a herald of the bad weather on its way. Picking up my pace, I jogged only when I was sure she was on solid footing to keep up. We had time, but I really wanted her to see.

Rounding the corner, I slowed. The street here was a little more cracked and less maintained. Ahead of us, painted across the whole side of the building, were my brothers.

All of them.

It was also the first time I'd painted them.

"Rome..." she whispered.

"That was our group home," I told her. "We grew up there."

"Here?"

She glanced up and down the street, then back to the building again. It was two stories, three if you counted the attic rooms, but those were only used for storage.

"The roof always needed repair. There used to be playground equipment," I told her as we walked closer. "But every year, a new piece broke and they didn't replace it. One of the matrons kept a garden, it was small, but she grew tomatoes."

I'd almost forgotten about them, but I could taste them on my tongue as we neared the building.

I paused a hundred feet from it while she stared up at the painting. Milo sat on steps, his expression thoughtful and distant. He always looked like that. Always planning. Jasper wasn't far away, but he stood with Freddie like a sentinel and part of the reason for the fight.

Vaughn and Kellan were leaning on the old jungle gym, Vaughn laughing and Kellan frowning. The day I'd painted had been our first argument. Well, their first argument. I hadn't really cared whether we wanted to take the summer job or not. If they went, I'd go. If they didn't, I wouldn't.

Leaving Freddie for the summer wasn't something they wanted to do. Liam was there, not in fact, but in spirit. I'd—

"That's Liam's shadow, isn't it?" Emersyn asked as she pointed to where I sat in the painting on the old stone wall that used to surround the playground. Like the playground itself, it had crumbled away. I almost hadn't painted myself into it, but Freddie said it was weird.

"Yes," I said. "He wasn't there that day, but he was always with us. Where I am, he is."

She smiled and wrapped her arms around mine.

"The guys wanted to take a job up the coast." The day was right there. "It was a neat job, they liked the pay and if they got permission, it meant freedom from here. They wanted that."

"You didn't?"

I shrugged. "Not the same. I—did what I wanted."

I always had.

Except...

Glancing down at her, I had to ask, "Do you see?"

A frown tightened her brow, then she looked back at the painting. "You were free because you were with them."

That was part of it.

"Not everyone is happy about the plan." She dug her fingers into my arm and I held still. Had she seen it? "But you're all together so—happy or not—you'd make it work?"

Yes, she saw.

"Not alone."

Exactly.

23

Rome's idea of getting out wasn't just the first stop; he took me to see some more of his art. It was everywhere, if you knew what to look for. I'd seen some with Doc when he drove me back from the hotel to the clinic. Then there were the pieces tucked away from common view, like the one of Liam beneath the bridge.

Every single piece he'd painted held some element of a story or a truth he held valuable. When I asked him about the one near Doc's clinic with the dancers, he'd changed directions. It took me a minute to realize he was actually taking us to the mural.

Traffic had grown heavier, as had the skies. What sunlight had been present earlier disappeared behind the heavy curtain rolling in from the water. Rome cut into a different parking lot, then backed the car into a slot near the exit. I'd grown so used to it at this point and I liked the freedom it offered.

He glanced outside then at me. "Stay in the car?"

The fact that there was a hint of a question mark at the end of the statement made me nod, even as my stomach bottomed out.

"I won't be far." He pointed to the little kiosk where you could pay for parking. Blowing out a breath, I tried to quiet the fear bubbling up in my system. Of course, he wasn't just leaving me here.

Rome didn't leave the driver's seat until I finally glanced over at him again and nodded. "I'll be right here."

He smiled, then with one brief caress of my cheek, he slipped away. As promised, he wasn't long. Though I could see him the whole time, I still fidgeted for every prolonged second. When he opened the door to let me out, rain splashed my cheek. We both looked upward, but the sky didn't follow up on that promise of more than those random drops.

Hands clasped together, Rome led me right out of the parking area and along the busy sidewalk to the corner, where we turned then ducked between two buildings and jogged along the alley. Weird as it might seem, ducking away from the people seemed to make us safer.

Then the alley opened onto another block, one a distant part of my mind recognized as being close to Doc's clinic. There, on the huge side of a building, was the mural I'd asked about.

It was a series of dancers. They were adorable little girls in pink tutus going through their routines. As before, it threw me back to when dance had been fun. There was a girl in the background dancing away from the others. Her hair wasn't perfect, even if her steps were, but she was completely out of sync with the rest of the troupe.

The wind rushed against us, but with Rome pressed to my back, I barely felt it. "What do you see?"

His question pulled a smile out of me. "I see—me." Shaking my head, I leaned back against him. "I don't know how you did that one."

Clearly, I couldn't see the little girl's face. Honestly, none of their faces were distinct, even with the mirror and the barre he'd added for the studio. If anything, they were even less apparent in the reflection, muddied out. But the girl who danced away, she was clear, but with her back turned to us—

"She could be anyone, I guess."

"She's not," he assured me.

"How?"

A little shrug lifted his shoulders and he wrapped his arms around my middle, shifting his grip until he was holding my hand again.

"Milo," he answered.

"You guys were watching me."

"Sometimes. It made Milo feel better."

Tilting my head back, I looked up at him. "Just Milo?"

"No. I liked watching."

From anyone else, that might have sounded creepy, except... "Not alone."

He nodded, then dropped a kiss to the top of my head. "Never."

The oath and the words stirred up a longing inside of me. "I wish I'd known," I whispered, more to myself than him. Then, "But if I had—I don't know that I wouldn't have run away sooner. You guys would have been in the middle of all of that."

Before they were ready.

He tightened his grip on me. "I'm sorry."

Turning my gaze away from the mural, I twisted to look

up at him. "You have nothing to be sorry about. *Ever.*" None of them did.

"You were hurting."

"If you'd known?"

"I will kill him."

Not would have… *will.* Apprehension crawled up my spine. I couldn't let him go after him.

"Rome—" But I didn't even finish the thought before Rome sealed his mouth to mine. The kiss was both gentle and demanding. Liquid heat scalded my system, burning away the apprehension and the sinking feeling of fear even as it consumed the longing and loneliness. Fresh drops splashed against my cheeks, and I swore it sizzled.

The lightness of his touch as he slid a hand to cradle the back of my head stood in direct contrast to how he stroked my tongue with his. Electricity sparked through me with every teasing brush of his lips over mine. A groan tore out of my throat, or maybe it was his—the vibration passed from his chest to mine, and my nipples went taut.

More rain fell; the fat, spattering drops struck and glided down my cheeks. Some clung to my eyelashes. One snuck down to where our mouths pressed together. Thunder rolled across the sky like so many bowling balls being flung down their alleys and light flashed against my closed eyelids.

Our breathing came out in matched shallow pants as he lifted his head, and we both looked up as lightning arced over the storm clouds that billowed fat and threateningly. The chill in the air couldn't compete with the heat simmering off my skin.

Licking my lips, I could still taste Rome along with the rain and the hair on the back of my neck lifted at another tumbling roll of thunder just before a jagged flash of lightning danced from cloud to cloud.

"Sometimes," I confessed as the wind pulled at us, "I wish I could dance on those."

He dropped his gaze from the sky to me. Delight flashed in his blue-green eyes. "We should go."

But he was in no hurry, and I couldn't say I was either. "We won't melt," I told him as thunder cracked so loud overhead it might as well have been a gunshot. For all my bravado, I still jumped and he laughed. Another kiss, this one biting and quick.

"No, but you can get cold." He glanced at the mural, then back at me. "I'll bring you back."

"I never left," I told him, grinning. "I've been right there since you painted me."

His answering smile ballooned around my heart and sent me soaring. It was my turn to clasp his hand. "You belong here."

The words, so heartfelt and real, offered up in a fleeting moment, took wing and lifted me even higher. I told Ezra, Adam, and Lainey that I wanted to be here.

This was where I wanted to belong.

Belonging meant so goddamn much.

Rome didn't leave me long to dwell on that thought as he turned us away from the mural and we retraced our path, heading back to the car. The rain chased us, but we didn't try to run from it. If anything, as it began to come down harder, I skipped letting Rome move faster rather than shorten his longer stride to accommodate me.

I leapt one puddle, and he lifted me clean over another, twirling me as he moved. It was a smooth transition from hurrying to dancing. When we were almost to the car, he picked me up and spun me around. This time I let my arms go wide and dropped my head back.

He wouldn't drop me and the spiral left me both dizzy and elated. Another kiss, and then he pulled the door open. The rain waited just long enough for him to climb into the driver's seat before it turned into sheets.

I clapped my hands in pure delight. The thunder and the lightning were still up there, a soundtrack to accompany us on our drive. He checked on me frequently as he drove. When I slid a hand over to his leg, he put his on top of it and kept it there.

When he pulled into the garage at Liam's, I laughed. He glanced over at me, but at the simple question in his eyes— I nodded.

Wherever he wanted to go was fine with me. The drive had definitely been longer than getting back to the clubhouse, but I didn't complain. We were still wet when we left his car in the garage and went through the security doors to the elevator.

He had a bag with him, and I did a little pirouette on our way into the elevator itself. The smile on his face grew once we were inside. I leaned against one wall and he stood at the other. Nothing would happen in the elevator, but the air between us seemed as stormy and tempestuous as the weather outside.

At Liam's floor, Rome put a hand against my abdomen before he glanced out of the elevator first. Then he beckoned me out and went to the door. He made no motion to hide the code he entered before he unlocked the door and let us inside.

With no lights on, the interior was dark and I tugged off my wet shoes before I went too far. The hallway off the living room had a single, dim nightlight glowing and the door to Liam's room was open.

"He's not here," I said, turning and running into Rome's chest. He put his hands on my hips to steady me.

"No," he agreed with me.

"So, we're alone."

With one slow nod, he plucked the shoes from my hand and dropped them on the floor behind the sofa. The bag was already sitting there on the back, along with his jacket.

Unzipping mine, I began to walk backward and kept my gaze firmly on his. Not once did Rome look away as he followed me. When I pulled the jacket off, he took it from my hands and threw it back over his shoulder.

A laugh escaped me.

"Liam won't care," Rome said as we reached the door to his room. I paused, leaning against it and then he was just there, his mouth locking onto mine in another heated kiss that set my nerves on fire.

He found the hem of my shirt, the warmth of his fingers trailing over my skin. With a gentle bite to my lower lip, he dragged it out as he pushed the sweatshirt upward.

"What do you want?" I asked him, a little breathless. All the times we'd made out in there, he'd been so careful with me. That same care was still present, but hunger punctuated his movements. I wanted that hunger.

I wanted all of it.

I wanted all of him.

"You," he said, as if it were the simplest answer on the planet. A shudder cascaded through my system.

Gripping the hem of my sweatshirt and the tank underneath it, I ripped them both up and over my head. Balling them up, I tossed them over his shoulder.

"More," he whispered, tracing his fingers over the tattoo on my abdomen. Aware of the liquid heat in his gaze, I pulled the sports bra up and off. It followed the sweatshirt and tank top.

Another kiss, this one soul-stealing, sucked all the breath out of me. He covered my breasts with his hands, his touch gentle but certain. My nipples were two hard peaks aching for the roughness of his palms. Too soon, he left them, trailing his hands lower and I groaned.

Then he dropped to his knees and gripped the leggings. They, along with my panties, peeled right down until I could step out of them. Grinning, he pressed a kiss right to my pelvis, just above my cunt and the soft swipe of his tongue made everything in me clench.

It wasn't even my cunt itself, just the soft skin above it. "Freddie calls me Pretty Pussy Girl," I said, almost an afterthought, really.

"He's right," Rome said. "You have a very pretty pussy, Starling." With a smile, he balled up my leggings—sans the panties and tossed the leggings into Liam's room behind him.

A laugh escaped me. I fisted his hair as he stood and he gave me another kiss, sliding a hand behind me to open the door to his room.

"Bed," he said, as much an order as a request. "I want to kiss your cunt while nothing else is in it."

Desire pooled in my belly and my stomach bottomed at those words. Direct. Hot. Inviting.

"I want that too—" I promised him, retreating across the cool darkness of his room where the storm outside kept flashing against the closed blinds. "I want you."

Not once did he take his gaze off me as I settled on the bed. A statue at the door, he waited until I'd laid down and spread my legs, just for him.

"Yes," he said. "Very pretty pussy. I should paint it."

Shock vied with delight at that declaration. "Maybe not on the side of a building?" Not that I'd say no.

Rome could do whatever he wanted.

"No," he agreed and then hung my panties on the door handle before closing it. He ripped his own shirt off on the way to the bed in an absolute economy of motion.

My heart hammered.

"Only for us—I'll paint it on a wall here."

His jeans went the way of his sweatshirt. Then he was right there at the edge of the bed, his cock jutting out, thick and erect. Pushing up on my elbows, I reached for the light, but he beat me to it and the soft yellow light filled the room, closing us in a circle together.

Since the first time I'd seen the ink *of me* on his dick, I'd never grown less fascinated with it. I wrapped my hand around his base and gave him one long, gentle stroke. He lacked the thickness of hair there, as well. I wasn't sure if it was because of the tattoo or because it was softer than the often springier hair.

I really didn't care. As he thrust against my palm, he drifted his hand down to cup between my legs, fingers dipping into my cunt with care.

His gaze riveted to mine when I looked up at him, and I understood the question in them.

"Yes," I promised him. "Everything is alright."

I swore it was like someone released him because he thrust his fingers into my already soaked cunt as he dropped forward, pushing into my hand and then his mouth was on mine.

Heat blanketed me, but even better.

Rome did.

24

Starling let out the most delightful sound as I kissed her. It wasn't a moan or a groan, but something that seemed to come from far deeper inside of her. The feeling of her hand around my cock was so damn good. Almost as good as when I pushed it between her lips.

I bit down on her lower lip again. I liked scraping it and making it darken to a deeper pink. The catch in her breath whenever I used my teeth suggested she liked it. Vaughn hadn't been that gentle with her when he fucked her from behind.

Still, I wanted to be careful and find out what she liked and didn't. Starling had known too much pain. I didn't want her to have any pain with me. I curled my fingers inside of her, she soaked my hand and when I found that spongy area Liam told me about once, she arched her hips up to the contact.

Oh, she liked that.

With more biting kisses, I trailed a path down her jaw

to her ear. I bit down on the earlobe gently. She had the indentions for pierced ears but no piercings. Sucking it against my teeth, I glanced up at her as her lips parted and another of those soundless gasps escaped.

When she flexed her fingers around my dick, I curled my fingers and stroked that spot. I varied the pressure, sometimes light, sometimes more, and I alternated it with thrusting my fingers in and out. Every time she arched her hips, I did it again. The play of the golden light over her face left her eyes in shadow but not her expressions.

"Starling?"

The writhing of her body slowed as I stilled my hand, and she tilted her head. There were her eyes. Light catching on the soft brown gave them a hint of gold to go with the shadows. "You're doing it very right," she told me, each word punctuated with little explosive breaths.

"Thank you." It sounded like a compliment and should be treated as such. Her eyes lit up and then she let out another laugh. The sound was magical, and so was the way her muscles moved when she laughed. The bruises on her flesh were still there in places; some had faded to green-yellow. However, the handprints were gone.

Anger fountained inside of me, but I shoved it to the side. They were not allowed here. Not now. Not ever.

I took too long because she lifted up on her elbows, and I'd slid down enough to pull away from her touch. All at once, I missed both her distraction and her touch. "You wanted to ask me something?"

She understood me. Saw me. I liked that about her. Liked that she saw me.

"Will you say my name when you make that sound?"

Confusion flickered over her face and then she flexed

those inner muscles around my fingers. The movement was so precise and intense, it made my dick hurt for a moment.

"When I moan?" she asked finally, biting her lip.

Curling my fingers, I stroked slowly over the spot that made her tense up and her abdomen flex even as those muscles began to spasm. A shuddering rippled up and down her body. Her nipples seemed to pebble even more, and for a moment, the wings on the birds appeared to move.

"Rome," she managed, the syllable of my name trembling on her voice was like a drop of paint coloring the air as it shivered in response to the ripples in the air or in the sound.

"Again," I whispered, adding to the pressure so when she lifted her hips all the way, and a little scream tore out of her, it gave my name wings.

A flush spread the pink across her face. Sweat dampened her skin and the quaking seemed to spread to all her muscles. "Rome," she called out and stretched a hand to me. I wanted to keep playing, but I couldn't tell her no.

Easing my fingers from her, I sucked them clean before climbing up to where she wrapped around me. No more words, just her mouth opening to mine and her hands teased over my skin. The hot velvet of her hand closed over my dick again, and she began to stroke me against her cunt.

I broke the kiss to lift my head and watch. All the times the guys had mentioned this part, there had been a wonder in their voices. Liam had been—crazed with his enjoyment of the act. But it never appealed to me before.

With Starling, I wanted everything.

"Did you like it?"

The soft question captured my attention, and I looked up to find her watching me as she stroked me back and forth. The tingles spreading over the head of my dick were hard to ignore, especially with the wicked wetness slicking up my skin. I wanted to go and taste her again, but she wanted me here.

I struggled with the question, uncertain. "Like what?"

"Me calling your name."

The echo of another conversation surfaced and I grinned. I couldn't help it. "Yes," I told her. "I liked it a lot. I want you to always call my name like that."

"Okay," she whispered, hooking her leg up and over my hip. "I promise. Are you sure...?"

"About you? Yes." No questions. No hesitation. "Are you?"

If she had any, I could wait. This had already been so much. "I want you, Rome," she responded, and it was my turn to shudder. I didn't know who moved, if it was me or her or both of us. But I was sinking into that velvety heat.

All the air seemed to squeeze out of me. "Tight," I whispered. It was so hot and tight, like the perfect fit. Too perfect. "Not hurting you?" I braced a fist against the bed, ready to pull away if it was.

"No," she said, her voice dipping as she flexed her thighs around me and then tugged me close as I sank all the way into her. It was—everything. It wasn't until her lips parted beneath mine that I even realized we were kissing again.

Moving with Starling was like dancing, only not. It was like flying, only not. I didn't have the words for it. The feelings burning inside of me were almost too much and not enough. I clung to her as she arched her hips and pulled me into her. When she rolled me over and I lay on my back, I stared up at her in wonder.

"This is your first," she whispered as she rose and fell,

hips rolling and pulling me in tighter only to release me again to sweep back into her again. It was—like thrusting, only she controlled it.

"Our first," I told her fiercely. "Not last."

"Oh, no," she said and then laughed again. The feeling that shuddered through her took me by surprise as her body fisted my dick. I kept losing the rhythm, but she covered my hands on her hips with her own and set the pace. "Our first and most definitely not last."

A thrill went through me. This was like sinking into the perfect painting, only Starling was living art. Art that I didn't create, but I could worship, appreciate, and mimic.

Our mouths fused again when she leaned down and the pace increased until all I could see, feel, and taste, was her. The molten heat in my spine radiated out. My balls ached—maybe for the first time—there was motion from her hand and I broke the kiss to see her playing with her clit.

Brushing her hand to the side, I imitated her motions. The swollen nub seemed to have a pulse, and every time she sank down on me, I pressed up a little harder.

The ragged sound of her breath echoed under my own. Everything went low, hot, and tight— "Starling..."

"Oh yes, Rome," she exhaled my name, and it was as magical as the first time she'd uttered it in pleasure. Gripping her hip, I increased the pressure with my fingers as my eyes whited out. The first hot jet escaped and it was...

It just was.

She was shaking as she jerked against me, then her breath came out on a low scream. "Too much—too much..." It wasn't until she pulled at my hand that I realized she meant me, and I let go of her clit.

Later, I promised it in a haze. I would play more with it later.

I dragged my hand up into her hair and kissed her like I needed her for air. Nothing else existed except for Starling. She was the whole world and she wrapped completely around me.

Time ceased to have meaning as she lay in my arms, the steady hammer of her heart echoing my own. Spent and weak, I cradled her close and it wasn't until her breathing slowed, deepening and evening, that I opened my eyes to look down at her.

Sprawled against my chest, she looked so delicate and perfect. My starling, the perfect dancer. My dick softened gradually and I almost hated it when I slid out of her. We needed to get another erection.

Soon.

I wanted back inside that—what did Freddie call it?

Perfect pussy.

But I didn't want to disturb her either. So, I lay there, stroking her hair and savoring her. Moving my arm took all of my concentration. I'd never been so weak. At least, I didn't think so.

A sound from beyond the room penetrated.

The door closed.

I focused, listening for a familiar tread. It didn't take long. A huff of laughter alerted me to the fact that he was right on the other side of the door.

"Really?" he muttered and I grinned.

My other half found her panties, as I'd intended when I left them for him.

"She's asleep," I said in a low voice.

The door opened and Liam filled it. Starling still blanketed me, her bare body hardly on display, but Liam moved over to pull the sheet across our lower halves before taking a seat on the side of the bed.

"How you doing?" he asked in a low voice. When he would have put his hand on her hair, I moved mine. He still hesitated.

"It's better than you said," was my only comment.

He chuckled. "Everything would be better with her."

"Then it was worth waiting for."

"Yeah, brother, she is definitely worth it." Finally, he lifted his hand and touched her hair. "I should go before she wakes up and finds me sitting here like a creeper."

"She won't mind." She cared about him too.

Liam shook his head. "Not everyone sees things the way you do, Rome."

I studied the bruises on his face. "You had another fight." He wasn't supposed to go on his own.

"Kind of," he said. "Don't worry about it."

I just stared at him, and he sighed, but he kept his gaze on her and not on me.

"How is she?"

"Scared." I didn't like the fear in her eyes. I liked it even less when it appeared around any of us. "Hurting."

Liam's frown darkened. "Why is she hurting?"

"Doc has her doing exercises. It hurts her arms."

"Physical therapy," Liam muttered. "Dammit. We should have taken longer to carve that fucker up."

"He's dead." That was all that mattered.

Liam nodded, but we both went still when she stirred. The way she snuggled closer to me and the warmth of her breath on my skin had my chest tightening.

"There are more who need to die," I warned him, but Liam knew. His single nod and the lack of surprise said as much. "When she's ready..."

"We might need to do it before then," he cautioned me. It was my turn to nod. "She just needs to trust us."

"I do," she murmured in a sleep-laden voice, and we both focused on her as she lifted her head. "I just don't always want to talk about it."

"Well, Hellspawn," he told her. "You might have to—at least enough to give us a direction."

We had one. I had one. Liam could probably guess.

"Why are you all bruised? Who hurt you?" The fierceness in her voice made me smile. Liam's expression gentled. She was good for him.

"No one you need to worry about, Hellspawn."

That didn't make Starling happy, though. She squinted at him and pushed up a little. "Do you need us to beat up someone for you?"

The offer was so easily made and so genuine that I chuckled. Liam joined me, and she glared at both of us.

"Don't make fun of me," she argued, but Liam just gripped her hair and kissed her. It was fun to watch. They kissed so differently. It was a fight but also a surrender. She didn't want to give in easily, but she did want to give in and he almost didn't want to let himself take, but he needed her.

The whole thing just made my dick hard. Again.

Good. I wanted to play with her more. When Liam let her go, I gave him a shove. "Go away now, don't go out. Don't get hurt. I want to play with Starling."

"Damn," Liam said as he stood, touching two fingers to his lips before brushing them against hers. "I thought you didn't mind sharing."

"I don't. Later." I flipped him off for good measure, and he laughed, then he stroked a hand down her back and gave her another kiss.

That one was nearly as provocative as the first.

"I'm going to go jerk off in the shower now, you lucky bastard," Liam commented.

"Have fun," I told him as I rolled Starling over and met her breathless gaze. Laughter chased the sleep from her expression. "Think of Starling."

"Oh," Liam said and Starling's eyes widened a fraction as she looked past me. "I intend to." The door closed behind him, and she switched her gaze back to me.

"He has my panties," she admitted with a playful expression.

"Good," I said, beginning to trail kisses down her chest. "You won't need them."

25

Jasper had been back when we arrived at the clubhouse the next morning. He greeted me with a kiss and hug that had me gripping him tightly.

Morning with the twins had included a quick breakfast before we'd left Liam. Awareness skated over me a split second before Liam had given me a kiss that had my toes curling inside my shoes.

Being welcomed back to the clubhouse by Jasper with an equally heated kiss had left me more than a little dizzy. "I want to stay here with you," he admitted. "But I have to run these deliveries after Milo and I take care of some things."

A shadow of a bruise was visible on his cheekbone, but it vanished into his beard. Trailing my fingers over the mark, I confirmed the swelling was recent and still warm.

"Looks worse than it is, baby," he said in a low voice. "Promise."

"Will you tell me what happened?" I worried about

them. Milo hadn't said much, just given me a kiss on the cheek before he'd strode inside with a purposeful walk and Rome lifted the duffel to carry it in after him.

The duffel that held his bear and my stapler, both of which he said he'd put back in my room. A smile ghosted over me. I hadn't needed them, but he'd made sure to bring them. The sensual ache lingering in my body was a definite improvement over the bruising cramps in my arms from the day before.

"I don't really want to tell you," Jasper confessed, even as he hooked an arm around my shoulders and pressed a kiss to the top of my head. "I will if you need to know but…"

"But you don't want me to know?" I struggled with that a little.

He sighed. "Some of the things we do—it's not pretty. Fuck—a lot of the things we do aren't pretty, Swan. That part of our lives, we never want it to touch you."

"I'm not that fragile," I told him. "I know it doesn't look like it—"

"Hey." He cut me off with a single word and a finger beneath my chin. Frowning, he studied my expression. "I know how tough you are. Doesn't mean I don't want to protect you. Doesn't mean it doesn't turn you on when I torture someone for you either."

I parted my lips to respond to the first part, but the last sentence made me snap them shut as a laugh escaped. Clapping a hand over my mouth, I stared at him as he began to grin.

"See, I know you're tough, Swan. You even being able to laugh—you letting us look after you—those are all signs of your strength. And your trust."

Still not certain I wouldn't laugh again, I lowered my hand and he caught my fingers, tugging them away from my face. "Will you tell me if there's something I can do to help? Please. I want—I want to help you guys. I want to fit in here and be part of this."

"You are a part of 'this,'" he said and I could practically hear the air quotes. "You have always been a part of us, but —I hear you. If I think there's something you can do beyond healing right now, I'll ask you. Deal?"

It was my turn to sigh, but when I reached up to wrap my arms around his neck, he curled around me. "Deal," I whispered.

"Thank you." His beard tickled my throat when he tucked his face against my neck. While he was hardly the first to pick me up, it always entertained me that they all liked to bring me up to level with their faces. Still, I hugged him tighter. There were different trucks parked inside the warehouses. One of them had been driven straight and faced us rather than away.

Odd.

Clearly, they could drive it straight through if they moved the cars and then take it out the other doors, but that wasn't how they normally parked. He took a deep breath like he was inhaling me. "Still on for our date?"

I leaned back to look up at him and nodded. "Today?"

"Fuck, I wish." He made a face. "Probably not until the weekend, I want to do you right." His pause was near comical. "I want to do *it* right," he corrected slowly, and I giggled.

"Pretty sure you can do me right," I teased. "You have before."

"A sweet girl would have let me get away with that slip," he said with a mock sigh.

"Yeah, but I never said I was sweet." I pressed a quick kiss to his lips. "And I liked your slip."

His grin faltered to a scowl when one of the rats called out to him.

"You have to go," I said, rubbing his chest. "I have to do physical therapy anyway." Though I managed to say it without a grimace, Jasper narrowed his eyes.

"Doc bothering you?"

The word no was on the tip of my tongue. It wasn't a total lie. Jasper didn't handle Doc well, and it wasn't all that long ago—just a few months—when he put a gun right up to Doc's chin. My issues with Doc...

"Swan?" Jasper gripped my biceps lightly, his expression darkening. "If Doc—"

"Doc isn't bothering me—exactly."

"Then define how he is bothering you, please." The absolute calm in his statement was such a contrast to the storm in his gray eyes.

Taking a page from his book, I settled on, "I don't really want to right now." His frown deepened, but when I pressed a hand to his chest, some of it eased. "I need to handle this one on my own and I don't want you to get angry with him."

"Uh-huh."

"Jasper..."

"I'm listening, Swan."

But he was not happy. "Doc—Mickey and I had a misunderstanding. Working so closely with him isn't totally comfortable, but it's not just because of the misunderstanding." I had to choose these words so carefully. "I know how you feel about Doc..."

"Well, that's good," he said with an air of resignation and just a hint of sarcasm. "I don't always know how I feel about him. But if you don't want him doing your therapy, we'll find someone else."

That was the problem. "I don't know if that's what I want or not."

"Okay."

"That's it?" I studied him, the bland answer so not what I expected.

"Okay, that you don't know. Okay, that you want to handle it." He grimaced. "Okay, that you don't want to tell me. Well, it's not *really* okay, but I can't ask you to trust me if I won't trust you."

Warmth blossomed in my chest.

He stroked his thumbs in circles against my arms. "Same deal applies, though, yeah? If anything changes or you *need* me, you say the word. I'll even promise to not kill him."

My lips trembled from the effort of keeping the laughter back, but his slow smirk told me I wasn't successful in the least. "But torture and maiming are still on the table?"

"Hell, yes." Jasper dipped his head again. When his lips were a whisper from mine, he added, "Torture turns you on, especially when they deserve it."

A full-body shudder rippled through me at the electricity skating up my spine, and it didn't matter how achy my cunt and breasts were, I was clenching up at the temptation Jasper added.

"Hawk!" a voice called from the far side of the warehouse and Jasper muttered something under his breath before giving me one firm kiss.

"Go on, Swan, before I end up shooting one of them for interrupting us."

I didn't even try to laugh that off, I just kissed him back and then headed for the door. He'd meant that last one, no doubt in my mind at all.

Vaughn was on his way out the door. He curved an arm

around me, scooping me up for a quick kiss, then a wink, before depositing me inside the clubhouse. Pausing, he touched my cheek. "Happy looks good on you, Dove."

Then he was gone before I could respond.

Happy?

Was I?

Closing the door, I stood there for a moment when soft voices carried from the hall above and I glanced to where Milo and Lainey stood together. Milo had his hands on her biceps like Jasper had just held mine. The intensity in how he spoke to her had me turning away.

Lainey deserved the best and I wanted Milo to be happy, but I also didn't want to intrude—even if I wouldn't mind tweaking him a little. I just wouldn't do it at her expense.

I headed toward the kitchen. Doc sat there, sipping his coffee when I came in and he gave me a measured look. "You're late."

Chin up, I met his gaze. "Couldn't be helped." I was not going to apologize. "I also don't recall setting a precise time."

"Little Bit, I said we were gonna need to do it every day. For the first bit, we need to avoid adhesions and too much scar tissue."

I was so not a fan. "I'm here. Do you mind if I get coffee before we start?"

I'd had coffee earlier; Liam had made me some.

"Feel free," Doc said, gesturing toward the counter and I paused. The shiny new espresso machine sat there, with everything ready to go. It was *exactly* like Liam's. Of course it was, he bought it, but at the same time—it was here, and it looked kind of out of place in the kitchen.

I wanted to make it nicer for them. I still had the cash

Lainey sent for me. Maybe she could help me get access to some of my accounts. No sooner did the thought dawn, but then I dismissed it. I didn't want her going anywhere near my accounts.

Maybe Adam could help. Of course, that would mean talking to Liam about Adam again, and he wasn't a fan and had his own questions. Questions he hadn't fully answered yet.

"Little Bit?"

I jumped and spun to meet Doc's concerned gaze. Fuck, I'd half-forgotten he was there. Putting a hand to my chest, I tried to laugh it off, but his expression didn't change.

"I'm going to make the coffee," I said and glanced at the doorway. I kind of hoped that Lainey and Milo would come in, but no one had appeared. Rome had probably gone to sleep or to paint. He knew I had therapy today. "Do you want one?"

"I'm fine," Doc said, leaning back in his chair. Even concentrating, I only managed to scrape together about five minutes before I had the coffee ready. The cappuccino was good, not quite as good as what Liam made, but the shots of espresso were desperately needed.

Large cup in hand, I joined Doc at the table. "Guess I can't procrastinate anymore."

"I'm sure you can," Doc offered. "If you really need to, but I'd like you to trust me to get you through this."

"I'm trying." As soon as I said those two words, I realized how true they were. I was trying to trust him. I trusted the others, but with Doc, it was harder. "It's just..."

He waited me out, not prompting me. Even as I stared at my cappuccino and the foam on the top of it, I was aware of his gaze on me.

"It's just that," I repeated, pushing the words out. "It's hard because you know."

"I know," he said in a quiet if neutral tone. "I know a lot of things, Little Bit."

Dragging my gaze up, I wasn't prepared for the sympathy in his eyes. Sympathy I didn't want and at the same time... Why did it have to be so hard with him? Why... "You know what he did."

"I know some of it," he agreed with me. "I know what I saw in the exam." Raising his hand, he asked me for patience while he continued. "I know what your x-rays showed me when they brought you to me—the patterns of the bruising. I saw the toxicology. I know the types of medications they had you on... and I saw the scarring, internal and external."

Focusing on the coffee again kept me from throwing up. Barely.

"When you're ready to talk about that, I'll be here," he said. "But what I know goes absolutely no further than me, Little Bit. Not just because I'm your doctor."

I stole a look up at him.

"But because I want to be your friend again. I want to earn back the trust I lost."

"I don't know how." Maybe that wasn't fair. He had told me he was sorry but...

"I don't know either, so why don't we just do this one step at a time, you and me, all right?"

The sick feeling burning inside passed, and I nodded. "Does that mean you have to do more with that rolling pin? Cause that really sucked."

He chuckled. It wasn't effortless and it wasn't as deep as his laughter could go, but it was real enough. "We're going to start with that. The new ultrasound will be set up tomorrow, so I want you to come to the clinic a couple of times a week. We're also going to set up some exercises that you can do when you don't want to see me."

Wincing, I jerked my gaze back to his. A half-formed apology stuck to my tongue. That was so dramatically unfair.

"Don't worry, Little Bit," he said, his tone more soothing than teasing. When he stretched a hand over, he hesitated to touch mine until I pushed mine under his. Then he clasped my hand lightly. "Some days are going to be better than others. I remember, sometimes too well."

And he had the scars to prove it. The scars and the patience. Even if he had been cruel, he hadn't been since I came back—not once. "I'll keep trying—and I will do my exercises."

He held my hand for a long moment, the same way he held my attention. Whatever he looked for in me, he must have found because he nodded. "Good, let me get set up here, and we'll start."

All business, he let go of my hand and the sound of a step in the hall made us both look.

"Excellent," Liam said as he strolled inside. "You're both here." He crossed right to me and slid his hand over my hair and I tilted my head back at the light touch. The press of his lips to mine was still so new and a little breathtaking. Heat scalded my face as Liam lingered in the kiss, intent on me even as he lifted his head.

"Liam," Doc said, and there was a distinct testiness to his voice that hadn't been present earlier.

Grinning, Liam winked at me before he hooked one of the chairs over to sit next to me. "Doc," he said as he took a seat. "Here to back you up on the physical therapy since I'm Hellspawn's trainer."

Wait—I blinked. He was, but...

"And because you have a clinic to run and I want her back in training sooner rather than later."

I might as well have not been there for all the attention they paid me as they stared at each other. Maybe Jasper wasn't the only one who had issues with Doc.

"Besides, I know a little something about rehabilitating injuries too," Liam continued. "You don't mind, do you?"

26

I'd treated enough injuries over the years, and I had a solid idea of what Doc was attempting to do here. "What about a percussive massage gun?"

"Eventually, we're working up to that," Doc said. "I have a TENS unit we can use if this doesn't start loosening up more and I want to treat it with ultrasound."

Arms folded, I nodded. "That's at the clinic."

"In about four hours," he said, his tone clipped and short. I didn't grin, though Doc should know better. Whatever he'd done to upset her and hurt her feelings still stung, the fact she dreaded coming to physical therapy today made me more inclined to cut my own meetings short and join them.

Besides, I wasn't kidding when I told her I wanted her back in training. I'd given her time and distance, but the threats were still out there. Therapy for her scarred arms so she could dance was good. She also needed to fight, and one of the skills she relied upon so heavily was her speed.

And her ability to climb.

She needed her arms for both of those. I needed her stronger and more prepared to confide in me. She was talking to Rome. That was a good start. Rome already said there were more people who needed eliminating.

"I don't really want to go to the clinic."

"Not really an option to bring it here, Little Bit." His rough voice always softened for her. As if aware of my judgment, he cut a look toward me. "We're going to start with three times a week, and I can come to pick you up—"

"Someone will bring her and stay with her," I interrupted. No way Kellan would go for her leaving solo with Doc every other day or whatever. The clinic was too open and had too much foot traffic.

He glared at me, but when I raised my eyebrows, he just shook his head. *That's what I thought.*

"How much pressure are you using to roll her arm?"

For a moment, I didn't think Doc would go for it but then he reminded me why we'd all relied on him for years. "Come here. Put your hand over mine and feel it. You don't want to do too much because we don't want to tear anything. The point is to get blood filling the area. We're encouraging repair without causing more damage."

I followed the motion, not adding or subtracting pressure. Hellspawn's expression served as a visceral reminder that she was not enjoying this at all.

"How uncomfortable is it?" I asked her and she gritted her teeth. Doc stopped the pressure before I even straightened. "You need to breathe, Hellspawn."

She sucked in a noisy breath and glared at me. "I know what I need to do—it hurts like hell."

"Then you tell me." Doc picked up the thread. "I want to help you, not inflict more damage."

"Pain can be compartmentalized and overcome. I've trained through pain my whole life."

The dead even tone and the fact that her eyes didn't even flicker at that statement just set fire to the fuse on my temper. She wasn't kidding or bragging.

"This is different," Doc said in a patient tone I didn't have a fucking prayer of emulating. So, I went and made coffee for us. It was something to do while he put away the roller and took her arm in his hands.

The massage I could do. And would. It was gentler. I had a percussion gun back at the apartment. I'd order a few more. We'd make sure they were everywhere. It was hard to ignore how inflamed her forearms were or how angry those slashes were. The jagged nature of them betrayed just how much damage the fucker had really done to her.

We really should have taken longer to kill him.

"I can handle it," she replied in that same dead fucking tone.

"Well, I can't," Doc said, sternness creeping into his voice. "What's more, you don't have to. You will dance, you will perform, you will do everything you want to do—but you aren't on a deadline. You don't have a show to go and do."

Stony silence met his statement, and I turned to find her staring at her arms and not at him. "Maybe not," she said finally. "But I have the deadline in my head and that's the most important one. If I can't do these things, then I'm weak. I can't be weak."

Nothing Doc said to her after that penetrated that thick skull. While I agreed with him, I didn't do him any favors. Instead, I just made the coffee and waited out his massage and then I iced her forearms.

"Take it easy again today," he told her, which was

tantamount to waving a red flag at a bull. He fucking knew it too. That was clear in the way he glanced at me. I nodded, but only in as much to acknowledge what he said.

This was the other reason I wanted to be part of the physical therapy. I wanted to see what her limits were and what we were working with, and her temper was right at the top of the list.

"I'll see you at the clinic tomorrow?" Doc asked and she made a face.

"I'll see who can bring me," she finally conceded when I didn't intervene. Doc paused after packing up his stuff and pressed a kiss to the top of her head. His grip on her shoulder was light, but the tension radiating off her redoubled at the intimate contact—she didn't pull away though.

I rolled my head from side to side, cracking the vertebrae and stretching out the knots yanking at my muscles. Once Doc was gone, she glanced at me.

"You need a break, Hellspawn? Or you just want to get right into it?" Because a night in my brother's bed and she was this fucking tense? Doc had definitely knocked some scabs off the wounds.

Wounds she wasn't allowing to heal.

"You were serious about training?"

"Yep," I said before draining my coffee and moving over to rinse out the cup. "You need it."

I needed it. But I kept that part to myself.

"I'm tired, Liam."

"Uh-huh, well, you're not the pampered little rich girl who can't work through her pain and exhaustion, so that excuse isn't gonna fly with me."

From zero to inferno, her eyes blazed as she rose abruptly. The weariness that had her spine drooping evaporated as she snapped her head up.

There was my little hellspawn. Come on, baby, come fight me.

"Let's go before I throw you over my shoulder and drag you down there. It's time you got over this little pity party fest everyone is insisting on throwing for you."

Cruel to be kind, that was me.

"Besides," I continued, ignoring the way she half-stomped over to the sink to rinse out her cup. "We need to talk."

"I thought we have been talking," she protested and I smirked. Yeah, I was a dick. Fuck, I was gonna be jacking off by myself for a while after this, but it had to be done.

Sorry, Hellspawn. Hopefully, you'll understand this later.

I headed for her studio without waiting for her, as it forced her to hurry after me. Shifting the balance more in my favor and getting her off-kilter. Her defenses were all raging high. Deflect. Deny. Change the subject.

Throw in those wounded eyes, and no wonder we were all fucking toast for her. At the door, I waited for her and snapped my fingers to hurry her up. Her hands balled up into little fists.

Yep, I was totally getting punched today.

Worth it.

I waited until she was inside and I followed her, locking the door behind us before I said, "We haven't had a real talk about Reed and Graham."

"Adam?" I really hated his name on her lips, particularly after the bomb that he asked her to marry him. He was still being a fucking stone-faced ass over his reasons too. No matter what she said, I didn't think he'd made the offer just to protect her.

Protecting her was definitely a perk, but he wanted

something out of the deal. Then there was Ezra's claim that she belonged to them. Yeah, that shit wasn't going to fly.

I went to pull out the mats. "Yes, Ezra. Lose the shoes and the heavy shirt, Hellspawn."

"Liam, I don't want to do this right now. My arms are sore."

"Well, the next time you voluntarily give yourself up to an enemy, be sure to let them know how you're feeling before you try to get away. Maybe they'll even go easy on you."

"Why are you being such an *asshole*?"

"Because you're not a wimp and you're not that fucking delicate. You're retreating into your pain. Fine, I get it. But that's not going to work with me."

"I'm not retreating into *anything*." But the sweatshirt and the shoes were off. She had her hands on her hips, and violence lashed the air around her. Yep, her temper was just about ready to spike.

"Then tell me more about Adam—why would he want to marry you."

"I don't *know*," she said, confusion flickering across her face. "I told you before, he wouldn't tell me why. That he would when I agreed."

"Yeah, you weren't going to agree." Even if she hadn't met us, she wouldn't have gone for the deal. Which was great, because I would have had to make her a widow and that would have been problematic for us.

"You know that?"

I kicked off my own shoes and then crooked a finger at her before pointing to the mat in front of me. At least in the studio it was soundproofed. We weren't likely to get interrupted, and I could let her work out some of her anger.

"I know a lot of things, Hellspawn," I said, raising my

hands to show her the empty palms. "Like, you aren't the type to stab your BFF in the back. Whatever is going on between Reed, Benedict, and Graham, your brother is about to be in the middle of it, and he still doesn't know about Reed's offer..."

Her eyes widened. "You can't tell him."

"I can and will do whatever I need to—"

Snap, her fist flew and I turned her to the side. There she was. Come on, baby.

"As I was saying," I taunted. "I can and will do what I need to do where you are concerned. You're not marrying him, so there's no purpose in defending it."

"I'm not defending it." Sharp jab, then a slice; I blocked both. Her expression tightened into a grimace.

"Then why did he ask you to marry him?"

"I don't know!" Jab. Jab. She went low with the third blow, and I was moving to keep her from catching me in the gut. I didn't mind a solar plexus hit, but that wasn't what she'd been aiming at. My dick was already sore enough, thank you.

"You have some idea—who in your family does he hate?"

She stopped. "Liam—"

"Come on, sweetheart, keep swinging. You need to get it out, and I need to know why you're tangled up in Royals business." Before something jerked the rug out from beneath us all.

"I know them because I know Lainey, and they—" This time, she paused again, her breath coming in little pants. The hint of tears around her eyes reminded me I was being an asshole on purpose.

"They," I prompted.

"They know my uncle." The last word came out on a

wheezed sound, like she didn't dare say it aloud. "Adam hates him."

"So, he wants to marry you to get at your uncle." I already wanted to get my hands on this asshole. This just amped up that need. "Does that sound right?"

"I don't know how it would…" But she didn't even believe herself. "I hate talking about him." Yeah, I got that. "But yes—that sounds right. Maybe it was always about punishing him."

She looked so fucking defeated, I closed the distance. I could be an asshole, but that wasn't what she needed.

"I don't know. Maybe it was just for Lainey."

Which translated to not about her, and I wrapped an arm around her.

She slammed her fists against my chest. "Why are you making me do this?"

I didn't let the blows shove me away. I just held onto her until she got it out of her system, which didn't take long. She really was tired and I was the son of a bitch pushing her. When she gripped my shirt, I held her tighter.

"Hellspawn, we're going to figure this out," I promised her. "Then we're going to eliminate every single threat."

"You still haven't even told me how you know them," she complained and there was a mournful note in those words.

I hadn't. Sighing, I cradled her closer. Fuck it, she deserved to know. "A long time ago, we figured out someone was sniffing around the Vandals, our territory, where they ran—the things they did. More, they were looking into Milo. It didn't take me long to figure out the guys I was going to school with were in on it and it took time and patience to cultivate a relationship."

"You're a spy?"

"Something like that," I told her. "I found some interesting allies but far more secrets. Those secrets are what I need to help me break them open so I can—"

Then my fucking phone rang, and I glared at the mirror, though her face was still tucked against my chest.

I had to answer that call.

"I'm sorry, Hellspawn," I apologized, then let her go so I could pull the phone out. Touching my finger to her lips to ask for silence, I answered.

"Yes, sir?" I skipped the "your majesty" part, which we often did—in public. No way was I giving Hellspawn more to worry about right now.

"I have a job for you, O'Connell. It's time to earn your keep."

27

Liam's abrupt departure two days prior had left a sour taste in my mouth. He promised he couldn't do anything else about it right now, but he would be back. Then he was gone.

Secrets with secrets. He was a spy for the Royals? Or on the Royals? Definitely on the Royals. It made my head hurt. More, it made my heart hurt, but I couldn't linger on that thought with so much going on around us. Jasper kept vanishing. He would show up long enough to give me a kiss and check on me, then he was gone again.

Vaughn was here, and that helped. In fact, he was almost always around the clubhouse and he'd begun doing sketches for possible tattoos for my arms. But something was off with him. Only when I asked, he just said it was fine. I needed to press more, but I'd spent every hour I could of the last couple of days with Lainey.

The time for her to go home closed in like some existential threat. I wasn't the only one who dreaded it. The tension between her and Milo had been so high that she'd pretty much just moved into my room the night before last.

At her request, I made sure Milo was gone before we slipped into his room so she could collect some of her things.

"I know I said I didn't want the dirty details," I told her. "But you can talk to me."

She glanced over her shoulder as she folded a top. "There's nothing to say, not really. He doesn't want me to go. I have to go. End of story."

I frowned, propping my chin on my fist as I watched her from the back of the sofa. "I told him about Andrea."

"I know." She cast me another smile before walking over to the dresser. There were more clothes in the drawer. "But he wants more details than I'm willing to give him."

Yeah. "They do that." I sighed then because this was important. "How are you feeling?"

With her back to me, Lainey went still, the shirt she held was much too large for her. I had a feeling it was Milo's, but I didn't say anything.

"Between you and me?" she asked as she turned to face me.

"That goes without saying, but if you need to hear it—then I'll take it to my grave."

"Well, let's not get that melodramatic," she scolded with wide eyes, but neither of us laughed. Settling back against the dresser, she looked down at the shirt. "And I don't know how I feel, Em. The last few weeks have been—a rollercoaster. I was worried about you, terrified, then here I've gone from terrified to furious to—he drives me crazy. Your brother isn't like anyone I've ever met. He's stubborn, fierce, brutally honest at times, and a fucking mystery at others."

Tears flashed in her eyes, but she turned away to fold the shirt and shook her head.

"I *have* to go home. I should have left a week ago."

"I should have encouraged you to go home sooner. But I was selfish."

That earned an almost wet laugh. "Me too." Another couple of items came out of the drawer and she carried them over to the bag she had on the bed. "We barely ever get to spend time like this—time where we can actually breathe without worrying the other one will be stolen away."

"I know," I said. "I wish I could go back with you to help."

"No, you don't," she said, chuckling. "And as much as I adore you, you're right—you're safer here. I don't want you anywhere near our world anymore."

"I don't think it was ever my world."

That earned me a haughty lift to her chin as she gave me a look. "It *is* your world. You belong there every bit as much as I do. We just have to knock a few players off the board permanently. Then you can reclaim what belongs to you."

"Lainey..."

"Nope," she informed me as she added the last of the things to the bag then closed it. I guess she really hadn't brought that much with her. "You're going to stay here and be safe with that mad crew of violent misfits who adore you. Also, if we're picking favorites—I really like Rome."

I laughed. "I am *not* picking favorites because I adore all of them."

"Even the doctor?" She watched me from beneath her lashes like I wouldn't notice.

"Doc—Mickey is different." I slumped back down on

the sofa. "And he's not one of them anyway. Or at least, they all say that he isn't." Instead, I ran my hands over my forearms. He'd been there the day before to do another therapy session when I hadn't shown up at the clinic. It had just been me and Lainey until Vaughn joined us.

"Well, I'd argue he's just like them," she said. "But..." Crossing over to where I sat, she dropped the bag on the table and then fell onto the sofa next to me. "You know I have your back. You want me to knock him on his ass, I'll make it happen. But maybe after he's done helping you..."

When she reached for my wrist, I turned to sit and let her hold my arm. She stared at the scars. "I know some good doctors—" She eyed me. "We might be able to do some surgical repairs, maybe even get rid of these scars."

The ointment Doc had me using was supposed to help, but I couldn't really tell. Then again—it hadn't been all that long since I got back. The sinking feeling in my stomach returned and I sucked on my lower lip.

"Maybe don't take this the wrong way—not sure I'm up for going to any medical facilities." No matter the reason.

Linking our fingers, she nodded slowly. "I get that. You know, you might want to tell Doc if he keeps insisting you need to go to the clinic."

I shivered, then shoved that aside. "I'll be fine. You need to focus on you and Andrea."

"Uh-huh." She wasn't convinced. "I'd recommend a good therapist, but I have a feeling that's a non-starter."

I just stared at her and she winced.

"Sorry."

"No," I said with a sigh. This time I pulled my hand away after squeezing her fingers, then rubbed my face. "I'm a mess. I know I am. But if I look at any of it for too long—" I shut down. Liam had been provoking me. Vaughn and

Rome were cosseting me. Kellan had given me a safe place to just be. So was Jasper.

Freddie—Freddie had walked into that Hell to get me, and he kept disappearing on me now. Then there was Doc... he wanted...

"I'll be okay," I said after a long minute, then glanced at her. "I promise. I just have to get my shit together." Maybe I could go talk to their friend again, but as much as I liked Ms. Stephanie, everything in me revolted at the idea of confessing any of this to her.

"You're also going to stay in touch with me," she told me firmly. "You have a phone, and we have our chats. Every day, you message me. Even if it's just 'I'm alive bitch, and I'm getting laid regularly. What are you doing?'"

Blinking, I stared at her. "Um..."

"Hey, you can choose the content, I'm just saying I expect to hear from you and—" She raised a hand when I would have countered with my own argument. "So will I. Though I rather doubt I'll have much to report on my sex life. It'll probably be more about wanting to throttle Ezra. Maybe my mother."

At the face she made, I laughed. "I really don't want you to go, no matter how much I know you have to."

"Same," she whispered, then we were hugging and I held her tight.

"Thank you for helping them find me."

"Anytime," she said with a sniffle, then leaned back. "However, I think never having to hunt for you again is a good plan."

"Deal."

She swiped at her cheeks, then checked her watch. "Time to go."

It was almost noon.

"You're taking a car?" I asked as we stood and she grabbed her bag.

"Something like that."

We walked out to the front. Vaughn glanced up from where he was working on a laptop in the living room and swept his gaze from me to Lainey and then back. Eyes narrowed, he frowned. "I thought you weren't leaving until tomorrow."

The question was definitely directed at Lainey. As far as I knew, it had always been today, but I hadn't discussed it with the guys.

She gave a shrug as her phone buzzed. Checking the screen, she said, "My ride is here. You're walking us out, right?"

His gaze jerked to me as he stood, and I shook my head. "I'm just walking her to the car." I could almost feel his relief as he blew out a breath. "No bolting for me."

Not anymore.

The corner of his mouth kicked up and he shut the laptop. "Yes, I'll be walking you both out there. Does Milo know you're leaving?"

Lainey didn't answer him as she pivoted and strode to the door. Worry speared through me as I caught Vaughn's expression. He was not happy. I hurried after her and ignored the jangling of my nerves as we stepped out into the warehouse.

There was only one truck parked out there, but there were more than a few rats offloading it. While Lainey and I hadn't made any excursions from the clubhouse together, she didn't even glance in their direction before striding toward one of the doors that led outside on the opposite side of the warehouse from them.

"You didn't tell him," I murmured as I fell into step with her.

She shook her head. "He wanted to take me back. That would not have gone over well."

I sighed. Milo was gonna be pissed.

The outer door opened and Freddie popped in. His hair was a mess, like he'd been raking his hands through it over and over. That worried me less than the dark shadows under his eyes.

"Boo-Boo," he said, a grin twisting his lips when he spotted me. "Ball-Cracker."

Then he dropped his gaze to the bag.

"Oh, that explains the dickhead."

Dickhead...

The door behind Freddie jerked open and he didn't jump, like he'd been expecting it. Ezra filled the doorframe and I wanted to groan. Oh, this could be bad. Lainey, however, didn't slow down.

"Ezra," she said as she neared him, and he dragged his gaze over her and then looked at me.

"You're both coming, right?" He didn't wait for an answer as he hooked the bag from Lainey's fingers.

"No," Vaughn said from right behind me, the warning more than enough to quiet my nerves when he slid his arm around my waist. "Not even sure *she* should be going with you."

Ezra didn't even look at him before he looked at Lainey. "Come on, the car's outside and we're going before any more of those assholes show up." Then he glanced at me. "Are you sure you don't want to go?" It wasn't until he moved to block Lainey behind him that I caught sight of the gun beneath his jacket.

And I wasn't the only one, because Freddie moved in front of me and had his knife in his hand.

"She's sure," he told him. "Just like I told you outside."

The tension crackled in the air and I groaned. This was just going to end badly. Patting Vaughn's arm, I said, "I'm fine. I promise." Then I settled my hand on Freddie's wrist —just two fingers. With light pressure, I nudged the knife down.

Kellan's warning echoed inside of my head.

"I'm not leaving," I assured him.

"Oh my god," Lainey said with a snap. "Leave her alone, Ezra. I told you when I called that you were just picking *me* up. If you're going to be an asshole about it, I'll get a rideshare or something."

"The hell you will," Ezra snarled as he jerked his head back to look at her. "You're going back with me and staying with me. No more crazy schemes or going off on your own."

Any minute now, someone's head was going to catch on fire. I circled Freddie and headed straight toward them, not slowing until I was right in front of Ezra, and it was me poking him in the chest. That earned me a startled look.

"Be nice to her, or I'll be the one kicking your ass. You don't have to be a dick *all* the time. We know you were worried."

"Do you?" he countered, not backing off in the slightest. "Do you even know who these people are around you or the war that's going on?"

"War?" Lainey rolled her eyes. "Stop being so dramatic. You're here because you already had one freakout, and I need a ride. Don't make me regret calling you..."

"Come with us," Ezra said, dropping his voice. "You two are happier in the same place anyway—it makes it easier to keep you both safe." He caught my hand then frowned as he studied the scars on my arms.

"Get your fucking hands off my sister." There was no mistaking the warning in Milo's voice. "Who the hell invited you here, anyway?"

Oh, it was going from bad to worse. Ezra closed his grip on my wrist and then I was suddenly behind him and shoved into Lainey. We looked at each other as Milo and Ezra glared at each other—only Milo wasn't alone. Kellan and Vaughn were both there, along with Freddie.

"Ezra, stop," Lainey said, gripping his jacket and tugging. "I mean it. I want to go now. We need to leave."

If I hadn't been staring right at him, I would have missed the hurt flashing over Milo's expression it was there and gone so fast. He glanced at Lainey. "You called him?"

"Yes," she said. "You have things to do, and I have a life to get back to. So, I suggest both of you boys put your dicks away. I'll be in the car." She jangled the keys she'd just fished out of Ezra's pocket. When Lainey turned to me, the pain I'd seen on Milo's face reflected in her eyes, but she gave the barest of head shakes.

They were killing me. "Freddie," I called before I snagged the bag that Ezra had dropped. "Can you walk us out?" Then before anything else could go wrong, I added, "I'll be right back."

This time, I looked to Kellan, then at Ezra and Milo before I looked back to him.

"Go on, Sparrow, walk your friend out. We'll take care of this."

Relief swarmed me, and I mouthed thank you. He looked so damn tired and I hated dumping more on him. Freddie glided around Milo and Ezra to open the door for us. The cold air washing in had me shivering.

I hadn't bothered with a jacket, but I wasn't going to stop now. Lainey murmured her thanks to Freddie then headed out with me right behind her. Trusting Freddie to have our backs, I followed her to the black Mercedes parked out in the alley that looked violently out of place.

The trunk opened and she took the bag from me before stowing it inside, then turned as the engine started up. I gripped her in a tight hug and she returned it fiercely.

"Be careful," I whispered.

"You, too."

Then the door slammed open, and Ezra stalked toward us. He picked Lainey up as soon as she let me go and she rolled her eyes as he marched her around to the passenger door.

Worry speared me, but I hugged myself as she slammed her elbow into him and he grunted. At least he put her down and she got into the car.

Relief seemed to soften his expression briefly before he looked at me. "Still time to come..."

"I meant it," I told him, aware of Freddie having moved right up to my back. "This is my home now."

He nodded once. "If that changes, you just have to call."

"Just look after Lainey, please," I told him.

"I *always* do," he said with a cutting look behind me, and I didn't have to glance back to know Milo stood there. When Ezra opened the driver's side door, Freddie leaned to the side and waved.

"See ya, Ball-Cracker!"

The lump in my throat grew as Ezra slid into the car. He didn't waste any time putting it into gear before accelerating around the alley toward the road as though we were already in pursuit.

Then they were gone.

Another shiver went through me as I stared after them. I'd always hated saying goodbye.

The door to the warehouse slammed and I finally turned to look back to where Milo had been. Freddie watched me quietly, then shrugged out of his jacket. "You're in socks, Boo-Boo." The quiet reminder had me looking down at them as he draped his jacket over me.

"Come on, there's probably gonna be a brawl inside, and we can get the good seats and the popcorn."

Tears sprang to my eyes as I laughed, but none of this was funny. When he gripped the jacket and leaned in toward me, I pressed my forehead to his.

"You'll see her again," he promised. "I'll make sure of it. Pretty sure the Ball-Cracker will too."

That made me laugh even as I swiped at the tears. He wasn't wrong, but it didn't make the sting any less. I missed her already.

28

Cooling my heels had never been something I enjoyed, but I'd done enough work as a driver to have perfected my skill at it. Anyone who thought patience was all you needed when you had to wait had never truly remained in place for hours with no end in sight.

Fidgeting. Pacing. Even eating and drinking—or in Jas's case, smoking, were often the methods utilized to while away the time. I leaned on none of those.

Instead, I rebuilt a car engine in my head while I waited. Most of the time, it was the first car engine I'd ever built—cobbled together from scraps. The time spent hunting for the right pieces had taken longer than building it had. The work had also led to a few professional friendships across the city with other mechanics.

Between working for them and studying in school, there wasn't much I couldn't do under the hood of a car. That first engine would always hold a special place in my heart. It was the first time I'd built something from nothing.

From the first rocking pings of the engine to when she began to hum with a rising purr that eventually became a growl, I'd been in love. Arguably, my first love. They say you never got over it.

The one piece of her I'd been able to salvage sat on a shelf in my room at the clubhouse. Eventually, I would build a new engine around that single piece... until then, I rebuilt her in my head, over and over again.

"Mr. Traschel," the receptionist called from where she sat behind her glass and steel desk. It was indeed an ugly tribute to modernity with all of its cold hard edges. "Mr. Warrick says he has ten minutes. If you need longer, you'll have to make an appointment."

Inclining my head, I said, "I only need five."

Chances were, my opening question would earn me quite a bit more time. But that conversation was for Jonathon Warrick and I alone.

She flashed me another quick smile, then pressed a button on her phone before speaking into her headset. "Yes, he said he doesn't need even ten minutes."

Around me, activity hummed with people coming and going. The Warrick Foundation managed a number of charities in and around Braxton Harbor, with some reaching nationally. The volume of money flowing through these offices in a week could probably buy the high-rise building they were located in five times over.

Volunteers hustled. Managers schmoozed. Then there were the spokespeople. The Foundation had more spokespersons and "ambassadors" on its payroll than they did on any other occupation. I would bet only a third of them were legitimate.

But it wasn't about what I could gamble on, but what I could prove.

"Thank you for waiting, Mr. Traschel," the blonde said as she leaned forward, offering a view of her stacked chest. Genetics—or a cosmetic surgeon—had been very generous with her. "You can take elevator three directly up to Mr. Warrick's private office. His secretary will meet you."

Yeah, I bet she would. "Thank you."

I ignored the way her face fell when I didn't rise to the bait. If it ever came down to needing to seduce one of his employees, we were already fucked, and I had zero interest in trading my skin or anyone else's. That was his business.

Not mine.

The elevator opened as I reached it. Pivoting inside, I glanced at the panel that had already been lit up. This was an express elevator. I spared a brief glance at the camera outside the elevator that had a little red light on it and the second one I imagined was above me in this elevator.

Yeah, they had security.

Sliding my hands into my pockets, I waited as the elevator carried me up to my appointment. This really was the last place I wanted to be, but we needed information, and Warrick needed to be put on notice.

The secretary was very much waiting for me just outside of the elevator. She was not alone, however, because a guy who stood maybe a quarter of an inch shorter than me accompanied her. He was well-armed, though his jacket had a bad cut and revealed the shoulder holster he sported.

Then again, maybe that was the point.

"If you don't mind, Mr. Traschel," the secretary said. Unlike the buxom blonde from reception, the secretary had steel-gray hair cut into a short pageboy. Her lined face was still verging on what I would call pretty, despite the wrinkles, and her smile was almost kind.

That stopped at her eyes, though.

They were deader than doornails.

"Not at all," I said as I stepped out with my hands extended at the sides. Having expected the pat-down as well as the metal detectors in the building's lobby, I'd left my weapons in the car.

The gorilla at her side wasn't light as he gave me a thorough pat-down, even grabbing my dick at one point. I glanced down at him. "That's attached and definitely not anything you have to worry about."

The guy ignored me. Finishing up, he stood and glanced at Granny Dangerous. "He's clean."

"Thank you. Mr. Traschel, please follow me."

She didn't wait, just set off through the opulent floor to where her desk was. The dark wood seemed to swallow all the light as the heavier carpet muffled steps. Everything up here seemed a little more expensive, a little bigger, and it definitely didn't "read" foundation.

It read rich prick.

With a cluck of her tongue, she pointed to a spot just before her desk while she picked up her phone. I'd had teachers like her in high school. Dour, unfeeling, bitter assholes—every single one of them. It was better to never turn your back on them because they'd be just as likely to drive a knife into it.

If they could be bothered to care at all.

"Yes, sir. Mr. Green has cleared him." She said nothing more, then nodded before hanging up the phone. "This way."

Without waiting for me, she set off again. The air

seemed almost frigid up here. Or maybe that was the company.

Pausing before a large set of double doors, she knocked twice, then opened both. "Mr. Traschel, Mr. Warrick."

With that announcement, she waited for me to walk in. There was another set of double doors opposite these. I had to wonder—had those belonged to Noel Warrick? There were no names on little placards up here.

Probably didn't need them.

Striding inside, I scanned and located my target sitting behind a large desk. His jacket was hung over the back of his chair, leaving him in a button-down shirt and tie. The color was almost painfully white, while his tie was some random geometric pattern in gray.

He didn't look up from the digital tablet he seemed to be reading on, not even when the doors closed behind me. Sliding my hands into my pockets, I waited. Finally, he glanced up and focused on me. It never failed to sink me when I was face to face with him.

Jonathon Warrick was some perverted, dark mirror version of me. In his fifties, his hair wasn't even gray, and the only concession to his age seemed to be the hint of lines at the corners of his eyes. He didn't even wear glasses.

Something to look forward to—but I'd take wrinkles, failing eyes, and balding, to be honest. Anything that didn't leave me looking like him.

"You have five minutes," he said, breaking the impasse.

"Your mother died."

His unreadable mask cracked at the edges as his eyes narrowed. "That means nothing to you. There is no inheritance for you to collect or demand."

"Good, I wouldn't take it if there were."

"As long as we're clear. There are lines, you being here is

crossing one of them." Maybe he shouldn't have told me that, but for the first time since I'd realized I had to walk into this building and meet with him, I relaxed.

He didn't want me around any more than I wanted to be here. Not bothering to contain the slow smile, I said, "You would know all about crossing lines."

Putting the tablet down, he rose and claimed his jacket from the back of the chair. "You had five minutes, now you have four. Would you like to get to the point? Or do you intend to waste more of my time?"

"Let's jump right in, shall we?" I fixed my gaze on him. This close, I also realized something I hadn't honestly thought about since that fucked up day I discovered the lie. I was taller than him. I probably had a solid ten pounds of muscle on him too. "You're running skin through this city. You've been doing it for a long time, but now you're running it through our trucks—or trying to."

He slid the jacket on and just stared at me. "I believe you are mistaken—"

"Save the shill and bullshit for the people you bilk for money to pay your transport fees and to launder your filthy income. I know what you do. I've known for a long time. Your mother died, probably took a whole channel of revenue and contacts with her. That's why you need the new charity—a new funnel for your income."

"Two minutes."

Now, I smiled. "Understand, your business in this city is done. You made a mistake involving us. A mistake we will be reversing. You should consider getting into charity work for real. Because you either shut it down, or I'll burn it down."

"Is that a threat?" His nostrils flared, and he pressed his

fists onto the desk. Leaning on his knuckles, he glared at me.

"It's a promise." I pulled my hand from my pocket. "One minute to spare. I have my eye on you, Mr. Warrick. You would do well to never get in my line of sight again."

With that, I turned on my heels and headed for the door. Only when I had gripped the handle did I pause and glance back. "Lest you think this is something you can ignore, understand what I did today is just a taste of the hell we're going to bring down on you."

He frowned. "What are you talking about..."

I didn't answer him, just let myself out and headed directly to the elevators. The doors opened as if anticipating my arrival. Granny Dangerous hurried toward me like she could slow my exit, but the doors were already closing.

I went straight to reception, then took the next elevator to the ground floor. I'd just slid into my car in the parking garage across the street when the FBI pulled up outside the building. They were noisy, the Feds. They came in a series of SUVs, all black, of course, and spilled out in their suits and dark blue coats with the yellow letters emblazoned across the back.

Jonathon Warrick was about to have a very bad day. If only it were as simple as just turning him in. No, he covered his tracks pretty well, but I knew where at least a couple of the bodies were buried. I also knew where to find more.

For now, I wanted him to be aware that he was on notice and questioning how much we knew. That might slow down his trafficking until we had a solid handle on the rest. The whole of the drive back to the clubhouse though only saw my internal agitation climb.

I hated the fact I shared even a particle of DNA with that

slimy son of a bitch. The information had been like a black skid mark on my soul from the day it fell in my lap. He had a family, wealth, power, and influence. He maintained it all through the buying and selling of people, and pumping the wealthy for their investments in his "projects."

How many of those assholes were his clients, and how many were just fools being defrauded? Who knew. But it was a fact we needed to deal with on all fronts.

It was late and quiet when I got back to the warehouse. No trucks were parked, they were all out and Jasper was on another run. This time, Vaughn had gone with him because Milo hadn't spoken to anyone in the last day. Not since the girl left.

I pinched the bridge of my nose. I needed to go talk him down, but what I really wanted was a very large bottle of alcohol. The door to the clubhouse opened, letting Freddie out. He moved in a hurried fashion across the floor to the side door and then out.

Not once did he even glance at my car. Jasper was right, we needed to be keeping a closer eye on him. I sent Rome a message. He didn't leave Sparrow that much lately. Hell, none of us wanted to, but if anyone could trail Freddie without being caught, it was Rome.

He sent back a one-word answer.

"K."

Well, that was better than nothing. Once inside the clubhouse, I debated just heading up for a shower and sleep, but the television was on in the living room. Adjusting my path, I checked to see who was down here.

Sparrow sat on the sofa, phone in her hand, texting and glancing up at the screen. It was some kind of game show. Weakest Link or some shit, I knew it. The host was kind of a dick. I liked her. She shouldn't be down here by herself. In fact, why was she down here?

Liam had been a ghost for the last few days. Milo wasn't much better. Jasper and Vaughn were out, so why wasn't—

A movement behind and I pivoted. Rome lifted his chin, then nodded toward Sparrow. I almost laughed. Right. He'd been with her when I messaged. I mouthed thanks, and then he was gone.

The television sound muted and I turned to find her looking at me. "Hey," she said with a smile, and for the second time that day, some of the pressure inside of me eased and I had no trouble summoning a smile for her.

"Hey," I said. "Since I sent your date away—need some company?"

When she patted the sofa next to her, I grinned. "Five minutes. Let me shower real quick."

"I'll be here," she promised and I blew out a breath.

"Be right back." Nothing from Warrick was going to be anywhere near her.

Ever.

29

After I snapped a quick selfie, I sent it to Lainey. She insisted she was fine, though she'd had a few choice words about Ezra since returning. Twice, she'd asked me about Adam though—apparently, he was missing, but we both knew he'd been with Liam.

Promising her I'd find out, I told her about my planned date with Jasper. I had no idea where we were going. The last time he'd taken me out, we'd gone for a wonderful drive up the coast to the resort where they'd worked one summer.

A thrill skated through my system, which seemed attached to a live wire. The only thing Jasper had said when he texted was that he was free tonight. He'd still been on the road when he sent the message and it had come in after I went to sleep—in Kellan's bed because Rome still wasn't back, and Kellan seemed to need the company as much as I had.

The only thing I'd asked him that morning was what

did I need to wear. He'd said be comfortable. It had left me with a lot of options. Fortunately, Lainey had plenty of advice, so I'd gone with a long-sleeved, wrap dress over leggings. I could lose the leggings if I needed to.

What had she said? The little black dress works for everything. The leggings were red, so they popped, but the boots were also black. The fun part was my dress was calf-length and my boots were knee-high so the leggings didn't show at all.

Using a little mascara and gloss, I'd skipped the rest. There were no bruises to cover. I'd braided one section of my hair so it would frame my face but left the rest loose.

Casual, but cute. I stared at myself in the mirror and then made a face. Jasper already liked me, so why was I freaking out over what I was wearing? They were clothes. So much of my life had been dictated by controlling what others saw. I didn't have to do that anymore.

I took one more picture and sent it to Lainey. She texted back a sweating emoji and I snorted. Then another message popped up.

Ezra says you look hawt too.

Right, yeah, that message needed to go. But all I did was send her a kiss face before I closed the app. I needed to bring up Milo, but I also didn't want to get in the middle. She'd promised she was coming back and we were in touch.

Milo needed to trust Lainey, but then she needed to trust him. I was still working on trusting everyone. Probably better to stay out of it all.

A knock on my door frame pulled me around and I grinned. Jasper filled the doorway, dark gray shirt matching his dark gray eyes and he'd even put on a *tie.*

Relief slapped me even as fresh apprehension scored

through my system. A tie meant we were going out some-where. What if someone saw? What if…

"Swan, you look," he said slowly, raking his gaze over me. "You look fantastic."

"You said casual, but you also said date." I bit my lip before I remembered the gloss, then forced myself to stop. "You look really nice… do I need something more cocktail hour or formal?"

"You're perfect," he said as he crossed the room to where I stood, "just like you are." This close, I couldn't mistake the fresh scent of him. He'd showered. I'd have noticed even without the faint dampness to his hair or the fresh trim to his beard. "I wouldn't change a thing. Well…"

I raised my eyebrows and leaned back a little. "Well?"

"Well, I might change one thing." He cupped my chin, running his thumb right over my lower lip and carrying away some of the gloss right before he kissed me.

Heat fountained within me, chasing away the appre-hension as I leaned into him. Mouth open, I groaned as he chased my tongue with his, teasing little licks. There and then gone again. His fingers were so warm against my skin, and I almost wished we weren't going anywhere.

Jasper had been gone so much, and I missed him. When he began to pull back, I let out a little sound that came out way too much like a whimper, but he only stroked my lip with his thumb again.

"There, no more gloss but all perfect and pink." Head tilted, he grinned. "Maybe a little swollen."

"Only a little?" Oh, I sounded breathless. Probably because I was.

He studied me then said, "You're right," before swooping down to claim my lips again. This time, I let the phone fall as I slid my hands up his chest. The hand on my chin fell away, but he wrapped an arm around me as he devoured my mouth.

Playful and sweet turned heated and demanding until I was straining against him. All I wanted to do was tug off his tie and spend a few hours just being with him again.

His groan suggested he wouldn't be wholly opposed. Lifting his head, he glanced down at me. This close, all I could feel, smell, touch, and see was him. If I licked my lips, I could probably taste him. "You're too fucking tempting for words, Swan, but I'm doing this right. I asked you out on a date."

"Yes, you did." Giddiness helped to keep the apprehension at bay. Well, giddiness and flat-out wantonness. "I seem to recall saying yes."

"You did," he agreed, then squeezed me gently. "Let's grab your jacket. It's definitely getting colder, and I don't want you freezing."

It was like being doused in cold water, the reality that, yes, we were going out. But I forced the knee-jerk reaction to back off. I'd been out—with Rome and with Milo.

I could do this. Especially for Jasper.

"Do I get to know where we're going?" I summoned a lighter smile as he let me go, and when I would have glanced around for my phone, he held it up.

Oh, he'd caught it. "I can tell you," he said. "If you need to know."

A laugh escaped. There it was again. The careful wording, but he wasn't hiding anything. He was simply telling me he didn't want to spoil his surprise.

I could accept that.

"Surprise me," I encouraged him and his expression lit up with excitement. Once I had my jacket, I tucked my phone into a little bag along with more gloss—which made Jasper laugh—and one of my new "fake" IDs.

He eyed it. "Do I want to know?"

"Just—trying something out."

When he held out his hand, I pulled the little wallet out and showed it to him. He stared at it for a long moment.

"You do not look like a Monica."

I giggled. "Well, no, but then no one looks like their name until they have their name. I could be a Monica. I could be a Tate. Or an Alyssa. I bet I could even be an Elisabeth."

"You're Emersyn," he informed me. "It's your name."

"One that almost none of you use." I glanced at the ID as he handed it back, and then I lifted my shoulders. "Emersyn is my name and I plan on keeping it. But—I don't want to use *my* ID anywhere."

Not to mention, I had no idea where mine was. Had they even taken it to Pinetree? A shudder went through me at the thought of that place and all the warmth seemed to just drain away.

"Hey," Jasper said, wrapping his arms around me. "You can be whomever you want. You can be you, you can be Monica—you can even be Jasper if you want."

The last pulled a laugh from me and I leaned back. "I don't know—I don't think I could do that beard justice."

His eyes glinted. "True, I'd rather wear you on my beard." Talk about making it warmer. Another squeeze, and then he tucked me under his arm. "Date first, beard-wearing later."

It was such a ridiculous idea, but I liked it at the same time. "I bet I could find some stage makeup and spirit glue to put on a beard. You can see if you like it."

The look he gave me was equal parts "hell no" and

"intrigued." Okay, that settled it. We were definitely doing that.

In the hall, I glanced toward Milo's door, which closed just as we came out.

"He'll be alright, Swan," Jasper assured me. "He needs to lick his wounds."

"She's coming back," I said, facing him. "She had to go home."

"He knows. But she also called that punk, and that's not sitting well with him. Give him space. We'll make sure he's all right."

I frowned. I didn't like the idea of him hurting. "A couple of days at most, then I'm going in."

"I'll back your play," Jasper said. "I'll even kick the door in for you."

He wasn't kidding. Hopefully, it didn't come to that. After one last look at the door, I let Jasper guide me out. No one was around. That had been the theme for the last several days. Only a few of them here at a time, sometimes only one or two.

My nerves flared again when he led me out to his car, but I focused on keeping my breaths even. Leaving the clubhouse was normal. Hell, I'd been so damn determined to leave, I'd escaped. Still...

Even with the music on, it was hard to focus on anything except not asking him to take us back. When he closed his hands over mine, I gripped his hand tightly.

"We don't have to go," he said, though we'd only just pulled out. We were barely more than one street away. "I know this is scary, but I'm not going to let anything happen to you."

"I know that," I snapped, then closed my eyes and squeezed his hand while forcing myself to take a deeper breath. "I do know that," I said slower and calmer. Glancing over at him, I found him watching me. The dashboard lights illuminated his face, creating a play of shadows. "I really do. I want to go on this date with you."

Nodding slowly, he lifted one of my hands to his lips and kissed it. "We don't have to stay out for long. If you need to feel the safety of being in the clubhouse, then we can go back."

That helped. But... "I'm safe with you."

A flash of his smile in the dark. "Tell me if you need to go back, okay?"

"Okay, but—I don't want to tell you that."

He leaned his head against the seat and laughed. "Fair enough." Frankly, the conversation *had* helped. It helped all the way to a *movie* theater. He was taking me out to a movie. When we parked in the structure next to the theater, I stared at it in wonder and trepidation.

"This is our date?"

"Someone told me she never got to see films in theaters —like *ever*."

I hadn't. "Only on DVD and then digital and streaming." Excitement threaded through me and I clasped his hand as he led us to the stairs—not the elevator—and we descended them.

"So, one of the classic ways a guy asks a girl out is to go to the movies."

I laughed. "I've seen rom-coms. They don't always go to the movies—well—they do in the high school flicks." Nose wrinkling, I caught him looking at me.

"So, first date—movies."

"Second," I corrected, hopping down the last two steps to land next to him. "Our first date was amazing, and you did get me dinner out."

He chuckled, hooking an arm around my shoulders. "That's true. I just had you for dessert, before and after our meal."

The more we moved, the more I relaxed. The theater was interesting. My stomach growled at the smell of popcorn—he got us a large bucket and a big soda to share, along with a bottle of water. When he caught me eyeing the candy, he insisted I get some.

And a hot dog.

"Really?" I eyed them dubiously. It wasn't that I didn't like hot dogs, but they weren't exactly a favorite.

"Popcorn, candy, and junk food. Movie staples. We can do nachos with cheese too." None of this was good for me, but it was all so irresistible.

The trailers were playing by the time we found our seats. I didn't even know what movie we were going to watch. I was too excited trying the different foods and then watching the trailers. More than once, I caught Jasper watching me.

The hot dog wasn't bad, but I let him have it after a couple of bites. The nachos were better. The chocolate-covered peanuts were the best. Especially with popcorn.

While I would have said I didn't care what we watched, the film turned out to be the second-best thing. The first being the fact that the arm of the chair between us folded up so I could curl up next to Jasper. It was an action movie, and I loved the fact the heroine was as badass, if not more so, than the hero.

She even took down a huge guy on her own. I might have cheered at that. While we weren't alone in the theater, I wasn't the only one enjoying the movie.

On the way back to the car, I was bouncing with excitement from it. "Wait—it's the fifth one?"

Jasper laughed. "Yes, it's the fifth one, the best thing is you don't have to watch the others to enjoy it. But we have them all, so we can watch them at home too."

Oh, I couldn't wait. It was cold outside, but at least it wasn't rainy. We were almost back to the car when he had to pull out his phone. His smile faded fast and all my earlier apprehension flooded back in.

"What's wrong?"

"It's Freddie..."

30

"This is a bad idea," Jasper growled as he accelerated. The warm buzz of our movie time disintegrated under the worry that Freddie had texted him for *help*.

"If you take the time to get me back to the clubhouse, that's time you waste getting to him," I argued. Not that I had any intention of going back to the clubhouse. Not if Freddie needed us.

"Swan." He cut me an aggrieved look, but I folded my arms.

"I'm not being stubborn."

He snorted.

"Okay, I'm not being *totally* stubborn. But Freddie came to get me when I was in trouble. I want to help him." I needed to help him. His constant disappearing acts had begun to worry me. Now, Jasper pretty much let me push the argument to go with him—that worried me even more.

If he was this—scared seemed too tame a word—concerned, then we absolutely did not need any delays in getting Jasper to Freddie.

"When we get there, you will do exactly what I tell you." It had been a while since he'd used that tone with me. "I don't know what the fuck we're walking into. If I say stay in the car, you stay in the car. If I tell you to stay behind me, you stay behind me."

"Sit and heel. Got it."

He shot me a look but didn't comment. I wasn't even going to protest the orders. As it was, I twisted the strap of my crossbody bag to give my hands something to do. While Jasper didn't fidget, I hadn't missed the way he white-knuckled the steering wheel or the way he pinned the needle on the car.

The drive from the clubhouse to the movie theater hadn't been long—fifteen, maybe twenty minutes. I hadn't really been clocking it. This trip, by contrast, seemed interminable, even if he seemed to know exactly where he was going. At the first red light we hit, Jasper paused to pull his phone out, then flicked the screen on before passing it to me.

"Go to the texts, fourth message down—it should be addressed to the Committee."

I found it.

"Type in 'Standby 911,' but don't send it."

We were already moving again.

"Done." I kept my questions to myself.

Another few blocks and he turned, cutting us between two buildings and then down a long, narrow alley that looked like something right out of a bad film with trash littering everywhere and dank pools of water.

Well, maybe not dank, but they looked more like ink

than water. The thud of my heart seemed louder and louder. He turned into another alley and then parked behind a row of dumpsters.

"Send it now," he told me, then reached over to open the glove box. The gun resting in there, holstered, didn't surprise me. I hit send. No one responded, but more than one acknowledgement popped up that it had been read. He tucked the phone into his pocket, then eyed the alley before glancing at me and down at my boots. "You have your phone?"

I nodded. "Do you need me to send the same message?"

"Just make sure it's on."

"They can track my phone." I wasn't asking, just confirming. It was part of why I'd left that phone behind in the first place.

"Yeah, Swan, we can. Right now, we want all the balls in our court. Purse strap over your head and arm, but under the jacket, then zip it up." He slid out of the car, and I wiggled out of the jacket before pulling it back on.

By the time he opened my door, I was ready to go. My pulse leapt at the way he scanned the area before he held out a hand.

Once I was out, he took my fingers and hooked them through the belt loop on his jeans. "This is as far from me as you get and where you stay until I say otherwise, clear?"

I nodded. "Let's find Freddie."

"That's my plan."

The smell in the alley was every bit as awful as the over-flowing trash cans promised it would be. We ventured farther along the alley. Jasper didn't speak, so I followed suit, tightening my grip on his belt loop. In the distance, traffic droned past. Wind tossed a discarded fast-food wrapper along until it hit one of the puddles, where it seemed to just stick in place.

We'd gone about a hundred yards, maybe, when Jasper cut to the left and pushed open a dangling wooden door. Okay, door might be a generous description for it. The long creak it released was straight out of a horror movie and I cut a look behind me as we went inside.

The alley seemed so much darker and more sinister for being devoid of life. The interior didn't smell much better than the exterior, only there was a far stronger scent of metal.

My heart fisted at the cloying smell and how it seemed to coat my nostrils and my throat. I recognized it, even as I shuttled the thought aside. To smell that intensely meant it had to be a lot of blood.

Sweat prickled over my flesh. It didn't matter if wind raced through the building like the walls were a suggestion, everything about this place made me cold and left me sweating.

A scuffle of movement ahead and I dared to peek around Jasper. He had his gun in one hand and a flashlight in the other. I thought he'd been using his phone.

When a rat scurried across our path, I swallowed the automatic scream. I fucking hated rats. Like, the real ones.

Wasn't all that fond of the ones back at the clubhouse either, but they didn't come near me, and I wished these little brown ones didn't either. I shuddered when a second one followed the first, but Jasper just booted it out of the way. If it wouldn't distract him, I'd just climb up on his back.

The smell of copper and metal grew stronger, and I did my best to just breathe through my mouth. At the end of the hall, Jasper shoved open another door and the tension in him seemed to drain away.

"Fuck…" He exhaled the word. "Freddie."

I pushed to look around him, but stayed where I was supposed to be, and I got a good look at the room as Jasper scanned it with his flashlight.

The room, with its dingy-looking pallets on the floor, stacks of slated wooden crates being used for shelves, and the half-dozen or so bodies sprawled everywhere.

Fear choked me. "Freddie?" I couldn't see if he was one of them and even as I started forward, another movement caught my attention and Jasper swung the flashlight toward it.

"He's alive, Swan," Jasper told me in a hushed tone.

"Oh man," Freddie groaned. "Why'd you bring Boo-Boo here? This isn't anywhere Boo-Boo needs to be."

Three things about his voice hit me at once. The first, he sounded so damn tired. It made my bones ache with how weary his tone was. The second, despite the tiredness coloring his words, he didn't slur at all. He wasn't drunk or drugged. Mental fingers crossed, it wasn't just that it hadn't kicked in yet.

The third—he was in pain.

"Can I go to him?" I'd promised Jasper I would listen, but it was killing me to stay here. Freddie was in pain and I needed to help him.

"Anyone else here?" Jasper asked, and when Freddie didn't answer immediately as Jasper kept sweeping the room with his flashlight—none of the bodies moved—he snapped his name.

"No," Freddie said. "Just these guys and they aren't. I messaged you and then waited…forgot you had a date. Sorry, Hawk."

"Fuck," Jasper swore again, then glanced back at me. He passed me the flashlight. "Avoid the blood, Swan. Freddie, get your shit together. You need to look after her."

"Shouldn't be here," Freddie argued. "Take her home. I'll figure something out..."

"No," I told him as I accepted the flashlight. Making my way across the room to where Freddie waited wasn't easy. Blood was everywhere. The scent was overpowering in here and I kept seeing the doctor's office, but Freddie needed me here. Another light flashed on behind me.

Jasper's phone, maybe.

"Boo-Boo," Freddie said, shooting me a pained look when I got to him. Blood was all over his hands and spattered on his face. It was even sticking to his hair. He was a mess. "Don't want you to see me like this..."

"See, my friend?" I asked as I crouched down, careful of how far the blood reached. At least he'd chosen the cleanest spot. At least the boots and dress were black. I dropped to my knees then reached for his hand. "You came to see me when I was drooling and strapped to a bed. This doesn't seem that bad."

The harsh release of breath behind me almost made me wince. Jasper may not have known all the details, but it couldn't be helped now and if this could help Freddie, I could deal with it. The doctor put his hand on my arm and I shook my head, shaking off the cobwebs of that memory.

"Can I touch you?" I asked quietly, and Freddie lifted his hand. The flashlight was in my lap, giving us light to see but not shining in his eyes. The red streaked his skin. "It won't hurt me. But I don't want it to hurt you either."

He sighed. "I have a lot of blood on my hands, Boo-Boo."

"So did I."

That finally got him to look up and meet my gaze. The pain reflected in his eyes hurt so bad.

"That was different," he said, but we both knew that wasn't true. "Bodhi said he killed the doctor, remember?"

Jasper's quiet murmurs on the phone stopped abruptly.

"I know what he said—and I know what I did." My arm burned from swinging the stapler. The smell of blood had been everywhere then too. "Let me help? Please?"

Not moving and taking his hand was so hard, because right now, he needed someone to care. That haunting look in his eyes cracked something inside of me, a broken place where so many shattered pieces just dusted all the surfaces.

I couldn't force this. It had to be his choice and when he sighed, my heart fell. But instead of rejecting the offer, he took my hand with his. I ignored the tackiness and gripped his hand tightly.

"I'm sorry, Boo-Boo," he whispered. "This is—one of the ugly parts of me."

"Ugly doesn't scare me," I said, not making light of it. "Confession?"

He raised his brows then glanced past me before focusing on me again. "Little hard right now..."

"I know, but remember, we're both broken."

His expression crumpled. I didn't know if he reached for me or I reached for him, but when he hugged me so tight he squeezed the air out of me, I held on.

"Broken isn't bad," I whispered the reminder to him. Freddie shook, but his grip was fierce. With the flashlight between us, it created a void of light where Jasper knelt next to us. He put a hand on Freddie's shoulder.

"I'm going to start cleaning this up. Think you can take Emersyn and head outside?" The question wasn't directed at me, but I had a feeling he was asking me as much as Freddie.

A whistle sounded, and I jumped a little, but Freddie lifted his head. The tear streaks through the blood spatter were kind of beautiful, if macabre. "Just Kel," he said.

The door to the room pushed inward and more light flooded the room.

"Yeah," Jasper said, his expression guarded and worried. "Just Kel and Vaughn. So, we got this."

"We'll go in a sec," I said. Maybe Freddie needed a minute. He hadn't let me go and I kept my grip on him equally tight. Those hugs in my room late at night when I realized he was there—he'd saved my life. I wouldn't move.

"Dove's right," Vaughn said. He squatted down on the opposite side of us and pressed a kiss to the top of my head before he gave Freddie's shoulder a squeeze. It didn't escape me that neither Jasper nor Vaughn lingered in the touch.

It twisted my heart that they understood.

"Liam's here," Kellan said. "He came with Rome, and they're bringing in a tarp. Does Freddie need Doc?"

I didn't think so, but then I hadn't checked the blood on him.

"No," he answered. "They didn't touch me."

Relief swam through me at that admission. I didn't doubt that he'd killed them for a reason, but if he said they didn't touch him, then I didn't have to worry about *that* reason.

"We're here," Liam said, then gave a low hum of what sounded like appreciation. "Goddamn, Freddie, you're getting faster."

"Good," Rome said, and I smiled against Freddie's hair

when he gave a little shake. I wasn't sure if it was a sob or a laugh.

"Less talking, more cleaning," Jasper said, then paused. "If you don't mind me taking point here, Kel."

It was droll, sarcastic, and a little funny.

"Asshole," was all Kellan said. "Let's get the bodies up, then we'll get rid of everything else in here. Are these all of them—?"

The conversation muted some as the guys went to work. I had my back to them the whole time, and honestly, I didn't feel too bad about not seeing them haul out bodies.

In one of the rare moments where one of the other five weren't in the room and all the bodies had been dragged out, I stroked my clean hand against his hair. "Think we can move now?"

"Maybe," he said, then sighed. "I'm being a fucking child right now."

"I don't think so," I told him and he loosened his grip to lean back and look at me. The way the shadows and light danced over his face seemed right out of a horror movie, especially with the blood. But it was Freddie—*he* was Freddie. "I think something went wrong, and you took care of a problem, but then you called for help. That's pretty damn adult—and brave."

"I told you they're always cleaning up my messes," he said, his wry grin self-deprecating. But he stood and pulled me up with him. Which was good, cause my feet had gone to sleep the way I'd been kneeling. I ignored the pins and needles dancing up my legs as they started to wake up.

"They also didn't hesitate." Or demand answers. "You were right when you said they'd forgive me and it would be okay."

He lifted his hand to my cheek, then hesitated, and I

stepped a little closer and ignored the blood to lean into the touch. His sigh made even the icky tackiness worth it.

"I'd forgive you anything," he said.

"One hundred percent the same. Anything and everything."

With a sigh, he glanced away from me and toward where the bodies had been. "Guess you can't say I don't take you to interesting places."

The hopeful tilt to the corner of his mouth made me laugh. "Maybe we want to try some less interesting ones? Cause my last choice was definitely not a winner."

"True, yours sucked more," he agreed, then dropped his hand from my cheek and the knife he'd still held in his hand this whole time disappeared into a pocket. "I'm a mess."

"You know, I bet they have something to fix that."

He snorted. "Probably."

Then step by step, we made our way out of the building. Jasper looked up as we stepped outside and he nodded. They'd given him the time he needed to get up and walk out on his own. I threw him a grateful smile, and Jasper just ran his fingers down my arm before claiming the flashlight. Freddie held fast to my other hand.

Together, we headed toward the cars. The guys were there; the bodies nowhere to be seen. It had been a couple of hours since we'd gotten here. So maybe they'd already gotten rid of them. I didn't want to ask.

Liam and Kellan both straightened at our approach, and even though I couldn't see their eyes, I swore I could feel the way their gazes raked over me.

"Let's get you two home," Kellan said. "And fed—"

A loud pop sounded, like when a stage light blew out when I was on the stage. I jumped at the sound, shock racing through me. The guys moved, even Freddie, and we went down against the trash-strewn ground. Water soaked through one of my leggings, then more pops sounded.

These were a lot louder and a lot closer. Sparks danced.

Someone was shooting at us.

All of us.

31

Shots came from multiple directions. Cars blocked either end of the alley, and their lights came on, blinding us. Or maybe to blind us, I just waited for a shadow to cross the light and shot it.

"Let's go," Kellan called. Currently, we were too far apart. I was nearest to Freddie and Emersyn. Freddie had taken her all the way to the ground and one of the dumpsters provided some coverage. But not enough.

More than one bullet sparked off the pavement close to them. They could not stay there.

"Three," Liam called.

"Two," Vaughn answered.

I yelled, "One," but I was already moving. I hauled Freddie up, and he brought Emersyn with him and I covered them as bullets flew past us. Trusting their aim wasn't an issue.

The cover fire bought us time to get Emersyn out of the fucking trap closing in around us. Fortunately, Kellan parked his car on the other side of mine, so once Freddie and Emersyn were between them, I said, "Are you hurt?"

I scanned them both, but the blood on Emersyn could easily have come from Freddie and he looked like he'd rolled in it after gutting those drug dealers. A conversation for another time.

"No," Freddie said, the wild-eyed shock from earlier gone. "Boo-Boo?"

"I'm fine—I think I banged my knee. I'll live."

Yeah, every single fucking bruise on her was gonna be extracted in a pound of flesh. Nodding, I pointed at them both. "Stay."

"Sit, Ubu, sit," Emersyn muttered, and I almost laughed. The temptation to say "good dog" was right there, but another time. The wild firing had dialed back to sporadic. I moved in a crouch from between the cars to where Kellan crouched near Liam's SUV. It offered the bulkiest coverage, but I wanted solid iron on either side of Freddie and Emersyn.

"How many?" I checked my gun. I had a couple of extra magazines in the trunk, but maybe five left in this one.

"Too many."

Rome ghosted out of the shadows. "Ambush. No exits."

Fucking great. "Then we're fighting our way out." Even if it wasn't my call, the banked rage inside of me flamed. "This was a trap."

"Yep." No debate at all. Kellan's expression turned grim. "They lured Freddie here and baited the hook."

Couldn't have planned on Freddie wiping out the dealers—so, fuck you very much. "Diamonds or Royals?"

"It has to be the Diamonds," Liam said before he rose up and fired two shots in rapid succession. The heavy thud of a body hitting the pavement reminded me of just how good a shot he was. "Royals business in this town *I* run. I sure as fuck didn't set us up for an ambush."

"You sure you still run it?" Vaughn asked without an ounce of judgment. But he also didn't wait for an answer. "They've got backup coming, and while the flophouse was open, this place is an old factory and locked up tight. We might be able to get in, but there are steel bars on the windows."

Fucking great. I tried to picture the layout of the area from when we pulled in. It wasn't the first time we'd had to come into the Downs—still named for Winter Downs, who tried to rehab the whole area and went bankrupt in the attempt.

As places for an ambush went. This was a good one.

Glass cracked above us, splintered and spiderwebbed but it didn't break. I shot Liam a look. "Bulletproof?"

"Armored," he commented. "Not enough to get everyone out if we have to ram their vehicles."

Fuck. I wasn't the only one thinking.

"Whatever we're doing, we need to do it soon," Vaughn said. "No way they're going to leave us here. They just need to run us out of ammo, and we're fucked."

"How much ammo do we have?" Yeah, we weren't running hot on a regular basis and tonight was about a date, not a goddamn war.

"Draw them out. We're going to need to pull them to us." The grim note in his voice echoed the internal one in my head that didn't like any part of this. Especially with Freddie and Emersyn in the middle of it. "Rome and Vaughn, you're both better in close quarters. Stay here and keep anyone who gets past us from getting past you."

"Yep."

"I'll take left," I said.

Liam nodded. "I've got right. Kel?"

"Just rack 'em and stack 'em." The stony attitude and expression I got. "Might as well use this chokepoint to our advantage."

Agreed.

"Go."

It was eerie to rise up with Liam in perfect sync. It had been a long time since we'd been in any kind of fight—guns or otherwise—where we were solidly on the same side. I had five bullets. Not wasting them was key.

Movement flickered against the too-bright headlights, and I put a bullet in one.

Four left.

Another guy came hurling at me from behind the dumpsters, like he'd been lying in wait. I shot him, but the angle was wrong and it went through his shoulder. Slamming my gun against his face twice, I let him drop after something in his face cracked.

A bullet hit the ground in front of me and another whistled past so close that I swore it buzzed my ear, but I went low after and pointed toward the direction of the bullets.

Three.

Two.

With one bullet left, I snagged the gun from the guy I'd shot in the shoulder and brought it up with my free hand. The rush forward was going to throw off my shots, so I just fired the unfamiliar gun. Three shots and the headlights were out, plunging the alleyway into darkness. It was almost too dark with my eyes dazzled.

One.

Clip emptied, I relied on the borrowed gun before throwing myself to the side as a bar swung where my head had been. Irritation flamed through me. That was my move.

I kicked the guy's legs out as he tried to swing the bar in a downward arc. With a grunt, he fell and I locked my legs around him as he came down, catching the bar in my free hand and putting the gun right to his chest as he landed on it.

The sound reverberated through me, but the guy collapsed, his air whistling and wheezing. Even if he wasn't dead, a gut shot or a bullet through a lung wasn't going to let him do much. I did him a favor, clocked him with the crowbar.

By the time I got to my feet, I had eaten a fist in the shoulder but managed to swing the bar, catching one guy in the side of the head and the next guy right in the wrist.

Three more were coming and they were pissed. Yeah, this is exactly what we wanted, so I laughed as I shot another one. Nothing got people more pissed than when their ambush went awry.

Retreating, I pulled them back with me. Another four or five bodies hit the ground. I was losing count and I was out of bullets. The crowbar was fucking useful.

Spinning, I checked on Rome and Vaughn. They were in the middle of taking down two guys when I saw another going for Kellan.

"Duck," I ordered and he just dropped. With both hands, I flung the crowbar and it curved a little but still smacked the guy across the face. He went down and Kel shot someone right past me.

Then Liam was there, and we hauled Kellan up and fell back. The plan worked. Maybe a little too well.

"How many of these fuckers are there?" Vaughn asked, almost breathless.

"All of them," Kellan said. Liam's SUV was a fucking wreck and both tires on the far side were down. But Kel wasn't wrong, I'd taken down six or seven, and there was easily another half-dozen to take their place. We were rapidly running out of options.

"Fall back," I suggested, and that got a solid round of nods. We retreated to between my car and Kel's. Freddie and Emersyn were right there, Freddie's knife was out and he'd put Emersyn behind him. Good boy.

"New plan," Liam said. "Put Freddie and Hellspawn in Kel's car." He glanced at his twin, but Rome glared. "Fine, Vaughn with them. Then the three of us cover them. If we do enough damage, they can punch a hole and get out."

"Not a bad plan." I patted the car. "Need more ammo." Damn, well, I wished I'd had my bat too.

"We're not leaving you," Freddie argued and I glanced back at him.

"Kid, you're going to do as you're told. Because if you don't go, she won't go, and this is the last place we need to be."

"Doors are chained from the inside. No lock to pick." Well, it was worth trying.

"It would help if we could get inside?" Emersyn asked, speaking for the second time since the nightmare started. A couple of bullets pinged off my car and I tried not to think about how much of the paint job they'd already fucked up.

"It's not an option," Kellan said. "This plan would have been better with Liam's SUV."

Sure it would have, but that was before we realized how many there were. "Your car can handle it. Put Em down in the well behind the passenger seat, Freddie with her. Vaughn, you angle to shoot anyone you can and watch out for Kel."

It was a shitty plan for a shitty situation, and there were way too many things that could go wrong. Not the least of which was Kel getting a bullet in the head. There had to be something else...

"Starling." The note in Rome's voice had me twisting and I wasn't alone.

"What the fuck... Hellspawn," Liam snarled. "Get your ass back down here." Her ass, which along with the rest of her, was currently ascending an exterior drain pipe like it was nothing. A bullet slammed into the brick next to her and I wasn't the only one who turned.

Liam handed me a gun even as he and Kellan fired their own.

"Fuck me," Freddie whispered in a harsh breath. We sent some of those guys scurrying back, but all they needed was one good sight on her. She was in a dark dress and boots, but the red leggings stood out like a flag when she shifted.

I glanced upward again, just as a guy slid around the back of the car and then I ate a fist. Mother fucker. All Hell broke loose and the only thing making this fight tolerable was Freddie, launching into the fray with his knife, and he was fast and brutal. Rome and Vaughn weren't being remotely kind and I managed to get another gun.

But Emersyn wasn't in the middle of it. No, she was scaling the goddamn building like Spider-Woman or some shit. Liam took a blow and staggered. I caught the bat the guy was swinging at him and yanked it out of his hand.

Yeah, bats were my thing. With one shot, I disarmed the guy, then slid the gun to Vaughn so I could two-hand the bat. In close quarters, this was fucking perfect.

A chain fell behind, the racket suggesting it was being yanked at speed and then a door swung open.

"Fuck me, Dove did it," Vaughn sounded practically

triumphant and proud. I would be too, after I made sure she was fine.

"In," Kellan ordered. Inside, it would be a running fight, but we would have room to run and we could create choke points. The fact the cops hadn't shown up already said either no one was around to report this, or they'd been paid to stay out of it.

Probably both.

"Get Hellspawn," Liam said, urging Rome ahead of him. I cracked another skull as the guys retreated into the building.

"Freddie," I snapped. "Let's go." He sliced another throat and I bashed in the skull of the next guy. "Now."

He shot me a manic look but moved when I body checked him. "I can get them," he swore.

"Yeah, I know you can," I crowded him, shoving him into the building ahead of me while Vaughn and Kellan covered us. "Later."

Heat burned through my side and it was like being kicked by a fucking horse. I lunged forward, tackling Freddie through the door. The breathtaking pain was immediate and my nerves were all screaming. Lightheadedness wasn't far behind.

Fuck me.

"Let's go," I said, staggering. Freddie got his shit together and stopped trying to get past me, and then we were up.

Rome beckoned from another door fifty feet away. "Here."

Yep. That was the plan. The doors slammed behind us and we were off. I made it into the next hall and then fell back against the wall.

"Jasper." Emersyn let out a harried breath, and I stole a

look at our Swan, her eyes were wide and terrified. Her pretty hair had been completely disheveled, there was blood on her face and her hands were scraped and bloody.

But she was alive.

"Just a scratch," I assured her. "Nothing to worry about."

Hopefully, it was Vaughn who caught me, because someone cut my strings and I dropped. I didn't want to fall on her, and I really didn't want to get her any bloodier than she already was.

Our little badass.

32

Sleep proved elusive, even though I'd pushed it, working through the day and well into the evening. I wanted to be tired so I could sleep, but like so many other nights previous—it just wasn't coming. My arm and leg both ached, but the soreness was just a fact of life. I could blame old injuries for keeping me awake, but it wasn't happening.

Shoving the sheets back, I abandoned the pretense of sleeping and headed for the kitchen. It wasn't my scars and wounds keeping me awake, it was Emersyn's. She went back to some virtual hell without a word to anyone but Freddie and came back bruised, battered, sexually assaulted, and scarred.

The whiskey was above the fridge, but I ignored it and opened the fridge itself. If I didn't have clinic hours in the morning, the temptation to just get blind drunk was right there. From everything I'd gleaned from the guys and from what she'd told me herself... the abuse had been going on since she was a child.

A fucking child.

What had I said to her?

Bracing a hand on the freezer door, I bowed my head. Getting her off with her hand and then telling her she was too young for me had been a dick move designed to distance myself.

To make it easier for Milo.

To make it easier for me.

It did not make it fucking easier for her.

That was the part that made me the asshole she wanted nothing to do with. Mission fucking accomplished. I snagged the orange juice out and unscrewed the cap before saluting myself and taking a drink.

Now, I not only had a battle to earn her forgiveness but to get her to trust me again. If she did, maybe I could coax her into the clinic where we could use the ultrasound. The guys running interference weren't helping, but then... I couldn't really say much, could I?

I wasn't sure I was helping at the moment.

Putting the juice down, I gripped my left shoulder and dug my fingers into the muscle and scar tissue there. The whole thing throbbed. The problem was a good chunk of the nerves there were dead. So, half of it was ghost pain and half of it was real.

When my phone went off ringing, I doubled back to the bedroom to grab my cell off the charger. Kellan's name on the screen sent apprehension slicing through me, cutting off my own pain.

"What do you need?" I asked, fighting the urge to ask if she was all right first.

"Jasper's been shot. We had a hell of a dust-up and

we're heading back to the clubhouse. I need you there now."

"How bad and where?" I put the phone on speaker and set it down while grabbing clothes. They had supplies there and I had stuff here. But the clinic would be better—and more sterile.

"Side, he's lost a lot of blood. It took us a while to get out of there." His voice was tight, controlled, like he had every single emotion on lockdown.

"It's a fucking flesh wound," Jasper argued, but the ragged note in his voice belied that.

"It is not a damn flesh wound," Emersyn countered and there was a sound of a slap. "Stop making light of it. Tell Doc to hurry."

Oh yeah. I was hurrying. "On my way."

I didn't wait for his response, just hung up, grabbed my bag, an extra case of medical supplies including sutures, and then I got my gun out of the gun safe.

They'd been in a goddamn gun battle and she'd been in the middle of it. Jasper first. Then answers after.

I pulled into the warehouse, only beats ahead of them. Rats had the door open and one of them, Shaun-whatever, jogged toward me. "Kestrel said to get you whatever you need."

We had the med room or we had the interior, depending on how bad it was… "Do we have an open room in the clubhouse?"

"Four currently," Shaun answered as Kellan's car pulled in, and it sure as Hell looked like it had gone through a fucking war. Freddie was the first one out of the car and he was covered in blood.

"Get everything from the med room and a flat table big enough for Jasper into an open room. Then wipe it all down. Go." The guy didn't slow down as he pivoted to run. Spotting two more rats, I whistled and they turned toward me. "Get these things and bring them with me, then stay close because I'm sending out for more."

Fortunately, neither of them argued as I moved to the back door where Little Bit emerged—the blood on her had my heart stalling for a minute.

"It's not hers," Kellan said as he slammed his way out of the car. "We need to move it. JD, get your ass over here as soon as you haul that crap in for Doc."

Leaving that for them to deal with, I nudged Emersyn out of the way so I could get a look at Jasper. He was gray-faced, sweating, and his breathing was shallow and harsh. There was a thick wad of bandaging around his mid-section and the blood was already soaking through it.

"Okay, first thing first, we're getting you out of here and into a make-shift exam room. How much shit are you planning to give me?"

"It's a flesh wound," he growled. "I can get myself there."

Right. A lot of shit. I straightened and looked right at Kellan. It was just the four of them. "Grab his legs."

I circled the car to go in the back, and he grunted when I gripped his shoulders. I'd climb across with him. Kellan was already in place.

"I said—" Jasper started.

"Jasper," Emersyn snapped, startling all of us—well, Jasper more than the rest of us. "Stop it and let them help you."

He grumbled, but he shut up. I'd take it. Kellan led the way. Unfortunately, there was no way to carry him inside without jostling him and I kept an eye on where the blood spot on the bandages was growing. In and up the stairs, we angled to the left when most of their rooms were to the right.

The first door to the left of the stairs stood open and there was a table, with bandages and more, along with my gear. I needed to triage, first, check that the bullet was out. We didn't have an x-ray here, but I could send them to the clinic for the portable one.

"I'm going to need stuff from the clinic."

"Give me a list," Kellan said as he helped me get him up on the table. Jasper's eyes had already closed, and his face had gone grayer, if that was possible. Emersyn was right behind us and the rats were clearing the room.

"I need the portable x-ray, it'll work with the laptop I have here. Get me clean bandages, a couple of banana bags from the locked storage, and IV tubing."

I pulled my keys out and tossed them to him.

"Code hasn't changed."

He nodded. "Stay here, stay locked in. The rats stay out." The rats in question left, then Kellan glanced at Emersyn.

"I want to stay with him."

"Not even a question, Sparrow." He wrapped a hand around her throat and then kissed her hard and swift. Anger unfurled in me at the clearly possessive act, but I jerked my attention from them back to the patient.

Great, his eyes were open, and he gave me a faint smirk. "Get used to it," he told me in a wheezing breath.

"Concentrate on taking deep breaths. I'm gonna cut this shirt off and get a look at that wound. But first, breathe for me."

I had my stethoscope out and a pair of gloves on. Emersyn appeared in my periphery, and when I glanced over, Kellan was gone. She really did look like a wreck.

"Clean up," I told her. "There's sanitizer and wipes in my bag. Get as much of that blood off you as you can, then glove up if you're staying."

When I turned back to Jasper, he gripped my wrist. It wasn't that tight of a hold, but his glare said it wasn't the point. "Watch your tone with her…"

I met his gaze steadily. "You can keep holding my wrist and pretending like you're a threat to me until you pass out from blood loss, or you can shut the hell up and let me work. Worry about my tone when you're not bleeding out."

"Jasper, please let him help you."

He scowled then cut a look toward her, then back to me and I blew out a breath. "I'm a little focused on helping you, Hawk. Let me do my damn job. I'll apologize to her afterwards."

"Acceptable." He dropped his hand back to the table and I swore he was fighting tooth and nail to stay awake. It would probably be easier on him if he just passed out.

"I'm not going to have time to be gentle," I warned him.

"Just do it."

Emersyn reappeared on the opposite side of the table. "What can I do?"

"Hold his hand and keep him focused on you. This isn't going to be pretty."

She didn't hesitate, taking his right hand in hers and clasping it to her chest. "I have a question," she said to Jasper. "Do all our dates end like this?"

He let out a wheezing laugh, and I nodded to her, then went to work. The bandaging was makeshift and definitely consisted of someone's shredded shirt. Blood began to pool as soon as I got it clear of the wound.

Definitely an exit, it was pretty clean. Low-caliber bullet. Close range. They were lucky someone hadn't been shot right through him. I glanced over to where Emersyn held his attention. She leaned over him so he didn't have to strain and she kept talking.

Blocking it out, I focused on the wounds as I packed the front to staunch the blood flow, then checked the back. He grunted every time I moved him. Entrance wound said it was definitely small caliber.

Good. He could breathe deeply, no sounds of water in his lungs. The blood loss was a concern, but he and Kellan had the same blood type. Same as mine.

We could both donate, if necessary. It wasn't long before Kellan was back with everything I needed. He wore a harried look, then cut a glance at Emersyn. Yeah, he was worried.

"She's fine. I'm armed, and I have them both. Go do what you need to do."

"Thank you," Kellan said, then looked at Jasper. "Don't get dead."

"Swan promised me a second date, got everything to live for," Jasper fired back. Yeah, his voice was getting weaker. I got an IV set up and loaded him up on fluids, then added something to help him sleep. He might not want to pass out, but the next couple of hours were not going to be fun.

Emersyn didn't move, even after he went to sleep. If I needed something, she got it. When I used the portable x-ray, she moved behind me and then helped pass me what I asked for.

It took next to an hour to make sure we had everything cleaned out. He'd been damn lucky, a half an inch over and it could have perforated a kidney or, worse, his intestines.

By the time I had him stitched up, he was sleeping for

real and not just from the sedative I gave him. His pulse was steady.

"Is he really going to be okay?" she asked. It was the first question she'd directed at me since we'd gone to work. I met her gaze and found a smile.

What she needed was comfort and good bedside manner. What she got was me. "It's a good thing he's a stubborn bastard."

A smile flickered on her lips. "Yeah?"

"Yeah, he's gonna need to take it easy—which will be a miracle if we can pull that off short of tying him to a bed."

"I'll sit on him if I have to," she promised, and I snorted.

At her frown, I shook my head. "Little Bit, you sitting on him might not encourage him to lie still."

Her mouth opened into a little 'o' and I shrugged. Then she had to bite her lip as though she were going to laugh. Instead of responding, she looked at Jasper again. It gave me a moment to study her. She'd cleaned up a lot of the blood, but while she was pale, she was also radiating determination.

She seemed more like the Little Bit I'd been getting to know when she first came here. Full of piss and vinegar, ready to take them all on. She could probably do it too.

"Soon as we get the all-clear," I said as I stripped off my gloves. "You should go grab a shower and change. Then we need to get rid of those clothes."

"I actually kind of liked this dress," she mumbled, then lifted her shoulders. "I know why we need to get rid of it, I just..."

"It's okay, Little Bit. Really. We can look into finding you—"

The door locks tumbled and I put a hand on my gun, waiting before it opened, and Kellan stood there. He was freshly showered and had new clothes on with clothes in his hand.

"You need to change," he said to Emersyn, then glanced at me. "We have cops incoming."

Son of a bitch.

33

The impending arrival of the police sent my pulse skyrocketing again. I shot a look to where Jasper slept. Doc said he'd given him something for the pain and it had relaxed the tension from his face. The only thing I'd done upon getting back was strip off my jacket. I even still had the purse strong across my chest.

Peeling it off, I didn't waste time with modesty. We couldn't afford it, and I didn't want to leave Jasper. Soon as I was out of the boots, I loosened the fastenings on the wrap dress.

"Fuck," Doc swore, and I spared him a look as he cut his gaze away, but he didn't turn.

"It's hardly the first time," I reminded him. Not that I should have to. "A body is a body."

"That's not the point," he argued, but he wasn't looking away anymore. I stripped down to the bra and panties. The leggings clung to me and it took some effort to peel them off. Blood stained my legs and there were crusty bits that had become tacky.

"Here," Kellan said as he moved over to me. "Can I?"

It took me a minute to realize he had wipes in his hand. "Yes." Fuck, they were cold against my skin, but he gripped my leg with a warm hand then scrubbed the flaking blood off.

"You have more on your back," Doc said. He had already cleaned up most of his scattered tools and sacked together the copious amounts of bloody gauze bits.

"There's blood on the floor too."

"I'll get her back," Kellan said. "You get the floor."

"Sure, I'll get the floor." The tone was almost wry, and I laughed. This was surreal.

"I'd offer, but I'm kind of messy too," I said, but the corners of his mouth turned up.

"You're a beautiful mess, Little Bit. We've got this." The thing was, for as calm as they were both being, neither of them stopped moving. Kellan went over both my legs and when he passed me another wipe, I went to work scrubbing my arms.

Goosebumps rippled over my skin. The room wasn't exactly warm, to begin with. Even with all of us in here. As when I'd washed my hands earlier, the scrapes stung when I handled the wipes.

Kellan caught my wrist lightly and inspected both of my palms. "Don't think I've forgotten you going up that drain pipe."

"The important thing is, it worked." Oddly, I had. But at the time, it was just what I needed to do. There were windows on the third floor that weren't barred. I got in that way.

Exhaling a breath, he just shook his head. "Later, Sparrow."

That sent another shiver through me that had absolutely nothing to do with the cold. With care, he went over my face, then my hair, using the wipes to scrub in several places.

"I can pull it up into a ponytail or something," I assured him. He didn't look wholly convinced or pleased, for that matter. But he passed me the clothes. The first was an over-sized sweatshirt. It had to be one of theirs, I didn't worry about whose. Fresh leggings from my room were with it and, oh, socks.

They were the thick fluffy kind. I shivered as I pulled them on and Kellan frowned. "You're cold."

"I'll be okay," I assured him when he cupped my cheek and covered his hand with mine. "What else do we need to do?"

Cause they were going to ask about Jasper being shot. Doc hadn't found a bullet when he'd explored the wound or when he'd x-rayed it. Also, I never wanted to see that again.

Like ever.

Kellan's steady gaze held me in place as he seemed to search me for something. "We need to get Jasper down to his room and in his bed. The chances are high they will search the place from top to bottom. They are going to ask you questions..."

"I can handle it. I'm staying with Jasper?"

For a moment, I thought he would disagree, but then he looked to where Jasper was out and nodded, even if he seemed to be a little reluctant. "Don't fight them if they come into his room or knock on the door. Be as cooperative as you can. Don't offer more information than they ask for —and Sparrow, I don't want to ask you to lie."

"You can," I assured him and straightened. "I'm really good at it, despite what you might think."

That earned me another frown. "A topic for another day." Then he kissed me. The hard press of his lips to mine was less sexual and more just a connection that I clung to before he finally released me. "I'll find you as soon as this is done. No matter what happens, you do not engage. Clear?"

The last was a direct order. The fact that he felt the need to give it to me made me roil with objection. But we did *not* have time for that. "Clear."

As much as I hated it, I nodded. The door to the room opened and Vaughn was just there. Like Kellan, he looked freshly showered. However, his bruises were more than visible in the red marks decorating his face.

"We have maybe five minutes," Vaughn warned. "Rats are spread out, but there's definitely two cars outside and a third coming in. They'll move soon."

Kellan nodded. "Let's get him moved. Take the whole damn table."

He let me go, and Doc caught my arm to tug me back as Vaughn took one end of the table and Kellan the other. Rather than stay with me, Doc moved with them, controlling the banana bag.

My discarded clothes were gone, but I snatched up my purse and then looked around the room. Rome was there, though. "Go, Starling, I will finish."

I caught his hand and he squeezed my fingers, then ducked his head for my kiss. "Are you all right?"

"I'm here," he promised and I blew out a breath.

"Liam is still all right?"

He shrugged. "He's annoyed. He'll yell at you later. Let him?"

I grinned, after tonight—I'd let all of them yell at me if

they had to. Even Freddie. Maybe especially Freddie. "I promise. I have to—"

"Go," he said. "Take care of Hawk."

I would. That was my plan. I hurried down the hall toward Jasper's room. Kellan and Vaughn were already coming out with the table. They paused only so Vaughn could sweep me up into a tight hug.

"You scared the hell out of me out there, Dove," he scolded as he squeezed me tight. "You were also awesome." Not giving me any time to respond, he set me on my feet before he picked up the other end of the table and they moved.

Doc was adjusting the bag to hang on something near the head of Jasper's bed. They'd tucked him in. He looked for all the world like he was asleep.

"He's got whiskey over here," Doc said, nodding to a couple of bottles sitting on the dresser. "If you need it." I didn't get it immediately until he nodded to Jasper.

"Got it."

If I needed to explain why he wasn't waking up. "Little Bit?"

"Yes?"

"It's going to be fine, believe that. That's how we get through this. It's all normal and it's going to be fine."

I really wanted to share the confidence he demonstrated in those words, but for now, all I could do was nod.

"Lock the door behind me."

"D—Mickey..." I said as I followed him and he paused to look at me. "Thank you."

"You never have to thank me. I did it for him every bit as much as I did it for you—and I am sorry if I snapped at you earlier."

"You didn't, or maybe you did, but your focus was

where it needed to be. He's just grumpy." This was an easy thing to forgive because it wasn't anything at all.

"I'll see you soon." He tapped the door to reiterate his earlier point, then closed it. I turned the lock and patted the door once. He answered it with a single muted knock, like he'd patted the door too.

Leaning back against the door, I closed my eyes and took a deep breath. I could do this. Pushing away, I crossed over to the bed where I could sit beside him—I chose the floor next to the bed rather than the bed itself.

The last thing I wanted was to disturb him. Leaning my head against the bed, I focused on the door. It was late when we left the movie, and I'd lost all track of time except for the fact that my eyes were sore. I didn't want to close them.

I half-drifted when a fist hammered on the door and I shot to my feet. Heart hammering, I glanced at Jasper. His eyes were still closed and his face peaceful. It was hard to tell whether I'd been asleep for five minutes or five hours.

Wiping drool from the corner of my mouth, I headed for the door. The hard knock came again just before someone tried the knob. The rooms were pretty proofed for sound, so if they were saying anything, I couldn't hear it.

Unlocking it, I took a deep breath and then cracked the door open. A part of me really hoped it was Milo or something in a bad mood, but no, there was a uniformed officer standing right there.

"Ma'am," he said, surprise flickering across his face. I hadn't put my hair up into a ponytail or even really brushed it, so it was a tangled mess that I had to shove out of my face.

"Can I help you?"

"Do you live here?"

I shrugged. "Sure."

"May we come in?" He motioned to another officer who approached. They were both rather large men, their outfits were bulky, and their expressions ranged from polite to severe.

"I don't think so," I continued. If they pushed their way in, it might be a problem, but right now, I'd take my chances.

The men shared a look then the one who'd knocked backed up a step. "Do you mind stepping out?"

"Will you go away sooner if I do?" I kept my tone as even as I could, but I was tired, so I opted for the truth. "I don't even know what time it is and I got to bed late."

The dark-skinned man hid a quick smile with a cutaway glance as the other man gave me a look. "It's possible. Please, ma'am, if you'll step out and just let us do our jobs."

My debating on locking the door was lost to the idea that I might need to get right back in. Instead, I opened it only enough to slip out and then closed it behind me. Arms folded, I leaned back against the door.

Vasquez and Sommerland.

"Miss," Vasquez said, his expression almost kind. "Your name?"

"No offense, but why are you knocking on my door in the middle of the night?"

"You are aware of where you are, correct?" Sommerland asked in a slightly harsher tone. Apparently, patience only went so far.

"Yeah, I know where I am. I also know I was sleeping. Anything else?"

"Miss," Vasquez interrupted the other man and gripped his shoulder. "We are sorry for waking you up. First—you seem awfully young to be here, do your parents know where you are?"

"Probably not, but they don't need to know. I'll be nineteen in a few weeks, so it's not really an issue."

The officer nodded slowly, but his frown grew in intensity. "You're Emersyn Sharpe."

Well, fuck.

"I'm aware of who I am," I said, then tried for a smile that I just wasn't feeling. "I know who I am. I know where I am. I even know you're police officers named Vasquez and Sommerland. What I don't know is why you're bothering me."

Also, mostly true.

"You've been missing—"

"I'm not missing. I'm right here."

"You were reported missing," Vasquez continued, his voice still kind but his gaze very grave. "You've been missing for some time since the show you had here in the city last winter."

"Oh." I shrugged. "To be honest, I needed a break. I've been pretty much working nonstop for the last decade, often six nights a week with two matinees on the weekends. Minor downtime here and there. It's exhausting, I'm sure you understand."

"So," Sommerland said, squinting at me. "You just—take off and join a gang."

I canted my head at him. "Don't be absurd. I left of my own accord. The situation with the company wasn't always pleasant, and I just got tired of it. Like I said, I was within my rights to leave."

"If that was the case, why would they report you missing rather than you just quitting? Not to mention, your boyfriend went with you."

I didn't know who pissed in his coffee, but Sommerland was definitely not a fan. "Who?"

"Your boyfriend, the dance partner—Eric Arlington."

Manufacturing disgust wasn't even hard. "He was *never* my boyfriend."

"He went missing at the same time you did," Vasquez said, cutting off his partner again. "You can see how that looks."

"Not really. I didn't go missing. I don't know what happened with him." I shrugged. "I don't really care either. Are we done now?"

"She's not going to cooperate. We do have a missing person's case, and we can just take her in..."

"No, you can't," I cut him off. "I'm not a criminal. I've done nothing wrong. The last time I checked, an adult going to do what they wanted isn't against the law. Under what pretense would you even begin to take me into custody?" Tired *and* annoyed, I raised my chin and pinned Sommerland with a look. "I'd love to call my attorney to report police harassment, along with possible wrongful arrest and false imprisonment. I really, really would."

If there was one thing I knew how to handle, it was pushy, overbearing men.

"Listen, you little..."

"Emersyn," Milo called, his rough voice carrying down the hall. "Are you all right?"

"I'm fine," I told him, flashing a smile toward him before letting it fall away and focusing on Vasquez. "I am fine, right, gentlemen? I can go back to bed? I answered your questions—" I spared Sommerland a brief look. "Even your rude ones."

"Yes," Vasquez answered, cutting off his partner again. "Thank you for talking to us. I understand that it is late and we did wake you up." He and Sommerland both backed up a little when Milo reached us. "This is my card," he continued, holding out the business card to me. "If you need anything—anything at all—you can call me."

"Thanks?" I didn't have to pretend to be puzzled.

"Officers," Milo said in a stony voice. "The rest of us would like to go to bed soon, if you're done."

Sommerland muttered something rude before he stalked off, but Vasquez eyed me then Milo. "Mr. Hardigan, we're just doing our jobs."

"Right, and harassing her in the hallway when she's clearly dead on her feet is your job. Not to mention your partner's stellar attitude."

With a sigh, Vasquez rubbed a hand over his face. "Look, I get it. You guys get rousted periodically. You don't like it. We don't like it. But it happens. We got a report, and we had to follow up on it. And now Miss Sharpe is here—" He raised a hand as he nodded to me. "Of her own free will, she's made the statement that she's not under duress, nor is she missing."

"Great." Milo clapped his hands together and pasted on a smile so false you'd have to be an idiot to fall for it. "Then we can walk you guys out and lock up while Emersyn gets back to bed." The smile he gave me was at least genuine. "You good, kid?"

"Just tired." I rubbed his arm. "Thank you."

"Go get some sleep. Lock up before you go back to bed."

I rolled my eyes. "I do know how doors work."

He chuckled.

Awareness of Vasquez's observation weighed on me.

"Look, I'm overprotective and you're cute. Deal with it." The droll remark actually did make me smile.

"I'll think about it." Then waving the card at the officer,

I nodded to him. "Thank you for being concerned, Officer Vasquez. If you need me to come in and fill out something so you can prove I'm not missing, I can do that."

"Might be helpful," he said. "But you don't have to do it right now."

"Thank God, I'm going to bed. Night." Not waiting for anyone else, I slid back into Jasper's room, locked the door and sagged against it.

The trembling of the card in my hand betrayed how hard I was shaking. I stayed against the door for another minute, half-worried someone would knock again. But they didn't.

On wavering legs, I walked back to the bed to check on Jasper. The fact he was still asleep helped, a lot. I sank back into my spot on the floor and took his hand before I tucked my head against the side of it.

When he woke up and told me he was okay, then it would all be fine. I would tell myself that over and over until I believed it.

34

The cops took forever to leave. They hadn't been kidding when they said they planned to do a search. Kellan refused to make them get a warrant and I got it, I really did. At the same time, I hated having them there.

Hated that my fucking weakness led to this. When the first cop took our names, I'd given him a look. Dan Vasquez had picked me up on drunk and disorderly, vandalism, and more than a few cases of loitering over the last few years.

"Dunlap," I snapped. "Frederick Dunlap. Want me to spell it?"

"Cleary," Rome said. "Not Dunlap."

Wait—what? I twisted to look at him. He wasn't kidding. Then Rome didn't always have a sense of humor, not really. Too direct for that.

"Cleary," Liam said as he came out of the kitchen with a beer. "Your last name. You're adopted. I know it was only a few weeks ago, but you're a Cleary now, Baby Brother, get that through your head."

Rome nodded and then looked at Vasquez. "Cleary. C-L-E-A-R-Y."

"Got it. You want to tell me where you were tonight, Mr. *Cleary*?" The faintest note of humor touched the name, but it wasn't funny. Like Rome wasn't funny.

I stared at Liam and Rome. Were they serious?

"You might want to answer him," Liam suggested as he moved to take a seat on the sofa, kicking his feet up like he didn't have a care in the world. Kellan and Vaughn were at the pool table. They'd started a game the second they'd come down, about two minutes before the cops knocked at the door.

"Where I usually am," I said to Vasquez. "Here or down at the convenience store—wait...I don't have that job. So, I was here. Or did I go to the laundromat? Nope. Didn't do that either. Not allowed to, after I mixed the reds and the whites. Guys think pink underwear is too much, but I kind of liked it. Better than streaked ones, you know..."

Vasquez sighed, then pinched his brow. "Are you using again, kid?"

I jerked my head around and glared at him. "I'm fucking clean. Want me to piss in a cup?" Okay, maybe not my best idea, so hopefully they wouldn't take me up on it.

"That's a rhetorical question," Liam said. "By the way, if you really want him to piss in a cup, you'll need a warrant and have to go through my attorney." He held up a business card.

With another sigh, Vasquez just shook his head. "No, I'm good. All right, let's move on to you, Mr. O'Connell."

I kind of tuned out a little as they went around the

room. When they went upstairs, I'd half-followed. We wanted to keep them away from Jas.

Jas, who'd gotten fucking shot because I called him. The minute Emersyn appeared, though, an army couldn't have made me move from where I stood like some fucking creeper, watching around the corner.

They hammered her with questions, but she didn't back down or give an inch. When she got haughty, I did a little fist pump. Then Milo strode up the stairs past me, and I wanted to cheer again.

Apparently, Raptor had decided to come out and play. Go him. It was still another couple of hours before the cops left—empty-handed. The one place I'd been worried about them going—the office—I shouldn't have. It had been redecorated with new bookshelves and there was a stack of invoices along with equipment and more.

Goddamn, Kellan was good.

Doc had been absent for most of the search and the questioning. I wasn't even sure how he got out of the clubhouse, much less *when*, before he strolled back inside with coffee and breakfast sandwiches. The sky outside had given way to dawn.

Fuck my life, no wonder I was tired.

"Hey," Liam said when I was heading back into the clubhouse. I needed to go to sleep, or I was going to do something stupider than I already had.

"Yeah?"

"You good?" The question didn't surprise me. Not really. I'd be checking up on my loser ass too.

"Fine."

"Right." The corners of his mouth dipped. "Freddie, you need something, you say it. You don't go looking to score without backup, got it? You don't dismiss shit."

"Fuck, you sound like Jasper." That made my gut ache.

"Probably because he gives a damn about what happens to you too. Even when you don't."

Jas, I got. Sorta. He'd always been right there, in my corner, as ready to lend a hand as kick me in the ass. I stared at Liam. "Why?"

"You get to ask me that once," he said, seeming to pick his words with care. "But get this straight. Rome and me? We cared *before*. But I meant it when I said you were officially our kid brother. I don't abandon my brothers—ever. Do whatever you gotta do with that, Freddie Cleary, to keep it in your head."

What was I supposed to do with that? I just lifted my shoulders and nodded.

"Good," Liam said. "Now, go get some sleep before you pass out." The guys were all talking, but I just didn't have planning in me.

Taking my out, I headed upstairs. I just needed to have a minute. My hands shook as I walked down the hall toward my room. The cops had been in it. I didn't care if they tossed it. Nothing in there could hurt anyone.

It was embarrassing, but privacy was not something any of us had for long. Instead of going to my door though, I went down to Jas's. I checked the door handle, but it was locked. Digging in my pockets, I hunted up my picks. I'd had those on me, not in the room. Safer that way.

With the way my hands trembled, it took me a second to get the lock freed, then I was in. The room was dark except for the fairy lights that Jas strung everywhere. His room was never truly dark. Nothing could leap out of the darkness to get you if you didn't let the darkness in.

I gave my eyes a minute to adjust. Jas's soft snore carried, that was something. I eased forward. He was asleep in the bed, the covers were up to his chest so I couldn't see any bandages.

Fuck, there had been so much blood earlier. Blood on him. On me. In the car. On Boo-Boo.

She wasn't in bed with him but curled up on the floor and sound asleep with her head against the mattress and her hand in his.

Man, Jas would be pissed. How fucking tired did she have to be to even sleep like that? I glanced up at Jas again. Yeah, she didn't need to be on the floor. This was about getting her up and into the bed where Jas would want her. Not me needing to just talk to her.

I still couldn't believe she'd sat with me in the middle of all that blood, even with the demons in her eyes, and stayed with me. I didn't deserve Boo-Boo.

"Hey," I said softly, crouching next to her but not touching. No, Boo-Boo decided when she got touched. No one else. "Boo-Boo."

It took me saying her name a couple more times before her eyes fluttered up. A frown creased her brow and she jerked to look at Jasper. Shit, I didn't think about it freaking her out and worrying her.

"He's fine," I told her, even if she could see it for herself. "Just wanted to get you off the floor. Jas would rather have you in the bed next to him."

"I don't want to jostle him," she said with a yawn, then stretched.

"I get it," I said, keeping my voice low like she was. The fact Jas slept through me getting in his room at all was enough to worry me. Maybe I needed to sleep in here too, guard the door or something. "If you don't want to get in the bed, we can haul that chair over here. Or something—I could go get a mattress and drag it in here."

Though it would not really fit in the room the way Jasper had it set up. The chair would work. At least it leaned back. He really liked those recliners when he bought them. They were in here so nobody spilled beer on his chairs.

"I can go to the chair, or I can move a blanket and pillow down here. I don't want to be somewhere else if he wakes up."

That sunk me. "Right. Okay."

Swinging around the bed, I grabbed the extra pillows from the other side, then went for an extra blanket. Boo-Boo got up while I was finding stuff and disappeared into the bathroom. The toilet flushed then she washed her hands before she came back out. I patted the floor next to the bed where I'd layered two of the blankets, then used the pillows for our backs.

As soon as she was seated, I settled next to her and pulled another blanket over us. When my hand brushed hers, I frowned. "You're freezing."

"I'm fine. This is warm." She pulled the blanket up and I shifted. I didn't like that she was cold. I'd thrown myself through a shower earlier and changed, but I didn't have a jacket or hoodie or anything.

"Can I put my arm around your shoulders?"

She blinked at me sleepily and I wanted to take it back. "Can I lay my head on your shoulder?"

"Yeah," I said, able to breathe again with her answer. I lifted my arm and she scooted over. Even in her sweatshirt, leggings, and socks—or maybe because of them—the fact her hands were so icy bugged me.

When she settled her head against my shoulder and I had my arm wrapped around her, we sorted the blanket some more. Pressing my cheek to her hair, I sighed.

"Are you okay?" It was a quiet question in the half-dark of the room and I tried to find a smile but I failed.

"I screwed up, Boo-Boo." The words just tumbled out of me. "I've been...struggling since we got back. I've gone to score three times."

Admitting that stung. It was hardly my first time doing it. Hell, it wasn't even my tenth or twentieth. But saying it to her was like trying to push the words out over broken glass that dug into my throat.

"I changed my mind the first time. Just bailed out and left. Came back here and tried to pretend I didn't do it. The second time, I bought it. I knew I shouldn't have, but I got it anyway—then I threw it away. Well, flushed it."

She said nothing as I opened my veins and poured it all out. But she also didn't pull away or make a disgusted sound for how fucking pathetic I was.

"Third time...third time I was fucking close. I was ready to snort it, shoot it, swallow it—whatever— to make it stop. Then I kept seeing that fucking hospital and remembered how zombied out you were, and I said that wasn't for me. Don't do it. Just don't—I tossed it, but I almost didn't."

She moved her hand and it appeared in my periphery, palm up. I slid my free hand into hers and she closed her fingers around mine, hooking our pinkies together. It was ridiculous how good that felt.

"Tonight—tonight I went cause I just needed it all to stop, and they started giving me shit, they wouldn't stop calling me fucking names and then asked me if I planned to whore myself out for my habit and... I lost it, Boo-Boo. I fucking lost it."

Water and salt slid down to my mouth and I licked it away.

"I fucked up bad, and now Jas has been shot and they could have killed you and the guys and..."

When I pressed my face against her hair, she wrapped her arms around me, and fuck, that hug was nice. It was like when she hugged me in that fucked up slaughterhouse of a room with all its bodies. Bodies I'd made. I'd just lost it and when I stopped, they were all dead, and I was the only one standing.

Gradually, through the tears and the roaring in my head, the fact she was talking penetrated.

"I'm here, Freddie," she said. She kept saying it. Over and over. "I'm here."

It just made me cry harder.

Not once did she let me go.

Not once.

I didn't know when it stopped, but I had to move, she was half-kneeling and wrapped around me and it was all awkward. I was a snotty fucking mess. Pathetic—except—I really couldn't remember the last time I cried.

And here I was snotting right into her hair. Real good, Freddie. Classy. That was me. Liam and Rome should reconsider that adoption thing. Finally, I dragged my head up. My eyes hurt like a bitch and my face was wet and hot. Instead of running away, she lifted her head to look at me.

"Am I dreaming?" I finally asked in a hoarse voice and the corners of her mouth tipped up. The fact that her eyes were wet gutted me. She should never cry, least of all for me.

"Am I naked?"

A laugh escaped, half-sob, half-chuckle, and I lifted the blanket to look. "Pretty sure that's a no."

"Then you're not dreaming."

As I pulled back, she withdrew and I scrubbed my hands over my face trying to get rid of the tears.

"Wait," she whispered, brushing my arm with her fingers lightly. It was a there and gone again sensation. "I'll be right back."

She ducked into the bathroom. The water came on, and she really wasn't long. When she came back out, she had a glass of water, some aspirin, and a washcloth.

"You can take these, right?"

"Yeah, they don't get me high." Not that I blamed her for asking, and my head fucking hurt. I took three of them and washed them down with water. Instead of leaving, she settled back down next to me and urged me to lay my head back against the bed.

Agreeing seemed the easier thing to do, so I did, and when I would have stared up at the lights, she covered them with the washcloth. It was cold and damp, the weight and coolness felt good against my eyes.

"Arm around my shoulders again?"

"You don't have to," I assured her.

"But I want to put my head on your shoulder."

Oh.

"Okay." I kept my eyes closed while she curled back up against me and settled my arm around her. "Boo-Boo?"

"I'm here," she promised as if I couldn't feel her leaning into me.

"I'm sorry."

"Not where I was going," she murmured and I frowned.

"No?"

"Nope."

"Oh." Wait. "I was the one who said your name. You weren't going anywhere."

"I know," she said, and I could almost hear her smile. It

was crazy, but that one little thing made me feel better—more better? Betterer? Fuck words—than anything else.

"Thank you," I whispered, but the soft sound of her breathing wrapped around me, slow and even. She'd gone back to sleep. Guess I was staying right here.

Here was good.

35

Not even twenty-four hours after the ambush, I stood in Liam's apartment with a glass of whiskey in one hand while facing off with two men I'd called brother for more than half my life. Milo had been reluctant to leave Emersyn. I got it. I didn't want to leave Sparrow either.

But she was well-guarded, as were Jasper and Freddie. *This* conversation needed to happen away from prying eyes, ears, and potential tempers. We'd already had enough problems lately.

This one?

This one I could do something about.

"So, let's talk about what we know," I began because the staring contest had gotten old before we started it. "The ambush was a coordinated effort. The trap was laid for Freddie specifically. The goal was most likely to get him high or grab him. Something to pull us there."

Liam sighed.

"Exactly. Now, as luck would have it, we played right into their hands. Not something I remotely regret because we will never leave any of us behind." I glanced to where Milo sat, his focus now on the drink he turned in a slow circle on the table. "It could have been a lot worse. We got lucky, plain and simple."

"It wasn't the Royals," Liam stated in a cool tone. "I checked into it afterward. The only people capable of pulling together that level of firepower in the organization currently are Adam and Ezra."

Milo stilled at the pair of names, and the muscle ticking in his jaw was a dead giveaway.

"They are both otherwise occupied. Ezra can and did check with the others. No one else is anywhere near here. Now, could the King have turned around and pulled some shit? Possibly. But those guys were Diamonds."

"A few of them," I corrected. "And they were low-level at that. The rest were hired guns, loose cannons, and free-lancers."

Which was why, despite their numbers, they were so fucking disorganized, didn't trust each other to have their backs, and generally left us openings where survival was possible.

If they'd had a decent leader or a first clue, we'd have had far more casualties than just Jasper.

"It was a coordinated effort, one meant to specifically target us. They got lucky in how many of us showed up—and damn unlucky that Emersyn was there."

Because she really had saved our lives, whether she realized it or not. As fucking terrified as I'd been seeing her scale that wall while people were *shooting* at us, she'd gotten in and opened the door, giving us a way out.

"They could have killed her," Milo growled.

"They could have killed all of us," I replied. "This is the life we chose. It is not the life she did…"

"Except she has," Liam corrected me, and when Milo shot to his feet, Liam didn't flinch. "Deal with it, man. This is where she wants to be and she wants to be with us. We're not hiding who we are."

"Some of us aren't," I stated before tossing back the measure of whiskey. It burned its way down to my stomach. Milo pivoted to face me and I raised my brows. "We think it's the Royals."

"I just told you—" Liam began but I cut him off with one raise of my hand.

"Maybe you're not as plugged in as you think. Reed can't be at all. He's playing dead right now. The other? Maybe he is plugged in. But it wasn't that long ago that someone came after *you* and took a shot at *you* at *your* club."

He scowled. "That feels like eighteen years ago."

"It hasn't even been ten weeks," I said in case he needed the refresher. "They shot up your club, and you took two in the chest. The body armor was smart."

His expression was dry. "Thank you."

"You're welcome. My point is, you're playing one game with the Royals." I fixed Milo with a look and he met my stare impassively. At least he was engaging again.

The girl leaving had left its mark on him, and I didn't like it. None of us did. But we couldn't do a damn thing if he didn't want to talk about it. We had never been the holding hands and skipping types.

"You and Liam made a deal a few years ago. Then you went to prison and he's been honoring your deal so much that he cut ties with all of us to make it happen."

Neither of them moved.

"I'm not an idiot. I can read between the lines, but this

little code of silence you two have been trying to maintain along with the boundaries between the Royals and the Vandals has pretty much fallen."

If I had to lay it out for them, I would. Moving over to the bottle on the table, I refilled my glass.

"Lainey Benedict, for one, is attached to the Royals."

Milo's fingers twitched.

"And Sparrow is attached to them." I glanced at Liam.

"Actually, she's friends with them, that's a little different."

"Semantics," I challenged. "Don't be a dick."

"What can I say?" He spread his arms. "It's my default mode."

"A few years ago, I got word that there was someone looking to make a move on Braxton Harbor," Milo said, his voice dark and almost monotone. "No idea who they were, just outsiders looking to put their mark on the town. They were testing the various footholds the gangs had. We were consolidating, but we hadn't managed the hold we have now."

When he paused, Liam said, "One thing he knew was they had financing and a lot of it. There were rumors of it being wealthier families. I went to school with many kids from wealthy families." Liam shrugged. "Bay Ridge came up a few times. Milo asked me to keep my ear to the ground. He already wanted me cultivating relationships, access points for us to penetrate higher society when everyone was ready."

That fit.

"But the threat increased with each passing month," Milo said. "Then they approached Liam at school."

"I got scouted by the Royals. I made them work for it but eventually let them persuade my bad boy side. The King had loyalty tests, and he liked leverage—he tried to leverage Rome. That didn't end well. I made it very clear if they ever touched him, I'd burn them down."

"But the rest of us are fair game?" It made sense, even if I didn't like it.

"Something like that, but at first, they weren't even interested in the Vandals, just wanted to know what I knew about us. So, I fed them trickles of information. Nothing useful, some of it just accurate enough to prove I knew what I was talking about." He grimaced. "Then they wanted Milo removed."

"Milo, specifically?" I glanced at him and he nodded.

"I'd had a couple of run-ins, near misses here and there. Didn't think anything of it. You know how it was back then. We had a lot of lower-level gangs coming at us, trying to take what we were locking down. But this was different."

"Yeah," Liam said. "They wanted Milo out of the picture. Cut the head off, and the body will die."

I stared at both of them. "There was a contract on your life and you didn't think the rest of us needed to know?" I scrubbed a hand over my face. "What the fuck is wrong with you? This shit is not how we work."

"No," Milo said grimly. "It was how I worked. I compartmentalized. I took on the high-risk because I wanted to shield the rest of you. Kel, you stayed because I asked you to. You could have gotten out. You could have followed Mickey into the military, like you wanted to. You wanted to put distance between you and Braxton Harbor, but I needed you and your mind here."

"I'm aware. I'm also a fucking adult who owns my own decisions. I don't need you or anyone else 'shielding' me. You splintered us right down the fucking middle with Liam's absence. Jasper lost his shit for months, pissed at

Liam for being gone, pissed at you for taking that fucking deal, and pissed at himself for not being able to prevent any of it."

"You're pissed," Liam said slowly. "Kel..."

"You're goddamn right I am. And don't Kel me, you had plenty of time while he was in prison to bring the rest of us in on this. At least tell us what you had to do so we knew it wasn't you walking away."

"You never thought he did," Milo said with a sigh as he sank back to the sofa and groaned. "You and Vaughn knew something was up, so you didn't cut him off entirely."

"We couldn't, even if that was what Jasper wanted, because he doesn't deal well with abandonment, or have you fucking forgotten that?"

"That one is on me," Liam said. "But he got too damn unpredictable for the work I had to do. Moving up in the Royals put me in a position to protect the city, and trust me when I say that the King does have plans for Braxton Harbor. But the Vandals are a thorn in his side, because you—because *we* control so much."

"Then it's entirely possible that the Royals *were* behind the attack and they just used the Diamonds to do it. The Diamonds and whoever else they could afford."

Arms folded, Liam glared but into the middle distance. "A few weeks ago, he called me into a meeting with him and Adam. Of course, he wasn't actually there. The King uses his anonymity and leverage to control the Royals. I'd bet a thousand dollars Lainey was his leverage over Adam and Ezra."

Milo flexed his fists.

"The same way he tried to use Rome with me and will try to use Hellspawn if he figures that out. In the meantime, the point of the meeting was another loyalty test."

"You had to do what?"

"Kill Adam and take his place as Bishop."

I tilted my head back to stare at the ceiling. "That's why you're hiding him."

"Yep. For now, he's laying low, and he can be our quiet man moving out of the line of sight of anyone else. He can do things we can't because they don't know he's there."

That seemed a little too neat. Too *convenient*.

After taking a sip of the whiskey, I moved to claim a chair. "Fill me in on everything, and I mean, everything. I need to know what pieces are moving where."

Because our enemies seemed to have just expanded, the fight was coming to us whether we wanted it or not.

36

Two days post-shooting, and not only were we still dealing with clean-up, but we were also still dealing with cops keeping a "friendly" eye on us. When was the last time we had law enforcement so focused in our direction?

To be honest, I couldn't think of a time. Rome and I had both taken turns just strolling around the warehouse, checking on the trucks coming and going. Keeping a finger on the pulse. Jas did so much of this, though, that we were having to double and triple-check everything.

Our company sat, parked, just a block to the east with a great view of the rolling doors. I strolled toward them without a care in the world, two nicely brewed cappuccinos in disposable lidded cups in my hands.

Vasquez dropped his chin toward his chest and shook his head at my approach. I didn't go to the driver's side, which was facing the street anyway. I just walked up to where Vasquez sat.

I didn't recognize the other cop, but at least it wasn't that prick Sommerland. He hated us. Well, hate might be too strong a word. He just acted like we were less than dirt and "wasting" time on scum like us really pissed him off.

Hardly the first authority figure to treat us like that. Course, Vasquez was the opposite. He treated us like kids on his beat. Tried to look after us—did look after Freddie— and didn't usually give us a hard time for no fucking reason.

"Vaughn," the man in question greeted me as I came up to the window.

"Hey, man, it's getting colder." It was early and my breath frosted on the air. "Thought you guys could use some coffee."

Chuckling, Vasquez shook his head. "Rome dropped off donuts a half hour ago."

"I know." He'd brought extras for Dove in case she was hungry when she woke. She and Freddie were both camped out with Jasper, so we'd been taking them food. As much as I hated that Jasper was in rough shape, I liked having the pair in a containable, shielded area, out of any line of fire.

After passing his partner coffee, Vasquez waved me back so he could get out of the car. He stretched before accepting his own and then leaned back against the vehicle. "You up for some questions?"

"Nope," I said, shrugging. "Just came to bring you coffee and make sure you fellas were fine. I got work to do."

"You haven't been to the tattoo shop in a couple of weeks."

"You checking up on me?" I pressed a hand to my heart. "I'm touched. Really. I didn't know you cared so much."

Exasperated amusement filled his expression. "Don't make me call Ms. Stephanie on you boys. Don't think I won't."

That actually made me laugh. "That's cold, Dan. You wouldn't rile her up for all the money in the world unless you really thought you had to."

Pretty much one of the reasons I liked this cop. He'd been a beat cop for years, never moved up, never wanted to —well, at least as far as I knew. We'd met him for the first time when we were teens and he was a rookie. But he'd also busted Freddie during the early days of him trying to score on the streets, and he'd been the one to turn him over to Ms. Stephanie rather than sink him deeper in the system.

He was good people.

But he was still a cop.

"Yeah, I'm not going to give her shit. But I do have questions. Temperature on the street is climbing—you guys seem to be catching most of the heat."

"You know, I keep hearing that. Weird." I shook my head. "I gotta get back, but if you need an appointment for a tat, let me know. I'll hook you up when I get back from my vacation."

"Vacation?" Vasquez said slowly, his brows raised. Incredulous didn't even begin to describe his expression and I kept my grin easy.

"Sure, why not? You know, before now, I'd never taken one." Not that I owed him an explanation. I rented my space in the shop, and I was paid up. I'd had to postpone a handful of appointments, but they were willing to wait. For now, where I needed to be was right here, and if I had to move out of my spot there? Well, there were other shops and I could just start somewhere else.

Nature of the beast.

With a wave, I strolled off. No hurry. Nowhere to be. If the cops wanted to watch us, well, let them watch. Vasquez wasn't on anyone's payroll—as far as we knew. We couldn't afford to start jumping at shadows now. His partners?

The new guy in the car with him? No idea. Sommerland? He was too much of a jackass himself to work for other people. Still, we couldn't afford to discount the possibility.

JD, Shaun, and Rocky were coming out as I walked up. Rocky plucked the cigarette from behind his ear and lit it up. He'd shown up a couple of years ago, starving, homeless after aging out of the system, and pretty much uncertain of what to do.

He was graduating from the community college in a few months. Not bad, all things considered. "Hey," JD said, lifting his chin. "Going on a stock run. Need anything from the store?"

Rubbing the back of my neck, I considered what we had in the clubhouse and what we might need. "Standard order," I said after a minute. "Head by the Coffee House and get freshly roasted beans too. And extra milk."

"You got it." JD cut a look past me and I shook my head.

"Just wave, be polite, and keep right on moving."

"You got it," Shaun said, then gave JD a shove. "You heard the man, let's get moving."

JD shoved him back, but they were all laughing as they headed to where the rats parked their cars. They didn't get to park inside unless they'd earned it.

Letting myself in, I headed back to the clubhouse door as the roll-up door on the far side began to open. Liam pulled in. I paused to wait for him. There was zero point in continuing to pretend he wasn't one of us anymore. I hadn't really cared for it anyway.

"Hey," he said as he climbed out. The car was way too

rich to be in this neighborhood. But his SUV was toast, so what choice did he have?

"Gotta ask," I said as he headed toward me. "Do you walk out and go eeinie, meanie, miny, moe to pick out what car you're going to drive or just drop your hand into a jar and blindly pick out a key?"

"I roll the dice." He smirked. "Twenty-sided die."

Laughing, I pulled the door open for him. "Dick."

"I'd let you suck it, but it's not your thing." He bumped his shoulder into mine on the way past, and I shook my head before following him inside.

Milo and Kellan were already in the kitchen when we got there. The tension was so thick, it threatened to choke us. Ignoring them both, Liam headed for Dove's fancy coffee maker. Rome rolled in right behind me.

He wore a hoodie, no shirt, a pair of sweatpants, and no socks. Probably rolled right out of bed from the look of him, if he'd managed any sleep at all.

When he dropped to sit at the table, folded his arms, and leaned back with his eyes closed, I had my answer. He might have just gotten up, but he wasn't awake yet. The door to the clubhouse opened, and I leaned back, checking who our new arrival—Doc. He lifted a hand.

"Morning," I said. "Liam's making coffee. Want any?"

"Triple espresso," Doc answered. "Over coffee."

I snorted but glanced at Liam. "Do I look like a barista?"

"Nope," Rome answered without opening his eyes.

"But you still want coffee," Liam drawled the words, more amused than anything else. "I assume that's everyone?"

"You assume correctly," Kellan replied in a clipped tone. The number of bad moods in the room grew exponentially.

"Everyone grab food, your coffee, and sit. We have things to talk about."

"Right now?" Milo asked with a sigh.

"There's never going to be a right time," Kellan answered, then bumped his shoulder with a fist. "There's only the time we make. I meant it when I said no more secrets."

And Doc was here too. His expression didn't shift at the announcement, but he studied them both.

"If we're discussing plans, where is Hellspawn?" Liam asked. "And Freddie?"

"They're with Jasper. It's where they both need to be, and she's barely sleeping as it is."

"She's asleep now," Rome said. "Freddie too. Jasper is awake but out of it."

Which meant the painkillers were working.

"I'll check on him after we're done," Doc said.

"I'll fill Sparrow and Freddie in later."

"What?" Milo said, rounding on Kellan. "She doesn't need to know this shit."

Kellan didn't respond, he just stared at Milo.

"With every other fucking thing going on, this is the last thing she needs. This isn't just about our business. Liam said they are also her friends. That's putting her in a position she doesn't need to be in."

"Milo," I said, folding my arms, and he jerked a look at me. "I don't know what all this is, but I have a solid idea. Kel's right. He can brief her on what she needs to know. She was right there when we got ambushed. She's right here for all of this. The last thing she needs is an emotional ambush. We're not doing that to her. Not again."

"Vaughn—"

"Don't," I said with a shake of my head. "Her not

trusting us is why she went back. She didn't trust us to protect her *and* us. Protecting us cost her. It cost her way more than I would have ever wanted her to pay. She's already bled for us, she's not going to bleed because of us."

Head back, Milo stared at the ceiling. The muscle in his jaw ticked as he flexed his hands. The only sound in the kitchen came from the steamer on the coffee maker as Liam continued making coffee, adding shot after shot to each of the cups he'd lined up.

"Kid," Doc said, shocking the shit out of me. "We get it. All of us. Keeping her safe has been the driving force behind every single decision you've made for two decades. You took responsibility for her when you were way too fucking young, and you have *never* tried to abdicate that. But this isn't about you making a decision or a call or trying to shield her."

"It's about giving her the tools to defend herself, to fight for herself. She's not fragile, Milo," Liam added. "She might look it, and fuck knows, she's been through enough that if she was, I couldn't blame her. But she's a fighter, tough as old boots, and way stronger than you're giving her credit for."

"She belongs," Rome added to all of that. "She gets to know."

"Any other questions?" Kellan asked. "I would have just gone with, 'because I said so,' but they all have points. She's your sister. You love her. But *never* make the mistake of thinking we don't care."

He didn't say love, but he didn't have to. Dove was ours, every bit as much as we were hers.

"I fucking hate that it's come to this," Milo admitted.

"It is what it is," Liam said. "We have done everything we could, but Kel's right. Now it needs to be all of us—and she does know them. Maybe even knows them better than I do. They also care about her." As much as it killed him to say it.

I snorted. "Yeah, they care enough that they keep trying to encourage her to leave and go with them. They're willing to do a lot to protect her, and don't forget her bestie."

That hit a mark, and Milo glared at me.

"Look, I'm just laying it out there. Stop reacting, man. Stop jumping at every damn thing like it's the enemy. Prison *sucked* for you. We know. But you're not in that goddamn cell anymore."

"You're not alone," Rome added as Liam put his coffee in front of him.

"You're not," Doc agreed. "None of you are. Maybe we didn't go looking for this fight, but no one is backing down from it."

Kellan glanced at him, and he wasn't the only one. "You don't like the battles."

"Still don't," Doc said. "But I'm in. For whatever you need me for, whether it's patching you up or taking the fight to them. This isn't going away because we don't want to fight it. It only stops when we end the fight."

Liam handed him a cup. "Been a long time."

"Too long maybe," Doc admitted. "That is also what it is." He flexed his left hand before he took the cup and then shrugged. "Tell me what you need me to know and what you need me to do."

That left Milo. We all waited him out while Liam passed out the coffees. Yeah, mine was a little too damn foamy and he'd drawn a middle finger in the foam.

Snorting a laugh, I grinned at him, and Liam just took a seat and stretched out his legs while we waited. No one hurried Milo along. He took a long drink of his coffee, then focused on each of us one at a time. It was Doc he studied the longest.

Finally, he said, "Kel's right. You all are. I hate it. I don't think I'm ever going to be 'okay' with her being in the middle of the fight."

"To be clear," Kellan said. "None of us want her there. None of us are 'okay' with it."

"Nope," I said, and Doc shook his head.

"Never going to like it," he added.

Liam spread his hand. "She's been in the fight longer than we have, I think. I don't have to like it to make sure she has the skills and the tools to win the damn thing."

Rome just stared at us like we were all idiots. He probably wasn't wrong.

"So, now that we've gotten through the holding hands and skipping a portion of the discussion," Kellan said, taking over even as he settled a hand on Milo's shoulder. "It's time to bring everyone up to speed on what's been going on. Take a seat. Save your questions and comments until the end; this is going to take a minute."

37

Milo and Kellan were with me, Rome and Vaughn back at the clubhouse. It had taken another couple of days to get Ezra to agree to the meetup. He was not a fan and preferred that I bring Adam to him. Considering the fact Adam wanted the fuck out of the house—yeah, not happening. Hopefully, he wouldn't bring Lainey with him, because that was just a cluster-fuck in the making.

I cut a glance back to where Milo sat in the backseat. He'd ignored both of us from the moment he climbed in. His temper was riding the edge. I wasn't sure what fucked him up more—the fact Lainey had ties to all of this and had chosen to go back or that Emersyn was also right in the middle.

Probably both. I felt for the guy. We all did. I wanted to tell him we'd fix this shit. Because we fucking would, one way or another. The problem was, it had already cost us—

cost him. It was likely going to keep costing us until this was done.

"Before we get there," I said, keeping my eye on our surroundings. The cops who were camping out the warehouse made me take longer, more circuitous routes to the old house. The last thing we needed was someone from law enforcement, or anyone else, following us. There was really no telling who those guys were working for. "I would like to reiterate that taking you both in there is not going to encourage them to talk or cooperate. They know me, and for the most part, they trust me."

I flicked a look at Kel in the passenger seat and Milo in the seat behind him. Milo's gaze remained fixed out the window. Yeah. This was going to go *great*.

"You're not going in alone to open this line of dialogue with them. You're a Vandal. You have always *been* a Vandal."

"I'm a Royal," I pointed out, even if I appreciated the fierce possessiveness in Kel's tone. "I made that choice to do this job."

"For us. For Milo. That means you're *still* a Vandal. You get backup. Period."

Hard to argue with that. Milo ceded his leadership to Kellan. "Leadership looks good on you, man," I pointed out, and he just rolled his eyes before he glanced out the window himself.

Yeah. I got that. Not a conversation any of us really wanted to have. Fuck, at some point, when we solved all this shit, I was taking Hellspawn and the guys, and we were going to have a fucking vacation—somewhere Rome couldn't just ditch if he decided to steal a car and leave.

Then again, I didn't think he'd ever get bored if she were there.

Yeah. That needed to happen. We were going to make a goddamn plan and then we could sort out how all of this was going to work. The five of us—well—fuck.

There were more than five.

Right. I scratched my jaw. Later. That was a matter to be dealt with *later*.

The Vandals. Our girl.

We'd figure it out.

Hopefully, we didn't have to beat the shit out of each other—then again, I'd win. That made me smile and I parked all of it in the back of my head. I needed my head in the game. By the time I turned onto the drive leading to the house I'd grown up in after I left them, I'd gone a solid hour plus out of the way.

We had no one on us and no one tracking us—another perk of swapping cars and sweeping them daily for trackers.

I was getting paranoid.

Getting?

"Fuck," Kellan said as I pulled around the circle drive and right into the garage. A cherry red sports coupe sat in there, along with a couple of older model cars I'd picked up, and the one sedan I left for Adam to use. "I sometimes forget just how much they have."

"It's easy to do," I said as I climbed out. "In the beginning, it was never about the money even though they had so much, you know?"

"Yeah." Kel sighed. "My parents weren't wealthy. But I remember what it was like." He shook his head, and the emotion clouding his expression was gone by the time he left the car and joined me.

Milo didn't exit the car immediately. Fortunately, even though Ezra was already here and likely plotting with

Adam, they didn't come out to meet us. I'd like a little more space before the fight that was likely brewing hit.

"You still sure this is a good idea?" I asked, keeping my voice low.

"He can handle it," Kellan said. "He's had to adjust to a lot since he got back. That girl and Sparrow are the only real things that have made him smile. He isn't taking the idea that they're involved in any of this well."

"That girl is going to be a problem."

Kel turned to look at me as the back door of the car finally opened. "She already is. We adapt, we adjust—we protect her and him."

Right. I nodded.

"You good?" I said to Milo and he shrugged.

"No promises. But Kel's right, you aren't doing this without backup, and I need to know more about these guys."

I motioned to the door with a jerk of my head and then led the way. The sound of male voices from the direction of the living room cut off as soon as I pushed the door inward.

"Ezra," Adam warned, and I moved, blocking Ezra's volatile ass as he charged forward.

"Don't," I warned him. "You're here because I called you, and you're seeing him because it's necessary. That can change *real* fast."

I met his hostile glare with a firm grip on my own temper. Ezra could be a really fun guy when he didn't have a lit stick of dynamite up his ass.

"Why is *he* here?" He glared right past me.

"Because I invited him. The same way I invited you."

Behind Ezra, Adam stood in the living room, hands in his pockets and his stare far more neutral but in no way friendly.

"We agreed to listen," Adam said. "That's *all* we agreed to."

"I'm aware." I kept my attention on Ezra, though. "You planning on making this a fight—again?"

With a harsh sigh, Ezra returned his glare to me. "You owe me a fucking apology for lying to me."

A laugh escaped me and I shook my head. "As I recall, you tried to ambush me and my brother. I didn't fucking kill you. That's about all the apology you get."

"You're an asshole."

"And proud of it."

Ezra rolled his eyes. "Fine." He stormed back into the living room and I eyed the shattered lamp on the floor as he passed it, then focused on Adam.

"Problems?"

"We'll see."

Yeah, we would. No one took a seat and no one turned their backs on each other. Adam and Ezra formed a front on one side of the room, while Kellan and Milo took up a stand in the archway leading into it.

"We have a problem," I began because I was the bridge. The island in the middle.

"We do," Adam said, but he wasn't looking at me. Like Ezra, his focus was on Milo. "For example, your continued loyalty to a group you said you had severed ties with."

"That's not *your* problem," I pointed out.

Adam snorted softly. "The King would not see it that way."

"The King ordered me to execute you," I reminded him. "You're *dead* because he wanted you dead."

"What?" Ezra demanded, then refocused on Adam. "What the fuck did you do that pissed him off?"

"We're not having that discussion in mixed company," Adam replied without looking at him.

"Actually, let's discuss that. A few nights ago, a well-armed group staged an ambush designed to kill most of the Vandals."

"And I care because?" Adam asked, his expression not even flickering.

"Because Emersyn was right in the middle of it."

"Is she all right?" Ezra's whole demeanor shifted. "She has to be all right, Lainey would have said if she'd lost touch again. Did she get hurt?"

Exhaling, Adam pinched his brow. "You think it was us."

"We would not send a fucking ambush to hurt her." Ezra's shock wasn't feigned, nor was his rage. His eyes narrowed and his lips compressed.

The dynamic between the pair had always been rather fascinating. Even more now that Ezra wasn't just falling into line with Adam. If anything, there was a divide between them. Now I kind of wished I'd upgraded the internal cameras here.

I'd have to make that change, and soon.

"We wouldn't risk her like that," Adam said. "As much as I think the Vandals are a pain in the ass—an obstacle to be removed—I know she's there. I know *Lainey* was there. I wouldn't risk either one of them."

"Lainey's home," Ezra stated, and I caught Kellan shifting his stance to partially block Milo. Good plan. I held my ground. I was in the perfect position to intercept either side. "She's safe. I offered to take Emersyn with us, but she refused."

"She told me the same thing." Adam's focus was definitely on Milo, but he shifted his attention back to me. "No, we didn't arrange for any ambushes. I hadn't spoken to anyone who wasn't you before Ezra got here. Still surprised you gave him the damn address."

"I'd be surprised you hadn't, except you gave me your word." Exhaling, I shook my head. "I didn't think it was us."

"You were certain," Kellan reminded me, and I glanced at him.

"I'm aware."

"But are they so certain?" Kellan nodded toward Adam and Ezra. "Cause Mr. Reed there doesn't appear to share your conviction."

"No, Mr. Reed does not," Adam concurred and shrugged when I looked at him. "He ordered you to kill me. Does it really strain credulity that he'd set up a hit on all of them to make sure you were on the leash? And if it took you out in the process? Well—we know how he feels about failure."

"Yes, we do." If he suspected me now...

"Why did he want you to kill Adam?" Ezra asked abruptly.

"When was the last time he explained himself to you?" I asked because if he ever had, I'd really like to know.

With a scowl, Ezra turned and stalked over to the bar. "I need a fucking drink."

"You have to drive," Adam reminded him. "You're not staying."

One of the bar glasses went flying toward the wall and shattered. "Keep it up, and I'm going to charge you for repairs," I informed him and then motioned Adam toward the chairs. "Look, we're here because there's some seriously bad shit brewing. We need to figure it out."

"You," Adam said, motioning to me, Kellan, and Milo. "You need to figure this out. This doesn't involve us."

"Normally, I would agree with you. The Vandals are not

Royals business. Unless the Royals are targeting them—I was directed to remove Milo. To weaken them." At least this wasn't news to Kellan or Milo at this point. "I handled those instructions my way. But if the King is making moves—having me eliminate you, then moving to take me out along with the Vandals. That means he's clearing the field."

It also meant I may have made a serious miscalculation. One we could not afford.

"So, what does he do next?" Ezra asked. "That's where you're going, right? Who does he take out next?"

Adam and I shared a look and I raised my brows, then we both looked at Ezra. "What did he ask you to do?"

Rather than challenge my question, Ezra just stared at me and went mute.

"What did he ask you for?" Adam repeated. "When did he ask for it?"

"It's not important," Ezra said with a sharp shake of his head before he cut a look back at us.

"Except for the warning that you might have to deal with me if I didn't get the job done faster?" I reminded him.

Ezra shrugged. "Like I said, not important."

"This is going fucking nowhere," Milo intruded. "If they knew anything, they wouldn't offer it anyway."

"Hey, we're on the same page now," Ezra retorted. "I wouldn't cross the street to piss on you if you were on fire either. Just to be clear."

Yeah, this was going well. Rubbing the back of my neck, I paced away from all of them. Let Kellan and Adam manage the Ezra and Milo shit show. If the King was making moves, the question would be, why?

That was the part Adam and I hadn't figured out yet. Why had he wanted Adam removed in the first place? What had he—

Pivoting, I focused on Adam. "Did you tell anyone else that you asked Emersyn to marry you?"

The dead silence that greeted that question was pretty fucking profound. Even Ezra seemed stunned. I ignored Kellan and Milo right now. I needed to know the answer to this. Because it was the only tie, ephemeral as it was, between the Vandals and the Royals right now.

Milo and Emersyn.

The sniffing around after Milo and trying to take us out.

Had that been because of...

Son of a bitch.

"There is no fucking way," Adam swore. "No fucking way."

38

Jasper's sudden thrashing in the bed had me up and stumbling to grip his hand before he ripped out his IV —again. The last four days had been an exercise in soothing him from nightmares and keeping him from hurting himself. He kept fighting the guys, especially Doc. The last time he'd gotten the IV out, I'd had to literally sit on him and keep murmuring to him to calm him down long enough for Doc to get the IV back in.

On day two, Doc swore because the area around Jasper's wound had grown inflamed and hot. He'd also started running a fever. That was the day the dreams grew worse. More than once, his muttering in his sleep would wake me up with only a few seconds before the thrashing would start.

Doc insisted he would be fine. "Little Bit," he told me while I stroked Jasper's sweaty hair away from his face. "I know it looks bad, and I'm not going to pretend this isn't ideal. However, we've got him on antibiotics. I'm not going anywhere. I'll keep checking the wound and we're going to get him through this."

"I hate that I can't make this better for him."

"I know," he said. "The hardest part of watching anyone fight a battle is knowing you would gladly take it on for them. While we can't fight this *for* him, we can fight it *with* him."

"Mickey," I said. "He *is* going to get better, right?" Maybe if I had been faster getting up that drainpipe, if I'd acted soon—if I'd done *anything*...

"Little Bit," he repeated, then touched two fingers to my jaw to lift my chin so I'd meet his gaze. "He *will* be fine."

Freddie came out of the bathroom, his hair slicked back from the shower and wearing fresh clothes. "Let's go, Boo-Boo. Tag, you're it."

I made a face and then glanced back at Jasper. What Doc had given him seemed to work, he calmed again and his eyes were closed, even if his expression remained troubled. "I need clean clothes."

"Trust me to get them?" Mickey asked and I stole a look up at him.

"Thank you."

"Then go shower," he said as Freddie neared the bed. "You got this?"

"I'll watch out for him, Boo-Boo. Doc's right." But when I hesitated, Freddie gave me a playful look. "I didn't want to mention it earlier, but you're starting to smell."

A snort escaped me before I could stop it, a snort that turned into a half-laugh. He grinned. When I slid off of Jasper and went to stand, Mickey offered me a hand to get down.

"Go on, Little Bit. I'll be right back with a change of clothes for you."

"Thank you," I said, and I meant it. Mickey had been in regularly. I believed him when he said Jasper would be okay, but I really needed Jasper to open up those stormy gray eyes and yell at me or something. A growl would do.

Mickey held on to my hand, so I squeezed his fingers then let go. His smile was fleeting and Freddie bumped my shoulder. "Food?" The question was light, but his eyes were serious. "You're getting scrawnier."

I flipped him off and his grin spread. "Now you're speaking my language, Boo-Boo. We can bribe *Mickey* to get us some burgers and non-limp dick fries." Freddie shot a wicked grin at Mickey, who gave him a narrow-eyed look but glanced at me.

"I'll get you whatever you want, Little Bit. You can even share it with the little punk if you want to."

"Wounded," Freddie declared, probably a little louder than he should have and we both froze and glanced at Jasper. But his expression hadn't changed. "Wounded," he repeated at a much lower volume with soulful eyes. "Still, limp dick fries are the worst. Crispy, hot, and salty or not at all. Am I right?"

I couldn't not smile at the hopeful words. "You're right, so, yes, please, Mickey—if you wouldn't mind."

"Let me grab your clothes, and I'll get you guys food," Mickey said, already on his way to the door. The interior of the bathroom was still humid and warm from Freddie's shower, so I stripped out of my two-day-old clothes, turned the water on, and slid right under the scalding spray.

The heat beat down on my taut muscles, and my neck and back protested as I began to stretch. I was probably a mess of knots from how I kept sleeping on the floor and sitting up, but I hated being too far from Jasper when he was—well, when he was vulnerable.

More than one dark dream had gripped him, but he would settle if I talked to him. Sometimes, his hand flexed on mine, and once, he'd gripped on so tight my fingers had protested, but the minute I kissed his hand everything in him relaxed again.

No, I could handle this.

"Stepping in, Little Bit," Mickey said as I worked shampoo into my hair. God, it was so nasty, I hadn't even realized how filthy it was. I hadn't showered since the ambush and I'd gotten by with the sketchy hand wipes for a spot clean before changing into clean clothes.

That thought just made my skin crawl.

"Thank you," I said, massaging my scalp. "I can't stand the thought of putting those clothes back on after wearing them while I was still dirty."

"There are worse things," he said, but he didn't come any closer to the shower. "You had other things on your mind."

"You're right," I admitted.

"She said so easily, without an ounce of stubborn spite." The teasing warmth made me grin. "And before you put me in my place with a well-deserved remark, just let me enjoy being right."

I giggled. "Okay. Food now?"

"Yes, ma'am, I'm going to get you food now. You and Freddie stay in and secure?" The extra note of warning wasn't lost on me.

"Not going anywhere. I promise."

"Good girl," he said, and the praise sang right through me. "When I get back, I want you to get some real sleep while I look after him. Deal?"

Worry pulled at me.

"Little Bit, you can stay in here, just—sleep, okay?"

I'd rinsed my hair, so I eased over to glance past the curtain. He was still by the door, his arms folded and his expression worried.

"I'll try, if I can stay in here."

"Done and done," he said, straightening. "Be back in twenty."

"Mickey?"

He paused.

"Thank you—for real."

"You're welcome. For real." Then he was gone and I sighed. I might have lingered in the shower a little longer than I intended. But I was scrubbed, and my skin didn't crawl, itch, or stink by the time I got out.

I smelled like Jasper's shampoo and soap, which settled some of my unease. Mickey had brought me a clean t-shirt, panties, bra, and a pair of yoga pants, along with a hoodie and socks.

It was only a little weird to use Jasper's antiperspirant, but Freddie had gone to get my toothbrush the night prior and I scrubbed my teeth thoroughly before I came out to find Doc was back with the food and Freddie had already dug in.

The scent of the burgers and fries had my stomach growling before I even reached where they'd set up at the pair of chairs. Mickey rose at my arrival and motioned me into the seat. I hesitated and glanced over at Jasper.

"He's still asleep," Freddie said. "Probably Jas at his most boring. Think we should get a marker and doodle on him until he wakes up?"

I really shouldn't have snickered. It wasn't funny. Well —it shouldn't be funny, but... "If he doesn't get up soon, I say we flip a coin," I offered Freddie, and he made a little fist pump.

"You are so my favorite person," Freddie confessed with a grin, and I shook my head.

"Hopefully, he'll wake before then."

"Yeah, Boo-Boo, I hope so too."

Freddie had already half-devoured his food, and I didn't realize how hungry I was until I started on it. Afterward, my stomach full, and the rest of me warm from the shower, I fell asleep when Freddie started reading aloud from a new book. Mickey promised to keep watch so I didn't fight the sleep reaching up to swallow me.

Vaughn came in, and so did Rome. Twice, Milo had come to sit with me. Between us, we got Freddie to sleep, and then Milo sat with me for a while. We didn't talk, but it was nice to have him there and when I held his hand, he'd been surprised but he'd accepted it.

Liam stuck his head in once, more to check on me than Jasper, I thought. But I hadn't missed the way he'd frowned in Jasper's direction.

The guys were planning some kind of retaliation. I didn't have to guess at that or pretend I didn't understand it. Hell, I kind of wanted to be a part of it. I hated that someone had hurt Jasper.

"Sometimes, Boo-Boo, it's better not to know." But Freddie didn't believe that any more than I did.

Mickey was a little more circumspect. "Let us handle it," he said. "I know how you feel, and I get the rage, the need to pay back what was done to you. We will get it, but what he needs—what we all need—is you here, safe and sound so that we can focus."

It was hard to argue that point, at least, right now. Especially when I didn't want to leave Jas. Four days—or was it five? I'd lost track—Jasper's fever broke and he was really sleeping. I gave into both Freddie and Doc, after we'd gotten Jasper's bed sheets changed and him washed down, and I slept in the bed next to him.

I woke to Kellan's hand on my shoulder. He pressed a finger to his lips, then nodded toward the door. "Come with me for a bit, Sparrow?"

Pushing the hair from my face, I slid out of the bed. Freddie was already awake and he had food as well as coffee. "I got him," he said. "When you come back, we'll pick up at the next chapter?"

I liked that idea. "Okay." I stole another look at Jasper as Kellan caught my hand and guided me toward the door. "Come get me if anything changes?"

Freddie crossed his heart. "Promise." I blew him a kiss and he mimed catching it, then putting it in his pocket with a wink. "For later."

The hall seemed almost violently bright after the last few days. Squinting, I let Kellan pull me to his room. Once inside, he closed the door behind us then tugged me around. "C'mere, Sparrow."

At the simple request, I stepped right into his arms and curled against him as he picked me up and held me tight. I'd seen very little of him the last few days, and I hadn't realized how much I missed him until this second.

"Do you need to talk?" I asked in the same hushed voice he was using.

"Soon," he soothed. "Just let me hold you right now."

I could do that.

39

"Have you ever used one of these before?" Kellan asked. We were in the kitchen at the clubhouse. Instead of the cooking lesson I'd thought we'd come down here to do, he motioned to the gun sitting on the table. The night before was the first time I hadn't slept in Jasper's room. Kellan needed me.

"Not really," I admitted. "We had guns, or they did, I guess. I never really thought about it. I was always focused on my dance and on—staying away." They hadn't even let me take basic self-defense. That was why I had a chaperone and a driver. Learning how to protect myself might have interfered with his plans.

It certainly hadn't worked out for him the way he wanted when I went home. Ice crept over my skin. That realization sank into my bones about how deliberate a choice that had probably been. What I didn't quite understand was why it never occurred to me to look for something more when I was on the road.

"Sparrow?"

I dragged myself to the present and met his worried gaze. "Jasper had me hold one once," I said, the memory helping to chase away the shadows shivering through me. "It was a little smaller than this. Said to point and shoot. So, I get the basics of it."

He let out a low groan and shook his head. "Why does that not surprise me?"

"Because he's Jasper," I said, folding my arms and moving away from the table and the gun. Kellan had showered before we came down. He'd dressed in jeans and a faded t-shirt that was old and so worn it had to be a favorite. It stretched over his frame like it had been painted on, not that I minded the effect.

Flashing me a smile as he cracked a couple of eggs, Kellan nodded. "I'm glad you see him that way."

"Me too." Leaning near the counter where he worked, I studied Kellan as he cooked. Today wasn't a cooking lesson, and I had a feeling it was going to be about that gun. "Can I ask you a weird question?"

"How weird?" His tone was light, and a hint of a smile kicked up the corner of his mouth. "Not sure I've had enough coffee for Freddie weird at this point."

Coffee. I could do that. I pushed off the counter and went to the coffee maker. I loved the espresso machine. It made all kinds of brews, but it also had a foamer and its own grinder. It tickled me that Liam had done this, I hadn't really had time to appreciate it, but as I set about getting coffee ready, I definitely owed him a genuine thank you.

"Not Freddie weird," I said, after starting the first two shots of espresso and then going to hunt up the big mugs. "I don't think it is, anyway."

Chuckling, Kellan leaned back and reached into the

cabinet I'd been heading for and passed me a couple of the larger mugs.

"Thank you," I said, and rose up on my tiptoes to press a kiss to his jaw. He turned his head at the last second, my lips brushing his before wrapping a hand around my throat and using his thumb to tip my head back.

All control and heat, he kissed with a wild intensity that demanded every ounce of my attention. Wet, deep, and back-arching, his kiss damn near consumed me and left me dizzy when he eased back.

"You're welcome, Sparrow," he murmured, stroking his thumb over my lower lip before he turned back to the eggs and flipped them. I swore my heart did a tumble with them. I lingered for a moment, trying to reorient my synapses back into their proper place.

Coffee.

I'd been making coffee.

Belatedly, I glanced at the mugs in my hand with a little grin and went back to work. Bacon sizzled, toast popped, and the kitchen began to fill with all these wonderfully tasty smells that weren't just Kellan. He was definitely delicious though, and I licked the cool burn of peppermint he'd left on my lips.

"You were going to ask me something?" He asked as he turned the bacon and started fresh eggs.

"Oh, I was… sorry, I think your kiss left me a little scrambled."

His chuckle sent another shiver up my spine. I started another pair of shots while I got the milk foaming. "I'm not going to apologize for that."

"Good," I told him, stealing a glance over my shoulder and grinning when I caught him watching *me*. "I don't want or need one."

"Then ask your question, Sparrow."

"Jasper's been more relaxed the last few weeks, or am I imagining that? I know a lot of stuff has been going wrong, and you guys have all been crazy busy. He's also been tangled up—or maybe you all are—in business you don't want to tell me about." I winced, then amended, "Business he doesn't want to tell me about. He said he would if I needed to know, but he didn't want to, and I respected that."

"That was very generous of both of you," Kellan answered as the sizzle and pop of the cooking bacon had my stomach twisting. I was dying for both the coffee and the food.

"I don't really have the right to demand anything, you know?"

"No," he said softly. "I don't know that."

When I'd added foamy milk to both of our coffees, I carried them over to the table and met him as he set the plates down. The gun was right there still, and I steadfastly refused to look at it.

"Sparrow, you have all the rights in the world here," he told me, catching my hand after I put his coffee down. "Look at me."

I snapped my gaze to his.

"I would guess he gave you the option because he didn't want to worry you. He also just wanted you to work on you. You've had a hell of a few weeks, we all know it, and we're trusting you to look after yourself."

"He said that too." I grimaced.

"Then believe him. Jasper doesn't blow smoke up anyone's ass, least of all yours."

That was a horrible description, but Kellan said it so seriously.

"You can demand anything you want from us…" He stroked his thumb over the back of my hand then turned it so he could trace my palm. "Maybe you don't understand it yet, but you will. You're one of us, you don't have a single battle that we won't engage in with you or for you. The other night—you got a far too close a look at one of the darker parts of our lives. You didn't flinch, Sparrow."

"That's not true—I was terrified." I frowned. "And mad."

To my surprise, Kellan chuckled. Lifting my hand, he pressed a kiss to my palm before letting it go. "You didn't flinch away from acting. You scaled that wall and went right inside that factory. I should want to spank your ass for risking yourself like that—but you did what any one of us would do—and did."

Warmth unfurled inside me at the pride in his voice.

"Now," he continued, pointing his fork at me before cutting into his eggs. "That doesn't mean you have a license to be reckless. Not by any stretch, but you trusted your instincts, and you helped save us."

"I just wish I'd been faster, then maybe…"

"Nope, we don't do that," he said in between bites. My stomach grumbled, so I dug into mine, using the toast to mop up the egg. "Good girl."

There was that sizzle of pride again at his compliment.

"We can look back at what we did, how we reacted, and learn from it. But we don't beat ourselves up. That was a first for you and you kept your head. That's more important than you realize."

No, I had already kind of come to that conclusion, but I appreciated hearing it. "Is that why there's a gun on the table?"

"Partially," he told me. "We're going to go over gun

safety today. Then I'm going to take you to a range so you can learn to shoot. You don't have to be an expert, but I want you to be comfortable enough that if you need to pick up a gun and use it—you can."

Chills chased up my spine.

"Guns are a tool, Sparrow. Liam's already been teaching you basic fighting. I want you to keep up on that. I'm going to ask Freddie to teach you how to use a knife."

Shock rippled through me. "I've seen Freddie with his knife…"

"He's flat out better with a knife than any person I've ever seen. He's also capable of taking down men far larger than he is with it. What he can teach you is how to get away if you need to and incapacitate if you can't."

The race through the woods flew through my mind. The orderly. He'd been so huge, charging after us. Freddie hadn't slowed down when he'd gone to engage him.

The blood.

I glanced down at the plate, my hand flexing on the fork as I stared at it. Only, I couldn't see the food. It was the office, and the doctor's—face was mangled and the blood was everywhere.

"I know this is a lot," Kellan said. "But I need you to learn. I want you to have every tool at your disposal in case something happens again—because it probably will." The last sounded so grudging and irritated.

He didn't want anything to happen again. And I couldn't blame him. The idea of someone shooting him or Freddie or Rome… any of them. We'd all been there, only Mickey and Milo hadn't been.

My heart squeezed at the idea of Milo getting hurt. I already loathed the fact Jasper had been and that he was struggling between the infection and the fever.

The blood.

It was spilling everywhere, and it was on my hands.

Did that much blood ever come out? Really?

"Driving is another thing I'd like to get you back to doing," Kellan continued, and it seemed to be coming from very far away. "I've got a car I'm working on for you, but you can have one of mine until I get it ready. Frankly, I'd rather put you in an armored vehicle, but we're going to work our way up to that."

The hot-cold feeling intensified, and I couldn't quite catch my breath. Blood splattered me as I struck the doctor over and over. The blood flecking through the air as Freddie struck with the knife. The blood pouring out of Jasper as we packed his wound and kept pressure on it.

A river of crimson...

I couldn't breathe.

"Fuck, Sparrow." He was so far away, it was like he called from a distant tunnel. "Come on, head down, breathe for me, sweetheart..."

The world spiraled.

My uncle.

The doctor.

The fence.

The burns on my hands.

Then Cole gripping me, shattering the glass before he dragged it down my arms...

Spots danced in my vision, and when arms closed around me, I struck back. A scream clawed up my throat and it wouldn't stop. Nothing stopped.

There was so much blood.

40

"**B**reathe, sweetheart," I murmured as I closed my arms around her and held her close. She flailed, her hands striking wildly, but I ignored the blows. The minute she'd sent the coffee cup flying and grabbed the broken shard, I'd moved. Shoving her chair back and the table to the side, I managed to get to her before she cut anything.

Ignoring the mess, I sat on the floor and cradled her as she stared off into some fucking place I couldn't see or shoot.

"Breathe, Sparrow," I repeated, rubbing her back in slow circles until the short, sharp, and shallow pants gave way to deeper breaths. Then she shuddered, and the tautness of her muscles relaxed briefly before a wet sob choked out of her.

What kind of fucking asshole was I to push her like that? Cradling her closer, I moved my hand up to her hair and combed my fingers through the mass as she suddenly wrapped her arms around me.

"There's my girl," I crooned softly when she let out a hiccupping sound of misery. "There she is. Breathe for me, my sweet sparrow. Just keep breathing. It's going to be all right…"

How long we sat there, I didn't track. Mentally, I just shifted every single plan I had for the day. Sparrow moved to the top of the list. Listening to her weeping through the wall had been hard e-fucking-nough, but this?

This was *Hell*. I clamped down on every instinct I possessed. Jasper's white-hot rage wouldn't be enough to satisfy me at this point. I wanted to kill anyone who'd ever even given her an unkind review or a hard time.

It seemed an eternity, but her breaths came slower and deeper. She stopped burying her face against my throat and moved her head to my shoulder. But I stayed right where I was, murmuring.

"I'm sorry, Sparrow," I said, wanting to add exactly why I was sorry but she didn't need a fucking repeat. "I am so sorry. Tell me what I can do."

"Nothing," she whispered in this empty voice, followed by a long sigh. "I just—I shouldn't…" Another hard swallow and I waited her out.

"Sparrow," I said, tipping her chin just enough so she would lift those red and swollen eyes to meet mine. "There's no shouldn't. Pain is pain. When we feel it, we have to let it out. Sometimes, we can do it by kicking a rock down the road or punching a wall. But keeping it inside is going to poison you and I can handle tears. I can handle rage. I can even handle you breaking every damn dish we own. I'll go buy some more if you need it—but the only 'shouldn't' is choking yourself into silence."

From everything she'd let slip, silence had held her hostage longer than anything else. When she licked her lips and actually seemed thoughtful, I carefully wiped the tears from her face. Her nose was red and shiny, her eyes puffy and bloodshot. Even her lower lip was reddened and chapped from where she'd dug her teeth into it.

Even when she was losing it, she fought to contain that wealth of emotion. My poor sparrow, the world had battered her, but she was still there. Still fighting.

A bare flicker touched her lips as though she attempted a smile, but it failed before it even processed. "I made a mess."

"We'll clean it up." Order was something that was important in times like this. "When I was a kid," I told her. "After my parents died, I didn't really know how to handle the grief. You know—it's a weird thing. I obsessed with the fact that if I'd let my mom drive me to school, they wouldn't have been in an accident."

I shook my head.

"The brain is funny, the things it will latch onto. It was raining, but I wanted to ride the bus. She wanted to drive me to school. They let me ride the bus, even if I got wet waiting for it. I loved riding the bus. Then they were in an accident later that day while I was at school."

With care, and balancing her, I stood. She barely weighed anything, and I definitely didn't want her sock-clad feet on the floor with the broken debris.

"I can still hear her sigh when I ran out the door. I can still feel the rain on my face." I caught her wide eyes as she stared at me. "I can still hear my dad telling her it was okay, to let me do it. But I can't always see her anymore. I feel all the things I felt when they told me about the accident. When they told me they were gone. The hurt, the tearing—

but I can't see her unless I squint really hard. Even when I look at the pictures, it's like—too flat, not the woman who gave me hugs and made me sandwiches or told me funny stories."

Setting her on the counter next to the coffee machine, I rubbed her legs.

"Stay here for a sec?"

After she nodded, I plucked the paper towels from the other counter and put them next to her. Then I cleaned up the mess. She'd barely eaten her breakfast; the coffee was a loss. But I'd make sure she ate.

"I'm sorry about your parents." Empathy resonated in those words. It wasn't pity, but loss. A loss she probably understood, though her parents and mine were lightyears apart. She'd blown her nose, but it didn't diminish the nasal quality of her voice.

"Me too, Sparrow," I said over my shoulder. "But I got to meet the guys and Ms. Stephanie—she was always an ear. One thing she told me that I've never forgotten was that sometimes, you have to feel what you have to feel."

Once I'd put the dirty dishes in the sink and the rest of the broken bits in the trash, I put up the gun. At least it hadn't gone flying, and I walked over to scoop her up off the counter.

"What are we doing?"

I studied her tear-stained face. "Trust me?"

"Of course."

"Okay, hang on." At my encouragement, she looped her arms around my neck and I strode out of the kitchen carrying her. At a suggestion of movement from the side, I glanced to find Rome leaning on the wall of the living area next to the kitchen.

He met my gaze, then glanced at her before looking at

me again. Worry radiated off him, but I lifted my chin. I had this. I had her. He nodded, then tapped the phone in his hand. Call him if she needed him.

Message received.

Thankfully, Rome seemed to trust me with her, and considering how close he'd been staying, I appreciated that. Up the stairs, I headed for my room and, by extension, hers—but for now, we'd settle in mine. Closing the door, I turned the locks, both of them.

The deadbolt wouldn't really keep out any of them who wanted in, but they'd reconsider if it was important enough. With that in mind, I carried her over and set her on the bed. "Stay put."

She scooted up to the pillows and gave a little watery laugh.

"Something funny?" I asked before stripping my shirt off and tossing it over onto the stack of laundry in the closet. I'd gotten coffee and snot on it.

"Just—you all do that, tell me to stay."

"Because when you catch a wounded bird, you have to be careful of its wings." In my closet, I reached up to the top shelf, then tugged the wood bracket to the side and slid it open. Pulling out the box, I carried it over to the bed and set it in front of her. "Wings are delicate things, they can heal, but they can also be re-injured if you aren't careful."

After toeing off my shoes, I sat down on the edge of the bed and popped the box open. It was a shoebox, nothing fancy, but it had a few surprises in it.

"Candy?" she asked, leaning forward.

"Caramels. Butterscotch. Dark chocolate. This one tastes like donuts and coffee with cinnamon." I pulled the package out and waved it at her temptingly.

"You have edibles…" Surprise filled her face.

"Yep, not a lot, and I don't advertise these or I wouldn't have any, but my secret stash is your secret stash, and I think we could both use a few hours off."

"Kel…"

No fucking lie, I really did love the way she said my name.

"You've been so busy…"

"Exactly." I pulled out my phone and fired off a text. We were in a holding pattern for the next handful of days anyway. Even if we weren't—Sparrow needed me.

I showed her the screen after I hit send.

"Sparrow needs me," she read. "Taking the rest of the day to let her rest—for real. Unless blood and bone are showing, don't bother us."

At her grimace, I quirked a brow. "Too direct?"

"It just seems—mean? Blood and bone? What about Jasper?"

"Doc and Freddie will look after him. Rome's here and so is Vaughn. We all do rotations, and we've all been worried about *you* because you weren't resting. Also, if you don't hammer it home with a bat, or as Jasper often points out, they aren't all big fans of subtlety."

She laughed, the sound genuine and filled with lightness. "I don't know—Rome can be subtle."

"Sure, as subtle as a brick," I agreed. "He prefers directness."

"That's true…okay. Hang on." She dug out her own phone and then took the package with the dark chocolate, donut, and coffee flavor. Yeah, I'd picked that one up just for her on a whim, I just hadn't had a chance to give it to her.

The guys preferred to smoke the weed when we had it, but when I needed something to help me sleep—I'd rather not stink. Her fingers flew over the keyboard on the screen then she hit send before showing me the message.

"I'm alive, bitch," I read aloud. "Not getting laid right now, but I'm definitely being well cared for. Love you. Talk tomorrow."

"Too much?" she asked.

"Depends," I said as she shut off the phone screen.

"On?" She peeled open the packaging as she eyed me. A part of me debated my next response, but then again, what had I just told her?

Sometimes, subtlety wasn't what we needed.

"On whether you want to be getting laid right now."

I broke off a section of the chocolate and held it up to her lips. Her eyes were still red and swollen, her nose still shiny. She was still the most beautiful woman I'd ever seen. The way she licked her lips went straight to my dick, but like I'd told her before, dicks got hard. They just did.

It could wait. I could wait too.

Even if I could definitely picture her mouth wrapped around mine.

When she parted her lips to take the chocolate, she didn't take her gaze from me once, not even when she sucked my fingers into her mouth along with the chocolate.

My beautiful sparrow might still be wounded, but she was far from broken, no matter what she thought. She rolled her tongue around my fingertips and I held them for her until she pulled back.

"Hmm," she murmured, still sucking on the chocolate.

"Good?" I asked, and her lips curved up for real. Yes, that was the answer I wanted, so I narrowed the space between us, dropping my hand to her throat as I said, "Let me taste."

The full-body shudder wasn't lost on me, nor was the

fact that she leaned into my hand as she tilted her head and our mouths collided. Beautiful girl parted her lips again and the swirl of coffee, chocolate, and cinnamon greeted my tongue.

Dark, decadent, and sweet—just like her. I didn't steal it away, just lapped at her tongue, curling the taste on mine and then reveling when she sucked the chocolate from my lips.

Her moan vibrated right through me and I laved her sore lip before lifting my head. "Hmmm," I said, echoing her earlier sound. "I think you taste better than the chocolate."

"How can you be sure?" Her cheeks flushed and her eyes were a bit brighter, despite the redness.

"That's a very good question." I considered her, then the box of chocolate. My fingers were still on her throat, and she tilted her head, lifting her chin to let me wrap them a little tighter. Her pulse beat a steady, if rapid, cadence. "Tell me something, Sparrow, truth only."

"What?"

"Are you all right with this?" I stroked my thumb over her pulse point and her heart rate seemed to leap at the contact.

"I like it when it's you," she whispered, almost like she didn't want to admit it too loudly.

"Only me?" Did I really want to know what she got up to with my brothers?

"I like when they kiss me and touch me," she said, almost hurrying. "Don't think I don't. No one is forcing..."

"Shh, sweet Sparrow, I know they aren't. They'd cut off their own dicks before they ever hurt you with them." That wasn't a doubt in my mind. "I just want to know you're ready for me...today might have gone sideways, but you've also had another shock, and I don't want to push anything."

"Kellan," she said, scooting forward until I slid my hand from her throat and just dragged all of her into my lap.

She straddled my thighs and pressed those sweet hands right over the wings on my chest. The contact answered an ache I hadn't even noticed.

"I wanted you before I fell apart..." Her lips hovered deliciously close to mine.

"I remember," I promised. "But if you want this, I have rules."

Rules for both of us, but right now, there were only a couple of important ones.

"Rules?"

"Hmm-hmm... you tell me where I'm allowed to touch, and then you let me pleasure you until the only thing you can see, think, and feel is me." Her sweet mouth opened into a perfect circle, and she blinked hard as she stared at me.

"Do I get to touch you?"

"You're touching me now."

She glanced down at her hands. "I meant..."

"I know what you meant, Sparrow. And yes, eventually —but right now, right now I want you. I want to taste you, tease you, and make you come. I want you to fall apart for me and come on my tongue. I want you to feel nothing but pleasure—will you let me do that for you?"

"What do you get?" The words came out breathless.

"You, Sparrow," I confirmed. "I get you." And I get to help erase some of your pain. "So...are you in?" I held up the chocolate. "Or do we eat this until we're both pleasantly stoned, and we can just float together? I'm with you, so I'll be happy either way."

But fuck, would I very much like to make you soar. Those words, I kept to myself because I wanted her to choose her own pleasure. Come on, little sparrow, give me the word.

<h1 style="text-align:center">41</h1>

The coffee, chocolate, and cinnamon flavors all lingered on my tongue. Even more, was the way Kellan had chased the decadence around my mouth. Edibles were something new, but the desire coiling through me at his offer was a far headier prospect than eating more chocolate.

Tempted as I was to ask about whether we could do both, I hesitated. Getting stoned and just letting my problems go for a while sounded like a great idea, but I wanted to *feel* Kellan, not just be numb to him.

The denim kept his erection contained, but there was no mistaking it beneath my ass, and I didn't want to pretend it wasn't there. I didn't want to *pretend* at all. "How much do you need to know?" I asked, running my right hand over the wing tattooed to his pec. There were wings on both. But nothing to connect the two. The wings of a kestrel.

They were also hawks. But a specific kind. I'd been

looking them up, trying to figure out why they'd chosen the ones they had.

"Sparrow," Kellan said my name with such command that there was no trying to pretend to look anywhere else. "I need to know what not to do so I don't hurt you. But you don't have to tell me anything, we can just get high, sweetheart."

There was something about the way he said sweetheart.

"Remember what I said about dicks, they get hard. Doesn't mean we have to do anything about it."

He had said that—many times. Looping my arms around his neck, I soothed myself by stroking his hair just above his nape. "When I came onto you when you were my driver..."

At my hesitation, he nodded. "You were very provocative and far too damn enticing for someone who was hurting so much."

"You didn't want to want me then."

"No," he agreed. "You were ours to protect, Sparrow. Taking advantage of that was wrong, particularly when I could see just how fucking lonely you were."

"But the attraction was still there?" I had no idea why this was important to me, but it was.

"The attraction has always been there," he admitted, then sighed. "Sparrow, you're almost nineteen, you were barely eighteen then. I'm in my twenties. The word jailbait does actually mean something."

A laugh bubbled out of me. "But I wasn't jailbait when I made a pass at you."

"No," he agreed. "But you weren't that far from it, and you may not see it—but on the surface, you seem almost painfully young. Then you dance, and you're ethereal, time-less, and so fucking beautiful."

Heat flooded me at his description.

"When I sat in that audience, and you plummeted, twisting and falling, only to lock eyes with me as you were suspended in the air before you danced up the silk again? You claimed every fucking part of me. Just took me a while to realize that I'd been waiting for that."

That had been months before, then not even an hour later—

"Yeah, then you were hurt, and we took you. Giving in to the way I wanted you would have been a bad move, then."

"Not now?"

"No," he answered simply. "We're on more even footing with you now. You're not here because we took you. And the secrets?" With that, he focused on me as he wrapped his hand around my throat again. That move had no business being as provocative and hot as it was, but I swore my whole body relaxed when he did it.

Nothing in his grip threatened me. If anything, it made the world a little better, easier—it was so hard to explain. "No more secrets?"

The question was more palatable with the way he held me, or maybe because he did.

"I would prefer that," he murmured. "I need your trust, Sparrow."

"I trust you," I protested.

"Then tell me where I should never touch you or what you don't want."

A ball of ice formed in the pit of my stomach that not even the languid heat released by his thumb stroking my pulse and the warm grip of his hand around my neck. Mouth dry, I stared into his eyes. They burned with their own fire, a cool, icy one that didn't threaten to consume me but to soothe me.

"I don't like ass play." Pushing those five words out was almost impossible at first. They seemed to turn sticky, clogging my throat, and I wanted to cough or look away—anything. But that would be hiding. He tightened his grip a fraction. The gentlest of squeezes quieted the rabbiting of my heart.

Well, quiet might be the wrong word.

"So—ass play as in anal penetration? Or you don't want anything cupping and squeezing your ass? No spankings?" The ease of his questions belied the utter serious note in his eyes.

I swallowed around the hard lump. "Squeezing is okay, I think. I mean—they have and I don't *always* freak." I frowned. "It's—the anal part." My face seemed to go up in flames, but there was no rejection in Kellan's expression. "When...when I was younger. That was how he would punish me if I didn't cooperate."

Kellan stilled.

"When you were *younger?*"

What little spit in my mouth there had been was gone now. "Yes. If I fought or didn't obey, he would—punish me by..." I could do this, I could say it. "He said once it was another way to play, but I never liked it—it always hurt. Especially if he was angry, and when he was angry, no was not a word he ever wanted to hear. I had to get stitches —once."

"He wanted it to hurt." It wasn't a question.

I had already figured that out. "It—it takes me back to that whenever someone grazes it or touches it—" I squeezed my eyes shut for a moment and dragged in a breath of air.

The soft brush of his cheek against mine as he pulled me close accompanied the gentle squeeze of his hand. The wild beat of my heart seemed completely at odds with the peace stealing through me at his nearness. Did I even understand what those words meant sometimes?

"Yes," I admitted, wrapping deeper into the cocoon he offered. "If I cooperated, it wasn't about the pain." I swallowed hard again. "I hate talking about this—about him."

"So, no ass play," he said, the timbre of his voice dropping. "Not until you're ready."

"I don't know—"

"Shh, you don't have to know." He pulled back a fraction. "Eyes open, Sparrow. Look at me. Remember, it's me that's sitting here."

My lashes fluttered upward. I couldn't forget it was Kellan. But then, I couldn't have forgotten it was Liam or Vaughn or even Jasper, yet I *had* at different points.

"That's my sweet sparrow. Three things—we will never do anything that hurts you. *Ever.* There are ways to make anal very pleasurable, and when you're ready, we're taking that away from him and giving it back to you."

My heart fisted so tight, I thought it might have stopped entirely. Then the thud came, like a pound on my ribs, a sharp, swift thump that promised I was still alive.

"Your body is yours. If you let me play with you, if you let me give you pleasure and make you come, that doesn't give me any more rights to your body than I have at this moment. You say when and you say how. That's your power. You only ever share it with whom you choose, when you choose, and how you choose." He touched his nose to mine. It was such a simple gesture, one that had me smiling despite the words.

"Better," he whispered, then ghosted his lips over mine. The touch so brief but also incredibly sweet. "Third…if anything makes you uncomfortable, you tell me. I don't care if I'm balls deep in your cunt and ready to come myself. If you need me to stop, you say the fucking word."

The last reverberated through me, a command that seemed to strike a place deep in my soul. It rang like some gong of a bell that seemed to dislodge all the ice and I sucked in a deeper breath than I'd managed since this conversation began.

"Do you understand?" He searched my eyes, and I swore my heart did a little flip-flop.

"You're—amazing," I whispered. That wasn't the right word, but it was all I had.

"Thank you," he murmured, a smile tipping the corners of his lips. "Do you understand, though?"

"No pain for me," I summarized his earlier statement. "My body is mine, but you will let me give it to you when I want to. If anything hurts or I need you to stop—all I ever have to say is stop."

He could have etched those words right into my bones; I felt them so deeply.

"Exactly."

"What about you?" I asked, sliding one of my hands from his nape to cup his face. He was so warm everywhere. These guys were all fire. Fire that chased away the frost. Fire that kept me safe and warm. Fire that filled me to the brim, and I still wanted more. I wanted them to just consume all of me and burn me clean.

"What about me?"

"What do you need?"

With his thumb, he tilted my head a fraction then kissed me, slow, deep, and soul-stealing. The sweep of his tongue demanded entry. The scrape of his teeth commanded obedience. But the way he breathed into the kiss, robbing me of breath only to give it back again, turned me inside out.

I clung to him, desperate for more even as he deepened the kiss, yet no other part of him moved. Even when my hips rolled and I pressed myself closer to him. It didn't seem like we could get any closer, but I wanted to climb inside of him or just surround myself in him.

Dragging my lower lip out as he lifted his head, he captured my gaze and my heart triple-hammered. But not from fear. No fear lived in me at all. Not right now.

Not with Kellan.

"You," he answered simply. "I get you, and I get to take care of you. Can I make you orgasm now?"

A shudder went through me at the simplicity of that provocative request. Kellan's control was a thing of absolute beauty. Was he even aware of how perfect he was? I let him go but didn't climb off him. Instead, I reached for the package of chocolate he'd opened earlier.

"Is one more piece of this all right?" If the earlier bit had done anything, I wasn't aware of it. I didn't feel high or even particularly floaty. Just—warm and safe.

"Yes," he murmured. "I don't want you to compromise your judgment, though."

"That's why you said we could get high, or we could have sex."

A brief shrug, but the motion seemed to also grind his very hard dick against my already soaked core. It drew attention to the fact I was already responding to him and my pussy spasmed around the emptiness.

"It won't always be one or the other, but for our first time? Yes, I want you to know exactly who is sliding between your thighs. I want you to know it's my tongue spearing into you and my teeth on your clit. More, I want you to know when I push inside of you that, it's my cock filling you up. When you come, and I intend for you to come a lot, Sparrow, I want you to *know* for damn certain that it's me giving you pleasure over and over again."

"Kellan," I whispered, unwrapping the chocolate. The scent of it really did remind me of chocolate. Awareness of his eyes on me as I ran the chocolate over his lower lip sent another electric pulse through my system. "I trust you, and I want you...thank you for showing me how safe I am with you." Then I slid the chocolate into my mouth, tucking it under my tongue so it could melt slowly. He never once looked away from me. "Make me orgasm now? Let me feel you—let me give my body to you? The control? Everything I can?"

I swore his eyes seemed to catch fire. "It will very much be your pleasure and mine, Sparrow," he said before he fused his mouth to mine and we dueled over the chocolate. Not that it was remotely a fight. My invitation and acceptance seemed to free him as he deepened the kiss, and then we were moving and I was flat on the bed.

Wildfire raced over me as he stared down at me. Then he tugged my shirt up and off before reaching for my pants. Whatever apprehension had been there earlier was gone. Not even the content of my earlier confession could penetrate this warm bubble.

He peeled down my pants, sweeping my panties with them and then my socks. Rising, he watched me and stroked his thumb over his lower lip as I pulled off the bra. Nudity really had never been anything to me. But the way he looked at me—the way they all did—it was like it wasn't just my body they saw.

They definitely seemed to like what they saw, but I wasn't just a body to them and no matter how fine they were—they were so much more than bodies to me.

"Fuck me," he whispered. "You really are beautiful, you know that..." With care, he traced his fingers over my tattoo. "Though I may have to have words with Vaughn, you need more than just a hawk and a falcon here."

The laugh that danced up through me shocked me with its freedom. Instead of lying there, I curled upward and went to my knees on the bed. The indulgence in his expression never shifted as I pressed a kiss to each of the wings on his pecs, then ran my index finger down to where the ivy-covered cross decorated his abdomen.

"You all have had me tattooed on you for a long time." I pressed a kiss on it, then I went to the fastening on his jeans. "May I?"

"Anything you want, Sparrow. But in about three minutes, I'm going to be between your thighs with my tongue, and I'm going to have your legs wrapped around my head."

I could do a lot in three minutes.

42

After freeing the button, I lowered the zipper. There was something about just staring into his eyes while I undressed him. "Can I tell you something?"

"You can tell me anything," he promised. I didn't miss the flex of muscle as I pressed on the waistband and began to shove his jeans—and boxer briefs—down. As much as I wanted to steal a look at his dick as it slapped against his belly, I didn't want to look away from his eyes.

If I thought the heat spilling from his chest had been intense, his hips and thighs were warmer still. I eased toward the edge, still watching him as I pushed the jeans lower and then pressed a kiss to his abdomen, right over the cross.

"Thank you for making me wait when I would have thrown myself at you before," I said. This would have been far more difficult to admit even a few weeks earlier, much less a few months ago when it all happened. "I know I got mad at you—when I realized you were part of these guys and that you'd all taken me."

"Hey," he whispered, cupping my chin. "You had every right to be angry at me. You thought I'd betrayed you, and in a way, I had."

"But you didn't," I argued. "You took nothing from me, even when I wanted you to—you could have said yes that day and I'd have given you anything you wanted. You didn't."

"It breaks my heart when you say things like that, Sparrow. You are so much more than a pretty pussy—no matter how beautiful your cunt is and no matter what Freddie says. Your loneliness cut me. The fact you thought you needed to trade your body for comfort? You never need to do that."

"And that's why I'm thanking you," I said, aware of the rapidly descending clock on how long he said I had until he was taking over. Dropping my gaze to his cock, I drank in the sight of it. The thick length, the blunted crown, how red and fierce it was.

Nothing in his manner gave away just how rigid his cock was or the way the vein along the underside of it seemed to throb. If I hadn't already been hot and slick with need for him, I would have been at this revelation.

Running my nose along his length, gently teasing, I grinned when his abdominals tightened. "You're a good man, Kellan Traschel," I whispered his name. "Kestrel... fierce, swift, and always there—hovering and ready to strike or to catch."

On the last word, I wrapped my hand around his cock and then closed my lips over the head. I wouldn't have long, and there was no doubt in my mind that what Kellan said would happen was about to, and I rubbed my thighs in anticipation.

Every ounce of wantonness in me was swirling into this wild mass of need. I pushed down, swallowing his cock as I stroked my tongue over the mushroom-shaped head, then along the underside.

His hand fisted my hair. "Tap my leg if this is all right, Sparrow."

I tapped his leg once.

"Good girl," he said in a low voice that was a caress all its own. "I'm going to fuck your throat now. One tap that you understand. Two taps to stop."

I tapped once and relaxed my mouth.

"Fuck yes, Sparrow, good girl." Then he pushed all the way to my throat, choking me on his cock for a few timeless seconds that had my eyes burning and my body aching. Then he eased back.

"Breathe," he ordered, and I took in a noisy breath. "Hold it." I had no time to react and then he buried his cock so deep, my face was pressed to his abdomen and he held it there until spots danced before my eyes and my hips rocked against the covers of his bed.

He repeated the command once more as he eased back, the saltiness leaking from his tip stroking over my tongue. Then he choked me again and again until tears streaked my face and I had my nails dug into his thighs.

It was fucking perfect. I was wholly focused on him, I wanted him to come in my mouth, but he eased from my lips. At my soft protest, he caught my chin and then kissed me. I was a drooling fucking mess, but it didn't stop him as he wrapped that hand around my throat and eased me back on the bed.

The command in his touch demanded obedience and I acquiesced without issue. I wanted to give him everything. Settling on my back against the pillows, I let out a hiss at how cool the sheets seemed against my fevered skin. His gaze fixed on me, searching until he found whatever he was looking for.

"What is your word if I do something you don't want?"

I licked my lips. The sensual glide of his skin against mine was something I was almost desperate for at this point. "Stop."

"That's my girl," he whispered, then kissed along my jaw. "Smart, sexy, and sensual. You're perfect, Sparrow. Never forget that."

I rubbed my thighs together, but whatever protest I would have made to the compliment died unspoken when he trailed kisses to my breast. He toyed with each nipple, as though growing acquainted with them.

A part of me wanted to just close my eyes and savor the sensations he provoked, but he kept glancing at me. Checking. Always checking, as he released my throat and cupped one breast. Every inch of skin he teased and touched, he also verified was all right for him to caress.

It turned my heart inside out, and I wanted to cry and shout. He trailed his lips down my abdomen, even as he kept teasing my nipples. It was hard to lie still, my hips arched and bumped against his chest. I swore he chuckled softly, but then he followed the line of my tattoo with his tongue until I was practically shivering from the contact.

"I love this art," he murmured, pressing a kiss to each word. "I love that you got it done while you were here with us."

A tear slid down my cheek and I reached for one of his hands. He released my breast to catch my fingers, and then he interlaced our fingers together.

"I'm right here, Sparrow," he whispered above my cunt. Even with his weight resting against me, he didn't pin me to the bed. I rocked my thighs apart for him and he glanced up to meet my gaze. "You still with me?"

"Yes." Even if it took me a minute to frame the word and push it out. "Absolutely, yes…" I shifted my weight, arching my hips again, and this time, his chuckle wasn't just soft and amused.

It was almost taunting and delighted. "You want something, Sparrow?"

Lifting my head from the pillows as I squeezed his hand, I hooked one leg over his shoulder and pressed the flat of my foot to his back. "I want to come on your tongue."

His smile damn near blinded me, it was so wide. "Yes, ma'am. Hands up behind your head and keep them there." He squeezed my hand once like a reminder, then let me go. My nipples tightened almost painfully as I put my hands behind my head, lacing my fingers together.

The act arched my back some and pushed my breasts up. He pinched one nipple before he tugged it. More liquid heat unspooled in my middle.

"Take a deep breath," he ordered and I complied. "Again." It wasn't until I'd flooded my lungs with air and taken another four or five deep breaths that he moved, and suddenly I couldn't breathe at all because of how hot his tongue and lips were on my cunt.

He didn't ease into it, instead, he pressed my thighs wide which forced my foot from his back. Then speared me with his tongue. The rapid thrusts were a tease, but he murmured against my soaked core a split second before he scraped his teeth over my clit.

The band of tension snapped like a rubber band stretched too far. I'd been riding the edge far closer than I'd realized as that first orgasm crashed over me. I tried to keep the sound in, but he pinched a nipple and I caught his gaze as he rolled my clit.

Fuck, I think my eyes rolled back, and this time I let out a scream. He nuzzled kisses along my cunt, like he was petting me down from the overwhelming sensations rioting through me. Then as soon as I caught my breath, he went back to lapping at me. The skill he employed with his tongue took me from repleteness to the edge, trembling with need all over again.

It was almost too much, but I didn't want it to stop, and this time, when he thrust his fingers inside of me to mirror his earlier thrusts with his tongue, I forgot to keep my hands behind my head. I thrashed, hips bucking, and he kept me in place, even as I strained to follow his mouth and ride his tongue and fingers.

"Fuck, you taste so goddamn sweet," he whispered when I lay quivering. He wiped his face on the covers and eased his fingers out of me. With care, he crawled up until we were face to face. The wicked smile, combined with a hint of swelling to his lips and the wildfire in his eyes, promised me we were not done. "Did you like coming on my tongue, Sparrow?"

"Yes," I answered in a raw voice. I couldn't stop the shaking that seemed to quiver right out from where my inner muscles kept clenching on nothingness. "And your fingers."

"Oh, you liked these?" He circled my clit with a thumb and it sent a shockwave up my spine. Too much and not enough. "Oh, you do like this. Eyes open and on me, Sparrow."

I flexed my fingers against the sheets as he went from stroking my clit to sliding his fingers into me. Three stretched me, but the burn was sweet, and I lifted my hips in entreaty.

"That's it," he said, the smile still there. "Fuck my hand, Sparrow. Make yourself come on my fingers."

I swore white-hot heat blew right through me and I rocked my hips, swiveling them to change the angle of his fingers as he curled them each time he thrust deep. Anticipation and tension both ramped up within me. Sweat slicked my skin, and I clamped down on his fingers as I thrust up, trying to take him deeper.

"You're so close," he whispered against my cheek, nuzzling a kiss there. "Aren't you?"

So close, but it wasn't quite—he stroked his thumb over my clit as he curled his fingers. Pleasure stiffened me until I went totally still. A soundless scream echoed in my throat as his tongue plunged against mine, mirroring his fingers.

The orgasm that burst through me damn near blacked me out, but I fought to stay with him. When he lifted his head, I shook everywhere, despite how boneless I was from pleasure and still...

"You're so beautiful when you come," he said. "I want to see you do it again."

Was that even possible? Words failed me though, so I just patted him. Once.

The intensity in his stare increased, and it set off a whole new wave of lust in me. When I tilted my chin up, exposing my throat, his eyes darkened and he wrapped his hand around my neck.

"You want this, Sparrow?" he whispered. "Are you ready for me?"

"Please, Kellan," I answered. Thank fuck my voice worked.

"Anything for you," he murmured. "Anything." He was

on his knees between my legs, and he stroked his cock with his free hand. "What's our word?"

"Stop."

"What do you want?"

"You."

He smiled, teasing the head of his cock along my slit and it took everything I had not to raise them up. His hand tightened just a fraction around my neck, and I obeyed the command to be still. To let him do it his way. I wanted him to do it his way.

"I want to come on your cock," I managed finally. "I want you to come inside of me."

The first push thrust him inside of me, stretching me around him and my inner walls spasmed. Fuck, I think my whole body spasmed in delight. Everything else had been leading up to this. He began to rock his hips and he gave my throat another squeeze, just a light one. It didn't cut off my air, just reminded me he was there.

Tethering me to him, as it were, keeping me grounded even as he drove me higher. The way he licked his lips as he gazed down at where his dick disappeared into me had me clenching around him all over again.

No words were necessary. He rocked us into a deliberate pace, alternating between watching his cock sink into my cunt, then lifting his gaze to mine. I covered his hand on my throat with my own. At his smile, I reveled in being able to touch him, but I couldn't hold the thread of my thoughts as he increased the pace.

His thrusts pushed me up the bed, but his hand kept me in place. When he slid his fingers down to search where we joined and pressed one in alongside his cock, I couldn't suck in enough air as my hips arched.

The pressure and the burn were intense. "That's it, Sparrow," he murmured. "A little more..."

Then there was a second finger added to the first, and the wild trembling from earlier came back.

"There it is, you're going to come just like this. The only thing you're going to feel is me."

The soundless yes fell from my lips as he deepened his thrust, slamming into me. He kept his fingers in place, stretching me wider and wider. The pressure was intense and then his hand flexed around my throat and I exploded as the world danced with sparks and light.

The slap of his flesh into mine, the soft grunts of his motion, and the constant stream of praise just set me on fire. The orgasm unraveling inside me was relentless, unstoppable, and it seemed to shred every part of me until I was nothing but electric pleasure catching fire everywhere we touched.

He stiffened and then the first hot jet of his own orgasm seemed to fill me, and I swore I came all over again. The world dimmed, then he released his hand and oxygen flooded my lungs. But I was spiraling so high, I was pretty sure he'd just fucked me right out of my body.

43

Kellan and I spent the day in bed. As decadent as that sounded, I was certain I slept almost as much as I orgasmed. I was sore in all the best ways when he left me long enough to get food. And I'd just showered when Freddie came to tell us Jasper was awake.

Excitement threaded through me. "We'll be right there," Kel told him. He'd dragged on a pair of sweats but didn't bother with a shirt. Crooking his finger at me, he held up a pair of panties he must have gotten from my room and then knelt so I could step into them.

Gently, he glided them up and into place, not once touching my ass. The care he demonstrated put another lump in my throat. He pressed a kiss to my abdomen before he stood, then grabbed a shirt off the bed. It was definitely one of his.

He tugged it over my head as I threaded my arms through the sleeves. "There we go, shall we?"

"Yes," I told him, then kissed his chin on impulse. "Thank you."

"Oh, it was undoubtedly my pleasure," he promised. "And if Jasper doesn't need you tonight, that bed is right where you're going after we see him."

The hum in my system was practically a full-on purr. "Anything you want," I said, with a little salute and he chuckled.

"Let's go, Sparrow. He's probably ripping Doc's head off cause you're not right there."

I grimaced because he probably wasn't far off the mark. Jasper's irritation with Mickey went far deeper and had developed well before me.

The door to his room was open a fraction and his voice reached me before I even got there.

"Fuck off. I can get out of bed and take a leak. So, take the damn catheter out."

Wincing, I pushed the door inward. Doc had inserted it on the second day because Jasper's fever kept raging and we needed to keep him asleep and resting as much as possible.

"You forgot to say please," I said as I closed the distance from the door to the bed swiftly. Vaughn's flash of a smile mirrored Rome's from where they were apparently keeping Jasper in bed.

Mickey was at the foot of the bed and Freddie sprawled in one of the chairs. "Thank fuck, Boo-Boo is here and she can settle your grouchy ass down."

Instead of responding to Freddie, Jasper tried to sit up, but he paled and Vaughn caught him and made him lay back down. "Easy man, she's coming."

I walked right up onto the bed, careful and light until I

reached the pillows next to him, and then I settled without disturbing him as much as I could.

"Hey," I whispered when he shot those gray eyes at me. Happiness ballooned within me, leaving me buoyant as he stretched out a hand and I caught it. Pulling his hand to my cheek, I leaned into his palm then pressed my lips to his forehead. "It's about time you woke up."

"You're all right?" He searched my face, and while he was awake, his forehead was a little clammy and dotted with sweat. His hair was still damp from it. The fever *seemed* gone, and I stole a look at Mickey.

"I'm fine," I said. "Did his fever break?"

"Yep, as promised," Mickey told me with a smile. "He's not totally out of the woods yet."

"Don't tell her that," Jasper snarled and I flicked his nose. The whole room went quiet as he jerked his gaze back to me. "Did you just..."

"Do this?" I asked before I flicked his nose again. He tried to scowl, but the twitching of his lips gave him away. "Yes, I did. Now behave. You've done nothing but worry us all week, and Mickey has been here every step of the way. So, thank him and be polite."

The corner of his mouth kicked even higher. "I love you," he murmured.

That...wow. I blinked as I stared at him. "Because I flicked your nose?"

All around us, the guys began to crack up. Even Kellan dipped his chin as he laughed and Jasper just raised his middle finger to all of them but stayed focused on me. "Maybe especially because you did that. I'd ask for a kiss, but my mouth tastes like ass and not even the good kind. So —raincheck, Swan?"

"It's a date." The fluttering in my chest turned into a whole flock of birds beating their wings as I turned those words over in my head. I turned my head to press a kiss into his palm.

"Okay," Jasper said, still smiling, but his eyes were not quite focusing yet. "I'm starving, though, and I would really like to go and take a leak, Doc. If you wouldn't mind, will you *please* remove the catheter?"

"I can do that," Mickey said as he approached the bed. "You can eat too, if you're up for it, but I'd suggest keeping it light. Soft foods for now. We're also keeping you on the IV. It's better for the antibiotics, but if the fever stays down for the next thirty-six hours, we'll switch you out to oral."

"Yeah, let Swan do the oral, Doc, if you don't mind."

It was my turn to giggle, though Freddie groaned. "That was bad, Hawk. Like dad-joke, bad."

"Leave him alone," I scolded, holding fast to Jasper's hand. Even glassy-eyed and pale, it was so damn nice to have him awake. I really was walking on air at the moment, despite sitting there on the bed.

"All right," Kellan said, sliding his hands into his pockets. "Vaughn and Rome, go get food for everyone, please. Freddie, grab a shower and fresh clothes. Doc—you have the patient."

"What about me?" I asked.

"Stay here," Jasper said. "Please. Just—you know, close your eyes for the catheter part. There's nothing sexy about a tube shoved up your dick."

"That," Kellan said. "I'm going down to make coffee, and I'll bring some up for everyone." He was probably right, with Jasper awake, I didn't want to move. Not yet. "Unless you need me here."

"I got this," Mickey said.

"Pizza, Jas?" Vaughn asked.

"That's not a soft food," Mickey stated.

"We'll get the soft crust," Rome said and I grinned.

"That sounds fucking perfect, thanks, guys."

Mickey's expression disagreed, but I caught his eye. "Pizza can be soft, especially if it's hot and fresh."

"Little Bit…"

"Please, Mickey? He's been out for days and he's hungry. One slice wouldn't hurt, right?"

Raking a hand over his face, he grunted. "Fine, one slice, and if you manage that, we'll try a second one."

Jasper grinned. "Done. Thank you."

Relief swarmed me, and the guys filed out, one after another, but only after they bumped Jasper's shoulder or made sure to take a good long look at him before they headed out. Only Vaughn, followed by Rome, circled the bed to press a kiss to my head and then another to my lips.

Freddie chortled and then slid over to my side of the bed and held out his pinky. "I'm with Jas, I'll brush my teeth before I kiss you."

Chuckling, I crooked a finger and he bent close so I could press a kiss to his cheek.

"Okay, that's pretty damn cool. Be back in a few." Then he was strolling out, lighter than he'd seemed in days. The guilt had been eating at him, and hopefully with Jasper waking up and being okay, Freddie could let some of that go.

It took Mickey about fifteen minutes to finish giving Jasper a once over; he also changed his bandage and checked the stitches. The inflammation around the injury was there, but it had gone down considerably.

The removal of the catheter was an experience I would rather have forgone for both of us. Mine had been *very* unpleasant, but Mickey had been relatively gentle and Jasper focused on me the whole time.

Between us, we helped him into the bathroom and went through the motions of brushing his teeth and washing up. "Chances of a shower?"

"Not yet," Mickey told him from the doorway. He'd backed off to give him a modicum of privacy while I'd stayed close, but he wasn't leaving him entirely. "Need to let that wound heal up some more."

"I can do a sponge bath—it's not perfect, but I bet we could work something out," I offered and he gave me a half-smile.

"Swan, that's about the sexiest, non-sexy offer I've ever received."

"Okay, lover boy," Mickey said with a chuckle. "Let's get you back into the bed."

"Oh, we should change the sheets." I gave Jasper a quick kiss. "Maybe move him to the chairs for a minute?"

"How about you just lean on me, Jas," Mickey said. "Little Bit has changing out your sheets down to an art."

"Wish you hadn't had to figure that part out," Jasper said and I blew him a kiss.

"Hush, Freddie had to show me how to do it. He's even better at it than I am, and we wanted you to have clean sheets." The guys had also done something with the dirty ones, they vanished, and clean ones replaced them.

As soon as I got the fresh ones in place, Mickey walked Jasper back to bed and we got him tucked in. Exhaustion covered his face and he was asleep long before the guys got back with the pizza.

Kel brought me coffee, though and more for Mickey. Freddie wandered back in as Kel said, "Real numbers, Doc. How long are we looking at for his recovery?"

"Long as the fever is gone and he remains infection free, I'm saying a week of total rest, then he can move on to a couple of weeks of light duty." He fixed Kellan with a look. "A month to six weeks before I'd even think about letting him anywhere near a fight."

I sipped my coffee but glanced between them. "Do you think we have that kind of time?"

Kellan considered me for a long moment. "No, Sparrow, I don't. That means tomorrow, we really do begin your lessons in earnest. And Freddie," he continued, glancing at him. "You need to get her a knife."

He grinned. "Can do. Boo-Boo is already a badass, and when I'm done, she'll be a badass who will cut you."

I wasn't sure whether to be happy about that, but the distinct frown on Mickey's face had me keeping my objections to myself. Kellan wouldn't suggest any of this if it weren't necessary.

"I need to up my physical therapy then, too," I said, capturing Mickey's attention. "Stretches and the rest—but I don't know if I'm ready to walk into the clinic. It's…"

"It's a medical facility," he finished for me, understanding in his slow nod. "You don't have to. We'll bring what we need here, Little Bit."

Relieved, I closed my eyes. Admitting that hadn't been as hard as I feared. It also took some of the pressure off to go to the clinic. Jasper slept through the guys getting back and Milo joining us. But our laughter woke him up and I helped him eat the pizza.

He managed three full slices before he was already falling asleep again. "Feels like Doc is drugging me," he complained.

"I'm not," Mickey told him. "Painkillers, but a low dose

and not enough to make you sleep. Your body needs the rest, let it have it. That's how you heal."

"Right," Jasper rubbed his face. "Go sleep, Swan, you've been staying with me for days...you need to rest."

"Will you behave if I go?"

He chuckled. "I might." Though the tiredness seemed to be just leaking out of his pores. "Kel, make her go rest."

"I will," he said. "But you *will* behave, even if she isn't in here. Because you're not going to worry her."

"I got him," Milo said, and I flashed a grin at him. "Go on, Ivy. Get some rest. Freddie—that goes for you too. I can sit here with the hardhead. Doc—you can crash in my room. It's late and you've been here more than your own place lately."

"I'll see you in the morning," I promised Jasper. I was reluctant to leave him, but if he was that tired, I wanted him to rest and not worry about me.

Kel lifted me off the bed and we left ahead of the guys, taking Freddie with us. In the hall, Freddie turned abruptly and crashed into me. I returned his hug and held on tight. Kel moved a couple of steps to the side, giving us space.

"He's okay," I whispered.

"Yeah," Freddie agreed as he let go of me slowly and backed up a step. "Also, I really like the little red lace panties. They're a nice touch."

I snorted. "Thank you, Kellan picked them out."

"Nice," he said, then sobered as he focused on me. "You good?"

"I think so..." I was...I wasn't sure what I was at the moment. "He's okay. That's the big takeaway for today."

"Yeah, all right, go sleep, Boo-Boo, knife training tomor-row. I'll show you how to slice, dice, and Julien cleavers."

"It's cleaves."

"Maybe," Freddie said, walking backwards. "But does Julian do it with an actual cleaver? Dream about me naked tonight, okay?"

"Sure," I called after him. "Just make sure I'm naked in your dreams too."

"Done."

He blew a kiss and then vanished into his room. I stared after him for a moment. Rome slid out of Jasper's room and followed my gaze, then said, "He'll be okay."

"I hope so," I murmured. He was too damn important to not be okay. Kellan caught my fingers and tugged me to his room. His soft laugh when Rome followed us inside made me grin. Rome glanced around the room, then at Kellan for a long moment. He nodded and said, "Your bed is bigger than Starling's."

"Yeah," Kellan said as he secured the door and plugged his phone in. "You're more than welcome to stay if she doesn't mind."

"I don't," I told him, and Rome gave me a kiss before nudging me toward the bed. It took us a minute to sort everyone out, but I was parked firmly between them. Kellan rolled me onto my side and tucked my back to his front so I was facing Rome.

When I settled my hand on Rome's chest, he covered my hand with his. "Sleep, Starling. No bad dreams."

"Only of Freddie naked."

That earned a grin from Rome and a soft snort from Kellan.

"And maybe the two of you as well," I teased, and that earned me the gentlest of pinches on my hip. The fact he remembered made me smile even wider. "Definitely both of you."

Maybe it was all the orgasms, or maybe it was the fact

that Jasper was awake and doing so much better. Maybe it was because I was snuggled securely between Kellan and Rome. Or maybe it was some combination of all of the above.

Sleep didn't elude me, and I didn't struggle; I was floating almost as soon as I closed my eyes. Floated securely between them into a place where people weren't shooting and we didn't have enemies, and the guys could laugh and tease while I danced.

44

The next couple of days started very differently. The first morning, Rome woke me with a kiss and it deepened until I was stroking him and he was teasing me. Awareness that Kellan had awakened at some point rippled over me, but Rome was teasing my clit with his cock. I stroked the lines of the gorgeous swirls that decorated his chest.

"Yes?" Rome asked, and I shivered at all the meaning he managed to intone in one single word.

"Yes." Still, I started to glance back at Kellan, but he merely kissed my shoulder.

"Let Rome have you, Sparrow. Let me see you dance with him." The shivers of delight cascading over my skin intensified as he stroked my skin. The electric tingling across my nerves grew when he slid a hand between my legs. No part of Kellan touched my ass.

The depth of emotion his care provoked swarmed me.

Rome kissed my eyes and as Kellan slid a finger inside of me, then another. He scissored them as he stroked.

"Rome," he said, his voice a little raspy and drenched in need. "She's soaking for you. Don't keep her waiting." The bed dipped and shifted as Rome eased forward. I was still on my side, and at the pressure of Kellan's thrusting fingers, I lifted my thigh higher to hook over Rome's hip.

Brushing my lips with his, Rome initiated the gentlest of kisses as I reached down to grip his cock along with him. Our fingers tangled and I tilted my hips, shifting the angle, and he began to push inside of me.

Kellan's fingers stayed there, like when he'd pushed his fingers in alongside his own cock, he bracketed Rome's. The stretch was incredible, the slow burn lighting a fuse as I squeezed tighter around both of them.

"Always something in the way," Rome muttered, but Kellan laughed, and I nipped at Rome's lip.

"He'll move if you want him to." These guys would do anything for each other.

"You like?" Rome asked. I'd never been so grateful for the darkness before, the blue light that lined the ceiling was far too dim to let me see their faces, and hopefully they couldn't see mine. Fire roasted my cheeks and my nipples pulled taut as I flexed my hips to match their surges. Fuck, Kellan added a third finger and between his hand and Rome's dick, I was going to split apart in all the best ways.

"I—oh yes—fuck..." Because at the first whisper of yes, Rome sank deeper into me and they shifted the pace. I was riding him, the angle ensured he hit the sweet spot inside me.

The burn, the press of Kellan's fingers, the hot wet kiss he pressed to my shoulder, and then finally Rome's mouth claiming mine. I arched into him as his chest grazed my nipples. The heat surrounding me was so intense that I felt like the friction would actually make me combust.

Our tongues dueled as we chased our orgasms together. The dancing metaphor fit as we moved, the three of us. Only instead of his cock, it was Kellan's fingers inside of me and the weight of his rigid erection pressed to my lower back.

I stretched a hand behind me to clasp his hip. The fact he remained so mindful of me penetrated the carnal haze they wrapped me up in. When I found his cock and cupped him, he began to thrust into my hand. The bite of his teeth scraped my shoulder.

"Beautiful Sparrow, let go," he murmured. "Keep kissing Rome, let him drive you mad. You can have my cock as soon as he's done."

The words submerged me as he continued to push into my hand, the wild motion perfect as I rocked toward Rome as he filled me. The stretch of his beautiful painted dick, along with Kellan's fingers, seemed to pull me apart.

I didn't fight the spiral, only gasped when Kellan's fingers pulled away and Rome let out a hum of sound. His pace increased, and the slap of our skin was the perfect symphony. With damp fingers, Kellan traced a path up my hip, not once touching my ass, and the urge to grind back against him had me moving without thought.

Rome devoured my mouth. Kellan cupped one of my breasts as he continued to push into my hand, mirroring Rome's deep thrusts, and the pleasure coiling within me exploded outward. Dampness trickled against my ass and I wanted more.

Head back, Rome let out a glorious sigh as he came, and now, I wished I could see. The wonder on his face when the pleasure stole over him was so beautiful. The rush of Rome filling me only lifted me higher. We shuddered together, his skin slick against mine.

We were still trembling when Kellan peeled my fingers from him gently. "Over," he commanded, and together, they helped me roll over until I straddled Rome and he could play with my breasts.

It was like being shocked again, only this time, I craved every sizzling connection that lit me up.

"Ass up, Sparrow," Kellan coaxed only with his hands on my hips. The adjustment had Rome slipping free of me and I groaned. "Don't worry, sweet girl, I'm going to fill you up." He pushed into me at the same moment, and I snapped my head up as he glided through Rome's cum, pushing some of it out while he shoved the rest of it deeper.

"Kiss her breasts, Rome," Kellan urged him as he wrapped his hand around my throat from the back. They surrounded me and every thrust of Kellan's dick into my still clenching cunt pushed a cry out of me.

If I thought it had been too much earlier, I wasn't prepared for how over-sensitized every nerve ending was. Or how much Rome would explore to see what I liked. By the time I came on Kellan's cock, I was sobbing from the overload. The spots across my vision whited out and I would have collapsed if they hadn't both supported me.

So many kisses feathering over my skin eased me down as I floated. The dampness between my thighs was a mess, but I craved it, especially with how empty I felt after Kellan slipped free.

"When you're ready," Kellan murmured. "We'll shower, then I'll cook you whatever you want for breakfast."

"Coffee," Rome said, and a laugh escaped me because my stomach let out a lusty growl. Whether it was hunger for them, the shower—we were all sticky—or for the coffee, I didn't know, and I didn't care.

"Need to check on Jasper." Oh, look at that, I could talk.

"We will," Kellan said, then he was sliding his arms under me and lifting me out of the bed. I would have protested I could walk, but I really wasn't sure. My cunt ached from the day before and the morning wake-up call. "Rome, you joining us or showering on your own? Sparrow, watch your eyes, light coming on."

I tucked my face to Kellan's shoulder as he flicked the light on. His shower was a stall without a curtain. But it also had two showerheads. Oh, that was nice.

Rome apparently decided to join us and it took a little maneuvering, but we all managed to get clean. It also gave me some ideas of what I'd like to do for them later.

It wasn't long before we were downstairs, my hair was still wet and Kellan was cooking. Vaughn trailed into the kitchen, pausing to take a long look at each of us as I sipped my coffee.

"I fucking hate all of you," he muttered, then winked at me. "Except you, Dove."

A laugh escaped me, then Kellan said, "Don't hate. You could have followed me last night and joined us this morning."

"Not enough room," Rome said. "He takes up too much space."

That had me choking on my coffee and my face flamed. Vaughn's chuckles joined mine and when he leaned over me, I lifted my face to meet his kiss. It was slow, sweet, and teasing.

"Sleep with me tonight," he invited with a murmur against my lips and that sent another shiver of anticipation through my languid muscles.

"How much sleep are we going to get?"

"Not much if I can help it," he teased, then kissed me again as my stomach clenched.

"Seriously?" Milo half-growled from the doorway, and I didn't jerk away from Vaughn, just glanced at my brother.

"It's wonderful," I said, choosing a different battle entirely. "They're wonderful. Just blows my mind."

The disapproval on his face eased and his expression softened. "You don't fight fair, Ivy," he muttered.

"Be nice, and I'll make you coffee."

"I've been very nice," Vaughn interrupted, then pressed a kiss to my temple and I laughed.

"Yes, you have."

"I think I just threw up in my mouth," Milo muttered, but he sounded a little less cranky.

"Then suck on a breath mint," Kellan advised.

"They're in the cabinet," Rome offered and a fresh wave of laughter rolled through me.

"Ivy, have I mentioned that my friends are all assholes?" He folded his arms and leaned against the fridge.

"You might have," I told him. "But then you can be one too, so I think it's a good fit."

Milo's mouth dropped open and shock filled his eyes.

I just raised my brows as Vaughn pulled out my chair when I went to stand. "You have only yourself to blame," I informed my brother. "You should appreciate the fact that being an asshole doesn't actually bother me that much."

"Much," he echoed and scrubbed a hand over his face, but he couldn't quite smother the laughter that shook him. Kellan grinned at me as I went to get the coffee made for Vaughn and Milo. I'd already made mine, Rome's, and Kellan's.

"Is Mickey still..."

"Here, Little Bit?" He finished the question for me, and I glanced over my shoulder to find him standing near Milo but not quite in the kitchen. "I am. Jas is doing fine, I just checked on him. The fever is staying down."

Relief added to the happy buzz in my system. "Coffee?"

"Please."

"If you start mooning at her, I'm going to punch you," Milo muttered.

"You can try, kid," Mickey said, and I had to look back at the coffee to keep from grinning.

Kellan chuckled. "No fighting in the kitchen. Someone set the table."

"On it," Vaughn said. The next hour passed in delightful warmth. Mickey and Milo joined us for food that Kellan dished out. Scrambled eggs, bacon, toast, and fried potatoes. The guys ate way more of the potatoes than I did, but they were crispy.

Rome skipped the eggs. Vaughn and Milo ate extras of everything while Mickey watched his portions. No one talked business, and no one—meaning Milo—complained about the fact that Vaughn and Rome both took turns massaging my neck.

I was going to end up a puddle before the meal was over, but I didn't protest in the slightest. It was easily one of my favorite moments in the clubhouse. Freddie wandered in toward the end and I climbed up to make him coffee while Kellan made him fresh eggs.

He peered at all of us through bleary eyes and grunted a sound. "You guys are way too happy." But when I raised my eyebrows, he gave me a quick nod and I pressed a kiss to his cheek. "Okay, you can be as happy as you want."

"Enough fun," Kellan said, but his gaze was on me. "Grab a jacket and shoes, Sparrow. Shooting lessons."

"What lessons?" Milo demanded. I grabbed the coffee I'd just made for Jasper and scooted past them.

"I'll just check on Jasper and let you deal with this." Because Milo had gone from fine to incensed. I didn't even make it to the stairs before Milo snarled something, so I double-timed it up them.

I loved how protective he was of me, but I really did hate the fighting it always seemed to lead into. Jasper was only half-awake when I slipped into his room. I set the coffee next to the bed and gave him a kiss before I whispered to him of their plans.

"Listen to Kel," Jasper said, stroking my hair. "I'll take you up on that sponge bath later, if you're up for it."

"I'll make time," I promised him. "How are you feeling?"

"I'd love to tell you I've felt worse, Swan. I really would. But getting shot sucks."

Grimacing, I rubbed his shoulder. "I'm sorry."

"Just teaches me to be faster next time," he said with a wink. "Besides, better me than Freddie." His expression sobered, and I didn't miss the way he glanced around the room before focusing on me again. "How is he?"

"Blaming himself, but—" I touched a finger to Jasper's lips when he would have protested. "He's handling it. We're talking, and he—loves you very much. He thinks if he hadn't gone to see those dealers, this wouldn't have happened."

"Ambush was planned," Jasper said without an ounce of rancor. "They used him, used a weakness to leverage. I'll talk to him."

Used a weakness like my uncle had. The thought left a bitter taste in my mouth. I hadn't asked Kellan who was behind it all, but what if it was my uncle? Fear sliced through the hum in my blood, followed swiftly by fury.

"Don't push him," I advised. "I mean—I know you know him better."

"Swan," Jasper eased up and moved onto his side carefully to cup my face with his hand. "I get it. Thank you for looking after him."

"I care," I admitted.

"I know you do."

I bit my lip. "Jasper?" At his raised eyebrows, I pressed on. "You said..."

"I love you?" he repeated those three gold-embossed words like they were as easy to come by as pennies. "I did." He swept some of my still shower damp hair away from my face. "I mean it. I love you."

He said it so easily that I leaned in and pressed a kiss to his lips, wanting to taste the words on his lips. The wealth of emotion that swamped me was staggering. His beard tickled my cheeks, and he lingered for a long moment, the kiss so much more than just passion or desire, though those lurked within his touch.

"I—"

"Don't have to say a word, Swan," he admonished me. "You coming back was everything I needed."

And that struck me as sad on some levels, but then the fierce loyalty and affection these men had for each other— for Milo—it was everything I'd never had in my life beyond Lainey. "I'm selfish," I whispered.

"Good," he said. "Cause we are too... Now tell me, what has you so worried when you should be relaxed? Considering I can smell Kel's shampoo on you."

My eyes widened and he chuckled. "I—Kellan's taking me for shooting lessons."

Sobering, he nodded and caressed my cheek. "Good. Liam said he's been teaching you to fight?"

"Yes, he can be a real dick about it—but he's a good teacher. Kellan told Freddie to teach me to use a knife last night when you were sleeping."

"He's going to enjoy that *way* too much." The pleasure in his voice gave him away. "I'm going to enjoy that too—see if we can swing a day-pass to get out of this bed so I can watch, yeah?"

"Maybe," I said. "You tried to die on me, but if you're very good, I'll come climb into bed with you after your bath, and if you're very good and let me do all the work…"

A groan escaped him. "Fuck, Swan."

"That is the idea," I whispered, then stole another kiss before a brief knock on the door announced a new arrival.

"Coming to steal my girl, Kel?" Jasper asked without looking away from me, a smile tipping his lips.

"Our girl, and yes. Lesson time."

"Good plan, I'll be here, behaving myself," Jasper said with a wink and I laughed. One more kiss and then I was up. Ten minutes later, I was in the car with Kellan, and to my surprise as well as delight, Milo joined us.

"Gonna backseat teach?" Kellan asked and Milo chuckled.

"Nope," he said, then glanced to where I sat in the back-seat. "Gonna make sure Ivy knows everything she needs to know."

When I put a hand on his shoulder, he grasped my fingers.

"Thank you, Milo."

"Not gonna say my pleasure, kid," he answered in a gruff voice. "I'd give anything for this to not be your life, but they're right. You're here, and you need to know."

I squeezed his hand. "And you want to make sure I can kick their asses if they need it?"

"That," he said with a kind of grim amusement, "goes without saying. Course, Liam's doing his part there."

Yes, yes, he was.

He was the only one I hadn't seen this morning, and worry niggled in the back of my mind. But Rome hadn't been worried, and I would trust his instincts on this. Of all of us, he knew his twin best.

45

EMERSYN

Shooting lessons did not go at all how I expected. It was more than just pointing the gun at the target and shooting. Yes, we absolutely did that part, but he had me try with three or four different types of guns. Milo observed, but he also added his own advice.

They finally settled on a Smith and Wesson M&P 380 Shield EZ and a Glock 19. Both were better suited to my smaller hands. One had a manual safety, and the other did not.

Kellan wouldn't even let me fire one until I could identify every piece of the gun. "There's no point in getting you one or teaching you how to use one if it puts you in more danger than it prevents." The implacable expression, coupled with his flat tone, quelled any argument I might have made.

Not that I was making one. The Glock 19 was a little heavier than the M&P. The reload on the M&P seemed smoother, but it didn't take me long to master both. When it came to shooting, Kellan braced me and then had me use both hands on the gun. One to hold it, the other to steady my wrist.

"You need to get as comfortable as you can with the firing. There's always a kickback, the recoil is lighter, but if you don't know it's coming, it can definitely throw off your aim." He offered every instruction in the same patient manner he had our driving lessons.

"We're going to work on driving again soon, right?" Excitement bounced through me at that idea.

"We will," he said. "Now, focus."

"Yes, sir," I said, then bit my lip at the flare in his eyes before I stared at the target again. "We're ready to let me fire?"

Milo settled a pair of earphones over my head. I'd forgotten them. He and Kellan had on their own. We seemed to have the range to ourselves, but Milo and Kellan knew the guy who ran it, and he'd actually met us to unlock the doors. He didn't ask for a fee or any paperwork, just sent us back to the range.

Weird, but these guys seemed to have a whole network of connections. Kellan framed me, his chest to my back as he adjusted my grip. Then had me line the gun up. That was the other thing, there was a site on the very tip. It was a slender little bit of raised metal, but they'd both been clear —all I had to do was line that up with what I wanted to shoot and it would help me hit my targets.

Squeezing the trigger took a heck of a lot more effort than I expected. I also jumped a little the first time I fired. It might have been embarrassing if Kellan didn't have me braced so I didn't fire wildly.

After the first three pulls, he eased one of the ear covers away so I could hear him. "I want you to empty the clip.

Don't worry about getting it in the center. Right now, anywhere in that target is a good hit. This isn't about accuracy—yet."

"This is a rehearsal to learn the steps. We can refine it later."

"Exactly."

That I understood.

Not that they had explained the stance they wanted me in, but I could guess. Feet braced and slightly apart for balance. One hand cupped the wrist of the other to support my aim. Keeping my eye on the target, though, made total sense.

It was like spotting when doing a pirouette series. It reduced dizziness and kept me in control.

This seemed about the same, I thought.

By the time I'd gotten "comfortable" firing both guns, my arms were killing me and Kellan called a halt when he caught me rubbing one of my scars. That earned me another lecture on not overdoing it to the point of pain.

I would have made my normal argument, but something in his tone and his expression told me he wouldn't take that well. So I just nodded.

"Wait," Milo said before we began to pack up. "Switch hands."

I blinked at him.

"You were firing right-handed. Try with your left."

"You think?" Kellan asked, but whatever they were debating, they did so silently.

Finally, Milo said, "I do."

My left arm and hand ached, but nothing compared to my right. Milo reloaded the Glock 19, and I gripped it with my left hand and braced it with my right. New muscle movement was something to get used to and it was always worse the first few times. I understood that.

"You mind?" Milo said to Kellan, who surrendered his spot and Milo stepped up behind me. He turned me slightly, so my body angled to face the right and I had to turn my head to look left. "Don't overthink it." He moved my right hand to cup my elbow rather than my wrist. "Just eye the target, then squeeze the trigger. Give me a count of three."

Then he let go to fix my ear protection and fixed his own. While he didn't touch me, his hand was right there to catch my arm if I needed it. Spotting me.

Something inside of me relaxed.

Three.

Two.

One.

I focused on the site, then the target and pulled the trigger. It *seemed* a lot easier to fire from this angle and I fired until I emptied the magazine. I didn't have the balance of being face-on, but I was used to compensating for my balance in any number of positions on the ground and in the air.

This wasn't *too* different.

The air stank of sulfur and cordite, the combination burning my nostrils a little, but Kellan hit the button to bring the target to us as I lowered the gun.

Of fifteen shots fired, nine were inside the eight ring, with three actually inside the nine and one on the line between the nine and the ten.

"Holy shit." I stared at it. Earlier, I'd barely gotten the shots inside the seven, and even then, they'd been in scattered groupings.

"Southpaw," Milo commented.

"Try the M&P again," Kellan ordered, so we reloaded then repeated the process.

Milo put his hand right between my shoulder blades. "Flex, squeeze my hand tight, then relax."

The stretch pulled the muscles and burned in the best possible way.

"And again."

I did it once more, then he adjusted my ear protection.

From the corner of my eye, I caught his three fingers, then two, and on the one, I cut my gaze to the white-dot site, flipped the manual safety and fired.

There were only eight rounds in this one, but all of them were inside the nine.

After Milo took the gun, I stared at the sheets as Kellan glanced at them. "You can probably sharpen your right, but you are definitely a southpaw," he said. "Milo can fire with both. But he's better with his left."

"Little sister has skills," Milo said, and the note of pride in his voice pumped me up.

"That was actually—fun," I admitted, even as I began to rub my arms.

"Good." Kellan gave me a speculative look. "You're more comfortable with the M&P, but the Glock has more rounds. I want you to be comfortable with both."

While it wasn't a question, there was still an inquiry folded into his words. "I can do that," I admitted. "Though, how good do you want me to be?"

They shared a look, but Milo's scowl darkened suddenly as he went back to cleaning up and stowing the guns in their cases.

Better than I was and good enough to kill someone.

Or at least wound them.

I blew out a breath, my next question I held onto until

Kellan and I stepped out. Milo said he would be with us in a sec. The guns we'd brought with us, so Kel carried three of the cases and he'd left the other two with Milo.

When we were in the car, I leaned against the passenger seat as I peered up at him. The car wasn't the one he normally drove, but that had been wrecked the night of the ambush. I didn't know where this one came from. "Kel?"

"Yes, Sparrow?"

"You're going after the people who ambushed us, aren't you?"

He did a sweep of the area around us after he started the engine, then glanced at me. "Yes. How much do you want to know?"

I resisted the urge to say *everything*, because while I did —it also seemed disingenuous. At the same time... "Tell me what I need to know to help. I'm in—they shot Jasper."

When he brushed his knuckles down my cheek, I leaned into the contact. "I need you to keep Jasper distracted. He'll know we're likely going to move, and he's going to want to be in on it—wounded or not."

"We can't wait for him to heal, and we don't want him to get hurt further."

"No," Kellan said with a slow smile. "No, we do not."

"This is why the shooting lessons and why you want Freddie to show me how to use a knife?" Did I really have time to learn all of that *before* they had to move?

"Yes and no," Kellan answered. "I meant it when I said I want you safe. I want you armed with the skills, the knowledge, and the weapons if need be. That said, you have some idea of how to use the weapons, and it is also safer for you to access what we have at the clubhouse. Those two are yours now. We'll go over cleaning them and how to store them. Also, *where* to store them..."

I frowned, and his smile deepened.

"We have a few secrets left to share with you, Sparrow. One is to be on you or near you at all times. Especially when we're not at the clubhouse in force."

In force, so more than a couple of them. I nodded.

He flicked his gaze toward the window as Milo exited the range, and the guy who'd let us in waved and closed the door behind him.

"We'll talk about the rest of this later, okay?"

"Okay." I leaned forward and kissed him lightly as Milo slid into the car.

He slammed the door and snorted, but Kellan had gripped my head and kept me in place as he returned my kiss with a much deeper one of his own. "Thank you, Sparrow," he murmured before he let me go and settled behind the wheel.

"You know," Milo said. "You could wait until I'm not around."

"We could," Kellan agreed. "But where's the fun in that?"

Between Milo's scowl and Kellan's smugness, I laughed. When Milo turned his "glare" back on me, I laughed harder.

"Eyes front, Raptor. No glaring at the Sparrow."

"Uh-huh. My sister," Milo grumbled.

"Our girl. Suck it up."

I met Kellan's look in the rearview mirror and grinned even as another bout of laughter took me. My arms were killing me, the guys were about to go and do something dangerous, and the fact *my brother* continually grumbled about my *boyfriends* just delighted me.

Maybe I was the cracked one in the car, but if I was, I never wanted to get better.

46

My phone rang as I slid on the vest. It had been a while since I'd put on any kind of body armor. It was not comfortable. At Steph's name, I sighed. Answering it, I left it on speaker. "Hey, Sis, what's up?"

"Not much," she said, though there was a fairly familiar note in her voice. She knew something that I had chosen to not share with her. So now she was calling to check on me. "Been a busy week at the office, and I'm leaving in a couple of days."

I went still. Leaving?

"You forgot," she said, amusement filling her voice.

Where the hell was she... "Vacation. Holy shit, you're actually going on vacation?" I pressed the last velcro into place then reached for my shirt.

"You don't have to sound like it's so wildly out of the ordinary."

I snorted and she laughed.

"Fine, I accept that I may not have taken many vacations."

"Many?" I retorted drily before pulling a light jacket over the shirt. I wasn't a small guy and the vest added to my bulk. The jacket was larger and would hopefully help hide it.

"Now you're just being rude," she corrected me primly.

"My apologies, Steph. You know I worry about you."

"That's my job, buddy. You need to remember that."

"Hmm-hmm, I did for a long time, and now I get to have a turn behind the wheel. Remind me where you're going, how long you plan to stay, and how you're traveling?"

"I emailed all of that to you a month ago, but," she said, still laughing. "Because I know you like to cross your Ts and dot your Is, I'll go over it again."

"I appreciate that. Sometimes—I'm an asshole."

"And I still love you, so we work it out." She took a couple of minutes to detail the place in Canada she was heading to. There would be a lot of snow on the ground, but it had one of those spas where she could soak in the hot pool outside in the crisp, icy mountain air. "It cost a small fortune, but—"

"You're worth it, no buts about it. I'm so damn glad you're doing something for yourself."

"There's still time for you to go with me. We might have to fly out separately..."

"I wish I could," I said, and I meant it. I did. We should spend more time together. Watching Milo with Emersyn reminded me of how damn lucky I had always been to have my sister in my corner. "Just too much going on right now to plan a getaway. Next time. I promise—we'll go do something fun."

"Hey," she scolded in a mock offended voice. "What I'm planning to do is fun."

"What you're planning to do sounds ridiculously fun for you. A place where you can unplug, be pampered, read all the books you want, and actually rest? It sounds *perfect* for you. I've got my keys, I'll keep an eye on the house and bring in the mail. Don't worry about anything. Do you need a ride to the airport?"

I fit the knife sheath over my jeans near my ankle on each leg, then tucked the knives into them before putting on my combat boots.

"No, I've already arranged for a ride share to get me because I'm leaving at like four in the morning, and the flight is at seven. You work bizarre enough hours as it is. I will let you know when I get there, and you should have all the info on the resort."

"I don't doubt it, you're the most put-together person I know." I walked back out to the living room ,where I'd already set out the guns I planned to take. One went into my medical bag, the second clipped on to my belt where my jacket would cover it and the third...

"What's going on, Mickey?" The quiet question riveted me in place.

"Don't ask, Steph. Go and enjoy your vacation and trust me to take care of things here."

"I do trust you, but..."

Eyes closing, I didn't sigh because that would definitely be me giving away the house. I waited, though. That *but* carried a lot of weight.

"You failed to mention Milo found his sister."

"Wasn't my place." Then, because there was no way Milo hadn't read her into some of it, I added, "He wasn't the one who found her. The boys did."

"So you've met her?" She was circling a point.

"Yes, I have."

Silence.

"You didn't say anything because of doctor-patient privilege."

"You know I can't comment on that."

A real sigh escaped her and I glared at my reflection in the darkened television. "I thought as much. I'm worried about them…I should—"

"Go on your vacation, sis, I mean it. I've got him." Then because the cat was out of the bag. "I've got them both."

Lying to her had never sat well with me. So, if I couldn't answer with the truth, I didn't say a damn thing. I meant it when I said I'd look after them. It took a couple of attempts to get her to agree. It was only when I promised I'd bring Milo and Emersyn both over for dinner at the house when she was back that my sister finally conceded the argument.

"Can I ask you one more question before I go?" The fact she asked to ask meant she wasn't sure I'd answer in the first place.

"You can ask," I said. "If I can answer…I'll try."

"Thank you." Warmth filled her tone. "What do you think of her? His sister? For so many years, she was the little baby *that* family swept away to wealth and privilege… but she doesn't read spoiled heiress to me at all."

"She's not," I confirmed. "She's a complicated young woman. I don't think—" I knew now, but before? "I don't think life has been very kind to her. She's more like Milo than he realizes, and they butt heads—a lot. On some levels, it's pretty entertaining. On others?"

"It's painful for him."

"Yeah," I said, rubbing the back of my neck. "It is. He has her up on this pedestal so high that she has no choice but to fall off it, because she's a real person, not an ideal." A beautiful, complicated person with a soul too old and too battered for her age. "But I think she's good for him too."

"He's always been so responsible."

"Agreed. And on that note, I need to run—you have a good trip. Take lots of pictures so you can make me jealous when you get back."

"As if," she said with a snort. "Be good, Mickey. I mean it. Whatever is going on that you can't talk about—take care of those boys and yourself."

"I love you, Steph."

"Love you too, baby boy." Then she ended the call and I tilted my head back. I really did hate lying to her. My phone had vibrated more than once with incoming messages.

Three in a row from the guys.

I fired back a text that said I was on my way. I had one stop to make—I wanted to refresh supplies from the clinic and pick up the ultrasound for Emersyn. I should have recognized why she didn't want to come to the clinic.

It had been bad enough when they brought her to me for an exam. We had time to get her past that, but right now, looking after her current need outweighed battling her ghosts. We'd get to them all eventually.

Thirty minutes later, I parked in the warehouse and met Vaughn, where he waited to help me haul stuff in.

"Where do you want this?" He loaded up the dolly with the fresh medical supplies while I offloaded the ultrasound machine.

"The room we used for Jasper," I said. "We can convert it to a treatment room if necessary. We can also secure it. The meds need to go into the safe."

"Painkillers?" Vaughn frowned.

"Yeah, not the heavy stuff, but I had to bring some in

the case of future injuries. Trust me, no one wants me stitching them up or digging out a bullet without it." But we didn't want it tempting Freddie.

"Got it. I'll secure that after I get this stuff upstairs."

"Thanks."

"Yep."

Ten minutes later, we convened in the kitchen. "Little Bit with Jasper?"

"Yep," Kellan said. "The plan we're discussing is for the six of us. The rats have their orders, and they're ready to go. Let me be clear—this isn't a hit and run. This is a full-on extermination. This isn't a skirmish, a lesson, or a retaliation. This is eradicating a problem that has gotten out of hand."

This was war. Not a task I ever saw myself volunteering for again, but Kellan was right. They'd escalated with that ambush beyond all measure. There was only one reasonable response to it, or we invited them to strike again.

Next time, we might not get so lucky.

With that, Kellan opened a folder and began to lay out photos. I spared them a glance. The truck with the human trafficking. The men, women, and children in that vehicle had been a wildly dissimilar group but all facing the same fate.

The next array of photos showed medical supplies. Some were equipment. More than one truck I recognized from the list of those missing. Then a cluster of bodies—a dug-up mass grave.

"Where did you get that?" I asked Kellan.

"Reached out to some of our customers in the Network. They did not care for the hijackings any more than we did. They sent out an investigator of their own." He put down the last photo. The photo showed clear torture. Freddie leaned away from the table and focused on the wall.

Of all of them, only Milo remained truly impassive, but Kellan's poker face didn't shift.

"He got the last bit of confirmation we needed where the Diamonds were concerned. This is Nate Rickels. He was the point person on which trucks were taken and he supplied the replacement vehicles."

"19 Diamonds," I said with a slow nod.

Milo glanced at me. "That's Juan Ricardo's enforcer. Personal hatchet man. I don't care if they were paid to do it, this means they were all involved."

"So, they all go." Kellan set the last image down.

Little Bit.

"What the fuck?" Vaughn asked.

"She was the target the night of the ambush."

Freddie whipped around. "What? Why would they use me—" He stopped just abruptly as he asked the question. "Pinetree."

"Presumably. The ambush, though, wasn't just about her, but she was the one they wanted to capture."

Ice slicked his tone and I didn't blame him. "Her family?"

"Those fuckers are *not* her family," Milo gritted out, but like Kellan, his tone was frozen solid. "Kellan's contact didn't give us that information, only that they had a photo of her and had orders to take her alive at all costs."

"The Diamonds are most likely just hired muscle, middle-men for someone else. That said, they are the most present threat but not the only one. Juan Ricardo is not smart enough to work out a multi-state hijacking operation, but he does have the people to do the work, and they probably hired out of state as much as possible to keep it below the radar here.

"Our primary goal is to erase them all. No survivors. No one to come back and rebuild. Scorched earth. Second objective, confirm who they are working for. If we have to reverse engineer, fine. We already have a few ideas."

"Where's Liam?" Vaughn asked.

It wasn't an unfair question.

"He has another job," Kellan told him. "This one is for us. We're moving out in thirty minutes. Gear up and get ready. We have to slip the cops watching the place first, then take this fight to them."

The guys pushed away from the table and left the room one at a time until it was just me and Kellan.

"What aren't you telling them?" I asked and he met my gaze.

"Nothing I can confirm. When I have more data, you'll have it too."

This was not a one-day job.

Hell, this might not even be a two-day job.

"Doc, you can sit this out…"

"No," I said before he could even begin to let me off the hook. "I'm in."

All the way.

When Kellan put out his hand, I clasped it. "Glad to have you."

"I got your backs," I promised him. "I'm going to give Jasper a quick look, then I'll be down. How much does Little Bit know?"

"She knows enough." The answer surprised me, but I preferred it to the secrets.

"Good."

"Hey, Doc…"

I paused to glance back.

"Thanks. We've missed you."

I just lifted my chin to him, then headed for the stairs. I'd missed the boys too.

War or no war, it was good to be home.

VAUGHN

One thing Kellan didn't tell Doc was how we confirmed key points of the data in order to turn it over to our contacts in the first place. Milo and Jasper had brought back two "survivors" from their ambush on the road. It had taken a few days to get it out of them, but we had determination on our side.

Then again, Doc didn't need to know. Those bodies were taken care of, and we wouldn't be worrying about them again. But they'd definitely told us who hired them. That was what we'd needed to know.

"Cops are still out there," Freddie warned as he slipped back inside. His hair was damp. "And it's raining."

"That actually works better for us." We'd swapped clothes with a few of the rats. Picking out the best ones to match us in size had taken a hot minute. "We want them to keep track of who is coming and going."

We had a Jasper and Milo climbing into a truck. JD and Shaun weren't the best matches, but they would do at a distance. They were both wearing hats and jackets. JD's beard needed work.

No one had Freddie's leaner build and hair, so we skipped on finding him a body double. It was rare for him to go on jobs like this anyway. Patrick was doubling for me, but he definitely didn't have my build, even if he had the red hair. We put him in bulkier clothing and he stacked a couple of heavier shirts under it.

He'd probably roast, but it would have to do. He was also taking my car. Here was hoping it was in one piece when we got back. Fuck, here was hoping they were all in one piece when we got back. If someone was gunning for us, they needed to be prepared for someone to come for them.

Every single rat was a volunteer, but Kellan only picked the ones he trusted to handle specific tasks. Everyone else had been cut loose or sent out to be ready to create mayhem when it was time. Milo pushed open the back of the truck and I gave Freddie a light push.

"Let's go," I told him. We were riding in the back. It was a huge shell game. Milo and Kellan were riding in the back of the panel van, with Rome actually driving that one. It was a painter's van, one he rarely used but he had been known to drive.

"Don't get dead," Kellan said with a lift of his chin. "We'll see you tonight."

"We'll be there."

Once inside, Freddie made a face as we slid through the containers to where we'd set up an actual place to sit. Nothing inside the truck was actually meant for delivery. It was cover.

Heavily armored cover. Pulling open the driver's side

door of the car we'd parked in here before we loaded it, I said, "It could be worse."

"We have no air conditioning or music and have to sit and stare at boxes for the next few hours." He leaned against the passenger side for a minute, looking thoughtful. "Oh, I could be in here with Raptor, and he could be talking about Boo-Boo. Yeah, that would be worse."

I laughed. "There's always worse. We just gotta remember that." I climbed in and then kicked on the pair of battery-operated fans we'd hooked to the dashboard.

"You didn't have anything with beans in it, did you?" Freddie asked, putting his seat all the way back and throwing an arm over his eyes.

"Gonna suck for you if I did, huh?"

He chuckled, and I checked my phone for the message. Kellan sent it a minute later, and the truck began to vibrate as the engine fired up.

We were rolling out.

"Vaughn?"

"Yep?"

"Why'd they stick you with babysitting duty?" As idle as the question sounded, a vague note of hurt crept into his voice. Maybe he didn't hear it, and maybe I was projecting. Either way, it needed to be addressed.

"One, no one stuck me with babysitting duty. Two, I volunteered to be your backup because you're the one getting us inside." I could almost feel the way his gaze jumped to me. "I can take way more hits than you can, and as fast as you are with a knife, when you get that door unlocked, I'm the one going through it."

He grimaced. "Vaughn..."

"Not done," I said, keeping my pitch even. "Three, babysitters are meant to keep people out of trouble. This isn't about keeping you out of trouble. This is about working together. I'm your backup, but you're mine. I trust you to have my back. You trust me to have yours?"

"I always have—I mean—no, I always have. The one I don't trust most of the time is me."

"Yep," I agreed with him. "Dove trusts you. That should tell you something."

The quiet settled over us again as the engine rumbled on. We were moving through the city traffic. Taking our time. With so many people watching the clubhouse, we had to use their observation against them. In this case, they see only a small group leave.

Patience.

We had to have patience for this part. We were playing against a stacked deck with various opponents. Some connected, but not all of them. It was the outliers that we had to keep an eye on.

"She shouldn't," Freddie said finally.

"You don't get to make that call for her," I reminded him. "You also walked into a dangerous place to get her out. You might be stuck."

"I'm going to fuck that up."

"Maybe." I shrugged. "I could argue we all have fucked it up at different points. Even Dove."

"Woah, when did she do anything wrong?" The sharpness of his defense wasn't lost on me and I didn't smile.

"When she didn't trust us to protect her."

"She didn't *know* she could. Not for sure. We lied to her."

"So, she had her reasons to not trust us—that means what she did wasn't wrong?"

He didn't answer immediately, then kicked his foot up against the dashboard. Not my car, so I didn't tell him to put it down. Frankly, a footprint on the vinyl was the least of our concerns. "She didn't feel like there was another choice," he said slowly. "Even when I tried to convince her to wait. Protecting us was more important than protecting herself."

That would never not anger me. "None of us are expendable." A decision we made a long time before. "She gets a little latitude because she didn't understand. She does now. But she got hurt, Freddie, and I think you know that better than any of us."

We hadn't asked him to tell us anything she'd told him. We hadn't even asked him to describe the conditions. What we had done was make sure *he* was okay while we also looked after her.

"Yeah," he admitted.

"And she trusts you." Now I glanced over at him. "What does that tell you?"

He blew out a breath. "That I really need to not fuck up anymore."

"Wrong lesson."

"Eh, I still need to not fuck up. I gotta not keep trying to score drugs, just get clean and stay clean."

Since he opened the door, I shoved it the rest of the way open. "Maybe change how you're doing that," I told him. "Instead of trying to do it all on your own—call one of us. Tell us you need someone to talk you down. Or you just need a friend. Stop trying to protect us from you and deciding that protecting us *from* you is more important than protecting yourself."

He jerked in place, the dance of his blade in the dark didn't worry me. It was what he did when he felt the walls closing in and he needed to think. Not once, in all the years I'd known him, had he ever turned that blade on one of us.

When he had no response for that, I closed my eyes and just leaned my head back to dose. It was hard to sleep while I kept replaying portions of the conversation with Freddie. If I could get those to stop, then images from the night of the ambush flooded my head.

Jasper bleeding, the gunfire peppering us. Dove going up the wall... They'd been firing at her even as she climbed the wall. Had they decided capturing her wasn't worth it? Or was someone double-dealing?

Fuck, I hated people.

If I could get those to stop. I saw Dove getting out of Liam's car, a ghost of herself, and I could feel her bones when she hugged me. That was a war I wanted. The war against the people who hurt her. The people?

Or the person?

The more I turned that over, the angrier I got, so I sat up and grabbed a bottle of water from the cooler in the back. The crackle of the radio punched through the silence, and Freddie jumped.

I passed him the water bottle and grabbed a second one before picking up the radio.

It crackled again. "Check-in," Kellan said via the radio.

"You're breaking up. We're awake."

"Good," Kellan responded. "We're about twenty minutes out. You'll get dropped off, then loop back to meet us."

"Copy," I said, unable to resist that particular lure. "Do we have eyes on them?"

"Yep," Kellan answered. "Or would you prefer that I say that's a 10-4 good buddy?"

I laughed, and even Freddie cracked a smile. "I'm good with yep, copy. I'll radio when we're in position. Copy."

"You're a dick," Freddie said, chuckling.

I grinned. "Sometimes, it's fun."

"See you at the meet point," Kellan said. "Copy."

"Copy that."

"Great. Get fucked. Copy."

"Oops, you're breaking up." I put the radio down and Freddie laughed.

"Not gonna copy that on 'get fucked'?" He grinned.

"Nah." I cracked open my water bottle. "He can tell me that in person."

"He probably will." He held out his water bottle and I tapped mine to his.

"Probably."

The truck was slowing down. At least the fans had run the whole time, so while it wasn't exactly cool in here, despite the temps outside, it wasn't sweltering either.

"Vaughn?"

"Yeah, kid?"

"I'll work on asking for help."

I nodded. "Can't ask for more than that."

"Sure, you could," he said as the truck continued to slow. "But maybe later after I master this first part."

"Good deal."

Ten minutes later, JD and Shaun were shoving the boxes aside so I could pull the car forward. They'd already set up a ramp. At the edge, I paused and glanced at JD. "You know what you're doing next?"

"Yep," he said, then glanced at his watch. "We'll park the truck at the depot, swap to a car, then we'll be in place in about an hour."

"Call if that changes."

"You got it." He knocked on the roof of the car, and I tapped the gas. The ramp was a sharp dip and then we were on the road. We were outside of Braxton Harbor by about thirty minutes. "Wanna tell Kel we're gonna be about an extra fifteen to be in place?"

Freddie snagged the radio. "Get Fucked to Daddy K, come in, Daddy K."

I damn near ran us off the road, but Freddie's shit-eating grin was fucking priceless.

48

We hit the first stash houses in rapid order. Our rats had already pinpointed their lookouts. Rome and Doc took care of them, then settled into their spots to keep an eye out while we went inside.

Tearing through the buildings, I missed having Jas with us. But these assholes were the reason why we didn't have him here. They took the job, whether it was their call or not. They'd been gunning for us, and right now, I was pretty sure—not one hundred percent certain—but pretty damn close that they were also behind the hit on Liam.

The hit that would have killed him if he hadn't been wearing a vest. It could have killed Sparrow. Yeah, I'd meant what I said. There weren't any 19 Diamonds walking away from this.

Every car we used, we swapped out the plates after each stop. They were all rebuilds with varying id numbers on different pieces of them. If we had to abandon one, they wouldn't trace back to us. We masked up going in, and we kept it clean and direct.

While we worked our way through their bunkers, stash houses, and money counters—that had been disgusting, a dozen women in their underwear shackled to their seats where they counted out the bills.

No collateral. Those women weren't 19 Diamonds, they got to walk. They couldn't recognize us anyway.

The rats were deployed in the city, tackling their businesses. By dawn, they would all be closed—one way or the other. Lights off, we moved through the neighborhood like predators on the hunt. They parked more than one of their cash houses in the suburbs.

Fuckers.

Using kids and families for cover was cold. Disrespectful. Dangerous. Callous.

We'd *never* use kids that way. Then again, we'd been those kids, running the streets and doing the deals. We'd been the camouflage because we were those kids.

I checked the GPS on the phone. We were almost to our next location.

"I don't like this," Milo said, and I didn't disagree.

House in the middle of the block? Soon as I got a bead on which house it was, I continued on past. My phone buzzed twice. The message from Rome that he and Doc were in place.

The lookouts had been cleared. "Every other stash house was a corner lot. Or in an industrial park."

One had even been in a strip mall. It had taken time to put the list together. We'd had a few of them. Liam had more. But the rats had actually turned up some solid leads.

Milo and Jasper's prisoner had also given us two addresses—including this one.

Every single one had been verified before we headed out.

"What are you thinking?" Milo asked as I turned the corner and then followed the block toward the cross street nearest our target address.

We'd go in on foot.

Neighborhoods like this had doorbell cameras and alarms. Some even had motion lights. None of the houses we'd driven past near the stash house had any. That was a point in our favor.

But it was in the middle of the block.

Why?

"I'm thinking this doesn't feel right for a stash house."

"No."

My phone vibrated, and I hit answer. "Hang on," I told Doc before dialing in Vaughn. He also answered on the first ring. They were right behind us—also idling in their car. "What do you have, Doc?"

"This feels off."

"Same," Vaughn said, and I nodded.

"I don't disagree." We got this address from one of the hijackers. He hadn't even been *from* Braxton Harbor. I flipped it around. "Tactically, this is even more secure than the others. They've got all sides covered by civilians."

I was talking aloud right now, but they knew where I was coming from.

"But it has the disadvantage of also having neighbors on all sides, which means people to observe what you're doing."

Corner lots weren't so impaired. Granted, they still had neighbors—but on one side. Being on the corner meant all traffic went by it, which made cars passing, parking, even stopping—less noticeable. Spillovers from other houses often reached up the street.

So why put *this* stash house in the middle?

"What are the chances this isn't a stash house but an actual *safe* house?" We'd discovered the 19 Diamonds used that name somewhat interchangeably. But the safe house didn't always refer to where you stashed your product or your cash.

They were for people.

"Juan Ricardo?" Milo looked thoughtful.

"Guy's been hiding since you got out. He has to know that sooner or later, you were going to be looking for him." We never had the proof we needed that he'd been behind the threats to Nikki and her family. But someone had attacked her, something Milo refused to discuss with us. She'd kept her distance for the most part, even though we kept an eye out for her and her siblings.

Rubbing his jaw, Milo said, "If he's in there—*I* want him."

I didn't doubt that for a second. Lifting the phone, I said, "Confirm for me that all the lookout positions have been cleared."

"Five by five," Doc said. "We have eyes on you and on the house. I've got forward, Rome has the back."

"We go in quiet, but we go in swift. Milo and I are taking the front door, Vaughn—you and Freddie go in over the fence and into the yard."

"They don't have a dog, right?" Freddie said. "I'm not hurting a dog."

"No dog," Rome answered. "Starling would probably like a dog."

I didn't roll my eyes, but I did grin. "We'll discuss

canines later. Get into position." Hanging up, I shook my head.

"We're getting a dog," Milo said with a grunt.

Yeah. We were. Rome had just said Emersyn needed one, and to be honest, I didn't find fault with the idea—but Milo was right.

We were gonna end up with a dog.

"Always wanted a dog," I admitted as we slid out of the car. Had since I was a kid. Behind us, Freddie and Vaughn pulled away and prowled to another location to park. My phone buzzed once to let me know they were in place.

"What happened to discussing it later?" Milo asked, then he groaned. "You're already trying to pick out the dog in your head, aren't you?"

"Sparrow is right," I said as I tugged the mask over my face before tapping him in the side. "You need to lighten up. Maybe you need a dog too."

"Bite me."

"Nah, keep up the attitude, and the dog will do that." I didn't have to look to know he flipped me off, and I swallowed the chuckle. Sometimes a little levity was all we needed to get through a day, and sometimes...

My phone buzzed again. The vibration slightly different. Vaughn and Freddie were in position. We moved down the center of the street, it was after three in the morning.

The part of the night where most normal people slept their deepest. One house away, I raised a hand. Five.

Four.

Three.

Two.

Lights out.

The block went dark.

Rome was good.

We headed up the driveway to the garage. Milo already had the wire hanger from earlier. He slid it through a depression at the top of the door while I watched the street. Two tugs and there was a pop.

The door was unlocked from the garage opener. He went low and lifted the door a fraction. I rolled under it and went straight to the security box on the wall. You didn't really need a code when you could just unplug it.

I used a power screwdriver to open the box, then yanked out the battery. The system went dark. Milo was at the garage door to the house when I finished and the door was shut.

Sliding the tool back into my pocket, I checked the vehicles. Both had their keys inside.

Gotta love lazy people.

After pocketing one set, I tossed the second set to Milo. I checked the time on my watch. We were in the right window.

Ten seconds, Milo unlocked the door and let us into the laundry room. If this turned out to be a bust, we wanted in and out without upsetting whoever lived here.

The laundry room had nothing in it—no clothes, no detergent, no dryer sheets—nothing. The washer and dryer weren't even plugged in. If I had to guess, they were here for the show. Gun in hand, I tapped Milo's shoulder.

He opened the interior door, letting us into the main house and where we went quiet to listen. No dog in the yard didn't mean there wasn't a dog in the house.

But nothing moved in the darkness.

My phone vibrated in my pocket. In the deep silence, it seemed almost loud. The backdoor to the house opened. The sound came from our left. That put the kitchen and living room there. We were in the hallway.

Milo held up a hand, four fingers.

Four doors.

I tapped his shoulder again, and we moved forward. A half-step before the first door on our left, it opened. Together, we went still. I had less than a second before whoever was in there came out and all I could think was *don't* be a civilian.

Don't be—*fucking Meeks.*

He had a pair of boxer shorts and nothing else, but the man looked right at us, his sleepy eyes barely registering, or at least taking a prolonged moment to recognize we were even standing there, much less who we were.

Milo didn't allow him time to reach that point. He slammed a hand over the guy's mouth and drove him right back into the bedroom. I was a heartbeat behind him. A woman sat up in the bed and opened her mouth.

Gun pointed at her, I put a finger to my lips and she clapped her own hand over her mouth.

Pinned to the floor, not a sound escaped Meeks with the speed of Milo's hammered fists raining down on him. There was more than one crunch of bone, but I didn't look at them, I kept an eye on the woman.

The room was dark, but her phone was in her hand and the screen gave just enough illumination to be clear that she was naked and her expression wasn't one of fear.

Her reaction had also not been one of absolute terror but far more controlled. The punches stopped and Milo rose to his feet. Her free hand moved from the phone in her lap to the handle just barely visible beneath the pillow.

I squeezed the trigger.

Suppressor on the gun or not, the sound of the bullet ripped through the room even as it went right between her eyes and splattered the wall behind her.

Shifting my weight, I cut a look back out to the hallway. None of the doors opened, but I didn't take my attention off of them.

"How the fuck did you see the gun?" Milo asked, his voice barely above a whisper.

"It wasn't the gun," I told him. It was the Diamond tattoo on her wrist. That was blood in the mark. She wasn't just his girlfriend, she was a Diamond.

I'd meant it when I said they all went.

"Later," I ordered, and we closed the door and continued down the hall. Vaughn and Freddie joined us with the simple hand signal that it was all clear.

At least knowing Meeks was here answered my question. This *was* a Diamond safe house. I pointed Vaughn and Freddie to the next door, then Milo to the third. I'd take the fourth.

We'd just gotten lucky. No way was I risking our prey rabbiting if we finally had him cornered. Juan Ricardo had been a nuisance, then a thorn, but he'd decided to become a real enemy.

I glanced down the hall. Vaughn held up three fingers. Milo two. I nodded and pushed open my door. They moved at the same time. The room I hit had two beds, two men, and one of them jerked awake. He had a hair-trigger and a gun in his hand. A bullet slammed into the wall next to my head. Bits of hot plaster and wood struck my mask. The burn of it sliced my jaw.

Two bullets in him. One in the chest, the second in the head. My second target launched from his bed, but I put two more in him and a third in his head. I cleared the closet, then moved back to the hall.

Vaughn and Freddie exited their room. With a sweep of

his hand in front of his throat, he indicated all clear. No survivors. That left Milo's room.

A woman raced out, and like Meek's partner, she was naked. Vaughn caught her and covered her mouth when she started to scream. Terror filled her eyes when Freddie shone the light on her and he grimaced.

They both looked at me.

"Secure her for now," I said, moving to the doorway.

"Got it," Vaughn hauled her with him and Freddie frowned, but at my nod, he followed them.

It didn't surprise me to find Juan Ricardo on his knees, his limp dick on full display and his hands behind his head. Milo didn't move, didn't say a word. He just stared down at the man.

"Long time, Juan," I said as I stepped into the room. "You've been a difficult guy to catch up with."

The man cut his gaze toward me. He licked his lips, and I took the time to unscrew the suppressor on my gun. I wouldn't be needing it. The weapon was hot, but I holstered it as I walked further into the room.

"What do you want?" he demanded, like he had leverage. "Name your price."

I'd give the guy a modicum of credit. He had Milo staring death down at him, while he was nude, unarmed, and about a half-a-heartbeat from dying—and he wanted to negotiate.

"You don't have anything I want," I informed him. Maybe once upon a time, but Juan Ricardo had firebombed any chance at a bridge.

"I might," he argued and moved like he was going to stand. Milo said nothing, just put the gun right up to his forehead. The man was lucky it wasn't my gun, or his skin would be sizzling. "You don't know what I do—you don't know all the people willing to pay me to fuck with your lives."

"You sound very sure," I countered as I moved to lean against the broken dresser. I paused to look at the cracked mirror. "You do know that's like seven years' bad luck, don't you?"

His throat bobbed as he swallowed hard. "I am sure…we were paid for the girl—"

Milo increased the pressure on the gun, and Juan Ricardo started bending backward.

"What girl?" Two words fired like the bullets they were but ground up into scattershot escaped Milo.

I waited. Juan made a sound that was pretty undignified.

"I'd answer if I was you," I suggested. "He has no reason to keep you alive."

The fact Milo had let him live this long was a testament to his control.

"Both of them," Juan said.

"Names."

Yeah, Milo wasn't playing. But both meant Nikki *and* Emersyn. If he thought admitting to being a threat to either woman would save his life, he was mistaken. The minute their names crossed his lips, he signed his death warrant.

"Only after I have a deal." Stupid. Brave, maybe, but definitely stupid.

In a swift motion, Milo cracked the gun across Juan Ricardo's face. Blood sprayed from his crushed nose as he collapsed. One solid kick pushed the man onto his side, then Milo planted his bullet on his chest.

"Wrong answer."

"You know who," Juan all but screamed, his agony

echoing in his words. "That cunt Nikki—the little rich bitch...fuck."

Milo shifted his stance and rammed his foot down onto Juan's pathetic cock. His gun never wavered as he continued to apply pressure.

"Names."

I folded my arms. It was the only way I didn't walk over there and take my own pound of flesh. Milo spent three years in prison and we damn well knew this asshole had been behind *part* of the charges. The assault on Nikki, the terrorizing of her family, and even when she fought against naming Milo, like they wanted her to—

Shoving that aside, I waited.

"We got a contract—one from Liam O'Connell—one he tried to renege on."

Bullshit.

"And the other?" Milo gave away nothing.

"There isn't—" The man screamed, his voice climbing an octave. If he had balls left, I'd be surprised. Choked sobs escaped him.

"We're out of patience," I informed him when his cries diminished to something in a reasonable decibel range. "You're dying tonight. The road ends here. How you die—is totally up to you. Who is the other?"

Gasping for air, face red and damp with tears and snot, not to mention blood, Juan Ricardo groaned. "Just kill me."

"You have one-half of your scrotum still intact," Milo informed him. "I can cut it off you, if I have to."

"I'd believe him," I offered. "In five seconds, he's going to do it whether you start to answer or not. One."

"Two," Milo continued.

"Three." This was not going to be pretty.

"Fou—"

"Warrick," Juan shrieked. "A man named Warrick. He wanted all of you dead. We were supposed to just use the trucks, but then he changed his mind. Exterminate you. Get the girl and turn her over. He had a buyer lined up—"

"Who is the buyer?" Milo asked.

"I don't fucking know!" he wailed.

I believed him. "Kill him."

Milo took a step back, then he shot him in the dick. It was definitely not pretty. He took out every joint before he shot him in the head.

I was pretty sure the guy was unconscious before then, but I didn't say a word.

The room stank of urine, blood, and gunpowder. Milo looked at me. I'd heard it.

Warrick.

"Tear the place apart. The proof we want is here."

And there was still the girl to deal with.

49

As hard as I tried to not keep checking the time or the door, the waiting crawled through me like an army of ants leaving hives in their wake. It should have been easier when Jasper was sleeping, but that seemed to make it worse. Mickey had come in briefly to check on Jasper. He didn't need the IV bags anymore.

Before he left, though, Mickey made sure I had three bottles of meds for him—one for pain, one for antibiotics, and a third for the swelling. "Little Bit, keep an eye on him. You don't have to change the dressing until tomorrow. It's better to keep it sealed. If he starts to run a fever, or if he gets numbness or swelling, those are the things to watch for."

He went over the instructions twice and left me with a bag that included a thermometer and chemical ice packs I could just activate. There was a host of other supplies in there for a just in case, including more of the scar gel for me.

"It's going to be fine," Mickey said, touching two fingers to my cheek until I lifted my gaze to his. "Tell me you believe me." As much as I worried, I'd done my best to tell him exactly that.

After pressing a kiss to my forehead, Mickey left, and even though I wasn't down there to see them go, I swore I could feel their absence in the building. It was unsettling.

Who was I kidding? It was terrifying.

They were about to deal out retaliation and it was dangerous enough that Kellan wanted me familiar enough with a gun to be able to use it if necessary. He didn't want it to be necessary, but it was currently secured with the bag next to the bed where I could reach both.

The hours since they left crawled by. Jasper slept, a lot. Even when he tried to stay awake, the fatigue swept him under. It took him especially fast if I sat there stroking his hair.

"Swan," Jasper murmured, yanking me out of my thoughts, and I spun to look at him on the bed. "You don't have to stay in here with me if you're this restless."

"I'm not—"

A smile flirted with his lips, and he patted the bed next to him. "C'mere."

More exasperated with myself than anything, I crawled up onto the bed next to him. He lifted an arm, inviting me to curl up, and I settled carefully, worried about his wound but it was on his other side.

"I'm not going to break," he admonished, then curled me to him with a squeeze. Some of the tension coiling in my muscles drained, but not all of it. "I know you're worried..."

Blinking, I started to sit up, but he tightened his arm and I had to settle for tipping my head back to look up at him.

"What? You thought I didn't know they were gone?" Amusement, not censure, filled his expression.

I winced. "I'm supposed to look after you and keep you distracted."

"I figured," he murmured, then pressed a kiss to the top of my head. "Best distraction in the world for me. But I'm not doing so hot distracting you—am I?"

"You need to rest," I muttered, then rubbed my cheek to his shoulder. "I shouldn't have woken you up."

"You didn't." He traced his hand in gentle circles on my shoulder. "In fact, I've been awake for a while, but you were so intently trying to not think about whatever it is that you're thinking about, you did about forty circuits of the room."

I groaned. "I'm sorry."

"Swan, stop apologizing. In fact, I'm glad there's something I can do for you—need to live up to my part of this deal and distract you."

"What you need to do is rest," I scolded. "I know I promised to do all the work, but I don't want you to rip any stitches."

A soft huff of laughter escaped him.

Wiggling, I shifted so I could turn enough to look up at him. "You weren't talking about sex, were you?"

"No, though I do appreciate your enthusiasm." A very real smile creased his lips. "In fact, I can't wait to reciprocate that enthusiasm—at length."

Heat flushed my face. Thankfully, we didn't have the lamps on, just the fairy lights, so hopefully he couldn't make out the blush. "I'm looking forward to it," I replied, nuzzling a quick kiss to his lips at his squeeze.

"Ditto. But for now… how about you help me up, and then we'll go downstairs and you can dance. That will give you something to do and burn off some of this nervous energy." He tucked some of my hair back behind an ear. "I know for sure you haven't since I got hurt. Kel's managed to distract you once or twice, and you went to your shooting lessons, but you've been in here the rest of the time."

"You're not supposed to strain yourself," I reminded him.

"Watching you is just what Doc would order." The retort made me laugh, even if it shouldn't. "Wait for it. Doc did order it. He told you what you had to watch for in me, right?"

There was no denying the way he searched my expression. "Yes," I said with a sigh.

"Okay, am I exhibiting any of the symptoms he told you to worry about?"

I frowned, then scooted up to my knees and pressed a hand to his face. He was warm but not hot. In fact, he wasn't any warmer than he would typically be. "No fever." I tugged the blankets down to bare his chest more and looked at the large, rectangular seal over his wound. There was a second one on his back.

As lightly as I could, I traced my fingers around it. Mickey said to make sure the injury wasn't hot. But it didn't seem any warmer than the rest of him. Goosebumps rippled over his skin, and I caught him grinning at me.

"Hey, not my fault if you find me irresistible," he teased. I managed to fight the urge to swat him, even if I couldn't hold back my smile. "What's my verdict, Nurse Swan?"

Now, I rolled my eyes. "No inflammation that I can feel and no fever. What about swelling?"

"If we're not counting my cock, I'm not feeling anything else swollen."

Laughter ripped through me and he settled a hand on my thigh.

"That's better. Now, I've been a good patient and you're the sexiest nurse ever, but I think if I can manage to walk back and forth to the bathroom, I can handle the long hike downstairs to the studio. Besides, I know for a fact that watching you move is going to be the best fucking medicine ever."

"I don't know if that's a good idea."

"Okay," he said with only a hint of irritation, but I didn't think that was for me. Or at least I hoped it wasn't. "Let's test the theory..."

Before I could ask him what theory, he log-rolled to a seated position and then, with care, stood. I knee-walked to his side of the bed, ready to catch him if I needed to. This was hardly the first time he'd gotten up.

He'd had to pee before. "I'm good," he informed me. "Just catching my breath. Want to turn the light on in the bathroom?"

Not hesitating, I sprinted over and flipped the switch. He'd already taken a couple of steps—including stepping down from the platform his bed was on—as he made his way toward the bathroom.

As carefully as he controlled his expression, he couldn't disguise the little beads of sweat.

"Okay," he told me when he reached the doorway and gripped the frame to rest. "That's step one. How am I doing so far?"

"Pretty damn awesome."

"Good. Got my girl to impress." He dropped a kiss on me before he eased into the bathroom. It took him a few minutes, but he emptied his bladder, washed his hands, then his face, and finally brushed his teeth. After, he sat down on the closed toilet lid. "Still impressed?"

"You have no idea how much," I promised him. "This is already a lot."

"Yeah, kind of lame how whipped I am. Better do a little more. There's this sexy little number who dances downstairs, and I bet, if I get down there and sit for a while, watching her dance will be the best medicine ever."

That was probably one of the sweetest things he'd ever said to me. "I almost miss when you were crabby at me all the time," I told him.

"Really?" He seemed surprised.

"It was easier to tell you no," I admitted.

"Got it, just be a sweetheart and you're putty in my hand."

Closing the distance to him, I stroked my hand through his hair. "I'm already putty—I thought you were hot and attractive even when you were an ass."

He grinned. "I'm not really sorry about these things."

Laughter shook me, but his smile faded.

"Since I'm so fantastic—why don't you tell me why you don't want to go to the studio."

"I'm worried about you..."

"I'll be fine, Swan. Why don't *you* want to go to the studio? You were stealing in there with your friend when you first got back and I know you pushed yourself too hard. So, tell me what's wrong. Let me see if I can fix it."

"Jasper," I said with a sigh. No more secrets. No more lies. "I—I haven't been in the silks since I got back...since I left even."

I glanced down at my hands. The burn scars on the palms had faded, but I could still see them like they were fresh. Could I tell him all this?

Could I tell him why when *I* didn't totally understand it?

"You're going to take time to heal," he said gently. "But that's not what is slowing you down...I've seen you dance and even fly when you were battered, bruised, and had cracked ribs." His voice dipped into a growl on the last. "Let me help you."

"I don't know if I'll ever be able to do it. My arms—the cuts they were so deep and how they stitched them. Mickey gave me scar cream, and he's got me on a plan to rehabilitate them, but they hurt so much when I do things that I used to be able to do without even thinking about it."

Catching my hand, he pulled it from his hair so he could examine my arms.

"And...when I first got there, I tried to get away." I hated admitting this part. "It wasn't the best plan, but I thought by cooperating and getting him away from here, you would all be safe. Then if I disappeared from there, he would have no reason to come looking for me here again."

His skeptical look echoed my own internal judgment. Yes, it was stupid.

"So, I made a run for it. There's a wall around his property. I'd gone over it before. Just two bounces up the tree and then hit the top of it and over."

"Only not this time?" It wasn't a guess.

"He electrified it." I flexed my hands. "It blew me back and burned me." When his expression went dark and his gray eyes stormy, I frowned. "Jasper, that part is done. I survived it. I know I did. I'm here, and it hurts, and it would hurt if I wasn't alive but..."

"You're scared," he said in a deep voice that seemed to echo all the way to the center of me. "I get it."

"Yeah?" I had a hard time believing it was that simple.

"Fear's an ugly thing, Swan. It gets inside you like an infection, it poisons everything, and if you don't face it—it can turn everything you care about against you. Worse, it can turn *you* against what you love." Taking my other hand, he squeezed them. "You love to dance. You love to fly. Maybe it won't be as easy, but I know you. I *believe* in you. Don't let that son of a bitch take this away from you. You take it back."

"Even if I fall..."

"You'll get back up again," he said. "You always get back up. I've seen you, remember... and if you struggle or need help? We'll help you."

I twisted my mouth, then played with his fingers. "Are you sure you can make it down the stairs?"

"Okay, now you're just being a brat," he muttered, but he smiled. "I can get down the stairs on my own. But it'll be easier if you help me."

"And watching me dance will really help you?"

"God, yes," he said. "Watching you dance is almost better than sex with you. Almost—never will beat it, but fuck, it comes close."

I laughed. "That's awful."

"Yeah, tell it to my cock later. Now, help me up—please —and we'll do this one step at a time."

While I should argue with him, or at least try to talk him out of it, I wanted to see his smile. "Okay, but if you need a break, we'll take breaks. Please?"

"Let me tell you a little secret," he whispered as he stood and wrapped an arm around my shoulders so I could help him. "I can't say no to you."

"Lies," I teased. "You told me no a lot."

"Told," he agreed. "Not anymore. You want it. You get it."

"How long is this offer good for?"

"For as long as you need it." The depth of meaning in those words wasn't lost on me.

It took us a while, we even sat on the steps for a few minutes, but eventually, we made it to the studio. I left him leaning on a wall while I went to wrestle a chair from the living room. It wasn't quite a recliner, but I grabbed a second chair from the kitchen so he could put his feet up.

He scowled at me when I panted from my efforts, but I put my hands on my hips and met him scowl for scowl. "You want to watch me dance, you cannot sit on the floor."

"You could have made one of the rats do the lifting," he countered.

"Maybe—but then I'd have to talk to them, and most of them are just—" I made a face.

"Just what?" His voice took a deadlier tone. "If any of them are giving you a hard time, point them out. I'll deal with it."

"I don't need you to shoot them or beat their head in with a baseball bat," I countered, flicking his nose. That knocked the scowl right off his face, and he laughed. "I just don't like them because I don't know them and a couple of them give me the creeps."

"Hmmm."

"You're not going to let that go, are you?"

"Nope."

I figured. "Okay, gimme two more minutes. I need to run upstairs for Mickey's bag and to get us water. Think about what songs you'd like me to dance to. I'll stretch and then see what I can do."

"Sounds good. And, Swan?"

"Yeah?"

"You're going to fly again."

"I wish I believed that." I really did. I stole a glance up at the silks where they hung. I really did want to do it, but what if...

"I can believe enough for both of us."

"Thank you," I whispered. "I just might need that."

It was more like fifteen minutes later that I was warmed up enough to dance, after I got us water and made him take some meds for all his running around. It was also after I stretched and Jasper asked me to dance to one of my favorite songs.

It actually took me my whole stretch to come up with a favorite song. I finally just dropped in the CD marked *Happy shit*. The upbeat music helped get me in the right mindset. I was a little off and stiff until the second song. By the third song—I forgot.

I forgot Pinetree.

I forgot the injuries.

I forgot the ambush.

I forgot his wounds.

I forgot my fear. I just danced.

There was always freedom in the motion, and even when I slipped or overcompensated, I pushed on. The playlist was almost forty-five minutes. When the last song ended, I dropped drenched in sweat and panting.

Jasper stared at me with something like wonder *and* worry on his face. "Holy shit, Swan—I always think I know, and then you dance and..."

I smiled, trying to get my breath back. "You were right," I told him between gasps for air. "I needed that."

"So did I," he murmured. When I finally dragged myself to my feet, I was sore—but at least I wasn't quite limping. I mopped a towel over my face. "Maybe after you shower," he continued with a grin. "I can convince you to do that sponge bath and relaxation technique."

"You think after all this, you're going to be up for a blowjob?" It was only the slightest of taunts, but his grin turned wicked.

"I know a challenge when I hear one, Swan. Trust me, I'm up for it."

"Well, we should get you back to bed then..." I hung the towel on a hook. I'd have to come back for it later. He kissed me lightly when I helped him up.

"Sweaty, hot girl," he teased. "I like it when you're dirty."

That sent humor and lust twinning through me. "Come on, big boy. Let's do this. I still have to grab Mickey's bag..."

I'd just reached for the door when it slammed inward and Liam crashed into both of us.

"Down," he ordered just as the bullets tore through part of the wall, punching through it like it was made of paper and shattering one of the mirrors.

50

LIAM

Goddamn it, Kellan was right. I'd trusted his instincts enough to do as he asked, but I'd rather hoped to prove him wrong. Sitting out their raid on the Diamonds absolutely rubbed me the wrong way. Rome going into any fight without me—I didn't care *how many* he had done in the past—would never be all right.

As the group moved out, I'd settled into my guard post on the roof. The cold temperatures didn't make it the most comfortable place to be. But not even the rats knew I was up here. I'd planted a few cameras in the rafters of the main warehouse and one in the living area of the clubhouse, and a final one focused on the door.

Not the best vantage points, but Hellspawn was down there by herself with a wounded Jasper. I wanted eyes on her. They were motion-triggered, so I'd seen her both times she'd come down for food or water in the course of that first day. Then again, when she'd come down in the middle of the night.

Her back was to the camera when she'd stared at the studio. "Come on," I'd murmured. "Turn around, Hellspawn. Let me see what you're thinking."

Only, she hadn't, and back up the stairs she'd gone. I took short naps, rousing only when my cameras let me know someone was close or in motion. It was how I'd seen her helping Jasper downstairs.

Goddamn stubborn asshole.

He had no business being up and moving, much less getting her to haul him around. She was so damn tiny compared to the rest of us, even if she was boot leather tough.

It killed me to just sit there while she dragged chairs into her studio. I also couldn't decide who was more stubborn.

Jasper or Hellspawn.

She reappeared once more, this time disappearing up the stairs, then back down and she had a bag with her. When she finally carried water bottles into the studio and then closed the door, I had to lean back and glare at the sky.

Why the fuck didn't I put cameras in there?

Next on my list. Being able to watch her dance would be worth a little invasion of privacy.

Maybe.

Fuck. She'd probably twist my balls off if she found it.

I'd ask. Safety and all that—I was in that debate when a camera at the front sent me an alert to movement. I switched my view to see the pair of SUVs pulling up.

Fuck.

Me.

A second camera in the back signaled movement. Two more cars. Kellan was right. Even if they limited how they left, with that many rats on the street and the majority of

Vandals moving on the Diamond stash houses and businesses, Jasper and Hellspawn would be vulnerable at the clubhouse.

Rising, I tossed the thermal blanket back and checked my weapons, then fired off a text to *my* backup.

It's time. Come in quiet. Come in hot.

Done, I headed for the roof hatch. There were three rats in the main warehouse, nowhere near enough for the numbers hitting.

"Someone wants her dead, Liam. They either want her dead or back under their control. There is no middle ground. I know you think it's her uncle, but I'm not one-hundred percent sold on that. Someone tried to kill her before, and that was when she was ostensibly still under his thumb."

The uncle was a problem one way or another. But he was a problem for the future, and the men in those SUVs were a problem for the present. Eight men in the front, seven in the back.

Good—they made it challenging.

I checked my phone one last time. Hellspawn and Jasper were in the studio. Bad placement. Get to them first. Eliminate the intruders second.

The hatch opened silently, and I let myself down just as lightly. No doubt the police babysitters were no longer in place, or they were already dead. Neither was a good option. I'd worry about them later. The catwalk was metal, and it wasn't long before I didn't have to worry about how much noise I was or wasn't making.

The side door blew open just as a shape charged, burning through the metal roll-up door of the front. A six-by-six panel of metal fell and the rat nearest that door didn't even make it to his feet before they shot him.

Flipping over the rail, I caught the rope along the side,

then spiraled down in a rapid descent. The fingerless gloves protected my palms, but I left skin on the nylon fibers regardless.

"Clear everything before we go in," a man from the group at the front issued the order and they split up—heading for both the office and the line of trucks. They had cars to clear too.

As soon as I touched the ground, I moved on lighter feet. Another two shots and a body dropped on the far side.

Two of the three rats were down. I kind of hated myself right now. These guys were here doing a job, and I was leaving them to their fate. But Hellspawn and Jasper came first. A shot pinged off a car and there was a shattering of glass.

I dropped, but not before the guy spotted me. Sliding the gun out of my holster, I stayed down until he came around the corner, then I shot him. It gave away my position, but I emptied the clip on the run for the door. Another bullet hit the wall and punched right fucking through it.

Fuck.

Whatever munitions they had, this was about to get ugly.

Uglier.

The door to the studio at the end of the hall started to open.

Oh, fuck no. I took off running, even as another bullet punched through the wall heading toward the kitchen. Good, let them think I was heading that way.

Plaster sprayed me as another hole punched through the wall in front of me. Fuck.

If they were going through walls, body armor was screwed.

"Down," I ordered as I shoved them both back. I

slammed through the door and took them to the ground. Covering Hellspawn's head wasn't going to be enough, and I couldn't stop Jasper from the hit he was about to take when he impacted the floor.

Bullets slammed through the walls and hit the mirrors. Glass shattered. It wasn't penetrating every part of the wall. Not yet. As soon as the firing stopped, I hauled Jasper up and caught Hellspawn's arm.

"In the closet—now."

It was at least partially reinforced. This whole area had been part of an old refrigeration before Jasper rebuilt and retrofitted it. The metal walls inside the closet and extending to the bedrooms were reinforced.

If I could get them upstairs, that would be better. Jasper grunted. "Gun," he said through clenched teeth.

I pulled my backup out and handed it to him along with a second magazine. "I've got help on the way, but there's fourteen of them and only two of us."

"Three," Hellspawn corrected. Her dazed eyes were focusing, but that thin trickle of blood escaping the cut on her cheek pissed me off.

"Three." I didn't argue. "Your job is to stay with Jasper. I'm going to tear a hole through their men. I can't do that and worry about you at the same time. They are heavily armed, and they know the layout. Stay in here, stay down."

I caught her looking at the ceiling then at Jasper, and when her gaze snagged on mine, I shook my head. He'd never make that climb. Not right now.

"I'll get us a window, Hellspawn. Trust me."

"Do it," Jasper said, though his face was pale and gray. "Don't get dead."

"You too, man, look after her."

"With my life."

She glared at him and it took effort for me to keep my face schooled. It was not fucking coming to that. I bumped his shoulder, then gripped her chin. When she blinked at me in surprise, I kissed her, hard and swift. Too swift.

No time to linger.

"For luck," I whispered. "Stay here."

More shots sounded from the hall, along with rough voices. Yeah, they were inside, and it violated every fucking part of me to realize these assholes were in our space.

Her space.

I shoved the door open with my foot then pulled back as bullets sprayed into her studio. It tore up part of the wood floor and slammed into the wall at the far side. Sorry, Hellspawn.

As soon as the bullets stopped, I went low and around the corner. The guy at the top of the hall was messing with his gun. It had probably jammed. I shot him in the knees. He went down screaming, and I shot the guy right behind him who rushed forward. The third one, I only managed to wing before he got his gun up, and I flattened back against the wall as he opened fire.

My phone buzzed in my pocket.

It was about fucking time.

Movement flashed in the corner of my left eye, and I scowled at Hellspawn. "Get your ass back in there."

"I need the bag," she told me in an equally hushed voice.

I spotted the bag in question. It hadn't been shot yet. That was a good thing. "Stay in there." At the next lull, I went high, sticking to the door and firing. The guy I'd winged lost part of his ear because he was trying to drag the first guy I'd shot out of the way. He snapped his head up and my next shot took him in the head.

A car crashed through metal and an explosion rocked the warehouse.

Oh, that was gonna leave a fucking mess.

I kicked the bag toward her and then darted out of the studio. The rat-tat-tat of gunfire from beyond the open door increased. There was a different caliber of firearm answering them, so I headed out to clear the clubhouse, pausing only long enough to shoot the one guy still alive in the hall.

At the corner, I collided with the guy coming down the stairs. He had a modified MK-18, that explained some of the shots from earlier. With a swing, he slammed the stock of the weapon against my face. I narrowly turned my head but still took a hit in the jaw. I clamped my hand over his as my gun went flying.

The guy with the bigger gun often won, but only if I gave him the room to use it. I lunged forward, head butting him, even as I kept his gun turned away. He pulled the trigger.

Bullets sprayed the living room, the television, and knocked out a lamp. It also caught the guy exiting the kitchen. The rapid-fire punched him a dozen times, and he danced in the air before he finally went down.

The gun clicked on empty, and I took a risk, letting go of part of it to drive my elbow into the side of the guy's head. He went down, and I wrenched him back up, using the gun to get up under his jaw, then braced him, knee to his back twisted.

The snap of his cervical spine didn't kill him, but his mouth opened in a soundless scream as he went down. He wasn't dead, but he also wasn't moving. MK-18 in one hand, I went for my gun and the rush of feet had me twisting to intercept the bruiser colliding with me.

Fucker had size. I ate two fists in a row, but I blocked the third punch and leapt, twisting my legs around him and pulling the behemoth off balance. He had size. I had leverage.

It drove us both into the wall. His head. My hip. Loosening my leg grip, I brought my elbow down on the soft spot at the base of his skull. Once. Twice.

The man groaned as I slid over his back, locked my forearm under his chin and dragged his head up. That got me on my feet, and my free hand to my knife. The blade came up and out of my pocket. Letting him go and switching my grip as he turned, I sliced and slammed the blade right through his neck.

Gurgling, he went down. The world rushed back in as I grabbed my gun and a bullet slammed into my chest.

Then another.

Three.

Fuck, I went down. The vest ate them, but holy shit, I couldn't breathe. The guy coming at me looked almost more terrified than he did pissed. The Glock in his hand didn't have armor piercing, thank fuck, but it didn't matter.

He only needed to raise that gun an inch. I reached for the handgun, it was just at my fingertips. The gun went off and I braced for it, but the bullet didn't hit me. His head jerked to the side and he staggered, turning and raising that gun.

I twisted and grabbed my gun, but a second bullet ripped through him, then a third. He took one in the arm holding his gun and it went down, then another in the stomach, and one went through his throat.

Emersyn stood there, feet braced, both hands on a Glock of her own. Movement rushing the door had me bringing my gun up, and she turned. We fired at the next guy coming through at the same time.

Goddamn, she caught him right in the chest. I went for the head.

A whistle pierced the air. "Friendly coming through," Ezra shouted. "Shoot me, and I'll haunt your ass, I fucking swear it."

Emersyn let out a wet laugh and I grabbed the wall to pull myself up. Adam followed Ezra through the door, step-ping over the body we'd just dropped.

I almost made it to my feet as Adam got to Emersyn. He nudged her gun down and away from him. "You hurt?" It was his first question and it was to her.

That was fair.

I cared more about her than I did me at the moment too.

Fuck, I was pretty sure that cracked some ribs.

"It's a mess in here," Ezra commented and I didn't even have the energy to flip him off. "For the record, it's a mess out there too. I've got people on the way to deal with the bodies, but I don't know if we can repair the damage at the same time."

"I got that part." I had to force the words out on a rough breath of air. Air that backed right the fuck up when Emersyn nodded to Adam and looked at me.

"I'm fine, are you...are you okay?"

"I'm good, Hellspawn." Really good. She was fucking perfect. Every bit the Hellspawn I'd always labeled her as.

An avenging fucking angel. She'd never looked better.

"But I'll take a kiss if you have it in you."

She glared at me, then marched over and thumped me in my bruised chest before kissing me. "I have to get to Jasper."

"I'll be there in a minute," I promised, then glanced at a bemused Adam and Ezra. "No fucking comments."

"She could be my fiancée," Adam pointed out. "I would have plenty to say then."

"Don't make me shoot you for real."

He chuckled, then shook his head as he walked over to give me a hand. "How bad is it?"

51

Jasper was on his feet when I got back into the destroyed studio. As much as the destruction hurt my heart, I didn't focus on it. We could put up new mirrors Jasper had ordered. Replace the shoes Rome had picked out. We could repair the floors—or replace them—we could *rebuild* a studio.

Nothing could replace Jasper *or* Liam.

"I got you," I said when he staggered. I got a shoulder under his arm as he gripped onto me. The blood seeping through his bandage had begun to redden his shirt. "We need to get you upstairs—"

But hesitation scored through me.

"Is it safe to stay here?" Kellan had warned me when I told him I was in. He'd said this could happen, it was why he wanted me to have a weapon and to keep it with me no matter what. The second gun was actually in the kitchen, so anytime I was downstairs, it would be within reach.

They had a few hidden spots for weapons but none in the studio. It was why I'd gotten my bag.

"It'll be safe, Hellspawn," Liam said as he limped into the room.

"You look like shit," Jasper managed to say, but there was no mistaking the pain in his voice.

"Right, and you look like a fucking daisy. You done sitting on your ass ,or do I need to carry you?" The concern in Liam's eyes belied the harshness in his tone.

"I'll get the asshole," Ezra said as he followed Liam in. Jasper brought up his gun, but I got his arm and Liam covered it to push it down.

"Why is he back?" Jasper asked in a harsh voice.

"He came to help," I said. "Let him, please?"

"Yeah," Ezra said, with a smarmy grin that was all him. "Let me help, cause Em said, please. She's also crying if you hadn't noticed, so be less of a dick."

"You too," Adam added as he cuffed Ezra on his way past. "I got him, Em. Where do you want him?"

"Fine, I'll help the other dick," Ezra muttered as he wrapped an arm around Liam, who just shoved him off. "Damn, no one wants my help."

"Upstairs," I said to Adam and to Ezra. "Thank you both."

Jasper scowled, but when Adam took more of his weight off me, Jasper let him. Liam got the gun, and I grabbed the medical bag. Ezra plucked it right out of my hands, then wrapped an arm around my shoulders.

"Lean on me," he said. "Are you sure you're not hurt?"

"I am going to beat the shit out of you," Liam said.

"Right, you gotta catch me first and she's in the way." Liam limped along with us as Adam got Jasper up the stairs. I was so proud of Jasper for not arguing. I also missed that somehow, I'd cut up my leg until Ezra waved me into a chair in Jasper's room. "I'd offer to bandage it, but O'Connell would give birth and he's already sore."

"I can do it," I assured him. "We need to check on Jasper's stitches, and he needs pain meds."

"No," Jasper countered, his voice firming up from the ragged notes downstairs. He was so pale. "Gun."

Liam sighed. "I'll check your wound *then* you can have a gun."

They glared at each other, and I put my hands on the arms of the chair to stand when they both said, "Stay," in the exact same tone.

Ezra shot a look at Adam, and he just shrugged. "What do you need, Em?"

Right now?

"To know everyone's okay."

"Message Lainey," he suggested. "Let her distract you, and I'll clean up that cut while those two measure their dicks."

Almost at once, Liam and Jasper stopped glaring at each other to focus on Adam. It shouldn't have been funny. It really shouldn't...

Still, I laughed, even as I wiped at the tears on my face. When my fingers came away with blood, I sighed.

"Fine," Jasper conceded. "Swan will be happier if you check it."

"All I'm saying." Liam moved like everything in him hurt. He pulled out his phone and checked the screen before setting it on the nightstand next to the bed.

The next few minutes passed in relative silence. Adam cleaned up the cut on my leg, then wrapped it. He then handed me a washcloth so I could wipe my face. My hands trembled, the exhaustion from dancing earlier coupled with the adrenaline rush from the attack had been swinging the pendulum, but the crash was coming.

"Your people are here," Liam said, and Adam nodded. When he glanced at me, I could almost read the offer but shook my head.

"I don't want to go anywhere. Thank you for coming, though." Honestly, I didn't think there were enough thanks for that. All things being equal, Adam and Ezra hadn't had the best experiences with the Vandals. They'd come anyway.

"Did you message Lainey?"

"Not yet," I said. "Not until I can tell her I'm alright without it being a lie."

His smile was grim, but he nodded. "Understood. You need me, you call me."

"Same," Ezra said. "Ignore the glaring. Just say the word."

"Stop baiting them," I suggested. "But thank you."

"Yep. I need to go deal with this shit then find a drink."

"No," Adam said as they left the room. "We need to clean this shit up and then you need to get back to her."

Their voices faded away and I dug my shaking hands into the arms of the chair.

"C'mere, Hellspawn," Liam said, and I lifted my gaze to find them both looking at me. They each wore varying degrees of pained expressions. Discipline helped me rise even when my legs protested and the shakes struck.

They both held out an arm. Liam was closer and when he wrapped me up tight, I closed my eyes even as I caught Jasper's hand in mine.

"You did good," Liam said against my hair. "Don't ever scare me like that again."

"Don't need me to save your life, and you have a deal," I

muttered. Jasper chuckled, then gave me a gentle tug. While I would have climbed up on the bed myself, Liam didn't give me the option. He swept me up and then leaned over to settle me on Jasper's other side.

"Done," he told me, then tapped my nose gently. "Rest."

"I'm sticky," I complained.

"Me too," Jasper agreed even as he curled his arm around me. The fatigue still drained his voice. "That blowjob is probably off the table, huh?"

A laugh bubbled up inside of me, and I kissed his jaw. "Later—when we're both up for it."

"How does one get in on this gig?" Liam asked as he dragged a blanket up over my legs and then set a gun next to Jasper on the nightstand before circling the bed and putting mine on the other nightstand.

"Get shot," Jasper grumbled. "Then we'll talk."

"He did," I said even as Liam smirked when he added, "I did."

Jasper glanced from Liam to me, then back. "Get in line."

It was—ridiculous and perfect. Jasper rubbed my arm and tugged me closer until my head was on his shoulder. My eyes were so damn heavy.

"You good?" Liam asked in a quiet voice. I needed to stay awake and help. Why the hell was I so fucking tired all of a sudden?

"I'll survive. Go watch your guys. I think she's trying to go into shock."

"No," Liam disagreed. "She's tired, but that's not shock. That's an adrenaline crash." Fingers brushed over my hair and then my cheek. It was them. It was safe. "She's a badass, Jas. Don't discount her."

"I won't." I felt more than heard Jasper's sigh. "Thanks for coming for us."

"Every time."

"Yeah?"

"Yeah—I know. I'm an ass."

"And a brother," Jasper admitted. "You shouldn't have left."

"Couldn't be helped." Then Liam brushed my cheek again. "Not going anywhere now."

"Good." There were no more words, but the door closed and Jasper rubbed his cheek against my head. "Go to sleep, Swan. I'll keep us safe... and Liam has your friends out there too."

My friends.

My family and my friends...

Thirty-six hours later, everyone was back—safe and sound —with only bruises—Milo, a cracked collarbone—Freddie, and exhausted but also angry. Liam and Jasper actually seemed the worst off, but Mickey had fixed Jasper's stitches, and Liam dismissed all concerns with the idea that his bruises would heal.

They were all *furious*. That fury wasn't directed at each other, though. At least, I didn't think so, even if they were sniping at each other.

"The clubhouse will need renovations," Vaughn said during one of the rare moments of quiet. I was sitting on the one chair that had the least amount of damage to it. The pool table was wrecked. The television shattered.

The coffee table had barely been standing, and when I'd

put a coffee cup on it earlier, it collapsed. Rome rescued my coffee. Thankfully.

Even my new coffee maker had been a casualty. There were bloodstains on the floor, even after they'd bleached them, and no one commented on the studio. The door to the clubhouse had already been replaced—with reinforced steel, and it had a drop bar on it now too.

"I can help," I offered. "You guys might have to show me how to do some stuff, but—I want to help."

"You don't need to be here at all," Liam said to me abruptly. "In fact, I'm more inclined to put you on a plane and steal you away for a few days while they get this all straightened out. The farther off the radar we put you, the better. At least for now."

"No," I said into the sudden silence. They were all looking at me and I didn't care. I didn't want anyone to agree with him. "I need to be *here* where I can help...unless you guys need me to leave."

Did they?

"Hellspawn," Liam said with a sigh.

"No," Freddie said abruptly. "We do *not* need you to leave. Like ever. You belong here." He glared at Liam. "Besides, *big brother*, who is going to protect us if Boo-Boo isn't here? Weren't you just bragging that she saved your life?"

Rome chuckled. The soft sound cracked the tension in the room. Jasper laughed and clapped Freddie on the shoulder. "She saved my life too."

"See," Freddie said. "That's two votes."

"Got mine," Vaughn announced.

"And mine," Mickey said. "Not that anyone asked."

I grinned at him regardless.

When Rome raised his hand, Liam just gave him a baleful look. "Et tu?"

Rome's response was his middle finger. Then we were all laughing.

"Right, no one is taking Sparrow away," Kellan stated. "Thanks for the suggestion, but we're passing. She wants to stay—she stays."

"Fine," Liam said, then motioned to Rome. "Let's go."

"Where are you going?" I stared at him curiously, particularly when he held his hand out to me. I let him pull me from my seat. Instead of answering me, though, he wrapped an arm around me and then kissed me.

It was almost like the kiss in the closet; hard, fierce, and demanding. But there was more give in it, and he coaxed my lips apart until he could tease my tongue with his. I fisted his shirt, pushing up on my toes to meet his lowered head. Even when my lungs burned with the need for air, I didn't let go until he nipped my lip.

"Going to get you a better coffee maker," he murmured. "Anything else you want?"

I blinked at him slowly. My lips tingled and my face heated even as my thoughts crashed. "Um...a wine fridge?" It was literally the only thought that came to mind. I wasn't even sure the kinds of wine I liked most of the time, but it sounded—useful?

"Done." He winked. "Be good until I get back, Hellspawn. I don't want to miss anything interesting."

"No promises."

He chuckled, then eased back as Rome brushed a kiss to the top of my head. Milo caught my gaze as I sat back down slowly and I raised my brows.

"I'm not saying a word," he said.

"Why do I not believe you?" Jasper fired back.

"Except this..." Milo continued like Jasper hadn't said a word.

"There it is," Vaughn chuckled, saluting me with his coffee.

"Any one of these assholes steps so much as an inch out of line with you..."

"I'll thump them," I told him sternly, even if I had to fight against my smile.

He considered that for a moment. "Fine, but I get to help."

Now that really did let my smile loose. "I'd like that."

"Does that sound like we're in trouble?" Freddie asked no one in particular, and they laughed.

"If we're done with threats of bodily harm," Kellan said as he moved to take a seat on the arm of my chair. "Let's talk about renovations and next steps..."

Next steps drained some of the humor. There were still people out there gunning for us.

What had Ezra called it?

A war?

The last few days had just been a battle, even if it was one we'd won.

52

KELLAN

It took a week to go through everything we took from Juan Ricardo's stash house—and to confirm, no Diamonds survived our purge. The woman we'd freed from Juan Ricardo had a reward out for her return. Turned out she'd been a hostage. We gave her the opportunity to go home if she wanted, but she'd declined. Liam took care of setting her up elsewhere.

"So, we're sure," I said, more as a follow-up than an actual question.

"19 Diamonds are done," Liam said. "That's a problem for me, but I'll deal with it." The King apparently liked to farm dirty work out to them. "Maybe make him think they're still around… maybe not. I haven't decided how to play that yet."

"Let me know," I said as we neared the downtown offices for Warrick and his foundations. "We'll back your play. What are you doing about Reed?"

"He's gonna keep playing dead for now." Liam exhaled.

"We've still got more questions than answers, but his 'death' gives him a lot of freedom. It also let him bring in cleaners for us and to back me at the clubhouse."

"He did good." I could admit that. "They both did."

"You sound surprised."

I shrugged. "I don't know these guys. I have less reason to trust them. They don't share our goals—"

"Not all of them, but enough to make them trustworthy in this."

"Sparrow."

Liam nodded. "Whatever Adam had planned when he asked Hellspawn to marry him, I don't think it was ever about just using her."

Not information I would ever be glad to hear. No wonder he'd been so damn determined to talk to her. "But you do think it played a part."

"Yeah, I do. He's too calculating, and his emotional investment is definitely in another direction."

There was another problem. "So, protecting her for his girlfriend?"

"Man, would you ever offer to marry Hellspawn's best friend? Just to protect that friend?"

"Fortunately, that's not ever a call I have to make."

He chuckled. "Well, I know I wouldn't unless there was something more in it than just protecting her. Don't get me wrong—Hellspawn needs Lainey. We'll kill to keep her safe, but marrying her? No, you need more than just protection to create a legal and binding contract."

Waiting at the light, I stared at it and drummed my fingers on the steering wheel. "Marriage is about a lot more than a contract." My parents had a good marriage. From what I could remember of it. They'd been devoted to each other. Maybe it was the fanciful thinking of the boy I'd been *before* the accident.

Or maybe it was the truth.

"No shit," Liam said as I pulled into the parking garage across the street.

"You can wait in the car," I reminded him, but Liam just gave me a look.

"You're a Vandal," he said without preamble. "You get backup."

Chuckling, I let myself out and gathered the folders from the backseat. As with the first time I'd come to pay a call, I took the elevator up to the reception. Liam moved with me, a half-step behind me and watching my back.

The receptionist gave him a flirty look that he ignored. This time, when she called up to let Mr. Warrick know I was here, he didn't keep us waiting.

Granny Dangerous was absent, but not her gorilla friend, and he brought a buddy.

"Friends?" Liam asked as we stepped out.

"Not really." Since I was wearing my nicer suit, I didn't pause. "Don't touch me, gentlemen," I told them as I stepped out. "You wouldn't enjoy the response."

As expected, the first guy went to grab me, but he never touched me. Liam caught his wrist, twisting him into an armlock.

"Cooperate," Liam told him. "Please. I don't want to have to break your arm."

The guy made a sound of protest even as his buddy tried to intervene. "I wouldn't," I advised him, but he chose not to listen. One sharp right to his throat left him gasping and choking as he staggered back.

"They never want to cooperate," Liam mused.

"You even said please."

"I know." He gave me a vaguely outraged look. "He should be glad Jasper isn't here."

"He really should. Manners are everything."

The sharp snap of bone echoed in the room, and the guy went to his knees with a howl.

A blow from Liam to the back of his head cut off the sound and knocked him out. Brushing off his suit, Liam nodded to me.

"Excuse me."

He bypassed me and caught the second guy in a similar armlock, flipping him around and slamming him down onto the marble desk.

"I apologize," he informed the second man. "But apparently, we're having a failure to communicate and my ribs are sore."

Twice more he knocked his head into the marble top and the guy ceased struggling.

"Your ribs hurt?" I asked after he set the guy on the ground.

Liam shrugged. Well, he attempted a shrug. "You take three in a vest and see how yours feel."

"I'll take your word for it."

"Generous."

He fell into step with me as I headed for Warrick's office. I considered not knocking, but fuck it. I knocked and then just opened the door.

The bane of my existence and cracked mirror glanced up in surprise. Yeah, we probably weren't expected. His pair of goons had been sent to deal with us. Too bad for them.

And him.

"Don't get up," I told him as I made my way to his desk. Liam closed the door and leaned back against it. It was also to give him room to keep an eye on Warrick and anyone else who tried to come in. I appreciated it. "You won't be here long."

Leaning back in his chair, the man stared at me. "Is that so?"

"Very much so." I opened the case and laid down the first file folder. "These are your copies—so feel free to keep them, burn them, shred them..."

"...choke on them." Liam tacked on.

"We have our own."

"And what are those?"

I did give him credit, he hadn't even reach out to flip open the first folder.

"Transcripts of every single conversation you've had with a pair of men named Meeks and Juan Ricardo. Business conversations..."

Warrick snorted. "Anyone can write down some words."

"Absolutely." I pulled out my phone and hit play on the audio file that included his voice.

"...I don't care what you have to do or how much it costs. I'm fucking done with those Vandals. Put a bullet in all of them. Then bring me the dancer girl. I've got a buyer who wants her—intact or not, it doesn't matter to me."

He paled.

I paused it. "Would you like to hear more?"

That clip was also why this meeting was supposed to just be me. Jasper had been damn near homicidal when he heard it and Milo hadn't been much better.

It was one thing to be told, it was another thing to hear it.

Warrick swallowed. "That could be interpreted and misconstrued without foundation."

"Sure," I said. Then played the next clip.

"...you were supposed to keep those deliveries on time. You lost twenty-four pre-sold candidates in that last shipment. Are you aware of the fines I had to pay out for failure to deliver? You'll replace them, and at your own cost, or I'll be sending you to take their place."

When he would have opened his mouth to protest that it could mean anything, I raised a finger.

Juan Ricardo said, "Warrick, you don't frighten me. You pay people like me to do your dirty work while you play socialite. For the threat alone, you're going to pay me another five thousand a head to replace the skin the Vandals took and if you don't—well, let's just say, I'll pay a visit to your wife and your daughter and take it out of *their* skin."

He paled.

"Pretty sure the Mrs. isn't aware that you almost got her and her daughter killed, is she?"

Now he stood. "You wouldn't dare."

"Sit. Down." Liam's snarled order carried, and Warrick went from challenging me to sitting abruptly. Shock gave way to embarrassment that he'd obeyed.

"Don't ask me what I'd dare," I informed Warrick. "You won't like the answer. When I was here a couple of weeks ago, I made it very clear to you that your operations were no longer welcome in this city. That what you do and how you do it is no longer sanctioned. Instead of taking the warning in the good faith that I made it, you decided to double down."

After pocketing my phone, I pulled out the last folder and set it on the desk.

"That is a list of every single stash house where the Diamonds held your funding that still needed to be cleaned."

He blanched.

"It's gone—every penny, farthing, dime, and ruble. You have forty-eight hours to get out of Braxton Harbor for good. Don't come back. Don't look back. Don't even *blink* in the direction of me, the Vandals, *or* that dancer."

"That's it? Just get out?"

"I didn't stutter and I won't repeat myself again. Forty-eight hours started when we walked in the door. You have…"

"Forty-seven hours and forty-seven minutes," Liam finished for me. "You can go willingly, or you can go ugly. Either way, you are going."

Because we had his money, he also knew we had the rest of his "shipments" that they had been sitting on. Those men, women, and children had also been removed far away from where he could touch them again.

I started to turn then paused. "One last thing…"

The man glared at me, and then panic flashed across his face as I reached across the desk and hauled him out of his chair. The crack of my fist slamming into his face and breaking his nose was damn satisfying.

He gripped his face as blood spurted and staggered back into his chair. I pulled out a handkerchief and wiped off my hands before picking up the bag.

"That was for my mother, you sack of shit."

Liam opened the door for me and we made our way to the elevator. There was a new gorilla waiting for us, but Liam trained a gun on him and the guy just backed up with his hands raised.

He kept the gun out until we were in the elevator and it began its descent to the reception level. We said nothing as we changed elevators. You couldn't tell from the ringing phones or the flirty receptionist that anything had gone on.

If I were a betting man, I would suspect that they would all show up in the next day or two to find the business gone, their jobs erased, and their bosses in the wind.

I'd feel bad—except I didn't. They worked for monsters, they just didn't know it, and if they did? Well, fuck 'em.

On the way out of the building, Liam had his phone to his ear. "Tag, Doc. You're it." He listened for a beat, then ended the call.

I glanced at him. "What are you doing?"

"You made a deal with him. You got to lay it out to him your way. I respect that. Doc's right, though—he goes down ugly regardless."

At the car, I frowned at him.

Liam met my stare without blinking. "You got him for us, for Hellspawn, and for your mom. We're taking him down for you."

Blowing out a breath, I stared at the vehicle and then nodded. "Thank you."

"We got your back," he reminded me. "None of us runs alone."

I chuckled and shook my head, even if none of this was funny. The drive back was silent. I was too fucking tired at this point to even debate it. Frankly, I was fine if Doc called in friends to deal with this. Shut it down, all of it, and make sure he suffered on his way out.

It would be better for his wife and his kids if he just ceased to exist.

Back at the clubhouse, it was late, but the repairs were well underway. We were reinforcing all the walls on this level and out in the warehouse.

We wouldn't be caught like that again. Rome was actually painting in the hallway and Liam and I both paused to admire the scene. It had no people in it—yet—just a mountain view. Nothing we could see here.

He'd probably seen it in a book somewhere. All she'd done was mention we could add a little color. Well, she wasn't wrong.

There were renovations upstairs, too. We were rebalancing the rooms, creating a private space that we could share with her—no offense to Milo, but his glowering every time one of us kissed her got old some days.

He'd get over it—eventually. Until then, we'd create a suite where our bedrooms surrounded hers and we could have private time with her together or apart.

It would take a while.

"I'm going to bed," I told Liam. He lifted his chin.

"I'll be around for a while."

Good. I bumped Rome's shoulder lightly when he paused, and he gave me a small smile. He was doing that more often.

It was kind of nice.

On my way upstairs, I loosened my tie. Hanging up the suit, I threw myself in the shower, then I would sleep. I hadn't really grabbed more than a couple of hours since we went after the Diamonds and I felt it everywhere.

We'd gotten damn lucky. Jasper would heal. We could rebuild. The Diamonds were gone and we'd forged a new— albeit tentative—alliance with a few Royals. The cops had nothing on Vaughn and the shooting remained unsolved.

Emersyn was home. She was healing.

Yeah. We'd gotten damn lucky.

When I came out of the shower, I paused to find her sitting on the bed. She'd barely left Jasper's side since he'd reopened his wounds but I couldn't blame her.

"Sparrow..."

She smiled and patted the bed next to her. "Come on, Kel. Time for you to rest, and I'm going to sit on you if I have to, but you're in this bed for at least the next eight hours. Milo is going to be on watch, Liam is going nowhere, and Jasper promised to behave. Freddie will tell me if he doesn't."

I chuckled. "Is that so?"

"Yes, it is."

"Well then, how can I say no to that?" The simple truth was I couldn't. Shutting off the light, I crossed over to slide into the bed.

Fuck, the sheets had never been this cool or the mattress this comfortable. When she curled right up into my arms and tucked her head against my chest, I groaned. This was... perfect.

"Go to sleep," she whispered. "I'll guard your dreams today."

"Then I know I'll be safe," I murmured and kissed the top of her head. "When I wake up, you can totally sit on my face to keep me in bed."

She shook with laughter and I hugged her tighter. We'd gotten damn lucky.

Lucky that our wounded bird was every bit the fighter we needed her to be.

Just—fucking lucky.

53

"N o," I said as I pulled on a boot.

"Why not?" Lainey complained. "We could be on a ski slope in Zermatt before you know it."

"You *hate* skiing, for one," I retorted as I laced up the boot. "And two, you still have Andrea, and you can't take her out of the country no matter how much you want to."

"Fine," she said with a groan. "Another week, and she'll be back at school and I'll head in your direction. I just have to lose Ezra."

"Be nice to Ezra," I said. "Maybe if you tell him where you're—"

"Okay, Em, I love you and you're my best friend, so he doesn't get to win *you over at all*."

I paused. "Fine, but...he kind of helped save our lives."

"Then he gets a cookie, but he's become an unbearable ass since I got back."

Both boots on, I checked for my wallet. I'd gotten used

to carrying a different ID on me. It helped that I didn't actually have my own stuff. None of it, really. "He missed you."

"You know, he was *almost* nicer when he was pleading with me to leave with him. Then I left with him." She made a disgusted noise.

"Maybe he's worried you're going to disappear on him, and Adam is still—"

"Gone? Yes, I'm aware. When he *deigns* to share with me they've spoken, it's usually to issue more orders. Also, Andrea is beside herself, and I think Adam's father might have noticed he's not returning his calls."

That could be a problem.

"Not that I'm worried about it. They both seem happier when they aren't reminded that Adam and I exist. As long as Andrea is happy, we're good. Now—tell me about you? How are you? Are you and Milo getting along better? Is he handling you dating—how many of them are you dating?"

Subtle. I grinned at how naturally she folded Milo into the call. She was always so careful about *how* she asked, but she always asked.

"He's—good, and I think we are. He and I went to see Ms. Stephanie again after she came back from vacation. She invited us to dinner with her brother. Seemed surprised that I hadn't met him yet but—I mean, why would I have, you know?"

"That's weird. What did Milo say?" The sound of a bed bounced in the background, and I could imagine her falling back on it to stare at the ceiling.

"He said I'd see, and don't you have a lunch date with your grandfather?" It was later there than it was here.

"In an hour, and he expects me to be late. You know how he is, if a woman is on time, then a man may think he doesn't have to work for her. A good man is always willing to wait for the women in his life."

I laughed. "I can't wait to meet him someday. He always sounds so funny."

"He's a curmudgeon and a judgmental old fuck. I adore him." Her voice softened at the end. "But you and Milo are getting along better?"

"Yes, we are. It's a work in progress. He wants so badly to protect me from everything. I think sometimes he wishes I were still a toddler, and when he realizes I'm not, he doesn't know what to do with it. But—he isn't threatening the guys' lives every other sentence, so that's a definite improvement." I laughed. "He has been giving me tips on how to incapacitate them, if necessary."

"Oh, I bet he has. He's a bit overbearing, isn't he?"

"Yes, but I adore him," I admitted. "I love that—he's just on my side, Lainey. Just like you. No questions. No hesitation. He's just—there."

"Good, you deserve everything. Now, who are we dating? Have we decided?"

"I like them all and I've decided I'm going to date them all, and they all seem to like it—even encourage it. Nope, don't ask me how it's going to work or what kinds of things can go wrong because—everything could, and I have no idea. So, it's one day at a time."

"Okay." Just like that.

"And, before you ask, physical therapy is going—well, it's going. We've got new exercises and I think the scar gel is working between the ultrasound, the vibration, and rolling therapy. I can actually do a handstand again without feeling like I want to die."

It was definitely an improvement.

"Yes, Em, that's fantastic."

I still hadn't tried the silks. Jasper came down to watch me dance as often as he could. I also divided my time between exercises, dancing, and training. More trips to the gun range, more fight training with Liam. Rome had started coming to those and so had Jasper.

It was funny until Jasper and Liam would argue over a technique. Then Rome would sneak me out. Freddie and I started knife lessons, but that was a lot harder than he made it look.

"It's actually been pretty great. I mean—if you don't count the shootings and people trying to kill us."

And the nightmares. The nightmares still came and they were still bad. Sometimes, I had panic attacks. Only two so far this week, so that was an improvement.

"Em? For real? It's good?" She'd sobered.

"Yeah, for real. We've even been doing renovations. Wait until you see what they've done, it's—it's pretty cool."

A knock sounded at my door, and I bounced up to answer it. Rome grinned at me and I smiled, then pointed at the phone.

"Rome is here, Lainey. Say hi to Rome."

"Hello, beautiful, Rome," she said, like she was playing Juliet in *Romeo and Juliet*. "How art thou Rome?"

He quirked a brow. "Fine. We're leaving. You should call Milo. He misses you."

I opened my mouth as he picked up the phone.

"Starling will message you later."

Then he hung up on her.

"Rome."

"You want to tell her, but you won't." He shrugged as he held out the phone. "I don't mind, so I told her for you."

My phone vibrated with messages from her. Three in rapid succession, so I opened up the app and cracked up.

I showed him the picture of her flipping us off, followed by the note below that said *For Rome* then *I love you bitch.*

"She is a good friend." He picked up my jacket. "So are you. You are also a good sister."

"And you're a beautiful man and a wonderful boyfriend."

He held up my jacket for me to put it on. "For you."

After I slid my arms in the jacket, I leaned back into him and he hugged me. "Thank you, Rome."

"Welcome. Ready to go?"

I blew out a breath. "Exposure therapy?"

He shrugged. "You need sunshine. It's a pretty day. I want to show you something."

So, yes, exposure therapy. "Yes, I'm ready. Did we tell the guys we're going?"

"Yes." He paused at the door. "But I didn't tell them it was for your birthday."

I blinked. My birthday?

What month—oh.

"I forgot."

He held out his hand. "I didn't."

Despite the signs of renovations, new wall framing— old walls being knocked down and redesigned—the club- house hardly looked like it had just what, three weeks ago?

It hardly seemed real. Milo glanced up from a book he had open on the card table—we hadn't replaced all the furniture yet. They didn't want to until they'd finished "building."

"Going out?" He frowned.

"Yes," I said, when we paused. "Rome wants to show me something."

"And he can't *show* you something here?" The droll question was *almost* funny.

"No," I said. "He can't. It's not about sex—"

"Ugh!" Milo grimaced.

"I didn't say that," Rome corrected.

"Kill me," Milo muttered.

"So, it could be about sex?" I pivoted to look up at him, then grinned as he canted his head.

"Stop," Milo said. "Don't answer that. Just—go show her something. Do you guys have backup?"

"Liam knows." That could mean just about anything, but it was enough to satisfy Milo.

"Great, go—look at things with the twins, and definitely don't tell me about them."

My heart wrenched a little cause he really was trying. I squeezed Rome's hand and then went to give Milo a hug. He paused when I wrapped my arms around him, and then —he crushed me gently.

"Lainey's fine," I whispered. "She's gonna be back soon."

He went totally still and his arms loosened. Kissing his cheek, I straightened. The question on his face threatened to break my heart all over again.

Hopefully, I hadn't overstepped.

"Thank you," he said after a minute, then cleared his throat. "Go—behave. You know—or not."

I laughed and then skipped over to where Rome waited. As much as leaving still fucked with my head, I refused to give into it. No more being a prisoner. Just staying here didn't keep danger away.

Liam

Traffic was a snarl coming out of the city. It took me

almost an hour to go a mile and a half. What a day to skip bringing the bike. But I didn't want to leave it behind, and I didn't want Hellspawn to freeze if she rode back with me.

I texted Rome that I was running behind, but he didn't answer. Not unusual. Besides, he was with Hellspawn. She would have all my attention too. And would, very shortly, if I could ever get out of the backup.

It wasn't until I prowled past the remains of an accident, that the road opened up again. An overturned black SUV that had apparently caught fire and burned. There were no ambulances, just a fire crew dealing with it and cops directing the traffic around.

The minute I could put my foot down, I did. The engine purred as I accelerated onto the open road again. The drive was a familiar one. We'd been meaning to bring Hellspawn out to the carnival grounds—well, Rome had, and he'd wanted me to be there too—we just hadn't had the time until now.

I stopped to get her a present, it probably could have waited, but Rome said her birthday was right around the corner. Wine and cupcakes were probably not the best combination, but she would likely have approved of a whole cake much less.

There was another box safely stowed in the glovebox. An impulse. It could wait for the holidays if today proved to not be the day. Patient, I could be. Besides, Jasper mentioned that she was reluctant to test herself in her silks.

The carnival had everything we needed to set up a safe practice ground. Out of habit, I kept an eye on my tail. No one stood out, and no one followed me off the exit I took. But for paranoia's sake, I exited two before I needed to and then followed the side road for one more block.

Taking a more circuitous approach added fifteen

minutes, but not risking someone following me straight to them was more than worth it. I wanted to relax with my brother and our girl today. We could be wary and have fun.

The road was a bit bumpy when I turned on it. The trees and underbrush had thickened near the entrance to the carnival grounds. I needed to make arrangements for a landscaping crew to get out here. Maybe a contractor, fix everything up nice—

Three things hit me as I cleared the trees and had a solid view of the parking lot and the front of the carnival, including the wall that had prompted me to buy it in the first place. A dark blue SUV—my SUV—parked diagonally across two spaces with both driver's side and passenger doors open.

The sun was shining, but the air was cold. Were they wait—no, they were not waiting.

I slammed on the brakes and pulled out a gun from the holster beside the seat. Phone in hand, I pressed Rome's contact as I climbed out of the car.

Scanning the area for movement, I did a sweep. There was nothing near either of my vehicles. Buzzing came from the SUV. Approaching, I kept a wary eye out and then swore.

Rome's phone lay on the ground just beneath the driver's side, discarded. This close, I couldn't miss the blood smeared on the side of the car or Hellspawn's bag open and everything inside it scattered on the passenger seat.

The keys were still in the ignition, but when I put a hand on the engine—it was cool. Not cold, cool. An hour and a half to get through traffic. Plenty of time for the engine to have cooled off, especially in this weather.

I did another sweep of the area, keeping my head on a swivel. No movement beyond the breeze kicking up a discarded fast-food bag and sending it tumbling. Not even the sounds of the road reached back here.

Ice slithered in my veins as I cut a look back at the vehicle and the blood on the side of it.

On Rome's side.

Rome didn't play pranks. He'd never risk her.

I shut it off. The fear. The worry. The pain. I buried all of it. I didn't have time for it right now. They didn't have time for it.

The ice closed in around me, and I lifted my phone. There were no bodies. If they'd killed them, there would be bodies. A warning. A retaliation.

But they hadn't—they'd left the car and the signs of struggle instead.

Someone had taken them.

My brother and our girl.

Someone was going to die.

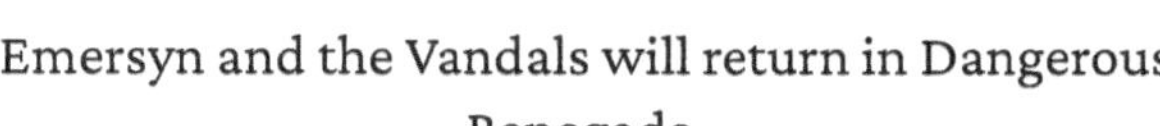

Emersyn and the Vandals will return in Dangerous Renegade.

To keep up with Heather and all her series join her reader's group:
Https://www.facebook.com/groups/HeathersPack/

AFTERWORD

So... yeah. That happened.

I know. That was definitely *not* a WTF-hanger, I hear you.

Right, you need to catch your breath so I'll wait.

Back with me?

Imagine for a moment that I am holding your hand in a totally non-creepy way and assuring you that the next book is coming.

So, let's unpack this a little. I have said repeatedly this is a dark journey. None of these characters had easy child-hoods. None of them have grown into adulthood in warm, safe, and secure environs. They have all had to fight their battles to become who they are.

They have had to build their families through a network of loyalty, trust, and reliance. Sometimes, when you have so little, you are terrified of disappointing those people or putting them in danger.

There is no easy way out. There never has been, but the collision course they have always been on has begun to rain down on their lives like a meteor shower. It's not just the impacts, but the ripples they have to worry about.

Every choice and action has a consequence. For now… let me thank you for reading. Truly.

So, what happens next?

I've got the notes started for Dangerous Renegade and I am currently writing the final Untouchable book. I need to take a few days off in June, but as most people who know me will attest, I am a workaholic.

So, if you need to curse my name or rail or debate theories be sure to head over to my group and spoiler groups on Facebook.

You will not only find your people there, you'll find me

xoxo

Heather

Reader group: facebook.com/groups/heatherspack

Spoiler group: facebook.com/groups/teammadatheather

ABOUT HEATHER LONG

I *love* books. Not just a little bit, but a lot. Books were my best friends when I was growing up. Books didn't care if I was new to a town or to a class. They were always there, my trustiest of companions. Until they turned on me and said I had to write them.

I can tell you that my own personal happily ever after included writing books. I've always said that an HEA is a work in progress. It's true in my marriage, my friendships, and in my career. I am constantly nurturing my muse as we dive into new tales, new tropes, new characters and more.

After seventeen years in Texas, we relocated to the Pacific Northwest in search of seasons, new experiences, and new geography. I can't wait to discover what life (and my muse) have in store for me.

Maybe writing was always my destiny and romance my fate. After all, my grandmother wasn't a fan of picture books and used to read me her Harlequin Romance novels.

Friends to lovers, enemies to lovers, friends to enemies to lovers, you name it, I love them and love to write them. I started with Earth Witches Aren't Easy, the first in the Chance Monroe trilogy, but my characters and I have traveled a long way since I created that urban fantasy world.

One of the series I hear my readers recommend the most is the Untouchable series followed in quick succession by the Vandals, and that just delights me. No lie, whenever one of my readers brings up my wolves, I do a little a fist pump.

I'm active on social media, and I love hearing from readers. Feel free to tag me with a question about any of my books, or just say hi!

ALSO BY HEATHER LONG

82nd Street Vandals

Savage Vandal

Vicious Rebel

Ruthless Traitor

Dirty Devil

Brutal Fighter

Dangerous Renegade

Merciless Spy

Always a Marine Series

Once Her Man, Always Her Man

Retreat Hell! She Just Got Here

Tell It to the Marine

Proud to Serve Her

Her Marine

No Regrets, No Surrender

The Marine Cowboy

The Two and the Proud

A Marine and a Gentleman

Combat Barbie

Whiskey Tango Foxtrot

What Part of Marine Don't You Understand?

A Marine Affair

Marine Ever After

Marine in the Wind

Marine with Benefits

A Marine of Plenty

A Candle for a Marine

Marine under the Mistletoe

Have Yourself a Marine Christmas

Lest Old Marines Be Forgot

Her Marine Bodyguard

Smoke & Marines

Bravo Team Wolf

When Danger Bites

Bitten Under Fire

Cardinal Sins

Kill Song

First Chorus

High Note

Chance Monroe

Earth Witches Aren't Easy

Plan Witch from Out of Town

Bad Witch Rising

Her Elite Assets

Featuring:

Pure Copper

Target: Tungsten

Asset: Arsenic

Fevered Hearts

Marshal of Hel Dorado

Brave are the Lonely

Micah & Mrs. Miller

A Fistful of Dreams

Raising Kane

Wanted: Fevered or Alive

Wild and Fevered

The Quick & The Fevered

A Man Called Wyatt

Going Royal

Some Like It Royal

Some Like It Scandalous

Some Like It Deadly

Some Like it Secret

Some Like it Easy

Her Marine Prince

Blocked

Heart of the Nebula

Queenmaker

Deal Breaker

Throne Taker

Lone Star Leathernecks

Semper Fi Cowboy

As You Were, Cowboy

Magic & Mayhem

The Witch Singer

Bridget's Witch's Diary

The Witched Away Bride

Mongrels

Mongrels, Mischief & Mayhem

Shackled Souls

Succubus Chained

Succubus Unchained

Succubus Blessed

Shackled Souls (Omnibus)

Space Cowboy

Space Cowboy Survival Guide

Untouchable

Rules and Roses

Changes and Chocolates

Keys and Kisses

Whispers and Wishes

Hangovers and Holidays

Brazen and Breathless

Trials and Tiaras

Graduation and Gifts

Defiance and Dedication

Songs and Sweethearts

Legacy and Lovers

Farewells and Forever

Wolves of Willow Bend

Wolf at Law

Wolf Bite

Caged Wolf

Wolf Claim

Wolf Next Door

Rogue Wolf

Bayou Wolf

Untamed Wolf

Wolf with Benefits

River Wolf

Single Wicked Wolf

Desert Wolf

Snow Wolf

Wolf on Board

Holly Jolly Wolf

Shadow Wolf

His Moonstruck Wolf

Thunder Wolf

Ghost Wolf

Outlaw Wolves

Wolf Unleashed